The Shekinah Road

by

Roberta Bedell Bausum

Bloomington, IN

authorHOUSE®
Milton Keynes, UK

AuthorHouse™
1663 Liberty Drive, Suite 200
Bloomington, IN 47403
www.authorhouse.com
Phone: 1-800-839-8640

AuthorHouse™ UK Ltd.
500 Avebury Boulevard
Central Milton Keynes, MK9 2BE
www.authorhouse.co.uk
Phone: 08001974150

This is a work of fiction. All characters and events not actually mentioned in the Bible are strictly from the writer's imagination.

First published by AuthorHouse 4/18/2007

ISBN: 978-1-4259-8277-5 (sc)

Printed in the United States of America
Bloomington, Indiana

This book is printed on acid-free paper.

All Biblical verses used in this book are from the NIV translation by ZONDERVAN Publishing Co.

Dedication

This book is dedicated to George, my husband, who is a beloved friend, critic and encourager par excellence. Thank you for always believing in me.

To my mother, Virginia Thomas Bedell, from whose lips I first learned about Jesus. To Ann... who promised.

In Appreciation

I would like to express appreciation to someone I have never met, Don Francisco. It was his musical representation of the King and Queen becoming the "gardener and his wife" in "Adam, Where Are You?" that inspired this book.

Chapter One

Beginnings

The cave was warm and dry; nevertheless, the woman tenderly pulled the mat over the sleeping boy. Gently she smoothed his hair, still wet with tears, away from his face. Eve sat back on her heels and observed her children. Her eldest, Cain, for the first time in his ten years, had sobbed himself to sleep. His six-year-old brother, Abel, and two baby sisters had seemed confused about their sibling's behavior. The mother sighed and stood up, giving all of the children a quick bedtime check. They were sleeping soundly.

Abel's hair curled around his face, but no tears had dampened it. He lay on his back with his arms thrown over his head in a relaxed manner. He was an obedient child, never questioning what he was told to do. The girls, Aluma the three year old, and Rina whose first birthday had occurred during the harvest celebration, were curled so tightly together that it was impossible to see where one began and the other ended. Eve smiled at the sweet closeness of her girls.

"Who would have thought that there would be such a fuss over the sacrifice of a little lamb?" Eve mused. And yet… and yet she allowed herself a fleeting memory of another sacrifice, so long ago in her first home. She too had sobbed, but for a different reason. Her sobs had been guilty ones; for no lamb would need to have been slain, had she and Adam not listened to the voice of the Deceiver.

Cain's sobs had been angry and defiant. He had tried to hide the lamb. He stormed and screamed when his father had firmly pried the animal from his arms, explaining that this was the ceremony that must be observed: the sacrifice of a first-born animal in order to atone for the sinfulness of mankind. Cain would not be consoled. He yelled that he hated God, that God was mean, and that he would never ever kill an animal just to please someone! He was sullen and angry throughout the entire dedication, refusing to partake of the feast afterwards, eating only a few grain cakes dipped in honey, which his mother had made and silently given him after Adam sent him to his bed.

Eve shook her head as if to clear her thoughts. She joined her husband outside the mouth of the cave, where he sat tending the fire. Every day the boys gathered fallen limbs and brush, so that their father could light a huge bonfire at night.

Adam had dug a pit for hot coals, which he kept burning at all times. He had started his first fire during those awful early days soon after they had left the Garden. There had been violent wind with great flashes of bright light raging through the heavens. One flash had landed on a tree causing it to burn to the ground. Never had they seen such a sight, and they thought they too would be burned. Fearfully husband and wife huddled together out of reach of the flames. Suddenly they began to feel the warmth from the fire and cautiously moved closer, for the day had been cold. Eventually they fell asleep, their exhausted bodies covered with ash as they lay near the fire.

When the morning came, the fire had become glowing red coals. Adam held a dry stick next to a hot coal and it flamed into fire. He had looked at Eve in awe and wonder. Carefully they had taken long sticks and placed the coals in a mud-hardened basket that Eve had made. They had guarded those coals as if they were life itself.

Indeed they had been life, for they had provided warmth for the cold nights and fuel to cook their food. The fire burning at the door of the cave also provided protection from wild animals, for the beasts were afraid to enter the area guarded by the burning flames. Now flames burned brightly, dancing and jumping up into the night as if to touch the brilliantly shining stars.

Adam looked up at his wife. The moonlight shown softly on her face. She looked tired and worried as she reached up and loosed the leather strap that held her long plait in place. As she shook her hair out so that it hung loosely down to her hips, she looked for just a moment as she had in the Garden: young and carefree. Then Adam looked at her hands. They were work-worn, calloused and scarred, with nails that were jagged and torn. He took his cup of hot wine from the outer coals of the fire, and leaned back to rest his head against the smooth rocks outside the cave. Memories began to flood his heart and mind. There had been that first day. That day long, long ago…when the animals had shared happy stories with them.

❋ ❋ ❋ ❋ ❋

The man's face was smooth and warm to touch. The white wooly animal allowed her nose to gently nudge his cheek. She giggled and jumped back, bumping into the large brown animal with gentle eyes, who stood peacefully chewing her cud.

"Hush," said a sleek small animal with large teeth and flat tail, "you'll frighten him."

"But, what is he?" asked the yellow bird that flew from tree branch to swaying flower and back again, warbling in song before and after his question.

"He's all alone," declared another creature, grinning broadly as he swung by his long arms and long tail from tree to tree. "Where is his other part?"

The creature's other part immediately took up the refrain: "Where is his other part? Where is his other part?"

"Both of you hush!" demanded the other part of the wooly animal who had dared to touch the man's cheek. "What will he think of all of us when he does wake up and hears us chattering so? Now, everyone be still!"

White Wooly bent his head down and gently pushed his other part back from the man. All of the animals in the garden formed a circle around this newly created being, and stayed very quiet and still.

Slowly the man began to move his legs, and then his arms, and then he scratched his nose. And then…everyone got very, very still, for the man had begun to open his eyes.

"He has blue eyes like the sky," said the bird with wings so large that he could soar higher than any other bird.

"Oh, but indeed he does not," said the little gray animal with the bushy tail. "His eyes are just as green as the leaves of this tree in which I am sitting."

"Pooh," said the small furry animal with big ears and a little soft ball for a tail, as she hurried out of the new burrow that she had just made for her home. "None of you are seeing correctly, for his eyes are just as brown as my house."

All of the other animals and birds began to give an opinion, so once again the chattering became quite loud. However, it stopped just as suddenly as it had begun; and all of the animals jumped back with a collective gasp.

The man had sat up and looked around, greatly disturbing the soft bed of grass and leaves on which the Father had placed him so gently. He looked at each animal, each bird, each tree and flower. He blinked; he looked again. Each animal stood side-by-side in pairs and looked back at him.

"How do you do, Adam," said the white wooly animal whose horns were just starting to poke through the fur. "Our Father said for us to welcome you to Eden."

The man looked around, his eyes full of questions. "Who…who is our Father?" he asked in a newly discovered voice.

Suddenly a cloud appeared, shining so brightly that it was as if millions of diamonds had been sprinkled throughout its sunbeams. The animals all lowered their eyes and bowed in reverence, for they knew that they were in the presence of the Shekinah glory of the Lord God.

"I Am your Father, Adam," spoke a gentle voice.

"Today I have created you from the dust of the earth. This Garden is your home," the Voice continued, "and you are to tend it and care for it. You are responsible for the Garden; and I will visit you each evening to see how you are doing, to give you guidance and to answer your questions."

The Voice then beckoned for the animals, which had been kneeling in adoration, to come forward for instructions. Each animal came forward eagerly, and looked happily towards the Voice and the man.

"These are your creatures, Adam. Every creature of the earth, sky and sea belongs to you. You must give them each a name, and you are responsible for their well-being. Name them carefully; for as you name them, so shall their nature be. You have dominion over them."

"Yes Father, Sir," said Adam bravely and firmly. "I will do everything that you say."

"Very well," said the Voice, "and Adam, you must always remember that you have been created in My Image. I formed you out of the earth, which I also made; but I have breathed into you that Life which can only come from me.

"You must be obedient to all the lessons which I shall teach you," the Voice went on. "You may eat of any of the trees of the Garden except the one in the middle. "Adam, if you do eat of that tree you will surely bring death into the Garden."

Adam had no idea what death was, but he was sure that it was something to be avoided at all cost. He looked in astonishment at the many, many other trees and bushes loaded with beautiful fruit, and resolved not even to look at the tree in the middle of the Garden, much less eat from it.

He looked around to see what else the Voice had to say to him, but the Voice had left. Adam jumped up and laughed with joy at being alive in such a wonderful place. He ran over to White Wooly and gave him a big hug. The animal lowered his head and gently gave him a playful push. They frolicked about the Garden for several minutes, with all the other animals laughing merrily and running about.

"Ahem, uh, AHEM…" said the animal who stood on his four legs with his tail swishing gently, and his long face earnestly regarding Adam.

Adam stopped his play and turned to the creature. "Yes Sir," he answered with respect, for the animal looked powerful and sleek, with a mane that flew back in the wind when he ran.

The animal bowed his head in submission to Adam. "Pardon me, for it is I who must address you as 'Sir'," he corrected gently, "but I just wanted to assure you that Adam is a wonderful name to be called and we know that you are man. We are grateful that you will care for us; but, uh, well, that is...what are we to be called? The Father said that you would name us; and well, we were all, uh, wondering, uh that is..."

"Oh, of course," said Adam. "I'm so sorry! Everyone line up right now, with all of you who are the same grouped together."

Adam tried hard to sound important and official as he made this announcement because he knew that the Father had given him a serious assignment. He motioned for the animal that had been talking to be first.

"You will be called Horse. Because you are strong and can run like the wind, you will be the stallion of horses, and your smaller, other part will be the mare."

The two horses liked what they were to be called and immediately touched noses, then bowed to Adam, and ran happily off, racing each other through the Garden. So it took place: the sheep, the cows, the kangaroos and bears; the lions, the frogs, the monkeys and rabbits; the sparrows and eagles, whales and goldfish; all the animals of the earth received their names.

The animals were very happy, and they wanted to have a celebration. They gathered fruits and herbs, flowers, leaves and grasses from the Garden, and frolicked joyfully around Adam, urging him to join their feast.

Adam sat quietly at the foot of a large weeping willow that was situated by a bubbling stream. "Oh that's all right, you go ahead and have a good time," he said in a very quiet voice. "I'll just sit here for a while."

The white wooly animal, whom Adam had named 'Sheep', quickly ran over to where the man sat. "What is wrong, Adam?" he asked gently.

"It's just that, well, that is, I mean...where is my other part? Every one of you has a mate, but I have no one like myself."

All of the animals began talking at once. They decided that the Father had surely made a mate for Adam, but maybe He had left her in another part of the Garden. They all agreed to begin a giant search through the Garden to look for her.

Alas, although each animal had started out in high hopes, and with many words of encouragement to Adam, they came back with their heads and tails hanging down; for there was no mate to be found for the man. All of the animals once again gathered around Adam, but no one knew what to say; for although every animal in the Garden loved every other animal, each one especially loved his own other part.

Adam had no other part.

The Garden became very, very quiet. No birds sang. No frogs chirruped. No fish splashed. No one made a sound.

Suddenly the beautiful light was present and the Voice of the Father spoke. "What is wrong, Adam?" asked God the Father. "Are you unhappy with the Garden that I have made?"

"Oh, no Sir."

"Has one of the animals displeased you in some way?"

"Oh no Sir, they would never do that; for they are wonderful friends, and each one is very kind."

The Voice surrounded Adam, soothing him tenderly. "I Am your Father, Adam, and I love you. You must always tell me when your heart is troubled."

"Father, Sir, where is my other part? Is there no one for me?" asked Adam hopefully.

"Well, well," said God the Father, "it is not good for man to be alone. Let us see what we can do about that."

All of the play and talk, and the busy work, had made Adam very, very tired; and be began to yawn and shut his sleepy eyes.

The Father carefully laid Adam back on his soft bed of leaves, for He had caused a deep sleep to come upon him. Then God did a wonderful thing. He removed a bone from the sleeping body of the man, and closed the open place back up at once. The man never moved.

God then took the man's bone and fashioned the most beautiful creature that the animals had ever seen. The newest creation had hair so long that it nearly touched the ground. This creature was very like the man, and yet not like the man at all. Where his shoulders were broad and firm with muscles, hers were smaller and softer; and her front had soft curves and bulges that gave way to a tiny waist. She was not so tall as the man, and her feet were tiny compared to his. Her face was the sweetest feature of all; for her eyelashes lay long upon her cheeks, pointing past her delicate nose to the sweet lips that looked like a newly formed rosebud from the Garden. Until now everyone in the Garden had thought that the serpent was the most beautiful of all of them, but no one's beauty could compare with her .

Suddenly the Voice spoke in solemn tones. "Adam, awaken!" He commanded. "Behold your other part. Behold your wife."

Adam awoke and gazed in wonder at the beautiful creature lying on the bed of leaves.

"Is…is she re..really for me?" Adam stammered in surprise.

The animals giggled, and the Voice had a chuckle in it. "Yes, my son, she is really for you. I took her from you, and she is bone of your bone and flesh of your flesh. Therefore she is a woman: the other part of man. You may call her Eve, for she will become the Mother of all mankind."

"The sun will soon be setting and there will begin a day which I have set aside. It is a holy day, a day of rest and worship. You must do no work on the seventh day of each week, for it is the day that completes the Work that My Hand has wrought.

"However, beginning on the first day of the new week you must take your wife and teach her everything that I have taught you. She will be your helper. Together you will bring forth young and replenish the earth. Awaken your wife now, Adam. Take her to your bosom and cherish her."

Adam gently called her name. "Eve, Eve my darling. Awaken, my love. Listen to the voice of your husband."

Joy was known in the Garden as Eve awoke to Life, and her husband's joyous laughter rang throughout.

The sun, which had been quickly slipping beyond the horizon, suddenly gave way to the stars and moon and the entire Garden settled down to sleep the night away. The animals gathered around the man and the woman where they both lay sleeping on the bed of leaves. They were filled with awe and gratitude that the Heavenly Father had created such marvelous beings to be the overseers of themselves and the Garden. They felt very safe and secure. The owl, of course, awoke from his daytime of sleep and sounded the call which told all the creatures created for the night watch to report for duty; it was his job to sit high in the tree and look out over the Garden all the night long. This he did happily, pausing ever so often to look down at the sleeping woman and ask, "Whoo, who?"

On the first day of the week, Adam obediently began teaching Eve all of the lessons that the Father had taught him. The animals cheerfully assisted, for each had a special job to do in the Garden. The bees showed Eve where they stored the sweet honey; the cows and goats, how to obtain rich foamy milk; and the birds of the air would flit from berry bush to berry bush encouraging her to pick the sweetest fruit.

Adam and Eve had a glorious place in which to live. They loved running from tree to tree picking the fruit; and they knew only joy as, laughing and running through the fields, splashing in the brooks and bathing in the waterfalls, they explored the delights of their world. At night they would fall asleep counting the uncountable stars and watching the moon attempting to find its place in the sky. Every animal in the Garden was their friend, but their most special friends were the wooly white sheep. One day the ram called excitedly to Adam and Eve.

"Come quickly, oh come quickly!" he urged.

The man and woman ran to the shady spot where the ewe was lying. They knelt down so that they could peer into the cave-like area under the thick vines and branches. There nestled up to its mamma was a tiny white wooly creature. The sheep looked proudly and tenderly at their newly born offspring. They were now parents, and suddenly they looked older and wiser; but just for a moment, because the ram boldly gave a great leap into the air, turned around three times and went tearing through the Garden yelling, "I'm a dad, I'm a dad, I'M A DAD!!!"

The ewe giggled and fell instantly asleep next to her little one. Adam and Eve walked away hand in hand.

"Is this what the Father meant by 'replenish'? he asked thoughtfully.

"I think so." nodded Eve.

Adam glanced shyly at his wife. "It's…it's really…wonderful, isn't it?"

She raised her long lashes and looked deeply into his eyes. "Yes," she said firmly, "it is truly wonderful!"

Shortly thereafter, other animals also bore young, and the Garden seemed even more alive, now that it included the playfulness of the little ones. So life continued joyfully in Eden; and although she had not yet had a child, Eve found contentment in playing with the many animal babies. Every little one was taught to address Lady Eve as "My Queen," and Eve was the most gentle, loving creation in that perfect world of beauty and gentleness.

There was only one tiny wind that was beginning to blow against the gentle currents of peace, and at first it was so subtle that no one was really aware of it. The serpent had begun keeping himself aloof from the other occupants of the Garden; and although he would have denied it, even to himself, he especially avoided having to call Eve, "My Queen."

He would hurry quickly away whenever he saw her coming in his direction. Certainly he was never actually rude; he was just always *very* busy. He would stand afar off and gaze at her beauty. There was no question about it he thought, as he peered at his own reflection in a pond, Eve was the most beautiful being in the Garden.

The more he thought about this, the more unsettled he felt. He had never experienced such feelings of unrest before, and he wasn't at all sure what to do about them. Little by little one of the friendliest, most beautiful creatures in all of Eden became distant and withdrawn.

His other part was happily absorbed in their new off spring; so after a few tentative questions about his behavior, she began to accept the situation.

One moonlit night the serpent stood silently on a nearby knoll, looking across the distance at the perfect features of the sleeping Queen. As he gazed at her he thought he heard a soft rippling sound in the nearby bushes, and then he was sure that something called his name. He moved closer to the bushes to observe. Just then the moon slid behind a cloud and the serpent was able to see only a vague outline of the one who had called him.

"Who are you?" the serpent asked, startled, for never before had he seen a stranger in the Garden.

"When I was given my due, I was called Lucifer," answered the shadows in a tone of voice that the serpent had never heard before.

It was as if the voice carried authority in the manner of the Father's Voice; and yet, and yet--the serpent's thoughts became a bit jumbled at this point--"and yet, it is as if the voice belongs to the darkness," he concluded with a shiver. He started to run away, but the voice of the one who called himself 'Lucifer' urged him to stay a moment; and in spite of his doubts, the serpent suddenly experienced a compelling urge to listen to the shadows.

"I, too, know what it is to be cheated out of my rightful place," moaned the voice.

The serpent looked sharply into the shadows, for he had never before heard sad, angry or unhappy tones, and he felt a chill run down his spine. He knew a strange urging, a curiosity to move closer into the shadows in order to hear more of what the strange voice was saying.

The moon came out from behind the clouds, illuminating the bushes. The voice scurried off calling, "We'll talk more later."

The serpent stared after the voice for a long time, suddenly vowing to himself that if this thing called Lucifer returned, he would listen to it no more. Shaking himself as if to be rid of the dark feelings, he hurried home to his wife and children.

The next day was the Sabbath; the day that the Father had set aside for rest and worship. All of the members of the Garden gathered together in their favorite meadow, and the birds led a choir of praise. Everyone joined in song, and the donkey got so carried away that his deep tuneless brays were louder than all the voices of the others.

The wolf family and the sheep family were sitting close together and the young lambs and pups looked at each other and giggled. The mothers sternly nudged the little ones, and the fathers quickly lowered their heads so that the youngsters wouldn't see that they too were about to laugh.

It was a joyful morning of praise and thanksgiving as the latest babies were presented to the group, and the Heavenly Father was praised for the Love that he had so freely given each of them.

After a lunch of berries and other fruits, which had been gathered the day before, the residents of Eden all settled down for a long afternoon nap.

The serpent gave a quick look around the Garden, but there were no shadows anywhere and no sign of the dark visitor. He gave a sigh of relief, deciding that it wasn't worth thinking about and would never happen again. He certainly didn't want to bother King Adam with such troublesome things on this beautiful day. He strolled calmly across the Garden to his home, smiling broadly at the Queen as he passed her.

Life in the Garden had a secure sameness about it with the bird choir greeting the dawn every morning and the rooster awakening his flock with his trumpet call of 'cock-a-doodle-do'. Each one arose eager to face the new day; for each had his special task to do, and knew that his task played an important part in the ongoing order of the Garden.

The King made daily inspections and encouraged each creature with kind words and friendly pats. He worked happily in the fields, which the oxen had helped him plow, and scattered the seeds that he had gathered from mature plants. He found his daily work pleasant and rewarding.

God had created a system of streams that flowed from the rivers to give water to the many new little plants as they grew. The streams sparkled and danced with the sunbeams, while fish jumped over rocks on their journey through the water. Adam enjoyed taking his lunch break by the water's edge and observing the enchanting scene.

Eve collected reeds and grasses from the shallow waters and wove colorful baskets and pretty mats. Every creature in the Garden had a sleeping mat made by the Queen. She also carved intricate pots from dried gourds.

In one part of the Garden there were bubbling warm springs, and Eve would fill a gourd with the warm water and make a tea from the herbs that she had gathered. She learned how to stew the fruit that she had sweetened with honey, and enjoyed watching Adam smack his lips when he ate.

"You are a good wife, Eve," commended Adam. And indeed she was a good wife; for Eve was very industrious and always set about her work with a smile and a song. She was content.

Each evening when the work was done, and the last meal of the day completed, the Father would visit them. They would walk together in the Garden. They would tell their Heavenly Father all about the day's activities, and he would kindly express His pleasure at their efforts. They felt very proud when God praised them.

The serpent had nearly forgotten the visit by the shadowy voice, and once again was taking a stroll in the moonlight. He had not intended to seek out Adam's home, but after walking past streams and through numerous groves of trees, he found that he had circled back around to where the couple was sleeping peacefully.

Once again he stared down at the lovely Eve whose features seemed to glow in the light of the moon. As he turned to go back to his own home, he was startled by the voice.

"God isn't fair. If He really loved you, He wouldn't treat you the way He does."

The serpent peered into the shadows trying to see the speaker, but all he could see was darkness. "Why, whatever do you mean?" questioned the serpent. "God made this beautiful Garden and placed us all here to live. He gave a kind and gentle King and Queen to have dominion over us. Life is wonderful. What more could we want?" he continued.

A long silence prevailed from the bushes with occasional snatches of a bone-jarring ditty which the voice sang.

The serpent shuddered; clearly the voice thought that he was being musical, but honestly the donkey carried a better tune than that!

The voice began to speak slowly, "Well, of course, there is just one small problem with your 'wonderful life'," he stated.

The serpent looked puzzled, but the voice hurried on with his story. Prior to the coming of the voice only Truth had been spoken in the Garden, and the serpent accepted the words that were being spoken, even though something deep inside of him felt ill at ease. "This world belonged to me until God took it away!" declared the voice brazenly.

"Wh…what??" stammered the serpent. "Why would God do a thing like that?"

"Oh, it's very simple," snarled the voice. "God was jealous because so many of the other angels loved me."

"You mean that you are an angel?" gasped the serpent in surprise.

"Only the most beautiful angel in all of Heaven, that's all!" the voice boasted. "It was because I was so beautiful and wise that God became angry with me and made me leave Heaven. I was so brilliant to look at that the other angels had to hide their eyes. Why, I was covered with rubies and topaz and emeralds and every precious stone that you can imagine--and some that *you* can't possibly imagine," he added scornfully.

The serpent strained hard to see if he could see any precious stones but the voice moved deeper into the shadows.

"I've got to go now, serpent, but think about this: look around you. What do you see when you look at all the couples in the Garden?" he queried.

The serpent looked around at the sleeping pairs, most of whom had young nestled up to them. In his mind's eye he could see how they each looked as they moved about in the Garden during the daylight.

"I see beauty," he said quietly.

"Yes, yes of course you do," impatiently interrupted the voice, "and who is more beautiful of each pair, the male or the female?"

The serpent paused and then spoke, "Well the male is of course, except for...that is..."

"Yeah right," spat the voice. "Go on and say it. Except for Adam and Eve. Why it goes against the very order of things for Eve to be more beautiful than Adam! God isn't fair. He only did it to be mean. God took away your rightful place as the most beautiful creature in the Garden and he did it with a female!"

The serpent started to reply but suddenly he realized that the dark angel was no longer there. He stared vacantly into the shadows and then slowly and numbly turned to resume his night wanderings.

By morning he was exhausted, and curled up on his warm rock to sleep all day. The others wondered at this strange behavior but said nothing.

Adam also felt concern, but decided to allow the serpent to continue in his unusual behavior for a while. After all, mother serpent had given birth to more offspring than any other animal; perhaps they kept their father awake at night. It would all work out somehow. He decided not to bother the Heavenly Father with the situation.

So life continued much the same in the Garden with the animals following the lead of their King. Everyone else accepted a small part of the serpent's daily duties and the change became part of the routine. The serpent and the dark angel began meeting nightly, except for the Sabbath. The dark angel never came around on the Sabbath.

During one nightly meeting, the dark one came up very close behind the serpent.

"I'm so cold," he whined. "Can I get near you so I'll be able to keep warm?"

Strangely the serpent found that he no longer felt repulsed by the dark one, and he allowed him to cuddle as close as he wished.

Several weeks later the dark one again complained of feeling the chill and got so close to the serpent that he slipped right inside of him. The serpent felt a jolt of surprise, but suddenly he was powerless to change the situation.

"I'll just live here for a while," the dark voice said firmly. The serpent could not say one word unless the dark one allowed it.

The serpent's behavior changed drastically, much to Adam's relief, for Adam had finally become ready to discuss the situation with the Father. He was relieved that now he wouldn't have to, for the serpent was again quite his jolly and helpful self. He did more than his share of the work, and every day he went out of his way to speak courteously to the Queen.

As a matter of fact he made a point to visit with Eve for a while every morning when she came in from her work. He began by complimenting her on the pretty things that she continued to fashion out of materials in the Garden. As the days went by, and it became obvious that she enjoyed his company, he began to comment on her beauty.

At first Eve was very shy about receiving such compliments, for in her heart she knew that she was simply as God had created her. She knew that any beauty that she possessed was not of her own making.

Eve began to confide to Mother Ewe how much she enjoyed visiting with the serpent now that he had become his old self again. Mother Ewe commented that it was rather strange how the serpent made such drastic changes in character; but all in all she too was glad that he was now doing his part of the work.

Mother Ewe also noted silently that Eve had begun some subtle changes. Several times she came upon Eve bending over the lake as she observed her reflection. Eve had never commented on her own beauty before the serpent began with his flattery, and the change made Mother Ewe uncomfortable.

Eve, however, was beginning to enjoy the warm feelings that she got from the serpent's flattery. She began spending less and less time on her duties and more time grooming herself. After bathing in the waterfall each morning she would run her fingers through her hair until it glistened in the sunlight. Adam noticed and presented her with a comb that he had made so that she could comb her hair until it felt like silk. He was proud of his wife's beauty, and at first didn't object to the extra attention that she was paying herself.

She would walk through the Garden, barely remembering to speak to the animals, searching for the sweetest flowers, which she rubbed on her body, enjoying the essence that they gave. Once, in the reflection of the pool, she rubbed juice from some red berries on her cheekbones and across her lips.

The serpent rhapsodized about how beautiful she looked; but when Adam saw her, he laughed out loud and playfully teased her about getting so carried away eating berries that she had gotten juice all over her face.

Eve quickly scrubbed the juice off her face; but, feeling for the first time rather miffed at Adam, she avoided him for the rest of the afternoon.

She became aware, in a way that she had never known before, that the serpent was an extraordinary creature. She began to enjoy just sitting and looking at the beautiful colors that blended vibrantly throughout his wonderful skin. Even more remarkable to Eve was how wise the serpent had become. She decided that, since Adam was so very busy, it was not necessary to bother him with her usual daily questions concerning the upkeep of the Garden. The serpent had such excellent ideas that she began seeking his advice. He was always available and was more than willing to advise the Queen.

One day Eve and the serpent were walking side-by-side deep in the center of the Garden. They had shared several minutes of silence when suddenly they found themselves near the Tree of Knowledge. Both stood looking up at the beautiful tree that was heavily laden with glistening fruit. The fruit was unlike any other in the Garden.

"Eve," the serpent asked so quietly that she had to strain to hear, "did God really tell you not to eat from any of the trees in the Garden?"

She looked at the serpent in surprise and laughed softly, "Why of course not," she replied. "We can eat of every tree in the Garden, except this one." Then to emphasize the point she added, "and He told us not to even touch it!"

She suddenly frowned, and for the first time since her creation her lovely face was furrowed; for she realized that she had invented the part about touching. Something didn't feel right, but she decided that it was a small matter and chose to ignore it.

The two stood silently looking at the tree until finally the serpent shrugged and turned to go away. Glancing back over his shoulder he called mysteriously, "I think it is a shame that is what God wants you to believe!"

"What do you mean?" queried Eve, but the Serpent had gone off into another part of the Garden.

Adam and the oxen were walking slowly home after a full day of working the fields, and Adam noticed Eve coming out of the depths of the Garden.

He waved cheerfully and began to tell her about the many new plants that were thriving in the fields. He was looking forward to another fine harvest. Eve seemed somewhat distracted, and after a few minutes Adam paused in his talk to look closely at her. He knew that there were changes going on with his wife that caused him to feel a nagging concern.

Much of her conversation in recent days had centered on the serpent and how wise, or beautiful, or clever, he was. Adam was beginning to feel shut out. It seemed as if the serpent was becoming more important to Eve than he was.

Adam shook himself as if to clear such unworthy thoughts. It would soon be dusk and time for their visit with the Heavenly Father. He knew that he should mention something to the Father about his concerns, but once again he was reluctant to share his problems with God. After all, God had placed him in charge of the Garden. He had given Eve as Adam's helpmate. There couldn't be anything *really* wrong.

Adam grabbed Eve's hand and they began to skip along the stream that led to their home. Adam's heart momentarily lightened, until he noticed that Eve kept turning her head back to look deep into the Garden.

❋ ❋ ❋ ❋ ❋

Adam leaned against a massive oak tree, which grew next to his favorite cool spot by the stream, while he waited for the Father to come for their evening walk. Adam loved this time of day. The sun was setting below the far hills, and purple rays were reaching up to meet the blue of the sky. Everything was peaceful and good.

Adam smiled. God had made a perfect world. Everything was perfect here.

Eve continued meeting the serpent on a daily basis. She would hurry through her duties so that she could venture deep into the Garden to seek him out. He was so very wise, and always very certain of his answers. She found that she had less and less time to spend with the other animals, and began even more frequently to take only the serpent's advice on matters. After all, Adam was so very busy, and the serpent always had plenty of time.

One day, several weeks after their first conversation about the Tree of Knowledge, the serpent brought up the subject again. They were standing underneath the tree, looking high up into the branches. The fruit seemed ripe for picking. It glistened in the sunlight and caused a glow to surround the entire tree and reflect off the upturned faces of the pair.

The serpent sighed a long, belabored sigh. "Oh well," he said, "I guess God has His reasons for not wanting you to be wise."

"Do you mean that the fruit from this Tree would make me wise?" asked Eve, with a hunger in her voice.

"Well, yes. Yes, of course. I thought you knew. I mean…Well yes. Yes indeed. That's why I think God doesn't want you to eat. God wants to keep you helpless and dependent on him: you know, like the baby lamb was when he was first born." The serpent signed again and shifted his eyes in Eve's direction.

"You are very wise," Eve said thoughtfully.

"Oh my yes, yes indeed I am," nodded the serpent smugly.

Eve walked completely around the Tree, never taking her eyes off the fruit. She heard Adam call to her and she turned, as if in a daze, to look at him.

He was standing upon a nearby knoll watching them. "Eve, come away from that Tree!" he urged in a worried tone of voice. "God told us that we must not eat of it. We will die if we do!"

The serpent laughed scornfully. "Oh you won't die," he assured them. "God would never allow that to happen. Why, He made you in His very image and He isn't about to kill you. He said that so you would be afraid to eat the fruit!

"I would certainly think, Adam, that you would like to be wise!" he continued.

Eve suddenly reached up and grabbed a piece of fruit and took a large bite.

"Adam, Adam, it is glorious. Look, I'm not hurt. Try some," she urged, handing him a piece.

He gingerly took the fruit from her hand and, looking long at the expression on his wife's face, took a bite, chewed and swallowed.

They began to laugh and dance around the tree, eating piece after piece of the wonderful fruit. They failed to notice that the serpent was lying limply on the rock close to them. Had they noticed, they might have realized that something, or someone, had left him; and he appeared lifeless with a glazed look to his eyes. So busy were they with their revelry that they didn't even hear the distant retreating sound of cruel laughter.

Overcome with their own laughter, they both fell to the ground and rolled languidly in the grass. As they lay completely still for a moment, enjoying the peacefulness of the white clouds drifting in the blue sky, they became aware of an unusual stillness. Sitting up they were surprised to observe the Garden animals gathered around them with shocked expressions on their faces. No one said a word. Even the leaves had hushed on the trees and the very air felt as if there was a heaviness about it.

Adam and Eve looked at each other and gasped, for a change had taken place in their appearance. Every creature in the Garden had his own special covering. The beaver had a sleek, magnificent coat that glistened like the dew-drenched grass when he played in the streams.

There were different kinds of rabbits; one had a soft white coat and another a sleek brown one, but each had a lovely covering. Each and every animal in the Garden had a unique covering; and for Adam and Eve it was the same. They were clothed with the Shekinah glory of God, for they were made in His Image.

But now something terrible had happened! They had no magnificent covering at all. Their bodies were naked, exposed, and they looked at each other in dismay.

Instinctively they both ran and hid behind the bushes. Peering around the bushes, they saw that all of the animals had left hurriedly; not one animal remained.

"Oh Eve, what are we going to do?" moaned Adam, with his head in his hands.

Eve suddenly jumped up, full of action, and what she considered to be a great idea.

"Why Adam, it is very simple!" she said gaily. "I shall make us a covering from the leaves. Am I not clever at weaving?! You watch, my love, for everything is going to be just fine--even better than it was before, for now we are very wise."

Adam gathered great mounds of grass and leaves, and Eve busily set to work weaving a covering for each of them. They dressed in the garments which she had made and Eve pronounced them quite elegant. She was proud of her handiwork.

Adam smiled and thanked her, but something in his chest felt tight and heavy. He went to sit down on the big rocks by the stream, and idly threw pebbles in the water. Eve glance around for the animals so that she could show off her new garment, but they were nowhere to be seen. She busied herself making daisy chains to wear as garlands around her neck.

The shadows began to lengthen and suddenly the Voice was heard in the Garden. The Father was speaking tenderly to the birds and creatures resting in the woods beyond the bright meadow. Adam and Eve looked up in alarm, their faces suddenly pale and frightened. Adam ran in a panic to a thicket and hid himself. Eve quickly joined him and they huddled together, their hearts beating so fiercely that they could feel the vibrations in their throats. Never before had they felt FEAR, and it caused beads of cold sweat to form on their bodies. Adam's breath came in short gasps. "Be very quiet, Eve," he urged. "Father must not see us like this."

The Voice was calling insistently, "Adam, Adam, where are you?"

The wind parted the vines in the thicket exposing the quaking couple. Adam stood shakily to his feet, his head hanging down and his eyes lowered. Eve was still on her knees, cowering behind him.

"Adam, were you hiding from Me?" queried the Father.

Adam gulped and in a strangled voice managed to croak, "Yes Sir."

The Father waited for Adam to continue. With his head still hanging down, the man scuffed his big toe back and forth in the dirt. Finally, unable to bear the searching silence of the Father, Adam blurted, "We didn't want you to know that we are naked."

In a very quiet voice God questioned, "Who told you that you are naked? Did you eat from the tree which I had commanded you not to eat?"

Adam began to tremble, for he had never before heard Father speak in that stern tone. He glanced quickly at Eve: "The woman that you put here to be with me, she picked the fruit and gave it to me to eat." He looked up hopefully.

God looked at Eve who had suddenly moved away from Adam and was looking around as if for another place to hide.

"Eve, what is this that you have done!" demanded God.

She spoke in a whisper, glancing swiftly to where the serpent was attempting to hide in the tall grass, "The serpent deceived me and I ate."

Turning then to the serpent, who still looked somewhat dazed, God began His judgment. "This is your punishment: You are singled out from among all the domestic and wild animals of the whole earth to be cursed. You shall grovel in the dust as long as you live, crawling along on your belly. From now on you and the woman will be enemies, as will all of your offspring and hers. And I will put the fear of you into the woman, and between your offspring and hers. He shall strike you on your head, while you will strike at His heel."

Then God said to the woman, "You shall bear children in intense pain and suffering; yet even so you shall welcome your husband's affections, and he shall be your master."

And to Adam, God said, "Because you listened to your wife and ate the fruit when I told you not to, I have placed a curse upon the soil. All your life you will sweat to master it, until your dying day. Then you will return to the ground from which you came. For you were made from the ground, and to the ground you will return."

For long moments Adam and Eve stood together alone and with heads bowed as they considered their punishment. Suddenly in the meadow they heard a pitiful scream and then a crackling sound.

They ran quickly into the meadow and there to their horror lay the body of the firstborn of Mother and Father Sheep. God had built an altar, and the flames were consuming the young body, while the blood ran freely down the sides of the rocks.

Adam and Eve had never before seen blood, nor had they experienced death, and both turned aside to share one more new experience as they vomited violently into the field. They now truly knew what 'death' meant.

God spoke again, explaining that when they had disobeyed they had caused sin to come into the World and that sin could only be paid for by the shedding of innocent blood.

He handed them the clothing that He had made from the skin of their playmate. It was still warm to touch and had the smell of the young sheep about it. With sobs racking their bodies they placed the covering on themselves.

They looked up to see Mother and Father Sheep watching them. Eve ran over to Mother Ewe and threw her arms around her neck. "I'm so sorry, so very sorry," Eve sobbed.

Both sheep ran off in fear. "Baa," they said, "Baa." A chorus of sound filled the Garden. Each animal began making the sound particular to its own species. No longer could Adam and Eve communicate freely with the animals.

Another sound was suddenly heard in the distance.

Huge gates, heretofore unnoticed, had swung open showing the vastness of the world outside.

"You must leave this Garden," thundered the Voice of the Lord God.

Adam and Eve and all of the animals and birds and everything that lived in the Garden were forced out into the world.

The couple stood silently outside the gates looking back at the Garden. The gates slammed closed, and angels with flaming swords stood guard before them, refusing to even glance at the deposed King and his Queen. All of the animals had fled into the new wilderness; darkness was falling; and the man and his wife, now strangers in a strange world, were alone.

* * * * *

Adam awoke from his memories with a start. The fire was still glowing, Eve was still sitting quietly by his side and the turmoil of the day was, indeed, reality.

Chapter Two

A New Home

Adam closed his eyes and let his thoughts wander once again. This time they took him back through the years that he and Eve had lived here in this cave. When they left the Garden, they had traveled aimlessly for some weeks, falling in an exhausted and discouraged sleep each night. One morning they awoke to see an angel pointing in the direction they should walk.

A long time later, the hills where they were to eventually make their home came into view. The journey was perilous and required many stops, sometimes for long periods. The beckoning hills, which had appeared nearby at first glance, seemed to take forever to reach. When at last they climbed up the jagged rocks that hid the little cave that was to be their new home, they knew that their journey was over.

His mind flooded with memories, Adam smiled a sad, rueful smile, "Oh that other home. That beautiful, peaceful, wonderful Garden home. Would there ever be another home such as that?"

Eve glanced in his direction and noticed the smile. "What are you thinking about, that causes you to smile so?" she asked curiously.

"Oh, I was just remembering the Garden, and was wishing that our children could have lived there, instead of here in this hard land," he said wistfully.

Eve was silent for a long time. When she spoke it was with a sadness and grief in her voice that Adam had seldom heard before. "God gave us that wonderful Garden home with all of our precious animal friends. He gave those animals to us, to nurture and protect, and made us King and Queen over them. He promised us young of our own and told us to replenish the earth. Work was not a drudgery, but a joy, and every morning was a bright new gift from our Heavenly Father."

Tears filled her eyes and ran down her cheeks. "It was I who lost it," she choked. "I was vain and greedy, and disobeyed our Father, and it was I who caused you to disobey!"

Adam placed his arms around his wife and held her close to him. "Oh no, Eve, that is too simple a solution to a problem we both caused. I sinned too. God created me first. I was placed in charge. I knew the command. Yes, we were King and Queen, but I caused us to become servants, slaves to this land. I wanted to please you, to show off, to be wise as the serpent; and I placed those desires above pleasing God. I am the reason that the sin sacrifice must be made. I am the reason that those wonderful animals were placed in this wilderness where they must fight and devour each other in order to survive.

"God gave me the most wonderful gift that He could possibly give. He made me, and placed me in a perfect world; and then, when He saw that I wanted more, He gave me you, my lovely, darling Eve. Time did not exist in that bright world. You know, sometimes when I think back, I wonder how long we were actually there. We did not reckon time then. There were just days and nights and the beautiful Sabbaths, but we just were, we just always *were*; time was not marked as it is here."

He choked for a moment and then continued, "And this is the gift I gave my children: toiling day in and day out in a land that gives frugally and harshly; watching our little son, our first to give us joy, bitterly reject the Heavenly Father whom we know to be loving and kind. Cain has a spirit of rebellion that came from us. Of course Cain hates death. It angers him that animals must die, and the hideous truth is that this is the gift that we gave our children. Death. God gave us life and we gave our children death."

He bowed his head in shame.

Husband and wife stood together for a long time with heads bowed, their tears mingling. Finally they silently turned to the door of the cave, and went to their bed.

They did not look back into the night; but if they had, they would have seen a bright light glowing over the altar where the lamb had been slain and offered as a sacrifice. The Shekinah Glory of God rested there, for God always accepts the sacrifice of a broken and contrite heart.

When the family awakened the following morning all of the anger, darkness and despair had abated. The children laughed and splashed in the stream while Eve prepared breakfast; and Adam began his morning as usual by offering up prayers to God for his family.

Everyone except baby Rina had a job to do during the day. Today Adam announced that they would begin clearing another field. He wanted the field cleared of rocks so that after the winter, which was soon to come, the spring planting could be expanded.

Several times a year Adam took a journey to a different part of the land. He would round up animals, as he was able, and bring them back to be used in the fields, or to provide eggs, milk and cheese for the table. Never, in all of his journeys, had he come upon the original animals that had been placed in the Garden. Only Horse had remained by their side. The mare, heavy with foal, had run away when the Gates had opened. The animals, which he caught, did not know him and would attempt to get away from the strange scent of man.

Eve had helped him to make leather harnesses and ropes. When he would trap the animals he would spend days, and sometimes weeks, gaining their trust by being gentle and kind, bringing food and water.

They would then follow him willingly, being led by the harness and leash, back to his dwelling.

Now Adam was able once again to use oxen to plow and till the fields. He was teaching Cain how to plow the earth and plant the seeds, and how to destroy the weeds and thistles that would so quickly crowd out the little seedlings. Cain loved to watch things grow, and Father promised that he could join him on his next journey, which would begin with the new moon. Cain was to search the wild fields for new and different seeds to plant. They would each lead a donkey behind then in order to carry the many plants, bushes and seeds that they would be bringing home.

Abel's love was caring for the animals that his father brought home. He took excellent care of them, for he had been taught to appreciate the many services that they provided for the family. These animals lived inside the stone walls that Adam had built as fences. This kept them from wandering off, or getting injured or even killed. Abel was especially pleased when Father would choose one of his own little lambs to offer as a sacrifice to their Heavenly Father. He loved the little animals; but he knew that it was God's will for the sacrifice to be made, and Abel accepted his parents' teaching that God's way was always best.

Mother had some animals of her own, and Aluma helped her take care of these. Aluma felt very special and important when Mother would give her a pot of grain to throw to the chickens, or tell her to take water from the stream to place in the rock basin where the chickens drank. Mother said that she was still too little to gather the eggs but someday she would be big enough. There were also ducks and geese, which swam in the pond at the foot of the hill, and milk goats from which mother made delicious cheese. It was great fun filling the wooden cups, which Father had carved, with foamy milk and seeing who could drink theirs the fastest. Aluma never won, but she knew that when Rina got older and drank her milk from a cup that she surely would be able to beat her!

After all the early chores were completed, the family began work on the new field. Rina was happy to sit on a woven mat, playing with toys, which Father had carved for her, and watch her family work. Abel liked to tease his baby sister, whom he loved dearly. He would tell her that she had been found in the field at harvest time when they were gathering the crops; and then he would tickle her and tell her that she was fat and lazy and urge her to hurry and grow big enough to help them pull rocks from the field. She would laugh and squeal and hug Abel tightly around his neck.

Mother and Father had woven a sturdy mat out of reeds, bark and leather, which they attached to a donkey by means of leather straps. The children would load the mat full of stones that they pulled from the field, and take them to the place that Father had shown them. If the stone was too large for them to lift, Father would stop the oxen and come help them place it on the mat. He showed them how to be careful to place just the right weight of stones so that the donkey would not become discouraged. Father was very kind to the animals. Sometimes the children would giggle, for they would hear Father talking to the animals. As if the animals could answer him!

"What are you going to do with this big pile of stones, Father?" asked Cain. "Are you going to build more walls to keep the animals in?"

Adam stopped his work for a moment and wiped the sweat from his brow. "No, Cain, I have a different plan for these stones. I intend to build walls to keep us in."

Eve and the children gathered round him in surprise. "What do you mean?" Walls for us! Tell us, please tell us, Father." They all talked at once.

Adam laughed and told Eve and Aluma to fetch their lunch and he would share his plans with all of them at once. Eve and the little girl hurried to the shallow part of the stream where they had placed their lunch in a basket, which Eve had made waterproof with pitch. The boys washed their hands, spread mats on the ground, and set the wooden bowls at each one's place.

After Adam had thanked God for the food and asked Him to bless the new field, he took a bark tablet from the pouch that he carried around his waist. Everyone crowded close to look at the marks that Adam had made on the smooth surface. "This is to be our new home," he explained. Four blank faces looked in his direction.

He smiled and continued, "We will build walls which are taller than I. We can be certain that they will hold fast for I have been testing a new mixture of mud, sand, lime and straw which I have been using to hold stones together for the fences. When it dries it is very hard. The walls will not move.

"We will secure long straight poles to the top that will hold the roof that we will build. I believe that we can cover the house with the same materials that we used to make the strong mat for hauling stones. We will add a layer of mud so that it will withstand the winds and moisture. We will make the walls so thick that the cold winds will become discouraged as they try to get in.

"We will build our new home on that knoll." He pointed to the high area that was situated on the other side of the stream.

It was an area where flowers and wild grasses grew. Eve had always enjoyed laying her wash out to dry in that area because it seemed so fresh and pretty, and the clothes always absorbed the sweet smell of the lush grass. She smiled and nodded at the prospect of a home there.

"The cave has been a good, safe home for us," Adam continued, "but we have outgrown it. There are too many of us now to fit comfortably in it, especially as big as you boys are getting!" The boys grinned and stretched as tall as they could. Their parents laughed.

"I will be glad to be closer to my chickens," Eve added. "Then I won't have to worry so much about the foxes eating them, or those hateful serpents eating the eggs!"

Adam agreed that it would be good to be closer to all of the animals. They were housed in the valley where they could graze in the grassy fields, and the cave was many long steps up the side of the hill. Each child expressed pleasure at some aspect of the new home. Everyone was thinking of the many trips up and down that it took to provide water and various other necessities for living in the cave.

No one complained that they already worked from first light to dark; for each was willing to work just a little harder and a little longer to have a house in the pretty valley. They quickly finished their mid-day meal and returned to the field, where they labored long and hard to add stones to the existing pile. Father said that soon there would be enough to start the foundation of their new home.

❋ ❋ ❋ ❋ ❋

The house took three long years of seemingly endless work. Finally, during the Festival of the Harvest, the family moved into their new home. The house had one large room, with a door leading to the outside and a window in each side wall. In this room they slept, ate and played. At the back of the room there was a door that led into another, very small, room with a cave-like enclosure just the right size to contain the fire they used for cooking and warmth.

This smaller room always smelled like herbs because Eve kept large bunches of dried herbs, onions and fruits hanging from the rafters.

There were stores of grain and other foodstuffs in various containers that sat on shelves that Adam had made. Eve spent as much time as possible in this room for it was her pride and joy. One side wall had a door leading into a shed which housed the chickens and the milk goats.

After the sacrifice of the lamb, solemn prayers of thanksgiving for the harvest were offered, along with a dedication prayer for the new house and the family who lived within. Even Cain, who usually had a stormy face and rebellious attitude during the harvest celebration, managed to look sunny and happy as they formally took possession of their new home. What a happy day it was! How cheerful the new house looked with all of the new mats that Eve had somehow found time to make. The children wondered how many long hours their mother had spent working by the light of the fire, long after they had gone to sleep.

Like millions of families which were to follow, the first family on this earth had good days and bad days; there were times when the children were cross and unreasonable with each other and their parents, and times when the parents wanted to get away for some quiet time alone. Eve especially missed Mother Ewe, for she had been a faithful and dear friend.

Adam and Eve had to tell the stories of the Garden of Eden, and about all the animals who could talk, over and over again. It was a favorite firelight topic as they rested at the end of the day. When summer days were long, they would all lie on mats and watch for the first stars to appear, while the parents would share their memories with the young ones.

Abel always thrilled to hear how the Heavenly Father would come every evening and visit with their parents; for now, although they spoke to Him every day in prayer, God usually only visited at the Harvest Festival. That was when His Shekinah Glory would hover over the gifts they offered Him.

Abel shared his father's sadness, when Adam would remember how he had failed to tell the Father about the Serpent's misbehavior. Adam knew that if he had confided his fears to the Father, the problem would have been solved at the very beginning. Adam stressed to his children that they should always come to their parents on this earth, and to their Father in Heaven, when they knew that something was not right.

Time was something else that fascinated the children, especially when their parents tried to explain to them that it had not been observed in the Garden. This was very difficult for them to understand, because now time was particularly important to the family. They knew that there was a time to plant, a time to care for the growing plants, and a time to harvest. There was a time for the animals to give birth; and now, their mother told them, there would soon be a time for her to give birth again. They watched the moon, and measured the weeks and months by the skies.

Once during a discussion of time and events, and how people grew older, the children wanted to know how old their parents were. Adam was able to tell them about how long they had lived outside the Garden, but he could never be absolutely certain how long he had lived *in* the Garden. The children found the idea of not getting older very difficult to comprehend. "But how long do you think you were there, Abba?" Rina persisted. Adam thought for long moments.

"Well," he said finally, "I know how long ten years is, and I would think that we probably had ten periods of ten years in our wonderful Garden. Would you agree, Eve?"

Eve looked thoughtful for a moment and then nodded her head in agreement.

"So, I guess," Adam continued, "that would make me about 119 years old; because Cain is seventeen, and we had him about two years after we left the Garden."

The children seemed to be satisfied, and both parents breathed a sigh of relief.

It was during the observance of Aluma's tenth birthday that Adam made a special announcement to the family. It was early spring and the air had its first sweet taste of warmth. They were sitting outside on mats enjoying a Sabbath afternoon.

Their father began to speak: "Children, soon we will have an additional child in this family. Your mother is due to give birth when the full moon is high in the heavens. She will be busy tending to the needs of the new one, and it is necessary for each of you to assume a heavier load of work."

They all nodded agreement.

Adam turned to address his firstborn son. Cain was a large boy now, recently turned seventeen, strong and well built. He was proud of his ability to till the field and produce healthy, vigorous crops. It seemed as if Cain's robustness flowed from himself into the fields. He could plow a section with a team of oxen in less time than his dad.

"Cain, God has given you a special gift of working with the soil," Adam began. "I have decided that it is time to place the full responsibility of the crops on your shoulders. In a few more years you will be a man, and we will decide whom to give you for your wife. You must become a man who accepts responsibility and toils well. Of course everyone will help with the planting and with the harvest, but you will now be the one to supervise us. I know you to be a hard worker, and value your love for the land. I trust your judgment."

Adam smiled at Abel, "My son, your gifts are of a different nature. You are kind and patient with the animals, and you never seem to mind the long hours that you must spend with them in the fields. When one wanders off, it is you who will not sleep at night until it is found. You are not squeamish to bind up their hurts or help with difficult births. The flocks are now your full responsibility. Although you are but a youth of thirteen, I know I can depend on you."

Abel could not hide the tears in his eyes as he looked at his father. "Oh Abba, I will try very hard to do a good job. Thank you for trusting me."

"No one works harder than I do," Cain said proudly, with his face shining and his chest thrown out. "I can certainly handle the fields by myself! Let Abel mind the smelly sheep. It gives him time for all that daydreaming he likes to do."

Eve spoke to her daughters. Seven-year-old Rina moved closer to her older sister for support. Aluma was given full responsibility for the chickens, ducks and geese. She smiled in delight for these were her favorite creatures. Rina would see that the cooking pots were cleaned each day with the ashes from the fire, and would assist Aluma in daily trips to the stream in order to maintain a constant water supply. "I like to bring the water, Mama, because Shimshon the big goat helps me by carrying the jugs on his back. He is proud to be called 'strong'! Eve shook her head in wonder because to everyone else the big Ram was a terror, butting with his head without any provocation. With Rina he was as meek as a lamb, doing her every bidding.

Each one was happy with his duties, and felt suddenly older and more special than before. After the family meeting, the children and Adam played games in the meadow, using a ball that Abel had made. He had gotten scrap pieces of wool from his mother as she wove, wound them into a ball, and covered it with strips of leather that his dad had given him.

When Adam laughingly threw himself down on the mat next to Eve, declaring that he couldn't keep up with the youngsters, she lovingly reached over and ran her fingers through his hair.

"Adam, it is time," she said quietly.

Adam jumped up, the laughter suddenly gone. He called the children to him. They came quickly and became very still as they saw his serious face. "I will be taking your mother to spend a few nights in the cave. When we return there will be another child. You know how to behave. I depend on each of you."

He assisted his wife up the neatly cleared trail to the cave. Adam insisted that the boys, using their tools and the goats, always kept the path cleared, although the family seldom went to the cave. When they did, it was usually just to fetch grain or vegetables that had been stored for the winter. During the past few weeks Father had led the children up there with supplies that would house people for several days.

That had seemed strange to them but they had cheerfully carried the jugs of water, mats and clothing. Mother had even sent a pretty basket filled with the softest of coverings. Now they watched silently as their parents climbed up the hill until they were no longer in sight, for the entrance to the cave was on the other side of the hill.

The children went about their chores as usual and the boys even helped prepare the meals. All were gratefully relieved when, after several days, their parents came back down the hillside carrying their new baby sister.

"What is her name?" they asked eagerly as they reached out to touch her baby softness.

"Names are very important, Children," their father told them. "First I will beseech God to give me the right name, and then we will have a special naming day when she is eight days old."

True to his word, Adam called for a celebration for the eighth day. Even though it was time to start the spring planting, they were able to take one day to have a special feast. Everyone agreed to work extra hours during the following weeks until the seeds were in the ground.

Abel brought his finest baby lamb to make a sacrifice of thanksgiving to God for the healthy baby and mother. Adam took the infant and lifted her towards the heavens in gratitude and praise to God. Having gone seven years without another child, both Adam and Eve had wondered if they would be granted any more children. Adam named her Simcha, which means joy; for there was much joy over her birth.

Soon it seemed difficult to imagine that there had ever been a time without little Simcha. Eve carried her in a sling across her chest as she did her work, and the baby was able to nurse even while her mother continued working steadily.

One day, after the crops were planted, Adam announced that he was going to make another journey. This time he took several donkeys and the two big animals that Horse, much to the family's surprise, had fathered by the little female donkeys. He rode Horse and led the other animals. The children were extremely curious at such a large number of animals going on the trip. They begged to know what he was going to bring home this time. "Wait and see!" he instructed. But before he left he dug a hole and placed marks on the ground. He told the children that everywhere there was a mark he wanted a hole dug just like the one he had made. The children could hardly contain their curiosity.

The days seemed to drag slowly by while Adam was gone. Each child took a turn maintaining a watch from the highest point nearby, looking far into the distance to try and see their father coming home. Finally after many weeks Abel, who was used to looking for his flocks, spied dust moving in the distance. The children quickly raised a banner up the pole that they had situated on the hilltop. They wanted to be certain that their father didn't accidentally pass them by. Adam and the heavily laden animals came wearily into the camp. The children were instructed to relieve the beasts of their burdens, brush their coats, feed and water them and turn them into their stable for a much-earned rest.

When all was accomplished as instructed, and Adam had also been fed a nourishing meal, the family was allowed to see the treasures that he had transported for many miles to their home.

They were terebinth trees! Over 50 tall, young trees had been wrapped in wet wool and carefully brought home to rest in the holes that were prepared for them.

"They will provide shade in the summer for us, and a wind break when the weather is bad. Terebinth-Oaks are sturdy trees and live long. In a few years we will be glad that we have them," Adam explained to his family as he carefully supervised the planting.

After several days the plantings were complete and every young tree had been watered with spring water. Everyone rested outside on the mats, observing their handiwork with pride. Little Simcha lay close to them in her basket, cooing and kicking her legs.

Suddenly Rina sat up, her face lit up with an inspiration. "Let's give each tree a name, just like we did Simcha!"

Cain put his head in his arms and groaned; but Abel smiled indulgently at his sister, and Aluma said that she thought it would be fun. They all looked at their parents who smiled their agreement.

Adam sat up and stated, "The grove shall be called Mamre; for we planted them with vigor, and the ground has received them with firmness!"

The children clapped with approval. Rina pointed to a tree with branches sticking up like horns. "I shall name that one Eyal because it looks powerful," she said.

"The one over there is Mahalalel because I praise God for our home," Eve smiled.

"I want to name that short, stubby one Shamir," declared Aluma, who was herself a bit short and stubby.

"Let's name that largest one Enoch," suggested Abel, "for the trees are dedicated."

Deciding to join in the game Cain suddenly sat up. "That one looks delicate, like a woman. I'll name her Elana."

The names continued, with the children contributing all the names that they could think of, including--when they began to tire of the game--some rather silly ones. They were all laughing when Adam declared that enough was enough, and Eve said that she certainly agreed and that it was time to start the evening meal.

Later, when the sad times came upon them, the children and their parents were to look upon that afternoon as one of the happiest in memory.

When Simcha was four years old and weaned, Adam and Eve had cause once again to make a trip to the cave, and once again brought down a baby girl. This child was named Tori.

Simcha was delighted with her baby sister and wanted to hold her and care for her. Her face beamed when Eve gently placed the baby in her arms and showed her how to support the head. Not fully understanding where babies came from, Simcha kept begging her father to take her to the cave so she could see if there were more babies up there.

Cain, who certainly understood where babies came from, began to dream of starting his own family. Aluma was no longer short or stubby and Cain found her most desirable as a wife.

In those beginning days upon the earth there was only one family, and it was necessary for the children to choose each other as mates. God had not yet forbidden this, as he did later, because the human condition was still new and fresh. No weak genetic aberrations had yet developed which could make the intermarriage of brother and sister dangerous to the offspring.

Cain approached his father to ask about taking Aluma as his wife. Adam looked at his son. "Have you built a place where you might house a family?" Cain admitted that he had not yet thought of such a duty. Adam stipulated that when Cain had built his own house, and made actual preparations to provide for a family of his own, he could once again approach the subject. Eve, who had overheard and had joined the discussion, added that Aluma would have to have her own mats and baskets woven, her bowls and eating utensils carved, and all the skills necessary for being a wife and mother polished.

For a while Cain went around in one of his dark moods, for he did not like to have to wait for any of his desires. When he saw that his parents were resolute, he began gathering stones for his own house.

Abel spent much of his time in the fields with his flocks. He loved having the time by himself to think his own thoughts, and to experiment with the numerous ideas that found their way into his head. Little Rina was a special favorite of his; but he knew that marriage was a long way off for them, and he was glad, for there was much that he wanted to do before he was responsible for his own family.

Being a quiet young man who never had the stormy moods that plagued his brother, Abel was content with his life, and wanted above all to be obedient to God and to his parents. He was a kind and thoughtful person, frequently bringing members of his family gifts that he had made, or found in the pastures. Once he found a shiny yellow stone in a stream of water that flowed high in the hills. He attached it to a leather cord that he had made and gave it to his mother to wear around her neck. She was thrilled with the pretty gift and praised Abel for his thoughtfulness.

The house was always full of flowers that Abel brought home from the fields, and Mother made luscious jams from the berries and honey he provided. The little girls played with toys that he had carved for them, and one day he shyly and silently left a beautifully carved wooden box on Rina's sleeping mat.

His favorite activity was what Cain scornfully called his 'scratches' on the smooth bark of trees. Abel could sit and work for hours at a time making symbols for words. He drew a man for the word 'man', a house for 'house', sun for 'daylight', moon for 'night' and so forth. When he had made an entire stack of pages from bark, he took the symbols and wrote simple stories for his sisters to read.

The girls thought the books were wonderful and they took special care of each one of them, reading them again and again. Cain thought that it was foolishness and a waste of time, and he voiced his opinion loudly and often.

Chapter Three

Cain

The elder brother loved hard work. Exceptionally proud of his fields, he was even more proud of his hard muscular body that had developed from all of his hard labor. He had no time for flowers when there were vegetables to grow!

When Cain was twenty-five years old, he once again approached his father about marriage. He took Adam to see the sturdy house that he had built with his own hands on his own time. He had enlarged the fields where they could easily support several families; and he had forged all of his own tools, so that he would not have to borrow his father's. He had worked hard and proudly displayed all that he had done to his father.

Adam looked at his son's accomplishments. He had to agree that Cain had worked industriously over the past few years. He asked himself why he felt so reluctant to allow him to take a wife. He remembered his son's frequent bursts of temper when things did not go his way, and thought how difficult Cain could be to live with when the black moods came upon him.

Nevertheless, Adam knew that he had given his word and could think of no reason for postponing longer. Certainly Aluma was ready to assume her duties as a wife. She could run the entire household by herself, and frequently did so now that Eve was expecting another child. She enjoyed pampering her mother, and would insist that Eve sit down and work on weaving or sewing while the girls did the heavy work. Yes, physically Aluma was fully developed and beautiful in her youth and vigor.

No, there was no reason to delay giving these two young people in marriage. Still Adam hesitated; it was time for spring planting. Aluma would turn eighteen during the autumn harvest.

Adam turned to his son. "The marriage ceremony will take place at the Harvest celebration, after the sin sacrifice is made. You will begin your marriage purified from your sin."

"But Father," Cain argued, "why can't I have a spring celebration and take my wife now? Haven't I waited long enough? I work hard; no one in this family works as hard as I do!"

Adam raised his hand to silence his son. "I have spoken and it shall be thus," he declared. He then turned and headed for his own house, giving no heed to the dark looks that Cain sent in his direction.

Once a week, the girls and their mother would make a trip to the house that was to become Aluma's home. They worked together to make the house snug and ready for the couple. They had enjoyed helping her make the many items that she would need to set up housekeeping on her own. Eve had allowed her to cull the poultry so that she would have her own chickens, ducks and geese. Even the little girls had been able to help; for they could weave mats for the floor and collect scraps of wood to place in the woodbin for kindling. Abel had surprised his sister by building a stable for the donkey he had given her and a shed for her poultry. He had worked during the cold winter days when he was unable to take the flocks to pasture. He also had a pair of lambs chosen for her marriage gift, but he had not yet told her.

One day, during the warm summer days, Aluma had carried a jug of water into the fields for her intended. Cain saw her coming, and watched as her young curved body moved in the gentle breeze. His blood ran hot within him. She waved when she saw him and called gaily, "I have brought you something to quench your thirst, Cain."

Cain waved back, but under his breath he muttered, "Yes, my Aluma, you certainly have!" There was no tenderness in his words, but a menace that would have frightened Aluma had she heard the tone.

Although she could not hear his words, she did see a look in his eyes hat made her apprehensive as she handed him the fresh water. He drank his fill, never taking his eyes off her. She smiled nervously at him, and taking the jar turned to walk back home.

Suddenly he grabbed her arm pulling her to the ground under him. He covered her face with kisses as he tore her clothes from her body. Aluma began to cry in real fear when she realized what he was going to do.

"Please, oh please don't do this thing, Cain. This is in rebellion against our father and therefore against God. It is not long until the Harvest Festival. Please wait until our vows are taken," she begged with tears running down her face.

Her tears were in vain, for Cain had his way with her and then roughly pulled her to her feet, shoved her clothes in her arms, and told her to "get back home and keep your mouth shut."

Aluma hurried to the brook that bubbled up at the base of the hills. She plunged herself into the water, mixing her salty tears with the crystal clear spring. When she was somewhat recovered, she dried in the sun, and then slipped her clothes on and replaited her long hair. With a heavy heart and shame on her face, she walked slowly home. She was glad that her mother and sisters were busy with the baking, for their faces were also hot and flushed from the fire. Her mother gave her a long searching look but said nothing, and Aluma prayed that the event would pass unnoticed.

The harvest was an exceptionally good one that autumn. There would be plenty to see them through even the coldest winter. Adam could not help but think of a strutting rooster as he watched his firstborn son displaying the size and abundance of the vegetables and grain that he had grown. Speaking quietly but firmly, Adam reminded Cain that the entire family, including little Tori, had helped with the spring planting and the recent harvest.

"And," he added, "God gave the increase." He watched closely, hoping for some small sign of humbleness from this son of his loins. Cain merely threw back his head and laughed. "I have a gift, Father, you said so yourself," he retorted proudly. "I labor longer hours than anyone, and I am wise in the ways of the soil."

Adam said simply, "The time is at hand to prepare for the sacrifice for sin. Let us prepare our lambs, for from henceforth we shall each man make an offering for his own sins and that of his family. I have agreed for Abel to have Rina as his bride during the festival one year from now."

Abel had brought numerous of the firstborn lambs of his flocks. He indicated that his father should take first choice; and when he had done so, and left to make his preparations, Abel informed Cain that he was to have his choice next.

"Thank you brother," Cain said boldly, "but I have something better to give to God. I am going to give the most beautiful of my produce, which I grew, with the toil of my own hands. It is indeed a worthy offering. See how skillfully I have arranged it so that the colors all complement each other?"

Abel stood totally still for a moment and swallowed before he said, "But Cain, do you not remember that Father taught us that there can be no remission of sin without the shedding of blood?"

"My offering will do just fine!" Cain boasted. "It shows what hard work and skill can truly do. Besides, what sin have I committed? Am I not a decent, hard working man?" With that he walked away to bathe himself and put on clean clothes for the dedication ceremony.

Abel stared after his brother for a long while with icy fear gripping his heart. What kind of man was this who did not see a need to be delivered from sin? Finally, he too went to prepare himself for the ceremony.

Three separate altar fires raced their flames toward heaven. Adam stood with his wife and his daughters at his side. Cain and Abel each stood alone, although Cain knew that next year he would stand with his wife. He resented the fact that she was not allowed to stand with him tonight; but his father had insisted he be cleansed from his sins before the vows were said.

Adam lifted his arms and face towards heaven and prayed a prayer of thanksgiving for the harvest, followed by a petition that he and his house be cleansed from their sins. He prayed to be a man worthy of the love of a loving God, and to be a kind and loving husband and father. When he had completed his prayer, he laid the fatty pieces of the lamb on the altar and poured the blood upon the fire in remission for his sins.

He stepped back, and instantly the Shekinah Glory of the Lord covered the altar. Tears of rejoicing ran down Adam's face.

Cain stepped forward next. He quickly thanked God for his strong body, his keen mind, and his gift with the soil. He held the basket of grains, vegetables and fruits up in the air and said, "I am very proud to be able to give this good gift to you, Lord." He then laid the offering on the altar.

The basket of produce burned quickly but there was no sign from heaven; no Shekinah Glory came in acceptance of Cain's offering.

Cain stood there looking stunned and embarrassed. Perhaps God would not accept Abel's offering either. Maybe it was because they were not yet married. He had told his father to let him be married in the spring! As his thoughts continued to ramble in this fashion he heard his brother's voice in prayer.

There were tears streaming down Abel's face, making a pool of wet soil where he knelt with his face to the ground. "Oh gracious Heavenly Father, I am the most unworthy of all of your children," he sobbed. "You know that I am sometimes impatient and annoyed with my flocks and sometimes I complain about the heat or the cold when I am out in the pasture. I am not worthy of the great love that you have shown me, my Lord.

"Please, I pray you, even though I know I am unworthy of your great mercy towards me, please accept this offering as a sacrifice for my many sins. Truly, oh Lord, when I am compared with your Glory, I am a sinful man."

Abel placed his sacrifice on the altar, pouring out the blood as his earthly father had shown him.

Instantly the Shekinah Glory of God shown down from heaven, covering Abel as well as the offering so that even Abel's clothes shown brightly.

There was silence for long moments after the ceremony. Adam cleared his throat and announced that the banquet would be held now, instead of after the marriage vows as had been planned. The women looked at each other in astonishment but hurried to put the food out.

Adam motioned for his eldest son to follow him. They walked towards the stream and had gone out of the others' hearing before he spoke. "God did not receive your offering. You must first make your life right with Him before I can ask His blessing on your marriage vow. The vow states that you will serve God with all of your might and all of your heart, and that you will instruct your family in the same way. If you are not willing to obey Him, I cannot, in His Name, join another life to yours. Go, I urge you; ask His forgiveness for your stubbornness and pride. Make the offering which He demands and then I will give you your wife."

With fists clenched and his face darkened with fury, Cain started to speak, but instead turned toward the hills and walked away with an angry stride. Adam watched him go and then quietly returned to his family.

"Cain had to go for a journey. We will have our meal without him," he announced to the family waiting anxiously with curiosity and concern on their faces.

Abel looked at Aluma's pale face and, slipping his hand over hers and giving it a squeeze, whispered, "It will all work out, little sister. Cain is suffering because his offering was rejected, but he will return after he has had time to clear his thoughts."

She offered a tiny smile but refused to meet his eyes.

Although Adam and Eve kept trying to make cheerful conversation, and the two little girls had a hundred questions about the sin sacrifice, the meal was strained and unnatural. Aluma ate a few bites, looked suddenly ill, and jumped up to run to the woods and lose her dinner. Eve sighed and shook her head, "She is very upset; I've never known her to be ill before." She went to her daughter and suggested that she lie down with a cool cloth on her head.

Cain had continued to run up the hill, over rocks and across meandering streams, until he came to a spot that overlooked the valley opposite theirs.

Suddenly he heard a voice behind him, and he jumped from surprise. God spoke. "Why are you angry? Why is your face dark with rage? Your face can be bright with joy if you will but obey."

"What do you want from me?" shrieked Cain. "I gave you the best that I had to offer. I raised beautiful crops, and gave you the best of each one! You're not fair! You want too much from me; and you let that sniveling Abel sit and dream all day, while I toil from dawn to dusk."

There was silence for a few minutes after Cain's outburst, and then God spoke again. "I want your heart, Cain. I want all of you. I do not need your gifts. I am the Giver of all good gifts. Watch out! For if you do not turn your ways to me and obey, sin will destroy you."

Cain said nothing, and suddenly he realized that he was alone. He walked until he came to the cave, where he lay down; not to sleep, but to make his plans for the next day.

* * * * *

Morning light pouring into the main room of Adam's home found the parents awake, talking softly in whispers about yesterday's events. Eve noticed that Aluma's mat was already rolled up in the storage area. She wondered if the girl had slept at all.

Suddenly Aluma hurried through the door into the room. "Mother, Father, it is Cain! I see him coming down the hill toward us."

Abel, who had been tending his sheep in their fenced yard, came through the back door at the same time. He had also seen his brother approaching.

Cain stood in the door with the eastern light shining over his broad shoulders. "Good morning, family!" he said cheerfully. "Abel, I am glad that you have not yet left for the pasture. Will you walk through the fields with me so that we might talk a while? I need your opinion on something."

"Certainly, my brother," was the answer, "shall we break bread together first?"

Cain hesitated and then nodded, "I see no reason why we should not have this meal together. Aluma, my *wife,* will you serve us?"

Aluma looked flustered and unsure, but she hurried to serve her brothers their morning meal. Adam, Eve and Rina exchanged glances as they arose from their mats and went out to wash in the stream. Something felt very strange this morning. It seemed as if Cain had made a decision, but what could it be? He certainly didn't seem any more humble than he had yesterday. Just more decisive. Simcha and

Tori continued to sleep soundly on their shared mat, completely unaware of any nuances.

"Shall I pack the noon meal?" questioned Aluma.

Cain assured her that it was not necessary. "Do fix a large meal for when I come home, though. I have a feeling I shall be very hungry."

The two young men, so different in build and attitude, walked down the path leading to Cain's fields. Cain talked cheerfully of inconsequential things--the clear sky, the fine harvest, Eve's coming child--until they were in the center of the fields.

Cain had planted his fields around a large circle of clover. There were six fields spreading out fanlike from this circle. He always planted each field with a different crop, moving his crops from left to right around the circle each season. He would harvest five of the fields, but the sixth field he would plow under, allowing the field to rest and nourish itself. There were a few trees and large boulders in the center of the circle of clover, and it was there that he sat with his brother to rest after the long walk.

"Tell me, Abel, do you honestly believe that God will only accept a blood sacrifice to make atonement for our sin?"

Abel looked eager and relieved to give testimony to his brother. "Oh, truly I do believe that, Cain. Mother said that when she and Father sinned in the Garden that it was necessary for the firstborn lamb to be slain. They were instructed to kill a lamb each year to atone for their sins, and they were told that someday God will send his own Shekinah Lamb to pay the full penalty of our many sins."

Cain stood looking in the direction of the field that had been allowed to lie fallow all season. He turned and looked at his younger brother. Abel stood a full head shorter than Cain; slender and wiry, where Cain was tall and broad.

"Well, Abel, I certainly want to please God, don't I! I shall make the blood sacrifice this very morning. Walk with me to that altar over there and you shall witness my sincerity."

Abel and Cain walked toward rocks that had been stacked as though for an altar, when Abel noticed an area where a large pit had been freshly dug. He turned to ask his brother about it, in time to see Cain holding a large sharp rock, which he brought down cruelly over Abel's face. Abel fell to the ground and feebly threw his arms over his bleeding face to protect himself. It was to no avail, for with many curses Cain brought the rock down on his brother's head and face again and again. When finally the blows ceased to the lifeless body, Cain stood back to survey the scene. His brother's blood was seeping into the ground.

"Here, God! Here is your blood sacrifice. Let this atone for my 'sins'! Here is your gift, God," he screamed into the morning sun. Finally he collapsed, exhausted, on the ground.

When he had calmed himself and regained his breath, Cain stood to his feet, dragged the body to where it fell into the pit, and set about covering it with soil, grass and rocks. When he was satisfied that no one could tell what had happened there, he walked to the stream and washed himself. He then went to his own newly furnished house, changed his clothes, and burned the old ones. He smiled, "No one will ever know what happened to you, my dear, righteous brother. Perhaps I will have Rina to wife also. Surely a ram such as I can manage more than one little ewe!"

It had been easy for Aluma to prepare the large lunch, which Cain had requested, for little of yesterday's banquet food had been touched. She and Rina pulled the storage containers from the cooling waters of the stream and prepared a lavish meal. Perhaps there would be much to celebrate today!

They heard Cain's cheerful whistle before they saw him. "Well, thank goodness, he is in a good mood." muttered Eve to herself.

The girls looked at each other and smiled, their spirits suddenly lighter. Cain came in and gave them each a hug, a most unusual act for him. "Abel had to go chasing after a silly runaway lamb; but that's all right because I'll just eat his share too," he said jokingly.

"You'll do no such thing," his mother said firmly. "Abel will certainly be hungry when he comes in, and his food will be waiting for him."

True to his prediction, Cain was ravenous. After he finished a huge meal, he yawned, stretched, and announced that he was going to the new house to make certain that it was weather proof before the first snow fell.

He grinned at Aluma and playfully pinched her arm. "After all," he exclaimed, "I expect to take my bride to live there before the end of this week!" Once more they heard his happy whistle as he walked down the path.

When he was well out of sight, he turned instead to check the area where he had buried his brother. He wanted to make certain that wild animals had not disturbed the body.

When he reached the site he heard his name being called. He recognized the Voice and began to tremble.

"Cain, where is your brother Abel?"

Cain spoke angrily in an attempt to cover up his fear: "How should I know? Am I my brother's keeper?"

The Voice of God became stern, and in spite of himself Cain fell to his knees.

"What have you done? Listen! Your brother's blood cries out to me from the ground. Now you are under a curse and driven from the ground which opened its mouth to receive your brother's blood from your hand. When you work the ground it will no longer yield its crops for you. You will be a restless wanderer on the earth."

Cain looked up in agony. Surely not. Surely God would not take his gift away from him. That was *his* gift. *His* soil. No one could work the soil like he could!

"No God, No," he whined. "This punishment is too hard. It is more than I can bear, and if I have to live in the wilderness I will be killed!"

"No, Cain," the Voice of God continued, "you will not be killed; for I will mark you in such a way that all will know that this curse is from Me. No one will dare to take your life."

Suddenly there was a great flash of light like a thousand tongues of fire. It was not the light of the Shekinah Glory, but like a fire of judgment.

Cain cried out as he looked at his hands. He then looked at his legs, his body hair,--he ran to see his reflection in a nearby pool--yes it was true, even his face and the hair on his head, and his beard were all white. He looked as if all of the blood had been drained out of his body. Even his eyes were so pale that they could hardly be distinguished from the rest of his body. He groaned and put his hands over his face. It was hideous. Who was this bloodless creature that stared back at him?

"Do not tarry in the land, Cain. Be gone quickly." And then God left him.

Cain stumbled up the path towards his parent's home. He was speechless and numb. When his parents saw him, they cried out in alarm. Aluma screamed.

"I have killed Abel," he stated woodenly. "God has cursed me and I must leave. I will gather my possessions; take my wife and go. I will bother you no more."

The women began weeping openly, and Adam had a look of rage on his face that no one had ever seen before: "You have killed your brother! I would to God that you were dead in his place. You have no wife. Be gone! Be gone!"

Cain turned around and walked out of the house without a backward glance.

In the midst of the deafening silence, a whisper was barely heard. "I am with child," sobbed Aluma.

Adam whirled around and grabbed her by the shoulders. "What! You gave yourself to him before the vow?" His entire body was shaking. He looked as if he might strike her.

Aluma turned away and bowed her head. How could she remain here and have her family provide for the child of a rapist and a murderer? She nodded her head. "Yes," she sobbed, "yes, I gave myself to him."

Adam staggered and reached out for the wall to support himself. "Go! He said in a harsh whisper. "Go with your husband."

Weeping silently, Eve and Rina quickly gathered food and possessions into baskets to send with Aluma for her journey.

Aluma stood stone-faced and silent while they packed for her. Her father did not turn around. The little girls, eyes wide with fear, looked from parents to sisters. What had happened to their family? "Go by your house and get your things from there," Eve whispered as she helped Aluma bridle one of the donkeys Abel had given her. The other donkey would follow along behind, with as many possessions as the women could get together in a hurry. Aluma walked over to her father who remained looking out of the window. She gently kissed his back, laying her head lightly as a feather against him for an instant. He did not move; but had he turned around, she would have seen the tears streaming down his face.

Aluma kissed her sisters and then her mother good-bye. With her head held high and a determined set to her chin, she rode off in the direction of the new house.

As she rounded the hill and crossed the stream to begin the path down to her house, she noticed a bright red glow in the sky. She hurried the donkeys in order to see what had happened. She arrived in time to see billows of fire rolling out of the house and stables. Cain was throwing bundles of dry straw into the house to make it burn more completely. She looked at him with eyes that seemed to hold no life.

"Well, my wife, my little one, so you have decided to join your husband. That was a good decision, my love, because those people are fools! They will never survive here without me. I am the one who kept the family going. They are nothing! I am the one!" He raved and raved as the flames jumped towards the sky.

Finally, leading the team of oxen, he motioned for her to follow him. They headed eastward, away from their parents' home.

❋ ❋ ❋ ❋ ❋

There was no evening meal prepared that night. Eve sat without moving, looking out the window toward the east.

Rina and Adam silently went about the evening chores; and when they were finished, Rina gave the little girls oatcakes and milk, and put them to bed. Then when she had prepared everything, she went gently to her mother, took her by the arm and led her to the sleeping mat. She covered her mother, kissed her cheek, and lay down herself by her sisters.

Eve would have said that she did not sleep at all; but surely she must have dozed off, for she was suddenly jolted awake by a familiar pain. She caught her breath and lay very still. It could not be. No, it must not be. In a very few minutes the pain came again. She quietly slipped out from her covers, stepped across her sleeping family, and went outside.

She walked to the stream to wash her face in cold water. She looked up at the sky. It was a new moon, dark in the sky.

She closed her eyes for a moment. It was too early. There must be a full moon and another new moon before the child was due. Her children had always come during the time that she had calculated for their birth.

The next pain doubled her over. She waited until she could catch her breath, then called for Adam, and started toward the house. There would be no time to go to the cave,

Suddenly a great gush of water came out of her body and with it she felt the baby being born. She screamed in desperation as she lay upon the grass and gave birth to her fifth daughter. Adam and Rina were suddenly at her side, cutting the cord, wrapping the baby. Adam lifted his wife and carried her into the house. Rina rubbed the tiny infant briskly, feeling a surge of relief when the little one screamed in protest. She placed the babe in her mother's arms.

"Here is your comfort, Mother," she said quietly.

And that is what they named her: "Nehama," which means comfort.

The weeks that followed were like a black blur. One crisis followed another so that there was no time to grieve, merely to survive. Within three days of the baby's birth Eve had a raging fever and was desperately ill. Instead of stopping, the bleeding that normally followed a birth became dark and malodorous.

Adam began to fear that Eve would die: and he clearly remembered the words, "You shall surely die." He went to the pile of stones in the center of the round field of clover and prostrated himself, in order to call upon his Heavenly Father. He prayed there for hours at a time, seeking the help and mercy of his Lord.

Rina never left her mother's side, giving Simcha full charge of the household. Although Simcha was barely ten years old; she became a woman during those difficult days. Rina instructed her how to fill a cloth with watered goat's milk and feed it to Nehama. And Tori, eager to show that she too could help, fed and watered the stock, her fat little legs running back and forth carrying vessels that were nearly as big as she was. She also kept jars of cool water from the spring close by Rina, so that the big sister could sponge her mother's body in a seemingly hopeless attempt to keep the raging fever down.

Eve had also shown Rina how to make poltices; and she made the strongest that she knew how, binding them upon her mother's abdomen.

During those evil days the meals were simple and hastily taken, and sometimes Tori would fall asleep as she was eating. Rina would make herbal concoctions that Eve had taught her, lessons learned in the Garden, and would force her mother to drink sips of it. At times, in her hours of worst delirium, it would simply run out of the corners of her mouth.

Rina soon lost track of the days. The children would come to her and ask instructions, and she had no idea how she answered them. Her father would bring her food, and urge her to take her rest lest he also lose her, but she would shake her head and take snatches of rest by her mother's side. Then when all seemed lost, when everyone felt that exhaustion would win the final battle, Eve opened her eyes and began to respond.

Chapter Four

Rina

Rina lay on her back looking at the night sky. She had watched the progress of the red star from the horizon across the heavens for the past two hours. It was now midnight and she still had not settled down to sleep.

Her sheep had long been still, their bleating sounds now silent, and their peaceful slumbers allowing sheep dreams to carry them unmolested through the night.

Even the wolf puppies were sleeping, their fat bellies full of warm goats milk. She turned on her side and reached over to touch the little female's silky ear. The male was sleeping on his back with all four paws in the air. She touched his tummy and smiled.

She had found them barely alive, their pathetic cries leading her to the den that their mother had so carefully hidden in a small cave in the hillside. She had found the big wolf's body several yards away, or at least what was left of the body after the vultures had finished with it. The wolf had obviously been killed by a craftier predator as she tried to defend her pups. There had been only two left alive when Rina found them. It seemed doubtful that the starving pups would survive, so tiny were they; but she had carried them in a wool cloth back to her camp and patiently fed them goats' milk until they were big enough to lap it by themselves. She kept them rubbed with wool from the sheep, so that their smell would not panic her flocks, and so that the pups would identify the smell as their "pack".

They kept her company, and the hours had flown since they had joined her in the fields. She wondered if it would be possible to keep them tame even when they were fully grown.

It would soon be time to move the sheep into the pastures nearer the house; for autumn was almost here now, and the winds would blow cold from the north switching suddenly from the hot easterly winds. Her two young brothers lay sleeping on their mats near the smoldering fire. How quickly everything seemed to be changing, she thought. It had never occurred to her that her life would be other than shepherding; for since Abel had been killed that was the path that she had chosen.

Now it appeared that she was to be married. She frowned and looked again at the clear sky. Could that be true? Was she really, after all these years, to become a wife and mother? She stood and stretched, walked over to place another stick on the fire. Well, why not? Her body was still as young and slim as it had been when she was a girl. After all, her mother--after Seth had been born--had given birth to six more sons and three daughters.

Now two youngsters were going to take over her job of caring for the flocks. Fourteen-year-old Adlai and twelve year old Kohav had been with her all summer, learning how to be shepherds.

She smiled: they were good boys, eager to learn; and, although they sometimes stumbled over their own feet in their attempts, they were more than willing to help. She knew that she would be glad of their help as they moved the flocks to the near pastures next week. Next week… Preparations for the Harvest Festival would begin at home. To her surprise, Rina's heart leaped in anticipation. There would be marriage vows spoken after the sin offering this year. She refused to allow her mind to go back to that other time, those other vows that were never spoken.

Three would become brides this year: Simcha and Tori, in addition to Rina. "And thanks to them I won't be getting married in the cloak of a shepherdess," she reminded herself.

That had been her second objection when her parents had consulted her wishes about the marriage proposal. (Her first had been that Nehama should be the bride.) She had argued that she had no way to prepare for the marriage. She had flocks to tend and she could not set up a household without the necessary items, indeed she didn't even have a proper garment to wear for the wedding! Her mother had spoken to her sisters and they had all put an end to her objections.

Nehama had insisted that she would prepare everything that Rina needed; she stated that it would be excellent practice for when she had to prepare for herself. Mother had said that she would sew Rina's wedding robe, and promised that she would greet her groom shining like the stars themselves!

"Or like the stars in your eyes, Mother," Rina mused. She had been a little startled when she realized how saddened her mother had been over the possibility of no life mate for Rina. "Rather silly really, because I was quite content with my flocks," she assured herself. But even as that thought came into her mind, Rina knew that she wasn't being totally objective, because until Abel had been killed there had been no room for any consideration outside of marriage. Abel had been her dearest friend for as long as she remembered.

Rina blinked her foolish eyes that were suddenly hot with tears, and thought back to that day, early last spring, which had so drastically changed her life. Memories flooded over her and kept sleep at bay.

She had been struggling with a tiny kid that had somehow managed to get itself tangled in a thorn bush. The mother was standing nearby adding her loud bawling objections to the screams of the kid, and the other goats and sheep were dancing around in the confusion. "Stupid, careless, dumb goat!" she had fussed in an uncharacteristically irritable voice.

This was, however, the third time that morning---and the sun was hardly above the horizon--that this silly little one had managed to entangle itself. "I shall name you 'Nehama' after my little sister who always got into scrapes," she declared as she suddenly sat down with a thump, the bush having decided on its own volition to release the kid.

At that moment a shadow had passed over her, and she had looked up to see Abel standing there with a golden halo round about him.

She gave a barely stifled scream.

'Abel' moved to the side so that the sun would not be right in her eyes. "I'm sorry," he had said in a concerned voice. "We didn't mean to frighten you."

"We" he had said. She looked around. Yes, there were two others. Rina realized that her mouth was hanging open. Abel...but no, not Abel. Eyes like Abel, hair like Abel, but taller, larger built than Abel. What? Who? Had she spoken? Was this a vision? Had Abel returned? No, no! Not Abel. Larger than Abel.

Slowly she had stood to her feet.

"My name is Abir and these are my brothers: Ravid," he pointed to the youth on his right, "and Tzevi," he added as he turned to the young man on his left. "We bring you greetings from our mother, Aluma."

Rina began to sputter, cry, and laugh all at once. "Aluma! Yes, yes, of course, you are sons of Aluma!" she managed. "My sister, my sister Aluma, yes of course, of course you are. It's just that for a moment I thought--well you looked like--oh never mind. Welcome. Welcome. I am Rina. You must tell me all the news. You must find my father. Oh, do sit down. Let me refresh you from your journey." Suddenly she threw her arms around each one, and they were all laughing and crying together.

They had stayed for two days and nights with Rina before heading north to meet their grandparents. The three brothers had many stories to tell about life with the wandering Cain, and the patient, loving Aluma. There were twelve brothers, and the first-born had been the child that Aluma was carrying when they left home. He was named Enoch and was in every way like Cain.

"I know how that can be," Rina interjected, "for Seth is the eldest of our boys at home, and he is exactly like my father."

There were also six girls, they had told her, the youngest still a babe in arms. Aluma had tried to teach all of them the stories about Eden, and how wonderful and loving their Heavenly Father is; but whenever Cain would catch her, he would stop her with blows. Only three of the boys had expressed a desire to know God.

"We are those three," said Tzevi. "We long to learn all that we can so that we may worship Him and make sacrifice for our sin."

Ravid joined in to continue the tale of their travels. "Mother made maps of the night skies as she and our father traveled away from home.

She had planned in those first years to run away and come back to your family, but then there were so many children that she knew she could never leave. She gave us the maps so that we could study the skies and find you."

And so, with Rina's careful instructions, they had gone on their way to find the rest of the family. When they left, Rina had felt a strange restlessness stirring inside of her.

Father had welcomed them, and Mother had rejoiced at the news of her firstborn daughter. They were both greatly saddened to know that Cain had continued in his rebellion against God. The three young men had listened carefully to all that Adam taught them about God, and about the road that one must take to receive the Shekinah Glory of God's presence. Each young man kneeled and vowed to serve the God of Adam. They soon fitted into the family as if they had always been there. They were grateful to be away from the coarseness and cruelty of their brothers and father. They missed their mother's sweetness and love, but found a likeness in Eve and her daughters that comforted them.

They had joined Adam's sons in the fields when the planting was to be done, helped build fences for the animals; indeed had cheerfully taken over more than their share of the work, and finally approached Adam about marriages.

Rina's sisters, hiding behind the door when the boys made their approach to Father, had shared the story with her on their next visit.

Ravid had spoken first and asked if he might be joined with Simcha. Then Tzevi, much more shyly, expressed his desire for Tori. Abir paused to hear Adam's response to his brothers.

Adam looked calmly at the three fine young men. "I suppose that you desire Nehama then, Abir?" he questioned. For Nehama was not only spirited, but also beautiful beyond words.

"Sir, Nehama is beautiful. To gaze upon her face is like looking into the sun; but no sir, it is not Nehama whom I desire."

"Well who then?" asked Adam in a puzzled voice. "Leeba is but thirteen. I will not allow her to be given to a man for several years."

Abir blushed. "Oh, no sir, I do not desire Leeba, for she is but a sweet little girl. It is Rina that I love. I wish to be joined to Rina. I will always be good to her, sir. I will treat her ever so kindly."

"Rina!!" Adam laughed to cover his embarrassment at having forgotten her. "Well, yes of course there is Rina. Rina is wonderful. Rina is everything that a man could want. Of course, Rina!"

"Eve, Eve, come here. Abir wishes to marry Rina! Isn't that wonderful!"

"Hush, Husband!" exclaimed Eve, only then entering the room. "You act as if you had thought no man would ever desire her."

"No, no not at all!" protested Adam. "Of course she is desirable. Why, we'll bring her in out of the sheep fields and clean her up. Yes, it seems to me that I remember that once she was especially lovely."

Eve groaned and promptly placed her hand over Adam's mouth. "Abir," she said sweetly, "you have her father's permission to ask Rina if she will marry you. You other boys may likewise ask for the one you have chosen."

She looked at Adam, who was by now totally confused, for he had no idea what he could have done wrong. "Come, Adam," she said, ruefully shaking her head, "it is time for bed."

Abir had left early the next morning to seek Rina. Adam, on the other hand, had suddenly realized that he was going to be minus a very fine shepherdess, and had asked Abir to take Adlai and Kohav with him for Rina to train. As he waved goodbye to the trio, Adam looked very happy with himself, for he was quite pleased with the plan that he and the Lord had worked out. Quite pleased indeed.

Rina remembered her sisters' giggles as they shared the story with her, and smiled sleepily to herself. She was snuggled down now in her blankets, and felt the waves of sleep engulfing her. The memories of Abir, as he approached her about becoming his wife, were the most tender and precious of all. Those were her thoughts as she dozed off to sleep.

* * * * *

The evening of the Harvest Festival was cool and clear. The Harvest moon had joyfully joined the merry event, donning its most resplendent hues and brightly illuminating the mounds of food that had been prepared. The brides all looked radiant, but Rina appeared especially regal in the exquisite robe that her mother had made for her. Eve had boiled purple berries until they made a thick dye, and had put the cloth in it to soak until it turned a deep purple. To this she had added a scarlet sash with long fringe. Never had there been a robe so beautiful.

Rina's brothers had fashioned a necklace from the shiny yellow stones that they had found in the mountain streams. They had always admired the one that their mother wore, and they wanted their eldest sister to have one too. She had wept when they presented her with their gift.

The children were each eager to have a part in the preparations for the ceremony. They had gathered so many arms full of flowers and ferns to decorate the grounds that their mother had finally begged them to cease lest no one should be able to view the marriage couples.

The marriages had taken place under the covering of the Terebinth-Oak trees which Adam and the children had planted those many long years ago. The couples had carefully and reverently repeated the marriage vows as Adam had instructed. The First Man, in his priestly robes, had blessed each couple with these words, "For this reason a man shall leave his father and his mother and cling to his wife, and they shall become one flesh."

There had been dancing and games, singing and much laughter, and then stories by the huge bonfire, after the Festival meal. The sin offerings, which had been made in the early evening, had imbued each person with a feeling of peace. Even the babies, Bracha and Chaya, had been quiet during the ceremony. It had been a time of blessing and joy.

After all of the festivities, Tzevi had taken Tori to the house that he had built for her. He had used the foundation of the house that his father, Cain, had tried to destroy. The original stones had been badly blackened; but the brothers had taken sap from the Terebinth-Oaks to clean them, and finished with a mixture of lime and water. They had covered the entire house inside and out with the white paint. Eve said that when the sun shone on the white house, it was dazzling to the eyes!

The other two young men had made temporary shelters by placing stakes in the ground and covering the top and sides with branches. They had covered the floor of the shelters with straw and sweet grasses, so each couple had a private place for the wedding night.

Having wearied of its own ostentatious display, the moon was now a pale silver ball, riding aloof, high in the sky. Its still ample light revealed masses of flowers, now trodden flat along the paths

The bonfire had also mellowed to a gentler blaze, and its shadows revealed numerous sleeping forms lying close to its warmth. The two youngest family members were asleep on pallets, blissfully unaware of smears of food on their faces and clothes. The half-grown wolf cubs were eagerly gobbling the banquet remains that had been placed on the ground for them. Firmly but gently a weary Nehama began to gather her younger siblings and herd them toward the house and bed.

Having kissed his remaining brood goodnight, Adam looked around for his own bride. She was standing silently by the bubbling brook that flowed at the edge of the meadow, her upturned face lighted by the sheen of the moon.

Adam slipped up quietly behind her. Placing his arms about her, he tenderly kissed her neck, and then whispered a question into her ear, "What do you see as you gaze up into the heavens, my own sweet lady love?"

Without turning, Eve leaned back into her husband's strong arms and murmured, "I see our children's children as numerous as the stars in the sky."

Nodding in agreement Adam added, "It is a great blessing to watch our children continuing the family line which God so graciously allowed us to begin. Indeed, our Heavenly Father has given us a wonderful family, Eve, and we can look forward to many more celebrations of marriage. May each celebration be as joyful and festive as this one.

Eve turned and smiled warmly into her husband's eyes. "I am happy for our young adults starting out on their own, but I am grateful that we still have young ones at home, or life would seem terribly quiet."

Adam's deep laugh rang across the meadows, its cadence reaching to the dwelling where the children, hearing their father, smiled securely in their sleep.

"Quiet? Woman when has our life ever been quiet? My earliest memory is of those noisy animals in the Garden giggling over me!"

Eve, snuggling more closely in his arms, laughed also, her laugh a tinkling soprano to his bass. "Yes, I guess that you are right," she agreed, "with our brood there will always be activity."

They stood together silently enjoying their memories and the tenderness of the moment.

"Adam?" Eve spoke so quietly that he had to bend down to hear her.

"Yes?"

"How did we fail so horribly with Cain? Why is he so bent towards evil? We hear such frightening, cruel stories about that family and it breaks my heart. Abir says that some of the younger children have even been born with that pale, colorless skin that Cain was cursed with."

"Oh my husband," she continued desperately, "maybe we can talk to Cain, reason with him, show him the error of his ways. He is our firstborn; surely we cannot allow him to continue like this. Perhaps we should try harder to see his point of view."

She felt Adam's arms stiffen around her. His voice was low but held so severe a tone that her bones felt a chill.

"Do not beguile me, Eve. We will never talk to Cain again. He has chosen an evil path; he deliberately leads his children in that evil path. He has set himself against God, and we have no part in him. We will never speak of this again.

"I urge you, my beloved," he continued, "do not let sad thoughts spoil this happy day. These children have chosen a straight and right path. Let us thank God for that decision. We can only love our children and teach them what we know to be right. We cannot choose their paths for them."

Once again the couple were silent. The man gently stroked his wife's long hair and pretended not to notice the tears that flowed down her cheeks. Adam knew that his words had seemed harsh to his wife, and he wisely left her to her bittersweet memories. He had his own memories and knew that he must never again fail his God or his family as he had once, so long ago, in the Garden.

Eve allowed the tears to continue unchecked as she relived the joy and promise of the birth of her first child. How thrilled she had been that God had allowed them to continue the human line. Every day that Cain grew had been precious to her. How she and Adam had laughed when, as he was learning to walk, Cain would fall and let out an indignant howl as he landed on his fat bottom in the process.

Eve knew that she could never cease to love her child, but she also knew that the child was gone. The stranger who lived in his place was full of hate and cruelty. She sighed deeply and took her husband's hand as they walked to the fireside to scoop up their two youngest. No words were spoken as they carried the babies to the welcome sanctuary of their home.

❋ ❋ ❋ ❋ ❋

Abir and Rina, and Ravid and Simcha, were leaving in two days for the seacoast where they were going to settle. Abir had traveled there as a youngster, with his elder brothers and Cain. He had marveled at the blue sea, the mild climate, and wonderful trees with abundant fruit on them. For years it had been his dream to return there to build a home in which to live, and a boat with which to fish the vast sea. He had shared his dream with no one except Ravid and Tzevi until they had left the land of Cain.

Tzevi had chosen to make his home near Adam's family; for Adam had given him a flock and a part in the planting. But it had been decided that each year after the harvest, Adam, Tzevi and all of the rest of the family would make the three-day journey to a point halfway between the two settlements.

There they would meet the others, who had traveled three days from the opposite direction, and they would celebrate the annual Harvest Festival together, thus reuniting the families for a few days. They would also be able to trade with one another the goods that were specific to each area. This plan helped ease the pain of separation, and gave everyone something to look forward to.

Each departing couple had donkeys laden with all the goods necessary for establishing households, as well as sheep, goats, chickens and ducks, and food to see them through the first few months. Sacks were filled with seed for planting in the spring.

There were many calls of "God be with you" as the two families left to cross the hill country on their journey to the sea.

And so Adam and Eve had begun the fulfillment of God's instructions to "replenish the earth". Cain had previously settled his family to the east in a land that came to be known as 'Nod', and now other families were moving to settle the western sea coast.

Adam stood for a long time looking to the distance, even though he could no longer see even the dust from the ones who had left. He had come a long way since being cast from the Garden of Eden. There had been sadness and joy, sickness and health, rebellion and dedication, but God had never left them nor forsaken them.

They had lost the literal physical clothing of the Shekinah Glory before being sent from the Garden; but now they were ever learning how to serve their Heavenly Father, as the journey continued on the Shekinah Road. Adam, glancing heavenward, smiled, winked and nodded, before turning back to his own house.

Chapter Five

Aluma

The children, laughing and running with merry abandon, collided en masse with the tall-dignified gentleman as he traveled the path, head down in thought, from the opposite direction. They stopped, momentarily speechless, as they looked up into the startled face. The eldest, a stub-nosed and freckled-faced boy of about ten, stepped boldly forward, electing himself spokesman for the troupe.

"Forgive us Father Adam; for we were playing a game, and were not watching where we were going."

As he spoke, the boy reached out an anxious hand to pull away a minute girl who was trying to brush the dust off the patriarch's robe. Another child offered her ragged bouquet of daisies to the man.

"Be still, children," Adam said gently. "I am not so easily injured. I see that you have lunches with you and I am hungry. Come and let us sit by that stream, and you will share your lunches; and I will share some stories, and we will have a good visit."

The children eagerly complied. What an honor! For many of them "Father Adam" was only a name, which they had heard from their parents. It was a name always spoken of with awe and reverence. They scurried to pull mossy grass and place it in an area of the rocks that they perceived as worthy of their esteemed guest. Placing their small cloaks over the grass, they urged the good grandfather to "Sit there Sir, for it is the best."

The sun warmed their backs and the gentle breezes carried with them the lovely fragrance of the wild anemones, lilies, and rose of Sharon, which throughout the long summer months had bloomed profusely in the fields. Time passed sweetly for the man and the children, as he regaled them with stories of the Garden. They looked at each other in wonder as he became misty-eyed with memories of Mother Ewe, the first of the mother sheep, and other good friends from a time long, long ago. Suddenly the lengthening shadows reminded him of the reason that he had been on the path.

"Oh my," he lamented, "I shall be in deep trouble with my beautiful Eve if I'm late for dinner! I must hurry on and make my visit to Seth's house to welcome his new grandson. We are to name him Cainan.

"Goodbye children, goodbye," he continued. "Thank you for a wonderful lunch. I have never eaten better. Hurry home now so that all of the mothers will not be upset with Grandfather Adam for keeping you out so late."

Bending to kiss the little tyke who had tried to dust his robe, he hurried along the path.

❋ ❋ ❋ ❋ ❋

Eve had attended to her own errand on this golden day in autumn. Still slim and sedate, eyes reflecting wisdom once gained in a world far apart from this one, Eve had climbed the craggy hillside to visit her oldest daughter, Aluma. She paused at a crevice where a crude bench had been carved into the side of the hill. Brushing errant hair out of her eyes, she sat to rest for a moment and to reflect on her mission.

On her arm she carried a basket made from reeds; in it were loaves of warm fresh bread and an earthen jar. The jar contained delicious pomegranate jelly, made from her treasured recipe, which Aluma had helped her to perfect many, many years before.

Eve sadly reflected that it was shortly after that wonderful day of jelly making that Cain had taken Aluma far away into a land unknown to any of them.

"Cain, Cain." Eve whispered to the cloudless sky.

Her heart never ceased to feel the agony of a mother whose son has gone far astray.

❋ ❋ ❋ ❋ ❋

Several weeks earlier Aluma had been found at the edge of the desert far west of Cain's City, near death and bereft of hope. Their water jugs nearly empty, the three young granddaughters who had accompanied her had made themselves shelters by using their blankets against the elements. Aluma had little strength with which to continue her journey; and when the traders stopped to investigate, they found the situation was nearly beyond hope for the older woman.

The girls had explained that they were on their way to find Father Adam because Aluma had wished to see the face of her mother and father once more before she died. They said very little more than that to the kindly traders; saving for the ears of the patriarchs, tales far too terrible to be oft re-suffered through the telling.

Eve lifted the soft white cloth from the top of the basket; lifting the jar out she held it close to her breast and allowed a deep sigh to escape her lips.

"Dear Father God," she prayed, looking up into the clear cool sky. "Please heal the heart and soul of my first-born daughter. She has been tormented and abased until she is more a frightened animal than a human. She hides herself in her cave, Lord, and disdains to be seen by anyone other than her father and me. Even Simcha and Tori have not been allowed in her presence. She is breaking our hearts Lord; we long to reach her, but she keeps herself just beyond our loving touch. Show us how to help her, Father, and we will ever praise your Name."

Eve bowed her head silently for a few minutes and then continued on her trek. She bid goodbye to the singing, splashing, south-flowing stream which had accompanied her on most of her journey; and taking a more westward path, entered a grove of trees planted by young hands many decades before. She startled a flock of crows nesting in the trees, and they scolded her vociferously as they took wing.

When the noisy birdcalls had quieted down, Eve became aware of the voice of another bird singing plaintively in the distance. She hurried her steps so as to hear more clearly the song that this strange bird was crooning.

Coming closer to the sound, Eve realized that the tune was not winged but mortal. It was Aluma singing, accompanying herself with a small stringed instrument. She was reclining in the warmth of the sunshine; her head, with still dark tresses tumbling unrestrained down her too thin shoulders, was resting against the back of the bower which her young hands had lovingly helped fashion for her mother, Eve, many years before. Her eyes were dreamy and for the moment un-haunted by ghosts of terrors past.

"Hel--llo, daughter," Eve called out, so as not to startle the dreamer.

Aluma sat up suddenly, nearly dropping the instrument. "Why mother, I had no idea that you would be coming today!" she gasped.

"Well dear, I saw no reason to send a messenger before me as it appears that you rarely leave your pleasant home."

Aluma had unconsciously drawn her scarf over her head as her mother spoke. The eyes were still blue and clear, but much of the face was horribly scarred: gifts from a not-so-loving husband.

When the traders had carried her daughter in from the desert, Eve had tenderly nursed the bruised and broken body back to wellness. She had been horrified at the condition of the once perfect form. Years of beatings had left grim scars upon a body that had been forced to submit to every whim of her husband. The little girls, who had been abandoned by the lustful wantonness of their own mother, had been given sanctuary by their grandmother, Aluma, and were forced to witness the abuse inflicted upon her by Cain.

Relief came only when Cain took off on one of his long periods of wandering. Always he would be gone for weeks and more finally for several months, seemingly unable to stay put when the spirit of restlessness came upon him. It seemed to seize him the hardest when he had just brutalized Aluma. When he would first return from a journey, he would seem somewhat content, happy even, to be back with his wife. After a few weeks of apparent newfound bliss with his loving and faithful wife, he would decide to give a banquet for his extensive family. He would lavish much praise on his numerous sons, and their sons, for the progress that they had made on the City, which was being built to glorify themselves. They would eat beyond surfeiting and drink themselves into stupefying sleep, awaking to revel in licentious celebrations of evil.

When Cain sobered from his welcome home banquet, he would be sullen and moody for weeks, gradually increasing in his complaints of Aluma's alleged worthlessness. At first the accusations would be of a minor nature: complaints about a tunic poorly mended, a cold meal, or then more severely, a cold reception in bed.

When this last accusation was arrived at, Cain would begin his recurring tirade by urging her to confess that she had taken another lover. He would strike her as she denied any such unfaithfulness.

The process had become so routine that Aluma would know instinctively which phase came next and would pray in advance that the blows would not be so severe this time. It seemed that God could not hear prayers uttered in the environs of the City of Cain, for instead of lessening, the blows became more severe.

The last time that Cain had come home, Aluma knew that she would have to leave her madman of a husband. For all the previous years Cain's blows had always been born by Aluma alone. He had long assured his children that their mother was a poor simple creature who did not deserve their love, and they willingly agreed with him.

It was only in believing their father that they could escape the Godly teachings of their mother; for no matter how difficult her life, Aluma had held steadfastly to her belief in God. She had never uttered an unkind word to her husband or to any of her children. She had been faithful always in her duties to her husband, and had meekly submitted to the surly, derisive slander of her children, and their children.

Her faithful testimony had appeared to bear little fruit. She was able to smile to herself, though, when she considered the sons who had escaped. Abir, Ravid, and Tzevi had left their father's City and journeyed to join their grandfather, Adam; to serve God as their mother had taught them.

Now she had the children of her last-born daughter to raise. Livia, the youngest, had been barely weaned when her daughter brought them to her. The children had obviously been neglected and sorely treated in the Godless environment in which their own mother thrived. She had thrust the three girls into her mother's home with these few words: "Take them. They are in my way!"

Aluma had received the girls during one of the longest absences of Cain. They had responded instantly to the love shown them, and had gained health from Aluma's nourishing meals and tender ministrations. Eager for love and attention, they had listened with open minds and hearts to her teaching about God, and had given rapt attention to her stories of her childhood. They marveled to think that such love could exist: love from God and from family. They dreamed of living in such a world, and shyly asked Aluma if they could all leave Cain's City and live with Grandfather Adam and Grandmother Eve. Aluma had shaken her head sadly, quietly explaining to the girls that the gulf was too great to be crossed to take them back to the old family.

Her decision had been dramatically reversed by the circumstances of Cain's last visit home. Cain, as usual, had chosen to ignore six-year-old Livia, ten-year-old Tova, and Sheera who had just turned 12 years of age. If they served his meals quietly and punctually, with the reverence he deemed due to him, he acted as if they were not present.

The children, who trembled in his presence, wondered anew at the change that came over Aluma when Cain was home, for instead of their laughing, cheerful friend and companion, she became quiet, eyes lowered to the ground, answering only when spoken to. She bid the girls stay in their room, safely away from their grandfather and his 'friends'.

His most recent time home had proceeded as usual, with the exception that the period of serenity preceding the feast was a very brief one. Cain had seemed edgy and restless, almost from the moment he had returned from his journey. Aluma noted that he talked to himself more; arguing with shadows and at times screaming at unseen others. She knew that this could only bode evil, and she spent many hours in prayer to God for protection of the girls.

One time Cain caught her at her prayers; and he became violently enraged, grabbing her by her hair and pounding her in the face with his fist until it was covered with blood. Her screams awakened the girls, and they rushed into the main room of the house just as Cain was pushing Aluma's face into the fire.

Little Livia, true to the meaning of her name, pounced on him like a lioness. She screamed at him to let go of her grandmother, and began beating him across the head with a stick she kept for her long walks in the hills with her sisters. Her tactic worked only too well, for Cain threw the writhing Aluma aside and grabbed the child. He beat her into unconsciousness; and then, taking the stick, he placed it in the fire until it glowed red, and he gouged out both her eyes.

Aluma roused herself to the screams of the child and watched with stupefied numbness as Cain angrily fled the house. Then she gathered herbs from the hills and woodenly made a paste, which she placed on the eyes of the wounded child, holding her and crooning gentle songs of love. Tova wept bitterly, begging her grandmother to forgive her for not protecting her younger sister. Sheera stormily paced the room, vowing to change her name from "one who is good" to Meri, "the rebellious one", and avenge her sister and her grandmother.

"Hush, children, and help me plan a way of escape. Cain has totally surrendered himself to the Evil One. There is nothing kind or good in him. I shall pray for him no longer; nor will I feel bound to him by marriage. None of my children in this City, except you three, serve Almighty God. We might as well die on the way to freedom as to be killed by a madman here."

Remarkably, Livia did not develop a fever from her wounds, nor did her lovely spirit soil itself with self-pity. She took strength from the plans which the four of them were making for their journey. Being careful never to discuss the matter when Cain was in the house, they were four conspirators laying plans for their escape to freedom. With her own hands, Aluma built a false wall across one end of the vegetable cellar. She stacked sacks of grain across the front of the entrance to her stronghold; and Cain, going into the cool haven for his fermented drinks, was totally unsuspecting.

For several weeks, the four stealthily prepared items for placement in the cellar. Livia declared that she had not lost the use of her fingers, and they moved with urgent speed as she wove baskets with which to carry wares on their trip.

The others gleaned early spring fruits from the orchard, drying them in the sun, and storing them openly in the cellar; but always a portion smuggled into the hiding place. Fish was salted and dried, vegetables carefully tended in the garden, and waterproof jugs made with special skill.

Cain watched this flurry of activity with great satisfaction. He assured himself that it took a strong hand to keep this willful wife submitted. Although at first he had resented the coming of the three children, he now was glad that they were here. Now, through the children, he had firm control over Aluma. All that he had to do was threaten a child, and his wife would kneel and worship her Lord and Master: Cain.

Aluma waited and watched for the old restlessness to come, as she knew it would come, to Cain. He began to take longer and longer walks in the hills; until one day at dawn he saddled his donkey, and without any farewell, or even a backward look he left.

She waited two weeks, and then she told the girls that they would leave during that very night. There was to be a festival that night, and Aluma knew that the revelry would go on until the early hours of the morning. When the drunken participants could no longer escape sleep, would be the time when the four would make their own escape.

With curtains pulled tightly over the windows, they began filling the sacks with supplies to be loaded on the pack animals. Aluma bid the girls sleep, but the excitement of anticipation forbade it. Sheera sang quietly to herself as she stuffed goods into bags and thought sweet thoughts of happier times to come. Aluma paused in her work and placed her arms around the twelve year old.

"No wonder that your mother named you 'song' she murmured into the girl's sweet hair.

Sheera smiled up at her grandmother, and tears filled her eyes. "Mama used to sing too," she said quietly, "before she began to go with daddy's friends to the bad places."

Aluma reflected silently that, in spite of her many prayers, her youngest daughter, like all of her other daughters had chosen to go to "the bad places." She shook off the sad thoughts and abruptly told her granddaughters that it was time to load the donkeys.

They moved as quietly as they could to the stable that adjoined the house. There the donkeys stood in sleepy silence, probably wondering why their slumbers were interrupted at such an early hour. There were six donkeys waiting in the stable; Aluma had purchased two just the past week. They were great sturdy animals, perfect for carrying the tent and supplies that the travelers would need.

Without a word among them the three loaded the donkeys, allowing Livia to stand next to the lead donkey, crooning soothing endearments to keep it calm. Carefully tying the six donkeys together in a single file, Aluma placed Livia on the donkey directly behind hers, followed by Tova and then by Sheera, and finally by the two heavily loaded pack animals. Livia had placed her mother cat and kittens in a basket on her donkey; Tova had two hens in one side basket and a favorite red rooster on the other side.

After much pleading, Sheera had convinced her grandmother to allow her side baskets to hold a tiny baby goat each; with their mother bringing up the rear on a rope attached to the last donkey. Aluma had tied the mouth of the mother goat shut with cloth lest she call out to her babies and wake the sleepers.

Walking carefully ahead of her donkey, Aluma led this strange procession through the gates of the City, praying desperately that none of the revelers would awaken to see them leave. She had explained to the girls that they would travel mostly at night, following the stars that Aluma knew so well. She still had a copy of the map, which she had used to send her sons on their journey to find their grandparents so many years ago.

"Well," she thought ruefully, "I'll find out the hard way how good a map maker I am."

They had found it more difficult to travel by night than Aluma had anticipated. They had left Cain's City during the dark of the moon and the firmament that gave them moisture for their crops was causing a heavy blanket of wetness to engulf them on their travels. After two weeks of difficult night travel, Aluma decided that they could safely rest for a few days, begin their journey at the break of dawn and travel along the Great River. She had heard tales of a settlement at the apex of the barren land, where the Great River had changed to a northwesterly course and the path to Adam's land veered southwesterly.

Careful to avoid contact with any travelers until many days northwest of Cain's City, Aluma began to travel with a lighter heart as the miles passed by safely. Although she had no reason to expect that the wandering Cain had learned of her escape, there were hundreds of others in the City who would rather see her placed in a dungeon than allowed to leave. During high festivals Cain would insist that she dress herself in finery and be paraded before the crowds as his 'Queen'. The populace would not take the defection of their queen lightly.

There were occasional small villages along the River; and Adam's daughter allowed herself to speculate which of her siblings or children had been the source of that particular family branch. One time as the travelers passed a field, women who were working there cheerfully waved to them. They waved back; and Aluma, after closely studying the women for signs of being from the descendants of Cain, decided a short stay to rest there would be safe.

They stayed at that small village for a full week; joining the people in Sabbath worship and delighting to hear tales of life as these people knew it. Aluma was interested to find that a son of Adam named Efron, born long after Aluma had left, had decided to bring his family to settle near the Great River. He and his sons and their sons were able to provide a livelihood by fishing. They would salt the fish and sell them to travelers going along the road. The family business was flourishing and the people there seemed content and happy.

They did not seem to find it strange that a woman with three children was traveling by without companions, although Aluma correctly guessed that it was not a common happening. She said simply that she was a daughter of Adam and yearned to see her parents' faces while they yet lived.

When they left to continue their journey, their water jugs had been replenished, and they had sacks of fresh fruit and vegetables, and salted fish to sustain them on their trip.

After several more weeks of travel, they came to a large settlement where two main roads crossed each other. Aluma went to the well in the center of the town, and there asked the women if there was a place where the four of them might rest from their journey. Some of the women looked with suspicion at the wind burned older woman whose face bore ugly scars and whose manner seemed regal but timorous. They turned their eyes to the three young girls. Two of them had hair of such a light color that it was nearly white: a certain sign that they were descendants of Cain. The third child, a diminutive little thing with raven hair, had horrible burned sockets where there should have been eyes.

Aluma saw their unease and spoke up, deciding that candor would be the best course.

"I am Aluma, long lost daughter of Adam, and these are my granddaughters. We are fleeing Cain's City; for we have no part in the evil done there, and we are headed for Adam's settlement. Can you tell me which road will take us home to Father Adam?"

The women stood in stunned silence. Finally one of the young women spoke.

"The southward road is the one that you want. My husband is a merchant and he takes dyed linen cloth all the way to the Great Sea to sell. I have never been on the road for I was born here, as were my parents.

"This town has been here for many years, as I am certain that you can tell by the buildings. We have many places of trade here and we are quite prosperous, but it is our custom to share with any who are in need. Many years ago there were several grandsons of Cain who had a quarrel with other grandsons, and they left Cain's City to build a City of their own, but one without evil revelry. They worked hard and built houses and tilled the soil, and then they sent two of their men to visit Father Adam to ask for wives. They said that Father Adam asked them many hard questions and then he told them to stay and refresh themselves while he sought the Lord's will in the matter.

"After Adam prayed for many days, he spoke again to the men. He told them to return home and come back for the Harvest Festival the next year. He said that if they were faithful in this that there would be wives waiting for them. He said that all must come, for he wished to meet personally each man who would claim a wife.

"They did all that they were told, and after the Harvest Festival they each brought a wife back home with them. The next year some men and their wives came from as far away as the Great Sea to become part of our village and every year we have new families come to join us. You are welcome to make a home here if you do not find what you are seeking in Adam's City."

Aluma was choked with joy. "But I thought, --I mean I was certain, -- that is, I had no idea that there were any other Godly persons to come out of Cain's City. I thought all of my prayers and teaching fell on deaf ears. Oh how I do praise God for this good news!"

An older woman spoke up. "I am one of those whom Father Adam selected to marry and move here. Mother Eve talked to me about it at great length to make certain that I was willing to leave family and home and move away with a stranger. I was very young, and I remember that I told her that they couldn't be any more strange than the boys I knew at home.

"She laughed and then asked me to spend time in prayer, seriously asking God if this was what He wanted me to do. I did pray and I felt a sudden peace about my decision. I fell deeply in love with the man I married, and I have never had any doubts or regrets. I have had a wonderful life. My Samien is a good man and a kind husband."

A woman whose long red tresses fell, unshackled by hair covering, to her waist invited them to stay as long as they wished at her house. She said that her husband, a tanner, was away on business; and that she had a large house and would enjoy the company.

The girls had a fine time playing with the children of the community, for never had they been allowed to run so freely. They exclaimed over and over to one another that no one seemed afraid here, and that there were no loud parties at night. All of the children wanted a turn at helping blind Livia with their games, and none asked her unkind or probing questions.

Aluma's soul rejoiced to know that, seemingly from the pits of hell, God had brought this good place into being. Truly God in his mercy had established this City and she smiled at its name: 'Eliakim' meaning established by God.

The morning that the four were to leave, they were summoned to a City council meeting. There Aluma was presented with a wagon, to be pulled by two donkeys while the others traveled behind, attached by ropes. The wagon was piled high with gifts for Father Adam, but there was plenty of room for Aluma and the three girls to ride. Aluma was too moved to speak, but Sheera, with all of the self-possession that any twelve-year-old girl could demonstrate, looked the council members straight in the face and thanked each one of them for the wonderful treatment they had received.

The men warned Aluma that the roads were sometimes very dangerous as they headed south through the hilly country. There were animals that had left behind their nature of gentleness and, becoming savage beasts, lurked behind trees and cliffs, waiting to pounce on unsuspecting travelers. Sometimes there were even bandits, evil men who made their living by taking what other people had worked to earn. The elders of the City looked very grave when they warned the group that they were to avoid travel by night, but move only after the sun was well up into the sky and before the sun set behind the hills.

"Always stay together," the men warned. "For no reason should one of you go off alone."

Then they presented Aluma with a gift that seemed very strange to her. It was a dog. Not a dog like the wild ones that ravaged the garbage dumps, but a calm, obedient, well fed, tame little dog. Aluma had never seen such a thing.

"This dog will protect you," one of them explained. "Keep him with you at all times. It is said that Adam's daughter, Rina, began the taming of these animals many years ago when she herded sheep. This one is for you. Feed him scraps from your food, and give him water as often as you would one of your granddaughters. Treat him with respect and he will guard your lives; but he will never harm you. His name is Zevi."

So they left the good City. They were glad to be riding in a wagon instead of on the back of a donkey, and they were excited to be laden with gifts for their final destination. Livia thought that Zevi was a wonderful animal, and he rewarded her warm embrace with generous wet kisses on her face. The animal seemed to sense that Livia could not see, and he never willingly left her side; he was always there to guide her steps.

The trip went amazingly smoothly as they headed southwest towards the area where Aluma had last seen her parents. She rotated the teams of donkeys so that the strain would be shared by all of the animals. The travelers had spent two full weeks on the road when they found a curious disturbance just around the cliff ahead of them. Tova, tired of riding, ran joyfully ahead of the group for a little while, chasing and being chased by her sister's little goats. It was she who discovered the skirmish and came running back breathlessly to report to her grandmother.

"Grandmother, grandmother, they have just killed those people! There are terrible men just up the road."

Aluma quickly got the animals and the girls into the bushes and hid them behind some large rocks several hundred feet off the narrow road. After tying rags around the mouth of each animal, she admonished the girls to be quieter than they had ever been in their lives. She then covered the wagon with fallen tree limbs and bushes.

They hadn't long to wait until five boisterous men came swaggering around the road from the cliff area. The girls lay motionless, completely covered by long reeds of grass. Aluma hunched behind the mound closest to the road. She had tied two donkeys close to her feet. If the men discovered her perhaps they would not notice the girls.

Oblivious to any of the females, the men continued on their eastward trek. They were leading three large animals that were strange to Aluma. She had once heard Cain talking to his sons about such animals, and knew that he had offered a large sum of money to any who could provide him with one. The animal was similar to the donkey but had longer legs and a sleeker body; the ears were pointed, and of a different shape than the donkeys. Aluma remembered her mother's tales about faithful 'Horse' who remained with them after their expulsion from the Garden and she wondered if this animal was the same breed.

Also being led by the men was a large gray donkey, heavily loaded with baskets and bloodstained robes.

Aluma waited for a long time after the men had passed by before she attempted to move from her hiding place. The sun was nearly setting when she cautiously climbed down to creep along the path until she could have a clear view around the cliff road.

She gasped at what she saw. Three naked, mutilated bodies lay sprawled in the road. Cautiously drawing nearer, she was stunned as she realized that one of the bodies was female. The woman's face had been beaten to a bloody mass. Retching, she turned to hurry away, but then she heard a noise that sounded like a kitten mewing.

She stood silently for a moment, and was ready to think it was her imagination, when she heard the sound again, weaker now. Walking closer to the body, she knelt down. There was no sound from the woman. Death was obvious. A tiny gasping sound came from an area that appeared to be underneath the body. Shuddering, Aluma turned the woman over. She had fallen to the side of the road, landing on a small boulder which allowed a basket she carried slung over her shoulders to escape being crushed.

Aluma peered into the basket and was astounded to see a tiny infant; its face was a dusky color, and it had apparently just taken its final breath. Aluma hastily snatched the lifeless body from the basket and, for reasons she could never explain later, gave it a gentle shake and then blew her own breath into its tiny mouth and nose.

The infant began to scream, its face now red and angry. Laughing through her tears, Aluma tore off her shawl and wrapped the child snugly. She ran quickly back to the hiding place and began calling for the girls. They pushed the grass covering off themselves and, with Sheera holding tightly to Livia's hand, scampered to their grandmother's side. Sheera and Tova exclaimed with surprise at the bundle in Aluma's hands. Jumping up and down on one foot, Livia demanded to be told what was happening.

Both Sheera and Tova began to tell the youngest girl about the baby, but were interrupted by their anxious grandmother.

"Sheera, quickly milk the momma goat," she instructed. "We must feed this little one before he is too weak to eat. His parents are dead. We must not let him die.

Sheera immediately did as she was told, while Tova grabbed a supple leather skin to shape into a little funnel with which to feed the baby. Livia took off her soft head covering and handed it to Aluma so the new arrival could be covered warmly, for now the night stars were out and the air had turned cooler. Aluma allowed the girls to drink goat's milk and eat cheese and stale bread, but told them that they must not light a fire; for she feared that the cruel men might still be nearby.

When the children were fed, she surprised them by telling them to load the animals and prepare for travel. They had not traveled by night since they had first started out months before. The land then had been flat with no dangerous cliffs or sudden changes in the landscape. How could they possibly see the road on this dark night?

Aluma explained softly.

"I am leaving the road now, children. I fear that there are more bandits, and the common road is too risky. There is a path going up into the hills, and we will take it; for I believe that we will be true to our course as long as we continue southwest. We will travel until we are well away from this terrible place and only then will we rest.

We will tie all of the donkeys together single-file; and Tova, you must lead them. Your place will be directly behind me. Livia will ride on the fore-most donkey and hold the infant. Sheera, tie a rope to the dog and keep him by your side. You will walk at the end of the line and make certain that no animals wander off. If you see anything that worries you, release the dog and he will come to Livia."

"But grandmother, what about the wagon?" asked Tova.

"We cannot take it, child. It is well hidden; and if we are as close to Father Adam's as I think we are, we'll send someone back for it."

As if to hide them further, the moon settled itself behind dark clouds. Aluma chose her way cautiously along the path, probing each step carefully with a shepherd's staff before going ahead. For what seemed to the girls to be an endless amount of time they walked on and on, rarely pausing to rest their weary legs.

Suddenly Aluma came to a sharp halt, causing Tova to run into the back of her, and Livia to nearly drop the baby.

"I feel water on my face," Aluma explained. She dropped to her knees and began to explore the ground in front of her. "The path drops off into the air. We can go no further tonight for I can see nothing.

"Tova," she directed, "follow the donkey rope to the end of the line, and tell Sheera to go back 100 paces and set up camp. I pray to God that we are in a safe place."

The sun rose on the sleeping travelers with enough brilliance to belie the awful darkness of the night. Aluma dragged her weary body from the bed of grass where she had been sleeping, and stumbled down to the river to wash her face.

The cool water was so invigorating that she suddenly gave into the temptation to plunge her entire body into the river. When she finally returned to the bank, her body felt refreshed and her mind somewhat cleared.

A "river," she mused. "A wide river. And deep. What river could it be?"

She buried her head in her arms with a sudden feeling of despair. "Cain and I didn't cross a river in this area when we left all those years ago. Where have I led these children? I was so sure, and now I don't know. Oh God, dearest Heavenly Father, which way do I go? This river appears to be flowing in a southerly direction. Dear God, suddenly I am so very frightened. How do I go on? What do I do?"

She couldn't contain the sobs as she unburdened her heart to her Lord. Lifting her head suddenly her mind took in the beauty of the area. The river was continuing on its journey quietly and serenely, certain of its destination, gently giving a ride to the occasional tree or limb or leaf. She smiled to see a turtle catching a ride on a crudely cut board; looking quite content to warm itself in the sunshine.

Suddenly her body jerked to attention. A board! Something made by a man. A man who surely lived in a village. A village north of here. They would travel up the river.

When she stood, as if on signal the infant began to wail at the top of his lungs. "Well, there goes this day's serenity," she smiled, as she headed back to the camp.

Following the river proved to be a difficult task; for heedless of the needs of its pursuers, it twisted and turned at will. Aluma and Sheera worked faithfully to clear a path as they traveled, but the work was hard and tedious. Before they had gone many miles, their hands were torn and bleeding. Once Aluma slipped down a bank, badly bruising herself and tearing a long gash in her leg.

Sheera begged her grandmother to stop for a day's rest, but Aluma refused. She knew many potential dangers that her granddaughters were not aware of: their supplies were running low, cold weather was coming, and there were likely even more dangerous men out there who had no hesitation to kill men, women or babies. She was certain that her husband had posted a reward for her return, as he once had for a servant who had tried to escape.

She grimly remembered the fate of that servant when he had been returned, barely alive, to her husband. Cain had ordered her to tend to the man's wounds and feed him well until his health returned. She had done this thankfully and gladly, grateful that her husband truly seemed bent upon showing kindness to the servant.

The day that the man was well enough to return to his duties, Cain had proclaimed a feast and had invited many. The servant sat in a seat of honor, and Cain drank a toast to him. At the end of the feast the servant had kneeled weeping at Cain's feet, and had pledged undying loyalty to his master.

The next morning Cain had called for his servant and tied him to a tree outside their house, where all who passed by could see. He began a series of torturous acts so horrendous that, merely by remembering them this long time since, Aluma broke into a cold sweat.

Slowly and systematically Cain killed the man. When, much to her relief, the servant was finally granted the solace of death, Aluma had never dared lift her eyes to her husband's face again, for fear that he would read there her measure of him.

No, there could be no rest now. They must hurry on. She drove the children and the animals harder and harder. Whatever lay ahead would surely be better than what lay behind.

One day, after much backbreaking labor to clear a path, Aluma realized that it had become impossible to continue to follow the river. The cliffs leading down to the river were now high and treacherous. One slight slip and they could all plunge to their deaths. She said nothing to the girls as they made camp that night, but she knew that at daybreak they must choose another way.

The girls were happy and excited because Aluma had allowed them to cease their travels while the sun was still high in the afternoon sky. They made their camp quickly and enjoyed having time to run and play: a rare treat.

They filled their water skins from the stream that flowed from the hills into the river. The girls enjoyed watching the fall of water that the stream made when it cascaded over the side of the bank and down, down into the river below.

Aluma leaned her head back against a tree, giving in to the pain of her leg, which didn't seem to be healing correctly since being injured during that silly fall she had taken. She pulled the rags from around it and frowned at the sight. The long jagged wound was bright red and oozing a thick drainage.

She sighed as she left it open to the air while she gave herself a few minutes to regain the strength needed to treat it. If only she had brought more of her precious herbs from Cain's City.

She saw nothing growing in this area that she recognized. She knew that if she did not properly treat her leg soon, the sickness would spread from it into her entire body.

While Sheera hunted for wild vegetables to add to their meager supper, and Livia fed the animals their limited ration of grain, Tova boiled the water and helped her grandmother wash and rewrap the injured leg. "What brave, brave girls I have," Aluma thought.

She gently ran her fingers through the silky hair of the infant who was sleeping at her side. Praise God that the milk goat was still producing a generous amount of milk. Enough for the little one and the two rambunctious kids. She smiled at the chubby infant. He had miraculously thrived in their care. They called him simply, 'baby', Aluma had decided that Father Adam must choose the name for this special one.

"Please, grandmother, eat some of this soup."

Aluma heard her granddaughter's voice as from a long way off. She opened her eyes and was startled to discover that the sun was well set and several stars could be seen in the darkening sky.

She felt disoriented and feverish. "What--what has happened?" she murmured. Looking over at small bundles snuggled sound asleep in mounds of grass, she realized that Sheera was the only one awake.

"You were so tired, grandmother," Sheera answered, "and you seemed to be sleeping soundly. I didn't want to bother you. Livia was good to help with the baby while he was awake, and Tova and I were able to handle everything else. We did fine. We were glad that you were resting. A bird flew up in that branch over your head and sang and sang, as if he was glad too."

Aluma pulled the girl into her arms and tenderly kissed the top of the young head. How could she possibly deserve such wonderful girls? How did they manage to have such sweet, gentle and kind hearts, after all they had seen in that horrible evil place where they had been raised?

Suddenly she playfully pushed Sheera away, demanding the soup that she had been promised. Sheera laughed and happily spread the makeshift table with a meal for her grandmother.

The next morning Aluma left the river and set her face towards the north. There was still no path to guide them, although the woods gave way to barren land, making the traveling easier, but causing Aluma to feel even more confused about their direction. To further complicate matters, the sky became so overcast that there were no shadows to give direction during the day and no stars out at night. Aluma, with the fever getting worse, became completely disoriented.

A morning came when the girls were unable to rouse their grandmother to full consciousness. They were frightened to find that she seemed to believe she was once again a little girl, and she kept calling out, "Mama, Mama, I am so thirsty."

The girls moved the animals close together and made a shelter of blankets around all of them. They tended Aluma the best they knew how, and prayed to the heavenly Father as they had been taught.

When all seemed hopeless, and the girls feared that they would all die, a trader chasing an errant lamb found them and took them to Father Adam.

They were home at last. The long journey was ended.

❋ ❋ ❋ ❋ ❋

Both Eve and Aluma seemed to be remembering that glad reunion when Aluma had called out 'Mama' to find that her beloved mother was actually holding a jar of water to her parched lips. What a wonderful blessing it had been to sink into nothingness, knowing that other hands would tend to the baby and to the girls. Knowing that, at long last, she felt safe.

But now, Aluma sighed; for the time had come that she had been dreading. It had been so very comforting to stay here in her warm cave, tending the needs of the infant, and hearing stories of the community that the girls would bring her. But now her mother was here, chiding her for staying hidden.

"But Mother, is it not enough that the girls go daily into the village to study at the school taught by the young women? They have adjusted well haven't they? You said yourself that they seem like any of the other girls of the village, who have lived here all of their lives."

Eve studied her daughter for a long moment, while Aluma lowered her eyes and squirmed under her scrutiny. The Mother of all Living began with a quiet tenderness in her voice.

"I have borne 17 children, Aluma, but you were my first-born daughter. You were the first copy of myself, and because of that you are especially dear to me. The girls are well, Aluma, and you have done a wonderful job of caring for them. They seem happy, and are making many friends, but it is you that I worry about. You are the one who is not healing."

Tears coursed down Aluma's cheeks as she stared into the depths beyond her mother. Her scarred face acquired a tortured look, and her frail shoulders began to shake under the burden of grief. In halting words she began to explain her fears to Eve.

"I am the mother of the children of that horrible place. It is the children of the children of my body that killed the parents of this little boy, and left him to die underneath his mother. My children curse God and seek evil. I gave birth to monsters, and I lived with them so long that I must be a monster myself.

"You know that it is true, Mother. Certainly father thinks so. Not one time has he climbed the hill to see me since I came back. I know that he is terribly ashamed of me, and I don't blame him. I do not understand why God allows me to continue to live now that I have delivered the children safely to your care."

"Aluma, dear, dear daughter, do you not remember that it is I who gave birth to Cain? Each person chooses for himself whether to serve God or the Evil One. No one can make that choice for another. Cain was taught the same way as Abel, but he chose a different path. Your father is ashamed because he sent you off to live with Cain all those years ago without giving you a chance to explain. He was angry when he learned that you were with child. He assumed the worst and didn't allow you to explain that Cain had forced you to lie with him. Now he is afraid that *you* cannot forgive *him*.

"As for your children, why do you choose to remember only the evil ones? Do you not have children who chose to build the good City of Eliakim? And how about those three wonderful men, children of your own body; Abir, Ravid and Tzevi! Why, Adam was proud to give your sisters in marriage to them.

"Someday, when you have pulled yourself out of this bout of self-pity, you must travel to the Great Sea, and see for yourself the wonderful cities that the children have built there.

"There is nothing that the Evil One would rather do than to keep us thinking about our failures in life. He doesn't want us to remember those things which are good. He wants us to feel completely discouraged and angry with ourselves all the time. That way there is only room in our hearts for ourselves and our regrets and failures. If we remember the good, then our thoughts soon fly to the Good One, and we begin to praise God for His goodness.

"Remember, Aluma, only God is good. There is no goodness in any of us, no matter how successful our lives may seem. Your Father and I explained to you, many, many years ago, how we chose evil and disobeyed our precious Heavenly Father in the wonderful home that He had prepared for us.

"God wants us to tell that story to all our future generations in order that no person will ever believe that he or she will be beyond God's reach, no matter how rebellious they are. The day is coming, Aluma, when God will send someone so perfect that he will crush the head of the Evil One; while we wait for the Shekinah glory of that day, we must continue to overcome evil with His good.

"Now, young lady," Eve continued, (for in all the years of time, no mother has ever looked at her daughter as any age but 'young lady', even if she was nearly 200 years old!) "I want you to get up in the morning, put on your best attire and come down to the village. You are to greet your father with a kiss, ask his blessing, and let him know that you forgive him. You must also give him a chance to ask for your forgiveness. Do you understand me?"

Aluma laughed through her tears. "Yes Mama," she said meekly.

Adam and Aluma, with many tears and joyful laughter, forgave, and were forgiven, by each other. As the days passed, Aluma began to feel a gentle acceptance by the women of the village. Eve helped her to realize that it was only natural that people were curious about the first-born daughter of the first couple on this earth.

One day several weeks after the refugees had arrived in the village, the search party which Adam had sent out to look for the wagon, returned joyfully. They had found the wagon, safely intact, and all of the gifts sent from the village of Eliakim were still completely untouched. But best of all, thought Aluma, her boxes of herbs and medicines had arrived. In the spring she would be able to plant her numerous seeds, so carefully saved and cataloged, and replenish her medicinal supplies.

Aluma soon found her niche in the village by helping in the building where the seriously ill and injured were brought. Her skills were so great that the younger women considered themselves fortunate to learn from her. Eve expressed immense gratitude to Aluma for her work; for every hour that Aluma spent tending the ill or injured, or teaching the novices, allowed Eve the freedom to tend to other matters.

The Harvest Festival arrived with the promise of the fullest, brightest, golden moon that the village could ever remember seeing. Excitement was great in Aluma's small household for the baby was to receive his name from Father Adam.

"And about time it is too, little one! You are much too big to be called 'baby'," Tova exclaimed to the three month old.

The girls and their grandmother had bathed and dressed carefully this crisp, clear morning. Today was the first Harvest Festival that Aluma had attended since that fateful day, so long ago, when Cain's offering had been rejected.

Aluma had told this story many times to the girls, and they never tired of its telling. Their spirits were high as they trekked down the hillside to attend the events, which began early in the day.

Adam looked with pride at the large number of babies that were brought to him by their parents. He placed his hands on each infant, gave the name which the parents had chosen and asked God to bless the child and the family. Finally the moment came for which Aluma and the girls had anxiously waited. Father Adam would give their baby his name. Aluma held the babe out to her father and bowed her head in submission.

"Oh Lord," Adam began, "I present to you this infant which you have given into the hands of these present today. When this child's birth mother was killed by a terrible enemy, you allowed your daughter Aluma to find the boy; and you gave her the wisdom needed to make him well. We thank you, dear heavenly Father for your many blessings, and at this time we wish to give this child back to you, to be raised for your honor and glory. We would not present him to you nameless, Lord, and from this day hence he shall be called Josiah because you have protected him."

Adam turned to Aluma and placed his hand gently on her bowed head. "Woman, this is now your son. Raise him to honor God and respect his fellow man."

Aluma raised her head and smiled into her father's eyes. Her own were shining, and the scars on her face seemed to have receded into the flushed happiness of her now radiant beauty.

She turned as she heard a male voice call her name from behind her. Aluma started as she looked into her father's face from her childhood. The surprise and confusion showed so clearly in her expression that Seth laughed loudly. "I am Seth, my sister; and, yes, I know that I look exactly like my father! I have heard about you all my life, and I give thanks to God that He has brought you home to us.

"Josiah is a beautiful boy. He is the same age as my recently-born grandson. He was presented to God during the Ceremony of New Life. Have you seen our little Cainan?" He turned and motioned for his wife Mira to bring the baby over for Aluma to see.

Aluma greeted Mira joyfully. This was one of the daughters of Rina and Abir and therefore Aluma's granddaughter. Aluma was nearly overwhelmed to meet her granddaughter, and thanked God again that He had spared Abir from the Evil one. She laughed to see that Mira looked as much like Rina as Seth looked like Adam. To Aluma it was as if her sister, age unchanged from when she had last seen her, was standing there smiling at her.

She gazed tenderly at her the baby. Eve had explained to her that God had chosen to produce a Godly line through Seth, and that it would be through his lineage that the Special One would come. She suddenly felt shy in front of her brother, and for just a moment the old doubts came rushing back. Seth's warmth and sense of fun quickly did away with her fears; and she soon found herself laughing with abandon at his shared memories of life with their siblings.

That night, under the full harvest moon, Adam -- the Father of all mankind, and priest of his people -- was for the first time assisted by

Seth and his son Enosh in presenting the burnt offerings to God. The many families came one at a time, bringing the finest animals that they had, to make a sin offering, in which the blood of a living being could cleanse each one of them of sin. The offerings were placed in the hands of an earthly father, to be taken into the presence of the Heavenly Father. All hearts were filled with praise to the One who had not only given them an abundant harvest, but had also added to their joy by bringing home those members of the family who had been lost to them for such a long time. Happy voices lifted in unison to sing praises to God, as the Shekinah glory consumed their gifts.

Chapter Six

The Journey

White fluffy clouds dotted the blueness of the spring sky. Rina had once told him that the vast sea, which lay but a brief walk from where she and Abir dwelled, looked like that; white froth on blue, blue water. Adam had never seen the sea, but standing there looking at the clouds he decided that he would someday have that pleasure. As soon as this matter was settled he would travel over the hills and plains and see such a wonder.

His mind reluctantly pulled itself back to the matter at hand. He returned to his seat of stone and looked at the grim faces of the men who had come to seek his guidance. How ironic it was that this particular meeting should take place in this spot.

Cain's field. How proud Cain had been of his fields. The men had chosen to meet in the clover field because of its flatness and privacy. It was a completely round field with spokes of other fields leading from it like petals of flowers. Cain loved symmetry, and he had delighted in the beauty of his carefully planned and tended fields. Adam glanced toward the small mound where, in his rage and jealousy, Cain had buried Abel.

Adam's sigh extended to the outer edge of the circle of men. The men ceased their quiet murmuring and with one accord looked expectantly in his direction. Adam cleared his throat and began to speak.

"Men, we have come here today because of the concern that many of you have expressed to me about your daughters. Adlai, you are the one who talked with the Trader, so please tell us what you learned."

Adlai nodded and stood facing the circle of men. Never before had be been called upon to talk in front of a group of people. His face and erect bearing betrayed his nervousness as he began to speak.

"As everyone here knows, Zalman the trader brings wares from the coast to us every new moon. He make trips to all of the villages and twice in twelve months even goes all the way to Cain's City. Many of the people who live in Cain's City are wealthy and like to buy the kind of special things that can only be brought in from the Great Sea. The City is also gaining great wealth from things that they make and sell to other people.

"We have all heard stories about great festivals. Well, Zalman says that he never goes there when the moon is full because he has heard rumors of strange happenings that take place during that time. Last month Zalman got sick the week before be was to arrive in the City, and by the time he reached the gates the moon was beginning to be full.

"When Zalman got to the City he was invited to eat dinner at Cain's house. He said that Enoch and his wife live there because apparently Cain doesn't stay at home very much. You know how Aluma has told us about his wanderings. Well, uh, I guess that is still how it is. And, well oh well, who should happen to be there during Zalman's last trip but Cain himself! Zalman said that he had never laid eyes on the man before but Cain asked him to sit at the table as his honored guest. It seems that Tubal had made some new instruments --- you've heard how he likes to make music, and all the villages buy the things that he makes -- and, well, everyone wanted to hear the new sounds that the instruments could make. And Zalman said that he really felt kinda scared because, well he said that there was a whole big crowd invited to eat and they drank until they were drunk, and they called in women and began dancing and making love, and …, Adlai blushed, … and well, just a lot of things.

"You know, Father Adam, Zalman is a pretty rough character, and he doesn't participate in the Harvest sin offerings or serve God like we think he should; but he said that he wanted to get out of that house and run away as fast as he could. He said that he felt like he wanted to take a bath and wash all his clothes and he said that he actually did that just as soon as he could; but, you know, he said he still felt like he needed a bath."

Doran spoke up impatiently, "Adlai, will you get to the point, and tell about the girls that you saw there!"

Father Adam walked to Adlai's side and placed his hand on his shoulder. "You are doing a fine job. I'm sure that this is a difficult story to tell. Just take your time and we will all be patient with you." Adam looked meaningfully at Doran who dropped his head.

Adlai took a deep breath, straightened his shoulders and continued his story. "Zalman said that after everyone had been eating and drinking, and all that other stuff, Cain stood up and said he had an announcement. He said how proud he is of the City and how there isn't any other place like it on this earth, and he said that the people who live there are the wisest and most clever people in the world. Then he turned to Enoch and praised him for how he keeps the City going when Cain is away. Cain said that from now on the City is to be called Enoch in honor of his first-born son."

The men in the circle began to talk all at once and Adlai stood quietly. Adam stood up and began to thank Adlai for sharing the story with the group.

Adlai looked startled. "Oh, but Father, I haven't told you the worst part yet. There is more."

Adam held up his hand for the men to get quiet, and nodded for Adlai to finish his story.

"Well," Adlai continued, "I guess that every full moon there is a kind of marriage ceremony for the young men who haven't taken a wife yet. Zalman says that many of the young women of the City won't get married because they don't like the way that the men treat them. The women are strong, like the men, and can even fight and hit just like a man!

"The women, well, they kinda do whatever they want to. They run shops and many of them even own men-slaves; but if they don't want to marry, they don't. Of course, they still take part in the goin's on at the full-moon ceremony, or whatever they call it, so a lot of them get babies anyway." At this point Adlai's face turned beet red, and the men were very, very quiet.

He turned to the older man: "Father Adam, I don't hardly know how to tell this part, but Zalman swears it is true. He said that they brought out 17 young girls, and none of them had on any clothes at all, and the unmarried men got to cast lots for the one they wanted. Zalman said that the girls had been stolen from the villages all around. That's all Father, that's all I know to tell; but Zalman says that it all really happened. I'm scared, sir, because we all have daughters and granddaughters, and how do we keep the evil ones from taking them into the City?"

Adam stood silently with his head bowed and eyes closed for long minutes. The men were also silent, each thinking his own thoughts, each forming a mental picture of the young girls of his own household.

When Adam lifted his head to speak he noticed that Eytan had stepped forward and was indicating that he had something to say.

"Speak, Eytan. Give us your thoughts," said the father of the race.

"Father Adam, I too have heard tales about the City. I was talking to Tabbai, who is the son of Eliakim and now Chief Ruler of that City. As we all know, Eliakim is a City based on God's love; and many of the people who live there once fled from Cain's City, or I guess I should say from the City of Enoch.

"Tabbai says that some of the girls who are taken to the City go of their own free will. He says that there are women who approach them while they are at the village Well, and entice them with promises of beautiful clothes and homes unlike any they have ever seen and riches that they cannot imagine.

"Some of these girls follow the women willingly into the City looking for 'freedom'. It is true that many, especially the younger ones, are stolen. But Father, the worst thing that I have heard is that some of the men from our own settlement have traded young girls from their family in exchange for a woman of the City of Enoch. It is said that these women are sexually exciting, and know things that our women do not know; and I am sorry to tell you that some of our men do not serve God as we would wish."

"Thank you, Eytan, for adding that," Adam responded, "for I too have heard those stories; and it is good that we know the whole truth of this terrible matter. Now men, let us go to God with this situation. He will show us what must be done to keep our children out of the evil place. For, no matter what name it goes by, its true name is *Death and Destruction.*"

Adam began his supplication to God. He prayed long and fervently, telling God in detail all that had been discussed at the meeting. When he had finished, he stood for a long while with his eyes closed and head bowed. No one stirred.

Adam finally lifted his head.

"I want an accounting of each family of every generation," he said, his tone suddenly brisk and business like. "I will place one of my seven sons in charge of this situation. Each family will report to his own Patriarchal head all information concerning the marriages of your Line. Each Patriarch will have his findings ready by the end of summer. We will have a meeting of the Priests and the Patriarchs at the Harvest Festival."

The men nodded with understanding. There was no one on the earth who had not descended from Adam; for Adam and Eve were the first parents. There were eight daughters including Aluma who had been the wife of Cain. Only three of the sons of Cain had chosen to serve God and return to live with the Godly line of Adam, marrying daughters from that line. Every man at the meeting knew from which of the original sons or daughters his lineage was derived. The head of that line, be it son or son-in-law of Adam, was Patriarch.

Adam glanced over the sea of faces until his eyes found the one for whom he was searching. He found him easily for he was a distinctive man. 'Young lion' he had named him.

He had arrived in this world a huge, hungry, squalling bundle. Masses of flaming blond-red hair had fallen in ringlets from his head. His beginning had not proved false. He towered over his kinsmen, and his disposition could go from sunny to stormy as quickly as a cloud could travel in front of the sun.

Guryon.

He had married the beautiful Nehama, and God had blessed them with a dozen children. Adam had heard that Guryon was replicated in a young grandson named Tal, and he smiled in wonder that the world could contain two such vital forces.

Guryon, second of his seven sons.

"Guryon, you will be in charge of this gathering of information; for I must know each man who has married a daughter from the daughters of Cain, each family who has lost a daughter to the City of Cain…."

He hesitated.

"…To the City of Enoch. We must find a way to put a stop to this evil practice that is bringing such wicked, sinful heartache into our midst."

Guryon had stepped forward until he stood directly in front of his father. "I will be honored to accept this responsibility, Father," he said in a voice amazingly quiet from one of such size, "but I will need some assistance with this duty."

"Whatever you need, Guryon, you may request."

Guryon walked purposefully to the stone where Adam was, and turned to the men gathered in the field.

"We must be very careful with our plans," he stated clearly. "We don't want any of Cain's men suspecting that we are going to prevent their dirty work. Even though the City of Enoch is many days travel from here, I have for some time suspected that there are spies everywhere we go. I hear stories of violence and cruelty coming from that place; and if we have any hope of rescuing those who want to leave, or keeping safe those who don't want to be stolen, we must be very secretive.

"Each man here is head of a family, and each of you has young males under your authority. I want each of you to select two young men from your household: men of good reputation and with the ability to keep their thoughts and words to themselves.

"I want those men here the first sunrise after the next Sabbath. Have them bring tools for work. I believe that we will dig a well in the middle of this ancient field of Cain's. The activity will give us a reason to meet and time to plan."

The crowd left in a determined mood; certain now that they would be able to do something to rescue sons and daughters who were straying from the fold.

Adam waved goodbye, and walked up the path that led to his home. He paused for a moment when he came to the spot where the path formed a V, dividing into two paths. Suddenly, on impulse, he chose the path leading away from his house.

❋ ❋ ❋ ❋ ❋

She was bending over the hives when he spotted her, instructing a young woman in the ways of bees. He stood at the edge of the woods and waited until the younger woman left for the honey shed. He then walked quietly towards the elder, gently calling her name.

The woman turned in surprise. "Fa-father Adam," she stuttered shyly.

"Good morning my daughter," he said, smiling cheerfully. He then looked at the sun in feigned surprise. "It appears that I should say instead, 'Good afternoon'. My goodness, how the time has flown away. No wonder that my stomach is growling in protest. Would you have some bread and honey for an old man, so that he could gain strength to travel on to his home?"

Aluma immediately relaxed, and laughed the tinkling laugh that Adam tenderly remembered from her childhood. "I think that I can probably provide a little something for your stomach, Father," she added. "I have freshly baked bread, honey, grapes, dates, and a pot of herb tea, and some hens eggs boiled just this morning. Come sit under the arbor and rest yourself. You are rather far from home this lovely day. Is all well?"

Adam began partaking of his food, and it was some time before he spoke. When he did, Aluma was concerned to see the sadness in his eyes.

"All is not well, my dear daughter," he admitted. He peeled an egg, took a big bite and washed it down with a gulp of tea. He looked around at Aluma's home. His first-born daughter had managed her life here well. She was hardworking and diligent. He nodded his approval.

"However, things do look well here. Your young women are active and appear to be content. And didn't I see Josiah fishing with other youngsters? He certainly appears sprightly enough."

She sighed and leaned back against a large grape vine, which twined itself as it climbed up the arbor. "Indeed, father, he is a handful. I had forgotten how different boys can be from girls to raise. He is busy every minute. I sometimes envy him his bursting energy. He is a good boy though, and so far he has chosen his friends well."

She sat quietly as her father drank his tea. It was obvious that he was not to be rushed in the sharing of his troubles; and yet she had the strangest feeling that the Patriarch and Priest of all the people of the earth had come to her for help.

"Father," she said very softly, "is there some way that I can help with whatever is bothering you?"

Adam looked at her for a long moment and then suddenly broke into a wide grin.

"Aluma, my dear, dear daughter, I believe that there is a way you can help. I believe that you are the only one who can help in just this way. How would you like to save many of our younger daughters from a fate worse than death?"

Adam explained the problem that the villages were facing concerning the young women. He asked Aluma if she would be willing to go to each village and talk to the women and maidens, telling them of the dangers. He was especially concerned about the women who were traveling from Enoch City to entice the young women away from their homes. He wanted Aluma to tell all of the village women what life in the wicked City of Cain was really like. He gently informed her that he wanted the women to see her scars.

"We will plan your trips carefully, Aluma," Adam went on thoughtfully. "You have time to visit many villages before the Harvest Festival. Your young women can take care of things here, and I will enjoy having Josiah in my own home for that time. I will send several of the strong young men with you to protect you on the trail, and you must choose a few female friends for your travel companions."

He paused for a moment, his eyes looking off into the distance, his thoughts obviously ahead of his words. He refused to look at Aluma's blanched face, drawn tight with fear. After a moment he continued.

"You will be taking honey and preserves to sell in the villages. That will give you a reason to call the women together. We must be careful to keep you safe, and to keep the real reason for the journey secret. I will speak to Eve, and she can speak to those women who might also have something to sell. I know that Doran's daughters have been using different dyes to make colorful materials for the making of apparel."

He paused at this point in his narrative to grin at Aluma. "You should have seen the color of the cloak that Doran wore to the meeting today," he chuckled. "It was as bright as the wild cranberries that grow in the bog. Well, brighter really. I have no idea how she got that orange hue. That is possibly something that would appeal to others as well."

He suddenly turned and gave Aluma a direct look. "What do you say, Aluma, are you willing to do this?"

Aluma could hear the determination in her father's voice. Her heart was pounding so hard that she was sure he must be able to hear it. She had been back in her old home for many years, and yet the memories of living in Cain's City were still so vivid and frightening that sometimes, when she remembered, she could scarcely breathe.

Oh how she longed never to have to wander from her home. She felt safe here, sheltered and loved. Couldn't someone else go? … and yet even as she allowed the thoughts to play in her mind, she knew that no one else could do what she could do. No one else had seen the horrible scenes that she had seen. There was no question but that she must, and would, go warn the young girls and women in the other villages.

She could not hide the sorrow in her voice. "When do I leave, Father?"

"The day after the next new moon, daughter. I will make all of the arrangements. And Aluma, when you have finished this task, after the Harvest Festival, you and I shall take a trip to the Seacoast. I have a yearning to look at the sea. We will see Rina's bunch!"

He rose from his seat, and turned toward the small but busy settlement that was Aluma's domain. He noticed the young blind woman as she sat at her loom; her voice singing a lilting tune as her fingers flew over the threads. The loom was an upright one with each warp thread held down by a stone weight.

Adam spoke softly to Aluma. "I am pleased to see that Livia is creating a worthwhile and active life for herself."

Aluma nodded. "There is no keeping that one down. She says that her fingers are her eyes. I never hear her complain, and she is ever a blessing to those of us who live here in my little cove. I shall miss this place while I am gone."

Having said his thanks for the meal, Adam resumed his journey to his own house. He felt pleased with the decisions that were being made; but had he looked back he would have seen his eldest daughter standing on the trail with tears streaming down her face.

As he passed the branch of the river where the boys had been fishing, he paused to see what they were now up to. They were engaged in some type of activity that required a great deal of scuffling and pushing, yelling and laughter. He smiled as he marveled at their energy.

Suddenly his face lit up with a thought that he considered to have come directly from God. Looking up into the heavens he nodded and smiled. "What a good idea Father, I'll get right to work on that!" He was bouncing with energy himself as he headed toward his home.

❋ ❋ ❋ ❋ ❋

Guryon and Adam watched from the knoll overlooking the center of the field. There were many men diligently at work digging the well.

"Zalman tells us that he travels to 29 villages on his trade route, not counting the settlement along the seacoast, or the City of Enoch. I am sending men to each village; to infiltrate the life there and see what news they can learn. Each man knows the situation and knows to be subtle and slow in his questioning.

"I don't want it to be too obvious when someone leaves the work here so I am sending them out on different days in different numbers: sometimes two, sometimes three or even four or five; never alone. There will be a group of men working here at all times. As far as our wives or others know, we are simply sending the workers to other villages for supplies."

Adam nodded in approval.

"You are giving much thought to this venture, Guryon, and that is good. It can be dangerous for these young men; for I have learned that there are those in the City of Enoch who have discovered ways of burning metal out of rocks. They make wonderful tools with these metals, but it is rumored that they also make tools for maiming or killing. Some claim that they use them only to kill animals who leave their natural ways, and become wild and uncontrollable; but I hear other, darker stories. It would seem that there is little peace in Cain's magnificent City. May God protect our venture."

"Amen, Father. Life used to be so much calmer. I just don't know what is happening to the world. There were many, many years when I wondered if there really was a City of Cain. No one traveled much; and Abir, Ravid and Tzevi lost all contact with that place. It was a long, long time before we heard of anyone else leaving there. Now life is so busy with all this trading and traveling; and can you believe 29 villages! That doesn't even count all the people living here in our settlement, or along the coast, or in that unspeakable place across the wilderness. Mercy father, what is the world coming to in these modern times?"

Adam shook his head in agreed wonder, and both men stood silent, once again watching the young men at work. Finally Adam broke the silence.

"I want you to send six of your bravest and strongest men with Aluma and her women, when they leave next week. They will leave the first day of the week, and will be taking supplies to trade at each village. They will not go east of Eliakim. There are still those who would like to force Aluma to return to Cain's City, if only for torture and imprisonment. She must be protected."

The man with flaming red hair looked at his father with a concerned expression. "I have the men, father, but I have no weapons such as you were describing. We have only clubs, and shepherds' crooks, and spears with sharpened stones in the end."

"Those will do for now, Guryon, and tell your men to keep their weapons out of sight. We do not want to be seen as aggressors in this venture. We only want to protect the weak."

As Adam and Guryon started to part, Adam remembered the day when he watched Josiah at play on the river. "Guryon, I have been dreaming of a way to channel some of that boundless energy that our boys have. I want to form a special group. I want them trained in ways of defense and endurance, and to show self-restraint and discipline. They will dress alike in robes of the same color; a color only for their use. We will have a unit trained and ready to protect our villages in the event that it is ever needed. Also, it will keep the younger men from getting bored; get them away from their mothers, and out of mischief that only young boys can think up. Be thinking about someone to train this group. It isn't something that has to start right now; just be giving it some thought."

❋ ❋ ❋ ❋ ❋

Aluma wearily sank down in the grass, removed her sandals, and sighed with delight as she placed her aching feet in the cool water of the mountain stream. The young women who had accompanied her were setting up camp for their night's stay, and preparing a fire to cook their dinner.

"I am going to sit right here and do nothing," Aluma told herself silently. "I am bone weary. We are loster than lost, even though those intractable boys won't admit it. I am not budging from this campsite until they can tell me that they know where on this earth we are headed!"

Having made her silent declaration, she laid her head back in the grass and closed her eyes.

The smell of smoke was pungent in the air, and stars were beginning to appear in the heavens, when Aluma opened her eyes again. Someone had thoughtfully placed a warm cloak across her body. Her feet felt as if they were no longer a part of her. Beyond all of those sensations, however, was the strong impression that someone was watching her. She slowly sat up and turned her head to look into the forest. There at the edge of the trees stood a woman that appeared more ancient than the hills. Aluma gasped.

"What an old, old woman," she thought; but said, "Hello, do you live in those woods? My name is Aluma, and I and my fellow-travelers are from Adam's City."

The woman simply stood and stared at her. Aluma's head began to clear from her heavy sleep; and she remembered that her mother Eve was the oldest woman on earth, but she didn't look nearly, *not nearly*, as old as this woman. Come to think of it, she, Aluma, was the second oldest woman on earth. Surely, surely she didn't look that old. Well not usually, anyway, she told herself, as she slipped her sandals on and smoothed her hair with her fingers.

The woman was as thin as a stick, her face hawk like and brown like the mud of the roads. Her gray hair hung listlessly down her bony shoulders in long dirty hanks. When she opened her mouth to speak, Aluma could see that most of her teeth were gone. Her hands looked like the claws of the great hawk, and her dirty fingernails were so long they curled around towards her fingers.

Just then a breeze blew, and Aluma caught a whiff of the unwashed creature. Her stomach lurched and she tried valiantly to control her facial expression.

"I am Aluma," she repeated. "What may I call you?"

Once again the woman ignored her question. Instead, she queried, "Are you the Aluma that was the Great Mother of Cain's City?"

Aluma caught her breath. She made her words calm. "I lived there once, yes. Long ago. I chose to leave; and now I live with my father, Adam, and the hundreds of young men who protect him.

"Forgive me, Lord," she prayed silently, knowing that she was exaggerating the protection that surrounded Adam.

The old woman laughed a loud, cackling laugh. She laughed and laughed until Aluma looked around to see which way she should run for escape.

The laughter stopped and the crone studied the much-frightened Aluma carefully.

"Well, well, well. So you lived. No one thought you did. And you got away. Took the brats didn't you! Did they live too? Heard that our noble Cain blinded one of them. Looks like you took a little damage yourself."

Aluma drew her scarf more closely around her face. Sometimes she almost forgot her scars, but the woman was staring openly at them.

"Who are you?" Aluma demanded. "What is your name?" She could hear the harshness in her own voice. She could remember no such creature as this. Surely she could never have known this woman when she lived in Cain's City.

"What are you doing here in my woods?" the woman suddenly demanded angrily.

Aluma jumped as a voice spoke from behind her. It was Tal, the leader of the men who had traveled with the group.

"We have carried our wares to trade to the villages around here. Would you and those of your village like to see what we have to offer?" he suggested calmly.

"I want something to eat!" the woman demanded.

Aluma motioned to one of the women who had gathered around her protectively, and a plate of food was quickly brought to the woman of the forest. They had never seen anyone eat like this woman. Aluma reflected that she had never even seen an animal eat like that. There was nothing with which to compare it. She averted her eyes.

The woman was suddenly gone; gone as if she had never been there, except for the lingering odor of everything stale, dirty and sour that one could imagine.

Eve's first-born daughter lay awake for a long time that night. Forbidden thoughts came tumbling into her mind; thoughts of more years ago than she could count. She had lived with Cain for a long, long time. From the moment that he had killed Abel, he had surrendered himself to his violent nature.

Aluma had never known the gentleness of a man taking his wife in a loving manner. He had always ravished her, even though after that first time, she had never attempted to refuse his advances. She had borne many babies. Babies who became men and women. Most of them had followed in the ways of their father. They had scorned their mother when she told them of a loving God.

Only three young men had listened. Those three had also escaped. Some of her daughters had appeared to listen when they were very young; but later, after Cain had given them to husbands, they would pay her no heed. They mocked the name of God.

She remembered her first-born daughter, Baila. How pretty she was as a little girl. Some of the other children were born with the translucent skin and pale yellow hair that Cain had been given, but Baila had raven hair and skin pink like a rose bud. She was a child full of laughter and joy, and Aluma taught her the stories that once, long before, Eve had taught her daughters.

Baila loved the stories of the Garden and begged her mother to "tell me about Mother Ewe, just one more time." Oh how Aluma loved that little girl. She had been the only little girl for a long time; for it seemed that Aluma could give Cain nothing but male children for years. By the time another girl-child was born Baila was old enough to be a wonderful big sister. She had loved helping her mother and was cheerful in everything she did. Baila had been the brightest spot in Aluma's life.

When Baila was scarcely more than a child, much too early for marriage, Cain had given her as wife to Enoch. Enoch. The child who copied his father in every way that he could; except for the wandering. How Enoch hated to leave their campfire.

When he was very little, he would cry when his father left. He would call after him…"Da, Da, Please don't go: Later the tears ceased and the anger came. He would stand at the edge of their settlement and stare long into the night whenever Cain, suddenly seized by the restless spirit, would take off into the wilderness, leaving his family behind to fend for themselves.

Cain promised his firstborn that together they would build the finest City that the world would ever know. He said that every time he went away he would bring back something to use in building the City. This was one of the few promises that he ever kept.

Gradually the little boy began to take pride in how he could care for the family while his father was gone. He would talk endlessly about what wonderful things his father would bring for their City when he came home next time. He never complained, but he never allowed his mother to hold or caress him, jerking angrily away when she would make such attempts. By the time Baila was given as bride, the drawings of plans for the City had been etched into flat rocks with sharp stones. The men would sit and dream late into the night about the grandeur they would create.

When Baila moved into Enoch's home she was allowed, at first, to visit her mother when her own chores were done. However, Cain returned from one of his trips to find Aluma and Baila teaching the little ones to sing songs about God. They were all laughing and enjoying the fun. His face was like a storm cloud when he entered the room where they were. He slapped Aluma hard across the face, knocking her to the floor. He told her that never again did he want to hear God's name in his house. He had no place for God in his life. God had failed him he roared. God had rejected him. He did not need God. Look at all he was able to accomplish without his Father's God! He grabbed Baila by the hair and dragged her to the home of her husband. Baila was never allowed to visit Aluma again after that day.

A sob escaped Aluma's throat as the memories crowded her chest until she thought she might suffocate from them. She placed her hands on her wet face and wiped away the tears. Why in the world was she having these thoughts? She hadn't thought about Baila for many, many long years. Her life, in recent years, had been full and rich. Why was she now dwelling on things that 'might have been'? She pulled her cover over her head and tried to force herself to sleep.

Aluma felt the wind gently playing with the leaves above her head. She opened her eyes, her body aware that the night had been much too brief and not very restful. She moved her body, a limb at a time, to see how pervasive the stiffness was. Even her neck rebelled when she turned her head. She sat up and looked into the woods. Nothing. Silence. No, wait: eyes staring out at her. A raccoon moved and startled a deer.

Encouraging her body into an upright position, Aluma made her way down the narrow path that led to the brook. There she completed her wash-up as the morning sun peeped over the horizon, scurrying the moon and stars off in sudden retreat.

When she returned to the camp, her companions had stirred the embers of last night's coals and had a bright flame going in preparation for breakfast. Aluma gratefully accepted a hot cup of herbal tea that had been generously sweetened with honey. She nodded in approval at the sizzling sound of the flat bread as it was poured out on a hot rock to cook.

The night fears gradually disappeared with the hustle and bustle of the activities of the morning. Aluma was even able to turn with a welcoming smile toward the group, led by the old woman, that was gathering at the edge of the forest.

They were the strangest collection of humanity that Aluma had ever witnessed. About twenty people stood there; each with a body that showed the ravages of a crueler time. They were bent, broken and misshapen; many missing eyes or limbs and horribly scarred. Most had running sores. All were thin beyond belief. Their eyes looked in unison toward the food. The longing in those eyes was palpable.

Aluma felt, rather than saw, Tal draw protectively close to her back. She was conscious not of fear but of sorrow as she surveyed the group before her. One by one they hesitantly came out of the forest, drawn irresistibly by the smell of food cooking. To say that they were dirty would have been but scant assessment of the state of their bodies. Aluma wondered why, with such ready access to water, they would allow themselves to remain so ill cared for. There were both men and women; although which were which required a closer study than usual. "Please, all of you, come and share our meal," Aluma invited.

The group was timid at first but then, motivated by the unrelenting demands of their bellies, ran forward and began grabbing the food that was offered them.

"There is plenty for all. Don't shove. There is enough. Whoa! Hey, slow down there! Take your time!" urged Tal as he attempted vainly to establish some order.

As their appetites began to wane, Aluma noticed that the visitors were furtively secreting food inside the rags that barely covered their bodies.

Now that their appetites were satisfied, Aluma began to look to the other needs of the forest group. She instructed her companions to boil water, and in each pot she placed some of her healing herbs. She motioned for those with sores to come forward. When they hesitated, the woman, obviously their leader, ordered them to obey. Aluma, with the help of her companions, bathed the sores. She then gave a packet of the herbs to the woman and instructed her as to how to prepare the medicine, and with strong urgings told her that the sores must be bathed every day until they were healed. The woman jerked her head in a hasty agreement and pointed toward the wagon.

"I want those things for my people," the old woman said with as much dignity as she could muster.

"What do you have to trade for such fine merchandise, old woman of the forest?" inquired Tal, raising an eyebrow in Aluma's direction.

The woman motioned to someone at the edge of the forest. That person ran into the woods and shortly appeared with a waif who appeared to be about five years of age. She had the appearance of a frightened fawn, but didn't smell as clean. The woman shoved the child in Aluma's direction. "Here, take this; you always did like brats."

The child reached down to the ground eagerly picking up fallen crumbs and stuffing them in her mouth.

With shock and stupefaction, Aluma gasped at the sight of the little girl. Her anger suddenly flaring, she reached out to shake the woman who would subject the little one to such cruelty. The woman snarled and bared her long dirty nails in defense. Tal moved immediately, placing his body between the two, warding off any blows that might injure Aluma. To her own surprise and revulsion Aluma began screaming at the forest people, years of pent-up anger suddenly being released. She shrilled, "How dare you feed yourselves while you let this little one go hungry? What horrible animals you are!"

As the men rushed in to restore order, Aluma's women hastily began to provide for the child; placing a full plate of food before her. The girl seemed unsure, at first, what was expected of her. When the women urged her to eat, she looked at them in unbelief for a second and then began stuffing food into her mouth with both little hands.

Aluma turned and fled to her quiet place by the brook, her uncharacteristic anger now dissolving in a sudden rush of tears.

Tal found her there, and for a long moment laid a comforting hand on her shoulder. She rose and walked over to wash her face in the cool water. He knelt down and began throwing pebbles in the stream.

His voice was quiet and consoling. "Perhaps they cannot be blamed for their behavior, Aluma. Only God knows what all they have had to do just to survive. Every one of them has obviously been mistreated in some horrible manner, and I cannot even imagine the violence they have had to endure."

She nodded and smoothed her hair. "We have seen the face of Sin, Tal. This is what a world is, without God. It becomes savage and uncaring, brutal beyond belief. I must tell Father Adam. We have been selfish with our knowledge of a loving God and there must be some way to share what we know and believe, with those who have never heard.

"Come, let us give generously to these poor people. Our journey is completed. Let us return home."

The travelers left the group not only with supplies of honey and material, but with much that had been traded to them along the way. There were rough bars of soap, candles and dishes with wicks that could be filled from the containers of olive oil they received. There were chickens and ducks; two milk goats with young and a young ram. There were abundant vegetables for eating and seed for planting.

A man came forward when the seed was presented, his eyes suddenly bright with hope. Because his tongue had been cut out, he was unable to speak; but he pointed excitedly to himself, to the seed, and then to the ground, his head bobbing up and down with his joy. Tal walked over and handed him some garden tools with which to till the soil. Tears formed in the man's eyes and ran down his face. The look he gave Tal caused the younger man to have to turn his face away.

Everyone in the group had received a personal gift. Their faces having lost their suspicion and fear, the forest people waved good-bye, smiling now as they clutched their treasures. They had gifts which, if put to proper use, could give them a better life. Most of all they had been given hope and dignity.

Aluma's young men had found the path they had lost in the failing light the evening before, and the travelers were able to begin their homeward trek. When they were nearly out of sight of the forest people, Aluma heard the leader call her name. She stopped and turned around to listen. The woman, with her hair now pulled neatly back by a pearl comb, held her hand aloft in a farewell salute.

Her words sounded clear and strong.

"I am Baila"

Chapter Seven

Ramie

Aluma looked at the little girl who was riding in the seat Tal had fixed for her in the wagon. "What is your name, Little One?"

The child looked puzzled and shrugged her thin shoulders.

The woman walked on silently for a while, and then turned back to the little girl. "You shall be called 'Derora', for today you have become free."

The little one smiled and nodded, quietly singing the name to herself until she fell asleep.

* * * * *

Adam received the footsore travelers with joy. "Welcome home," his strong voice boomed. "Come in, come in, and tell me all about your journey," he said as he attempted to embrace them all at once. "And who is this little creature?" he asked as he spied Derora.

"A long story, Father, and one that must wait until I see the members of my own house. Tal can begin our story, and I shall tell my part too, but not today. I am going home!"

There were shouts of joy in Aluma's little settlement when it was learned that she was home. She went first of all to the place of the loom where Livia always sat with her work. After embracing her granddaughter, she pulled Derora gently forward and placed the tiny hand in the larger one.

"Livia, this is now your daughter. Derora, I have brought you to your mother."

The hands of the blind woman traced over the girl's hair and face and thin little arms, and suddenly she was holding the child, kissing her and laughing through tears. Derora placed her own tiny hands on the face of her new mother, tenderly touching the place where once there had been eyes. She put both little arms around Livia's neck and snuggled contentedly.

A few days later Aluma, rested now, was enjoying the fellowship of her parents as they partook of tea and her mother's wonderful sweet cakes. Most of her siblings had gathered at their parent's home for dinner and now they were listening to Aluma's recounting of her journey.

"You know the saddest thing of all, Father?" Aluma said quietly in a heavy-hearted voice. "They don't know. They really haven't heard about Yahweh. They don't know the story of the Garden. Most of them have no idea of their heritage, outside of Cain being their ancestral father."

She paused thoughtfully and then continued. "Most of them think that I am long dead and the names of 'Adam' and 'Eve' are children's tales to them. Oh Father, even some of our villages that I visited have forgotten. Even them. They are good people but they are caught up in the busyness of their lives and they have no time for Yahweh.

"Your idea of trained guards is wonderful, but who will tell them about Yahweh, Father? Will no one take the message to them?"

Cainan looked at his father, Enosh, who nodded, and then back to Adam. "My father and I have been discussing this very thing. We, too, believe that there should be those who proclaim the words that Yahweh has told us through the years. Many come to take part in the Harvest Festival without truly knowing the significance of the sacrifice."

Enosh picked up the conversation. "Let us start a school of Proclaimers. Each village can have a specially trained person living there who is wise in the ways of Yahweh, and who can teach the village what they need to know."

Adam beamed. "A wonderful idea, my sons. I give my blessing to this plan and hereby declare that the school will begin officially at the next Harvest Festival. We will have a ceremony of dedication at that time. We must spend much time in prayer about the details of all this. We most surely do want the leading of Yahweh!"

Everyone began to talk excitedly. They were grateful to know that the knowledge of Yahweh would be taken to all of the villages. It would be a terrible thing for a people to forget their Creator.

❋ ❋ ❋ ❋ ❋

The white buildings of the City of Enoch glistened in the noonday sun, reminding Ramie of the white waves of the sea that he had known all of his young life.

He lay hidden in the tall grass on the gentle hillside that overlooked the City, as he amused himself by watching the people and animals moving about below like busy ants. He was astonished at the number of people, and at the almost hectic activity. There were many people along the seacoast where he, a descendant of Rina and Abir, had grown up; but they never moved with such haste. His life on the fishing boats had been more languid, spurred to haste only by sudden storms or some danger at sea.

Suddenly he was overwhelmingly, take-your-breath-away homesick. This had seemed a wonderful adventure when, encouraged by Father Adam's call to the young men, he had joined Guryon's band of spies. Now he wanted only home: faces and voices that he knew, sounds of the sea that he loved so.

Spotting a stream further down the hillside, he forced himself to put aside his fears and longings. There could be no turning back now. This was what he had trained for all of those long months, the reason he had left his home and family. He had lived for many months in Efron's settlement along the great river. By so doing he became aware of the commerce that flowed in and out of the City. He worked on losing his seacoast accent, and developed a way of speech more common to those in this part of the world.

After bathing in the creek until his olive-brown skin glistened, he smoothed back his long dark hair, neatly securing it with a leather thong which he kept in the pack on his back. He replaced his soiled tunic with a fresh one and concentrated on looking the part of a man of the world.

No sooner had Ramie gone through the great marble gates of the City than he was assaulted by the sounds and smells of the place. To a young man used to the comforting sound of waves breaking against the shore, and seagulls calling from above, the noise seemed nearly deafening. The smells were a strange mixture of animal dung, citrus fruits and melons in the market place, bread baking in the great ovens, and incense from various shrines.

Ramie gaped at the shrines. He had only known the worship of Yahweh, and never had he observed his elders making shrines to Him. The shrines in this City had many different beings carved into them; and all had little fires lit before them, and candles and incense burning upon them.

As he had been instructed by his leader, Guryon, Ramie found an inn and rented a room. He then went downstairs to the common room and ordered himself a meal and a jug of mulled wine. He ate slowly, allowing the conversation of the room to flow into his mind. When the innkeeper came to refill his jug, Ramie asked if there was someplace where he could learn the trade of tool making.

He was given directions, as he hoped he would be, to the home of Lamech, father of Tubal-Cain.

After a good night's sleep and an early breakfast he was able to follow the directions and eventually found the place he sought. He walked boldly up to the front courtyard gate and pulled the cord of the bell outside the huge gates.

While he was waiting for someone to answer his summons, he noted the intricate designs of the gates. They were of wrought of iron and inlaid with bronze. The work was unlike anything that Ramie had ever seen.

He started as suddenly the gates began to open slowly. There in the afternoon sunlight, her blond hair uncovered and streaming down her shoulders, her blue eyes alive with curiosity, was the most beautiful creature in the world. Ramie was certain of that. Never, never had he seen a girl so exquisite. She laughed a silvery laugh as he stood, mouth open, staring at her dumbfounded.

"Did you want something?" she questioned, unable to keep the amusement from showing in her voice.

Suddenly remembering why he was there, Ramie cleared his throat and stated, "I am Ramie of a land west of here, and I wish to learn how to make a gate like this one."

"You must talk to my brother, Tubal-Cain. He is the instructor in this craft. He is busy with a class right now, but you may come in and wait for him. My name is Naamah and we are of the house of Lamech."

Naamah shut the gates behind them and indicated that he was to follow her. For the first time in his life Ramie gave thought to his own looks. He was short and stocky, his face browned like leather from years on his father's boats. Most certainly a damsel of such comeliness would never give a second look in his direction. He sighed so loudly that the girl turned around to see if there was a problem. He blushed and ducked his head, embarrassed that his emotions were so near the surface.

She simply smiled and led him to a table fashioned of iron and surrounded by iron benches. His heart leapt at the fineness of the ironwork. Now he was thrilled at his adventure, for his instructions had been to stay here and learn the trade, as well as learning all that he could about life in the City.

He traced his fingers along the back of the iron bench. Could he ever make such a beautiful piece as this? Oh how he yearned to do so. He felt shy when he remembered his own tinkering with metal that had caught the attention of Father Adam. How proudly he had displayed the various tools and boxes that he had fashioned. They had been quite the pride of the seacoast. Never, never would he show them to the craftsman who had fashioned these magnificent pieces. He was suddenly ashamed. How could he possibly have thought himself to have any talent?

His reveries were interrupted by Naamah's returning to the arbor. He suddenly realized that he had been so enthralled by the ironwork that he had not noticed her leaving in the first place.

She carried a tray with dates and figs and some sweet breads on it, and a strange yellow looking drink that she poured for him. He had never before tasted the drink made from lemons and sweetened with honey, but he found it most agreeable.

She left again, the scent of flowers, which permeated the air when she was present leaving with her. He silently enjoyed his repast and wondered what he was supposed to do now. Wait, he decided. He looked around at his surroundings. Flowers. Kinds that he had never before noticed. Some with thorns. Some hanging on vines from trellises. Every color that could be imagined. What a pleasant place. How could the evil which Guryon had described possibly lurk in this goodly place?

He heard singing and the sound of an instrument being played as accompaniment. He stood and looked through the thick arbor, carefully pulling the vines apart so that he could get a better view. He caught his breath at the beauty of what he heard and saw.

Naamah was sitting next to a small pool of water, strumming a stringed instrument. Ramie was enthralled. Her voice was enchanting and, although he had heard of such music-making tools, he had never seen one.

"Did you come here to spy on my sister, friend?" asked a voice, gruff, but without malice.

Ramie turned quickly around, nearly dropping his container of lemon drink.

"No, no sir. Forgive me," he sputtered. "I came here to learn how to make beautiful gates and tables and other things like these here," he said pointing, "but I heard the music and I looked. I mean no harm."

The older man looked at the younger one for several minutes, as if taking his measure.

"Don't you know that students come through the back gates? How dare you intrude in my private home?"

Ramie looked startled. "No, I didn't know that," he responded. "I was directed here when I asked how to locate Tubal-Cain. I didn't know that there was another way. How would I know that? I traveled a long distance to be trained here, and I have money to pay for my training. I mean no harm and wish no trouble."

As he spoke Ramie squared his shoulders, looked his challenger in the eyes, and stood as tall as he could.

"Well, you have found me. I am Tubal-Cain. What is your name; and what makes you think that you will be found worthy to be taught by me even if you do have money?"

"My name is Ramie, and although I have no training with the fire that smelts metal, I have been told that I have some talent." He spoke bravely, as he reached into his bag and brought forth the tools that he had fashioned.

Tubal-Cain held the tools up in the air, letting the sunshine glance off of each angle, as he turned them round and round. After close inspection he looked again at Ramie.

"You have been told truthfully. There is talent here. If you become my student you will work long hours. You will never question my judgment, and you will not sit on my benches and drink mead made from lemons! Do you understand, boy?"

Ramie gulped. His thoughts were jumbled. This man who dared call him 'boy' in such a condescending manner could be but a few years older than he. How dare he treat an honored son of Adam with such disrespect? Ramie swallowed again. This was his assignment. He had been trained by Guryon, and oh how he did want to learn to work iron in such delicate patterns!

"I understand, sir," he said, forcing his voice to sound meek and his eyes not to snap.

"Very well, follow me and I will show you where you will lodge. We will start your training at sunrise tomorrow. We work every day."

Ramie stopped in his tracks. "Uh, sir, excuse me, but before we start this, uh, you need to know that I always keep the Sabbath."

Tubal-Cain turned around in surprise.

"You worship Yahweh?"

"I do. I worship only Yahweh. He is the true and living God."

"Well, well," mused Tubal-Cain, "a worshiper of Yahweh in the City of Cain. This should prove interesting!"

"Come, boy. You may have your *Sabbath* off, but you had best work diligently all the rest of the week. One lazy moment and you are out of here!"

With a determined look on his young face, Ramie hurried his short, stocky legs to keep up with Tubal-Cain's much longer ones.

If he had dared look back, he would have been interested to see the lovely Naamah intently watching his exit from the garden.

Chapter Eight

Tubal-Cain

The chatter of dozens of people ceased, as the horn sounded in the crisp morning air. Eve, Aluma and Rina turned in the direction of a large flat rock being used to elevate the speaker so that he could be heard. The excellent acoustics of the valley allowed for the man's voice to be carried clearly to each person present.

The young men stood in rows, twelve abreast, seven deep. Their short tunics were identical, the material having been dyed in dark cranberry red. Each waist was encircled by a narrow leather belt, and from each belt hung a beaded leather knife holder. The young soldiers stood rigidly, their shoulders squared and eyes staring straight ahead, bright with pride. Their commander, who wore a tunic of the same color but with the hem embroidered in gold, began to address the crowd.

"For two years these Shalomshamars have trained in the rigorous art of bodily exercise, and survival under adverse conditions. Now, they are to become commissioned into the official ranks of service to their people. These young men will be protectors of the people in every City that has requested protection. They will also guard roads, wells, and any area of commerce. Your sons and brothers have studied diligently to become the disciplined troops that you see before you this morning."

"Senior Commander Guryon, I now present to you these troops for your inspection." "Thank you, Commander Tal," Guryon said as he rose and turned to face the formation.

Guryon's tunic was similar to Tal's but a small inset of fur joined his gold embroidered hem to the rest of the cloth. The belt around his waist was made of silver. The knife in his leather sheath had a golden handle and in one end of the handle glistened a brightly colored stone.

Most of the people residing in Adam's domain had never seen such splendor and they were silent with awe.

Together Guryon and his junior officer walked smartly up and down the rows of Shalomshamars. Tal had taken his position two steps behind the Senior Commander. The young men stood perfectly still, never allowing their eyes or their bodies to change position.

After inspecting the troops, Guryon and Tal returned to the rocks. One by one, each young man was called forward to stand at attention, as a medallion hung by a cord was placed around his neck. Each medal was engraved with a six-pointed star, for the Shalomshamars were told that they must shine as the stars in the service of the people.

After receiving his medal, each young man walked over to the place where Adam was standing and knelt before him, as Adam placed his hands on the soldier's head and blessed him for service.

When the commissioning service was completed, Adam stepped forward and offered a prayer to Almighty God that He would bless and protect the young servicemen.

After the prayer, Tal dismissed the troops and invited everyone present to share in the lunch that had been prepared. Mothers ran, with tears of pride coursing down their cheeks, to embrace their newly commissioned sons. Proud fathers gave bear hugs, while younger siblings looked shyly at the uniformed men, their eyes like saucers. Grandfathers stood around in groups talking, wondering how much the world would change now that it was beginning to look as if even good men carried weapons. Grandmothers wiped the tears from their eyes and shook their heads.

The women had outdone themselves providing a celebration picnic for their soldier-sons, and for all those attending the graduation. Small children eagerly awaited their drinks of clear, cold water from the newly completed well. The fellowship was genuine and warm, lasting well into the afternoon.

Following the picnic, the graduates were given leave to return home for three days, visit with their families, observe the Sabbath, and return on the first day of the week for their orders. In two hours the field was completely deserted except for the three leaders.

Adam looked fondly at his son and grandson. "You did well men. You did exceeding well. We had hoped for fifty young men and we graduated 84 today. Our villages will be safer now. Those evil men who choose to prey on weak ones had better give a second thought before taking on one of these Shalomshamar 'stars'."

Guryon walked to the edge of the stone platform and looked over the circular field. He spoke softly.

"The field is hallowed now, Father. No longer will Abel's blood cry out for justice against Cain. Your sons of honor will forevermore defend against evil."

The three men softly said, "Amen ."

* * * * *

The evening sunset was spectacular over Cain's City. The sky was filled with hues of purple, pink, fuchsia, and blue. The three friends walked into the courtyard by the front gate, which stood open wide for celebrants to enter. Joyful sounds from the musicians joined with the soothing splatter of water from the fountain. A vast cage near the fountain contained colorful birds, their sleep pattern disturbed by the noise and light for the garden was filled with the light of torches. Gaily decorative streamers were hung from tree to tree.

Ramie saw his teacher talking to a group of businessmen from the City. When Tubal-Cain saw Ramie, he waved and motioned for him to join the group.

Tubal-Cain took Ramie's arm as he approached and turned to the men of the City. "This is my best pupil. Ramie is from a place far west of here, and over four years ago he traveled all the way here to be trained at our school. He has learned well. His craftsmanship actually excels mine."

Ramie shook his head firmly. "No, Master Teacher, do not say such a thing, for I have much to learn yet. It is with much gratitude to your expert teaching that I have done as well as I have."

The City fathers nodded their approval at the young man's speech.

"Who are your friends?" inquired Tubal-Cain.

"Let me introduce Josiah and Uri; two of my dearest friends and fairly recently graduated Shalomshamars stationed in the village of Efron. They have come to join me in celebrating my completion of schooling. This is their first visit to Enoch."

"Welcome, friends of Ramie. I dare say that this is the first time we have had Shalomshamars in the City of Cain. If Cain is still alive somewhere out there, in whatever wild place his latest journey has taken him, he is probably greatly shaken by the thought of someone representing such orderliness here in this City of chaos.

"I do, however, encourage you to be very careful as you travel through our City streets, for there are many who would take offense at your uniforms."

Although Ramie had often, during his four-year-course of training, heard Tubal-Cain make disparaging remarks about the City, he was amazed to hear him ridicule it in front of the City businessmen.

The businessmen laughed loudly as if Tubal-Cain had told the funniest joke in the world, but they let a coldness show in their eyes as they looked at the Shalomshamars.

Ramie felt a slight uneasiness as he realized how much his friends stood out in the crowd of of people.

Drinks on a silver tray were offered to the three men, and a silvery voice that Ramie immediately recognized caused him to turn quickly in her direction. She smiled. "I know that you do not wish to partake of the fermented drinks so I brought you the mead made from lemons."

"Thank you, Naamah. You are very kind."

He introduced Naamah to his two friends and he could see the questions in their eyes. As she returned to serving others, Uri playfully jabbed him in his ribs.

"You didn't tell us of all the hardships that you have had to endure while you learned your trade, my friend. It must be terribly difficult to have to look at such beauty all the time!"

Ramie laughed. "Forget anything you are imagining, Uri. It is a rare day when I get to talk to Naamah. Tubal-Cain is very protective of her. I have been invited into this Garden few times during the past four years."

Josiah spoke quietly, "Tubal-Cain seems different from the others that we have met in this place. It is as if he keeps himself apart from the filth and the shame."

"You have judged rightly, Josiah; his life extends but little beyond his craft and his love for his sister and mother. He has two brothers, much older than he, who also live in the City. They are both sons of Adah, the first wife of Lamech. He has two wives it seems.

"Jabal is the eldest, and he rarely comes to his City home; although he is immensely wealthy, and has a huge home made from sandstone and marble. His wife runs it with the help of servants and, it is rumored, the help of her live-in lover.

"I saw her once when she came here with a message for Lamech. I have never seen such a face. She had paint all over it. It was the strangest thing that I have ever seen. Whenever she walks there is a servant who walks behind her, holding up a piece of cloth that they call a 'train'. I'm afraid that the first time I saw her I just stood and gawked with my mouth open.

"When the woman left, Naamah came over and was teasing me. She said, 'You can close your mouth now.' Then she looked really serious and said, 'Isn't that the most awful woman that you have ever seen?'"

"How did you answer her, Ramie?" asked Uri.

"Well, actually, I wasn't sure what I should say. I mean, after all, the painted woman's brother-in-law is my Schoolmaster. So I just said something about her being 'highly decorative' or some such silliness."

Josiah was still curious and wanted to know "Where does Jabal live if he doesn't stay in his home in the City?"

"He has many large groups of people throughout the land who live in tents and raise livestock. He spends his time going from place to place to keep an eye on them, and I have reason to believe, to accomplish his real purpose."

"Which is?" Josiah and Uri asked in unison.

"Which is to capture young maidens, bring them to the City and give them to his wife to 'educate'. It appears that she too is a schoolmaster of sorts. When the girls have been starved and beaten into submission they are either sold to men, who purchase them for their own homes, or used as women for hire by men who want a variety."

The three young men sat in quiet reflection. Finally Uri spoke, "I don't think that I ever realized until this hour how important it is that we wear this uniform and defend the defenseless."

Josiah nodded in solemn agreement.

"What did you think of the graduation ceremony?" Ramie asked, deciding to explore another topic for a while.

Uri spoke up. "It was truly impressive, and we were most proud to see you take all those honors. It was so strange to see people offering burnt offerings to all those other gods. All that incense! And those girls that danced were nearly naked behind those gauzy veils. I tried not to look."

"Well you certainly didn't succeed, Uri!" harassed Josiah. "I thought your eyes were going to pop out. If our mothers had been there, we would have been pulled away by our ear lobes."

The others laughingly agreed.

"How can you stand it here, Ramie?" Josiah asked with a trace of sadness in his voice.

"It has only been learning my trade, and going about my assignment, that has kept me sane. That first year I longed to run home just as quickly as I could; but then Tubal-Cain began to trust me a little, and I was able to tell him about how life is when people are truly serving Yahweh. At first he scoffed, but then he stopped scoffing and began asking questions. One day he invited me to his home for dinner; Lamech was away as he often is, and I met Zillah, the mother of Tubal-Cain and Naamah.

"Tubal-Cain told Zillah that I worship only one God, Yahweh, and she began to ask questions. It seems that she had a grandmother who used to sneak away and worship with Aluma.

"She is the reason that Tubal-Cain and Naamah spend little time outside the walls of this Garden.

"Jubal is the younger son by Adah and he also has a school here in Enoch. He gives lessons in how to play the various instruments which he has made. He is greatly skilled; and he designs the instruments so that Tubal-Cain can forge them for him. I hardly find it believable, but it is said that he loves men like most men love women. I have seen him numerous times when he comes to have Tubal-Cain make an instrument. I know that you'll think that I'm joking, but I'm not; he paints his face too!"

The Shalomshamars shook their heads in astonishment. What a place this City was! Their attention was momentarily drawn by a man, very drunk, who was grabbing at a group of young women in an attempt to place slobbering kisses anywhere on their bodies that his lips could make contact. "Come on Lamech," someone said laughing, "leave those poor girls alone! They don't want kisses from an old goatish man. Let be!"

What a horrible, godless place. How strange that even with all of their gods, they had no God at all.

The men went to thank their hosts for inviting them to the after-graduation celebration. They had decided that it was time for them to return to the inn for the night. As they were walking toward Tubal-Cain, Naamah appeared soundlessly at Ramie's side. She did something that astounded him, for never once, not in four years, had Naamah touched him in any way. With a broad smile on her face Naamah took hold of his upper arm and held firm. With surprise, Ramie looked into her face. Only her lips smiled; her eyes did not.

"My brother says that the three of you are invited to lodge at our home tonight. He wishes for you to be our guests."

Ramie began to shake his head, "Oh no, we couldn't possibly intrude like that. We will go back to the …"

His voice trailed off as suddenly, unseen to anyone else, Naamah squeezed his arm -- hard.

"I insist," she said in a low firm voice.

Ramie was amazed. Could this be the delicate little girl that he always pictured as a butterfly fluttering around the garden?

He stuttered, "W..well thank you. We're honored. We will be honored, really honored to stay at your house." He looked desperately at his friends for help.

"Honored," they both added, foolishly. "Really honored."

Servants showed the men to their rooms on the second floor. Their rooms had an outside balcony and overlooked the far eastern edge of the City. The stars glittered overhead.

The three standing outside on the balcony were discussing the strange turn of events.

"What was that all about?" questioned Uri.

A voice startled them from the stairs that led to the balcony. "That was 'all about' your lives, my young friends," said Tubal-Cain. "Come let us go into the atrium where we can talk without the servants overhearing."

The story that Tubal-Cain had to tell was startling to the inexperienced soldiers. Before tonight they had somewhat romanticized their tour of duty. They had served faithfully in Efron, but with little excitement. There had been the occasional fistfight between friends, or a man who needed escorting home to his wife after an excessive visit to the wine shops. The young maidens, whom they were expected to protect from all evil, hastened to and from the wells, or fields, or pastures, with no incident. The girls had been taught never to go out alone and they all carried small reed whistles, supplied by the Shalomshamars, with instructions to blow only if help was urgently needed. They had heard the whistle blow only once and that was when a girl, not looking where she was walking, had fallen over a cliff and broken her leg.

Tonight, for the first time, they realized that they could face real danger related to their job.

Tubal-Cain told them of a plot that had been made to take their lives. His manservant had been told by the manservant of one of the would-be murderers. His manservant had told him. "So much for the element of surprise," Tubal-Cain observed ruefully.

"But, why?" asked Josiah incredulously. "We have offended no one."

"Oh but, rather, you have offended many, many men in the City of Cain, I assure you, my friend."

The three looked at Tubal-Cain; waiting for answers.

"You see, it is rumored that you are here to destroy the 'Palace of Pleasure' that is being run by my brother's wife.

"My dear brother brings the girls in; Laila trains them and sells them. A most lucrative business you see, and certainly not one that my beloved brother, or his wife, or the men of this City wish to give up. You would have been killed in your sleep tonight."

Tubal-Cain grinned at the looks on the faces of the men. "Stay here for a few days. No one would dare attack you in my home. Not even my drunken father, whom I feel certain you saw entertaining the young women tonight. When I feel it is safe for you to leave, I will send my servants with you until you are safely away from the City."

The two soldiers looked at each other shamefacedly. "But, we are Shalomshamars," Uri sputtered.

"Yes, yes my young friend, I know. But you see, don't you, that there is no peace in the City of Cain. Goodnight now. Sleep well. You are safe. May your Yahweh watch over you." Suddenly, inexplicably, he gave them each a quick hug before heading down the stairs.

❋ ❋ ❋ ❋ ❋

The sun rose rapidly over the trees that lined the banks of the Euphrates River. As the fiery globe flashed its rays upon his face, the golden lad stood looking to the East, both hands raised in prayer to Yahweh. He was tall, with long, reddish gold hair flowing freely down his back. Although Mahalalel was a special child, of the consecrated line of Seth, he was shown no special favors. Thus did he wear the bright uniform of the Shalomshamar, and recite his morning prayers many miles from his own home.

As he lowered his hands, he heard his companion watchman call his name. "Mahalalel, come on, our watch is over!

"Let's turn it over to Josiah and Uri. I'm starved and ready to get some shut-eye. Hurry up!"

"Alright, Yonatan, alright, I'm coming. If the village wasn't awake already, it surely is now. You make more noise than the black crows."

Mahalalel paused for a moment and a grin spread over his face. "Of course," he added, "considering the darkness of your skin, it is no wonder that you sound like your 'brothers'."

The boys began a playful shove and shuffle, as they laughingly headed up the hill to the village, greeting their replacements on the way.

They were carefully trained soldiers, conscientious in their duties; but young, inexperienced, and unaware of the fully evil resolve of the enemy. Therefore, not one of the Shalomshamar soldiers spotted the men huddled in the trees along the banks of the river.

A more experienced soldier might have noted the slight wisps of smoke escaping a carefully camouflaged campfire, or the glint of light as the sunshine touched the metal weapons that the men were holding.

The boys saw only the snowy clouds, the early sun, and the birds in flight. Their world was calm, peaceful: serene. They were content with their jobs, and soon their tour of duty would come to a close. They would return to their own homes to begin a new era of their young lives; they would learn a different trade.

Josiah and Uri knew that on the other side of the village there were two soldiers changing guard just as they had done.

Twenty-five of the twenty-nine villages had requested the Shalomshamars to protect them. Every year there was a new class of fresh young soldiers who would serve three years.

The village of Efron was large enough that it merited a unit of 16 soldiers; including two older men whose Shalomshamar rank was higher than the others. They were men who had chosen to make soldiering their lifelong trade.

Josiah and Uri talked as they walked the paths of their patrol. They had the easy comradeship of young men who had known each other all their lives.

"The moon will be full soon; perhaps Zalman the Trader will come bringing us news from home," Uri said wistfully.

"Yes," Josiah agreed, "and hopefully he will go through the City of Enoch this time and we will hear something from Ramie. We have heard so little since he sent that message that he would be staying on as a partner with Tubal-Cain."

Uri looked sober. "That was a surprise wasn't it? I mean Ramie seemed so ready to leave. I do pray that he isn't being tainted by the evilness of that City. Surely he won't spend the rest of his life there."

"I think he stayed on because he had orders to. You remember how he was packed and ready to leave when we did, and then Zalman came through. They talked and he stayed. Now you can't tell me that was a coincidence!"

"You're right Josiah. I think that only new orders could have made him stay...but still I wish he were out of that place. There isn't even a Proclaimer there; which is strange because they worship every man-made god that their minds can invent, and yet they don't want anyone telling them about Yahweh."

The friends continued their conversation as they went on their rounds, waving as they came into view of the other soldiers who were protecting a further side of the village.

"I like it when we have the Duty in the center of the town," mused Josiah, "it's nice there."

Uri laughed long and loudly. "Yes, Josiah, my dear friend, she is nice, and pretty too! I see you watching her when she goes to the well to draw water."

Josiah blushed. "Does she ever look at me? Do you think that Sharon, daughter of Elazar, likes me as I like her?"

Uri shook his head solemnly. "Who can tell about girls, Josiah? Sometimes I think they just like to tease and to play with a guy's heart. However, the baker's daughter certainly *does* see to it that you get the nicest sweet rolls for breakfast."

They stopped at a place on their patrol where they could overlook much of the area between them and the river. There they took out their slabs of cheese and freshly baked bread.

Every morning the women of the village provided the soldiers with their lunch, which they were able to enjoy when the sun was beginning the downward journey from its highest point in the sky. Their supper was eaten after sunset, when they had been relieved of their watch. Although they carried weak wine in their leather casks, they enjoyed stopping for water at a stream that flowed cool and clear and wended its way to the river below.

"Look," whispered Uri as he nudged Josiah, "those two girls taking the sheep to pasture. Isn't the tall one your Sharon?"

"Yes, yes it is; I mean not *my* Sharon, but indeed Sharon, daughter of Elazar the baker. Isn't she lovely?"

"Well....I have to admit, I have seen uglier."

The afternoon passed all too slowly. Josiah knew that at sunset, after she took the sheep to their pens, Sharon would be going to the well for water for the family. He had a plan: after he was relieved of his duty, he would hurry back to where she would be herding the sheep. He would offer to help her get the sheep in the pens and then casually walk with her to the well. That would give him a chance to talk to her. He smiled to himself and Uri teased him about his daydreams.

"It is our duty to do all that we can to help the fine people of Efron. I will simply go a little 'above and beyond' the call of duty," Josiah smugly asserted.

Uri guffawed loudly as the two continued their long afternoon rounds.

The sun was low in the sky and the Shalomshamars were weary when the whistle sounded, signifying that there were girls or women who needed help. Both suddenly came to attention.

"It's above us," yelled Uri.

The soldiers started in the direction of the village, but their attention was diverted by a disturbance with the girls and the sheep in the pasture below them.

Both girls were waving their arms and screaming.

"I'll go help the girls and you answer the whistle," called Josiah as he headed down the hillside.

"I'll send help!" Uri called back.

By the time Josiah reached the young shepherdesses they were being carried off towards the bank of the river. Sharon had been tied up and thrown over the shoulder of a rough looking man. Josiah, yelling for the kidnappers to halt, ran with all of his strength toward the man carrying the girl. Her companion, who was fighting valiantly; biting and kicking and screaming at the top of her voice, was suddenly silenced. From the corner of his eye Josiah could see that the burly man who was carrying her had suddenly punched her unconscious with his fist.

"Help me, Yahweh," pleaded Josiah.

Sharon's abductor suddenly fell over a tree root, dropping his burden to the ground. The girl began a wild attempt to crawl away.

Josiah was instantly upon the man whom he recognized as Lamech, father of Tubal-Cain. He began flailing him with both fists. With a fury that he did not know he possessed, he landed a blow to Lamech's jaw sending him crashing backward into the tree. Josiah heard Lamech moan and then curse loudly. The scuffle was over in a very few minutes, for the evil man possessed something that the guardian of the peace did not. He possessed a sword. Jumping to his feet, he drew the sword from the sheath at his side, and plunged it completely through the young man.

As he was bringing the sword downward his companion was yelling, "No, Lamech, no don't do it. Do not kill him. Such a thing must not be done!"

As if stunned by his own audacity, Lamech stumbled backwards drawing his sword away as he went. It was obvious that the life force had left the Shalomshamar.

Looking up the hillside, the two men saw a dozen men in red tunics heading in their direction. Leaving the girls behind, both attackers ran to the boat that was anchored in the river, jumped in, and quickly paddled off.

Uri was only vaguely aware that the bell in the village was wildly ringing its call for help. He even forgot that soldiers do not cry as he threw himself upon his best friend's body.

The whistle had been a decoy. A trick. Somewhere in the village there was a spy. An evil person who was aiding the men of Enoch in their stealing of young maidens.

Gentle hands lifted Uri from Josiah's body. Gentle hands took the ropes off the hysterical girls and calmed their fears. Gentle hands wrapped Josiah in clean cloths. He would be taken to the village, where the women would prepare him for burial. He was the first fallen soldier.

The business partners were sitting in the courtyard in the early morning sun, breaking their fast before starting their day's work. Naamah was serving them and, on occasion, cheerfully joining in their conversation.

Suddenly there was a ruckus at the gate. Both men turned to see a drunken Lamech entering the courtyard, dragging Adah with him.

Tubal-Cain shook his head in wonder, "How does he manage to get drunk before the sun is even well risen?"

"Get your mother!" Lamech roughly ordered Naamah.

Zillah had heard the commotion and was already coming down the stairs to see what her husband wanted.

Swaying back and forth, Lamech looked at his wives. "Adah and Zillah, listen to me; wives of Lamech, hear my words. I have killed a man for wounding me, a young man for injuring me. If Cain is avenged seven times, then Lamech seventy-seven times."

All present stood in stunned silence. Suddenly Lamech turned savagely upon Ramie. "Your pious friend didn't look so brave with all that blood on this fancy tunic," he snarled and strode off.

As Ramie stood looking helplessly at his friends, another person came quickly through the gate.

It was Zalman the Trader.

"Zalman, what has happened? What can you tell us? Who was killed?" Ramie pleaded.

Zalman placed his arms around the shoulder of his friend. "It was Josiah. He was attempting to prevent Lamech and his gang from stealing girls from the village of Efron. Lamech drew his sword and killed him."

Naamah gasped and her mother went to her side to embrace her. Ramie sat down abruptly and putting his head in his arms he sobbed brokenly. Tubal-Cain hit the tree with his fist.

Zalman waited a few moments and then he spoke. "This will be my last trip to this City of the Damned, and therefore my last message to you, Ramie. I urge you to return to your home. You must stay in this place no longer. This message is not from Guryon, for he has not yet had time to learn of the murder. This message is from Zalman. It is time for you to go home."

Ramie lifted his tearstained face to the weather-beaten old trader. "You are right my friend. I will go see Aluma and help her with her grief, and then I will return to my home by the sea."

He then turned to his friends. "Please come with me and live in my village, or stay in Adam's village. It is a good place to dwell. You are not like the ones in this City. Tubal-Cain, I know that you are searching for God. Come and meet Adam and he will tell you all that you need to know. Bring your mother, your sister and your servants. Bring your trade, for it is needed to improve the lives of decent people."

Aluma saw the group coming up the hillside long before they were in speaking distance. It was an unusual sight: Adam, Eve, Seth and his wife Mira, Guryon, Tal and, (could it be Uri?) yes, yes, it was Uri too. She felt a cold chill envelope her chest. Her breath came in short gasps.

"Sheera, heat some water for tea, we have guests coming," she called woodenly.

Her granddaughter, startled by the desolation in her grandmother's voice, hurried over to the older woman's side to see what had caught her attention. As the group came nearer, Sheera gasped, placed a hand over her mouth and turned, with tears in her eyes, to do her grandmother's bidding.

Her own daughters glanced at their mother's face and asked what was wrong. "We'll talk later," was Sheera's response. "Right now be a good girl, Kadya, and go fetch Tova and Livia. I fear that there is sad news to be borne. Livana, please prepare plates of fruits and sweet breads. Hurry now. Grandmother Aluma needs our help."

The old woman aged visibly before the eyes of her people. She did not cry out or scream. She had borne so much heartache in her adult life that there seemed to be no energy left for long protests against death, even such a brutal one.

The three girls who had helped raise Josiah were not so stoic. Death was a very rare occurrence in their lives. Adam and Eve had been alive for hundreds of years, and all of their extended family was enjoying long lives. Although they vaguely remembered that Josiah's parents had been beaten and left to die; that had been a most unusual happening. Their tears were profuse; their grief heartrending, and Eve and Mira were able to do little to assuage it. Adam sat silently and held his daughter in his arms, as he had done when she was a little girl.

His own face was a study in grief. He bore a grief that no one except Eve could possibly share. In his mind he heard the Voice of God saying, "...for in the day you eat of it you shall surely die." He and Eve had eaten and now all mankind must suffer death because of them. He truly believed that he had killed that young man, just as surely as if he had thrust the sword in his body. Tears coursed down Adam's face as he gently stroked the hair of his first-born daughter.

Eve tried to get Aluma to return home with her parents for a while, but she refused. She would stay here in her own special Cove. Here with her own people she felt safe, sheltered. Here she would endure her grief.

Several hours after their trek up the hillside, the solemn group made their way back down to their own homes. Aluma had told her family that she would go to bed early, and she lay down on her pallet, turning her face to the wall.

The next morning when her granddaughters went to call her for breakfast, they found her body cold and stiff. She had died during the night of a broken heart.

❋ ❋ ❋ ❋ ❋

Tubal-Cain emerged from the flat-roofed building where the Chosen had met to examine his belief in God. He must satisfy their inquiry before he could make his first sacrificial offering at the Harvest Festival. He took a deep breath of the crisp autumn air. For the first time in his life he had some awareness of what he was constantly putting his metal working students through.

He felt that he had answered well; after all, hadn't he been taught by the same master teacher that had taught the Chosen?

When Tubal-Cain had moved to Adam's village several years before, he had at first shown no outward interest in Yahweh. He had stayed busy with his commission from Guryon to forge weapons for every Shalomshamar soldier, for the Elders had decided that never again would a soldier be sent out defenseless.

At Ramie's urging, he had attended the Harvest Festival that first year; and he began to realize that there existed something much more than he had seen when the People of Cain had burned incense to their wooden or metal gods.

He had gone that next week and asked Adam how he could learn about Yahweh. Tubal-Cain knew that the Chosen were the only ones taught directly by Adam. Each chosen member of the line of Seth sat at Adam's feet to learn; so far Seth, Enosh, Cainan and the young

Mahalalel were his students. Tubal-Cain had been astounded when Adam invited him to join this group.

Adam had explained to him that every young boy of the House of Yahweh was sent to school from the time he was six years of age, to be taught about Yahweh by the learned women. When the boys reached twelve years of age they attended classes taught by the Proclaimers. He went on to explain that Tubal-Cain had much to learn, and that it was the wish of Adam, and of all of the Chosen, that his teaching be pure and without any possible error.

During the morning hours, while the Chosen were teaching at the School for the Proclaimers, Tubal-Cain conducted his own school for metalworkers. After the mid-day meal he washed his face, combed his hair, changed his clothes, gave assignments for his laborers, and headed for his afternoon lessons with the Chosen. He felt more honored than he could express. He had many, many questions; but Adam and the line of Seth never seemed to grow weary of giving answers, or, more often, helping him to arrive at the answer himself.

Mahalalel came to the door of the building and asked Tubal-Cain to return to the group. With a pounding heart and lungs that didn't want to provide him with enough air, Tubal-Cain went in to receive his judgment.

Adam spoke. The eyes of all the men were upon this transplant from the evil City. "Tubal-Cain, you have been questioned at length and found to be exceedingly knowledgeable of those truths we hold most dear. You have assured us that these truths are also precious to you. You have expressed a desire to become a believer and we believe that you are ready to make the sacrifice to Yahweh at the Harvest Festival. The acceptance of your sacrifice will be up to God; for only He can see into the heart of a man. We pray that your heart is much purer than that of your namesake.

Go now. Spend the rest of this day in prayer. God be with you, my son."

❋ ❋ ❋ ❋ ❋

The early dawn of the first day of the Harvest Festival was bright with the promise of a clear, crisp day. The trees had donned their autumn colors; and row upon row of wheat sheaves, bound by reeded cords, stood proudly at attention in the wide meadows.

Women of all ages had arisen while it was yet dark to begin the preparation of the feast that would be enjoyed tomorrow. Today was a day of fasting; a day to contemplate one's life and repent of sins. The celebration of the tithe offerings would begin with a prayer by Father Adam. He would ask for God's acceptance of the people and the offerings that they had brought. He would then preside over the offerings of the priests. When each one of the leaders had made their prayers of repentance and placed their offerings on the altar, they would then be commanded by Adam to be good and faithful priests and to minister to the needs of their people. At that time each priest would go to his own family group and preside over their offerings. All across Adam's land the altar fires would burn brightly throughout the night.

It was a holy time. A time when lives were open before God and before the people. The Shekinah fire received only worthy and true sacrifices. Only pure and repentant hearts were welcomed into the presence of God.

Tubal-Cain was amazed to find that tears were running down his face as he waited his turn to make his offering. Adam explained to him that he would make his sacrifice to the family priest of the descendants of Doran. This was his first sacrifice; his first time to declare that he was a follower of the One True God. What if God would not accept his offering? He had lived in the wicked City of Cain for so many, many years. He had lived there amidst the evil, shunning that which was distasteful to him, content with his own self-righteousness. In his secret heart he had doubted the existence of any god at all. Certainly he had not believed in the statues of wood and stone that the people of the City worshiped.

Tubal-Cain had felt satisfied with his life. He worked hard, loved and honored his mother and his sister, and provided a beautiful shelter for them from the corruption of the City. He had felt no desire to even think about religious things until Ramie came into his life.

During the early days of the lad's training the man had tried every way he could think of to break Ramie's calm spirit. Tubal-Cain had worked the young man twice as hard as the other students. Not one time did Ramie make a murmur of complaint. When Tubal-Cain demanded another hour of work, Ramie cheerfully gave an hour and a half.

Tubal-Cain had never known such a man. After observing the young student for several months, the teacher began to ask questions, and gradually the roles reversed. Tubal-Cain became the student, eager to know more and more about this one called Yahweh.

Now he stood before the altar fire with a young goat in his arms. A sweet young goat who looked trustfully into the man's face, its dark eyes seemed to ask if this was some kind of new game that the human wanted him to learn.

Tubal-Cain handed the goat to the priest and knelt before the altar. Quickly and expertly the priest slashed the goat's throat. The little creature made not one single sound. Suddenly there was a bright light that surrounded the priest, the goat and the petitioner. It was a blinding light and everyone in the surrounding area fell to their knees. Tubal-Cain felt a great peace flow throughout his innermost being. His sobs shook his entire body. He had no idea how long he knelt there praising God and singing joyful songs at the top of his voice. Gradually he became aware of the presence of others around him. He felt a strong hand on his shoulder.

Adam's deep voice sounded far, far away as Tubal-Cain returned from the spiritual journey that he had taken.

"Come my son. God has accepted your sacrifice. You are truly a follower of Yahweh. Welcome to the family of God."

Tubal-Cain stood and threw his arms around the Patriarch's neck. He wanted to shout. To sing. To run up and down amidst the people, hugging every one. He had no idea that his face was shining with a glow that was brighter than the firelight; he only knew that he had a joy in his heart hitherto not experienced in all of his lifetime.

❋ ❋ ❋ ❋ ❋

Everyone said that the Feast at the Harvest Festival this year was the best one ever. Tubal-Cain had a grin for everyone and astounded his mother and sister by sharing hugs with anyone who would stand still long enough. Never had they seen the man like he was today. He had always been devoted solely to his work, slow to make friends and never,

never demonstrative. Truly God had wrought a wondrous change in Tubal-Cain's heart.

Naamah had another reason for joy on this most special of days. Today would be her wedding day. Traditionally, marriage covenants were declared on the afternoon of the Feast day. This evening Naamah would become the wife of Ramie. Her heart was filled with overflowing joy.

They would spend the first night of their married lives in one of the gaily-decorated marriage huts. Naamah walked to the top of a knoll overlooking a broad meadow, freshly mown.

There were dozens and dozens of newly erected marriage huts widely spaced across the expanse of land. Her eyes rested on the one with robin egg blue ribbons flying from the top. The ribbons flying from her marriage hut matched the ribbons that she would wear around her marriage shift. Each girl knew her own hut by the color of the ribbons.

She heard an anxious voice calling to her from the village and turned to see her mother waving for her to come back. Naamah waved back cheerfully and made her way toward her mother.

"Child, what are you doing? Don't you know that it is time to begin your bathing and dressing preparations for your wedding? Your must not be late for your groom when he comes to fetch you!"

Laughingly Naamah grabbed Zillah's hand. "Lead onward mother! Go ahead and drag your poor little lamb to the sacrifice!"

They both laughed and ran across the field to the small house where Zillah, Naamah and Tubal-Cain lived.

Tomorrow all of their lives would be changed. Zillah would be leaving for the seacoast with the newlyweds; and Tubal-Cain, for the first time in his life, would be living alone.

At the very moment that the excited women were making their mad dash across the field, Adam had requested a private audience with Tubal-Cain.

"My son, I have a request to make of you."

"Father Adam, please, ask whatever you will and if it is in my power to do so, I will accomplish it. I owe you more than I can ever hope to repay."

"Tomorrow your mother will leave with Naamah and Ramie for the seacoast, where they will begin new lives. Ramie will be the chief metalworker in that area thanks to your excellent teaching. However, you will be alone."

"Yes, well, I will have more time to devote to my work and to learning more about Yahweh."

"There is one lesson that Yahweh taught me in the Garden that I would like to share with you at this time."

Tubal-Cain smiled uncertainly. "I am listening, Father Adam, what is the lesson?"

"God pronounced everything which he had made 'Good' until He observed my solitary separateness from all of the creatures in the Garden. At that time He said, 'It is not good for man to be alone.' He then caused me to sleep very, very soundly, removed a bone from my body, and created my beautiful Eve."

Adam stopped his lesson and looked expectantly at Tubal-Cain.

Tubal-Cain swallowed, attempted to speak, and swallowed again. "Sir, uh, just what lesson is it that you want me to learn. I'm not certain that I fully understand."

Adam, who stood at the same eye level with his young descendant, squared his shoulders and, taking a deep breath, plunged ahead. "Perhaps you wondered why I sent you to the priest of the line of Doran? Well, it is very simple actually, for you see I have selected a bride for you from the lineage of Doran. Atara is a lovely young woman who will make a fine wife for you. Your names will be called during the betrothal announcements this afternoon. That gives you a year to court her, and to prepare a home for your bride."

Tubal-Cain stood staring at the Patriarch, his mouth hanging open, and his face pale. He seemed incapable of speech.

Adam, straining to break the silence, said with a grin, "Look at the bright side, Tubal-Cain: at least you don't have to lose a bone!"

Eve had chosen that exact moment to walk into the courtyard where the men were talking. "Adam!" she remonstrated, "What in the world have you said to terrify this young man so?"

Both men turned suddenly in her direction. Tubal-Cain bowed reverently to the Mother of all. "I….I, um, …I think that I am going to acquire a wife," he said, a little too brightly. He suddenly grinned and added, "No bones about it!"

Chapter Nine

Achva

As years are wont to do, the ones following the marriage of Tubal-Cain and Atara flew by quickly. Much to his surprise, the master worker of metal found that marriage suited him extremely well. His wife was not only pleasing to look upon but of a cheerful disposition, and a godly spirit. She was a willing partner in all that Tubal-Cain chose to attempt, and he found his business better run because of her good sense. Their house always presented a warm welcome to others, and it was a frequent gathering place for the younger Proclaimers to meet and share their knowledge of Yahweh. Such meetings frequently led to hearty debates, and what they lacked in profundity they made up for with great cacophony. Adding in God's blessing of a dozen children in as many years, Tubal-Cain found it difficult to even remember his quiet, sober, bachelor days.

Lives were long, illnesses few, and offspring many. Adam's progeny began to occupy vast expanses of the earth. The seacoast first settled by Abir, Rina, Ravid and Simcha, and known as 'the sea of Avir', now had thousands of families living along its banks. Others spread to lands north, east and south of Adam's land.

Most cities contained a mixture of people, some which were decent, hardworking and God-fearing, with a small segment that rejected God and exploited man. A few cities were totally given over to a raucous and sinful lifestyle, the chief among these, of course, being Cain's 'City of Enoch'.

Only the area where Adam dwelt was considered a 'holy City'.

It was not a City in the truest meaning of the word, for no large buildings existed there. Mostly it was a collection of villages that had spread out enough to be joined together. Adam was clearly the Patriarch and allowed no sinful practices in the area that bore his name.

The area became known as 'Mivtzar' meaning 'a secure place'. The center of the City was the circle field that had once been Cain's source of pride; it now was a restful park with the faithful well still giving forth cool, clear water.

At the eastern edge of the park there was a large arbor that was covered with ancient grape vines. It was early morning of the first day of the week and the Patriarch sat on a stone bench enjoying the cool shade provided by the vines. He watched the young man whose legs so easily took the many strides necessary to bring him to the place Adam had arranged for their meeting.

When the young man was close enough for conversation, the long legs came to an abrupt halt and he stood hesitantly before the oldest man on earth. His face betrayed his curiosity, and it was obvious that he wondered why this great man had summoned him. He was, after all, only Achva, son and grandson of metalworkers.

True, his grandfather Tubal-Cain had the reputation of being not only the first, but also the greatest, metalworker ever born. All workers of metal since his grandfather had been but copies of the original.

Not that any of that fame had anything to do with Achva. His own fingers were clumsy; his talent for metalworking was non-existent. His father had accepted this. There were, after all, numerous other brothers and cousins to carry on the trade.

The problem was, Achva wasn't sure what his talent was. Crops that he planted seemed to wither on the vine. He had tried his hand at the potter's wheel only to be chased out of the shop by a furious potter when he found his wheel hopelessly clogged.

Achva had two great loves in his life: stars and scratching.

At least 'scratching' was what his brothers called the marks he made on papyrus sheets. Achva could lie for hours and watch the stars. He had carefully drawn their paths for every month of the year. As for his 'scratches', he had tried in vain to show his brothers that if they memorized his code and put the various marks together, words would form. From the words Achva could form thoughts, and from these he knew that he could write down the stories that the elders told.

The two men studied each other carefully. The thirty-year-old looked into eyes that had gazed upon things of this earth for 650 years. His usually glib tongue was silenced in awe.

He took a deep breath. "Sir, I am Achva, son of Josiah. I have been informed that you wish to see me."

"Be seated, Achva, son of Josiah, grandson of Tubal-Cain. Do you know that your father was named after Josiah, the adopted son of my daughter Aluma?"

❋ ❋ ❋ ❋ ❋

"Yes sir, I have heard that story. I know that the first Josiah died valiantly, defending the lives of Sharon and Diza. I know that his best friend, Uri, married Diza and that Mahalalel, of the sacred line of Seth, married Sharon."

Adam looked impressed. "Well done, young man. I am pleased to hear that you maintain knowledge of your heritage!"

"Thank you sir. It is all part of my 'scratching' as my brothers call it. I am writing down all that I know about the family and about the events that have taken place."

"Well then, Achva the Scratcher, you also know that Mahalalel and Sharon had a son named Jared who continues the sacred line."

"Yes sir, I do know that."

"Young man I need for you to make a long journey for me and bring back one of the sons of Jared."

"Sir?"

"Enoch, the seventh son of Jared, has been living for several years along the banks of the sea adjoining the settlement named for the man of wisdom, the great teacher, Ur. I understand that Enoch moved there because he wishes to build a fleet of boats to sail on the seas. I need him to come home."

❋ ❋ ❋ ❋ ❋

Achva looked in amazement at the great Patriarch. There obviously was no doubt in Adam's mind that if he sent word for Enoch to 'come home' that he would obediently do so.

Adam continued, apparently oblivious to the look on Achva's face. "You will be provided with the means to make the long journey. I would like for you to travel as inconspicuously as possible. If it appears that you are carrying much money you will be prey for every bandit on the road. I also have reason to believe that there is a certain group in Cain's City, named after that other Enoch, the evil one, that would love to see every man destroyed from the line that God has set aside. The hatred between Cain and Abel lives on, I fear."

Achva swallowed. Twice. "When do you want me to leave, sir?"

"You are to start on your journey right after the next Sabbath is over. I want you to be back here by the Harvest Festival. That gives you over four months for the trip. You will not want to tarry long in any one place."

Achva nodded silently his face still stunned.

"One more thing, Achva the Scratcher, I have a little gift for you. I found it among Aluma's things after she died. You see many years ago, when Abel was still alive, he too tried his hand at 'scratching'. He made little stories for his sisters. I want you to have this one. I hope that you will treasure it as I do."

Achva held the little wooden 'book' in his hand. His face was full of reverence. He reached out to shake his Patriarch's hand but Adam suddenly took the young man in his arms for a tender hug, and kissed him lightly on the cheek.

❋ ❋ ❋ ❋ ❋

Achva sat on the foredeck of the boat as it cruised slowly along the Euphrates River. It was his first ride on the water and he found it exhilarating. He had just come from below decks where he had checked on the well being of his donkeys. They were well fed and watered and acted as if they had traveled by this means of transportation all their lives. The young servant boy minding them seemed kind and attentive to his duty. Achva had paid him well.

On the way up to the top deck Achva had peeked through the open windows into the wide-open area that extended on both sides of the decks. The rowers, huge men with muscles of steel, sat three to a bench on this private deck, and propelled the boat slowly along the river. They rotated with an alternate crew, working in two-hour shifts from sunup until sundown. The boat did not travel at night but, instead, put into one of the small ports along the river.

Having finished the ample lunch recently purchased from the town where he had embarked, Achva was allowing himself to be lulled into slumber by the warm early summer sun. Suddenly he was jolted awake by a deep voice.

"Hello, my name is Nedav. I saw you board the boat at Eliakim. Are you traveling to Enoch also?"

Achva felt a moment of fear. The mans use of 'Enoch' for Cain's City had nearly thrown him off balance. For one terrible brief moment he had feared that his mission was discovered and that he was in the hands of the enemy.

He rubbed his hands over his face to chase the lethargy away. The speaker was standing on the port side of the ship and Achva looked up directly into the morning sun. The man standing over him was a dark blur.

Achva forced himself to speak calmly. "No, not Enoch, but Ur. I am a scholar and I am going there to the Tower of Learning to teach students about the constellations of the heavens. I am descended from the great Ur and I am called Uri."

Achva prayed that his voice sounded natural as he gave the name that he had been instructed to use until he reached Ur.

Adam had placed him in the hands of Guryon for hours of instruction in subtlety and espionage, and the novice emissary certainly hoped that his story was believable.

Nedav moved to a seat across from his new acquaintance and laughed a friendly laugh as his fingers touched the rough brown robe that Achva wore. "Being a scholar must not be a very lucrative position."

"No," Achva agreed good-naturedly, "riches mean nothing to us. We seek wisdom and contentment."

Nedav threw out his chest. "I go to Enoch to seek wealth and fame. Men say that these things are to be found in the City of Enoch. I travel from a land many miles above the beginning of the Euphrates River and I am excited to see the great City. Why don't you stop off with me?"

"I cannot for I must be at the Tower of Learning at a set date to begin teaching. There are many students there who wish to learn the secrets of the heavens."

"And you, Uri, know these secrets?"

"Well, I think that I know some of them. I have been charting maps of the heavens since I was a small child and I know the route that the stars take."

This information seemed to silence the inquisitive young traveler for a while. After long minutes of reflective quiet, Achva offered his new acquaintance an orange and some of the delicious fruit bread he had carried from home.

They munched together comfortably.

"I could go to Ur with you if I wished. There is none to direct my path. I am free of all obligation to family or home." Nedav spoke these words in a voice somewhat filled with bravado.

Achva said nothing for a moment and then cautiously. "You wish to become a scholar?"

Nedav laughed, but this time with bitterness. "I wish to be away, far away, from my father and his brothers. Their favorite sport was beating me with the whip they used to train horses. I grew weary of whippings."

Never having had a whip taken to him in all of his young years, Achva's face showed the astonishment that he felt.

"Come now, Uri, don't look so pale. Were you never whipped?"

"No, never. My father is a good and patient man. I probably needed whipping for I was very stupid when he tried to teach me his trade of metalworking. He never even seemed to get angry. He just put his arm around me and told me that God gave each man his own gift, and mine obviously wasn't metalworking."

"Where are you from, Uri? Where is this place that men put their arms around their sons and treat them with kindness, and serve a God that gives gifts?"

"Many days journey west of Eliakim, in the hill country."

Nedav stood and walked to the side of the boat and looked down into the green waves made by the oars. Achva noticed that he limped.

"Perhaps when I have made my fortune, I shall travel to this hill country west of Eliakim and see these people for myself." The young voice held a sad wistfulness for a moment.

Just as quickly as it had come, the dispirited mood seemed to pass; and Nedav grabbed 'Uri' by the arm and pulled him into the covered portico of the boat where men sat playing draughts.

The days passed comfortably; and by the time the boat reached the large port of the City of Enoch, the young men had cultivated a friendship. Achva yearned to urge Nedav to continue on the journey with him, but knew that he could not reveal the true purpose of his travels. Most difficult of all for Achva was his inability to completely share knowledge of the one true God with his new friend. Guryon had warned him to be very circumspect in revealing that he was a God-fearer. He stressed how essential it was to get Enoch safely back to Mivtzar.

Achva knew that Nedav had never heard of Yahweh. He was amazed that his new friend, obviously so cruelly misused by those who should have shown him love, could have such a gentle spirit. There was much bluster and bluff, but Achva knew that there was a tender heart underneath all of the façade.

The City of Enoch was the end of the line for the large boat that had carried the young men into its port. It would be in dock for three days before heading back to its farthermost northern port.

Achva and Nedav shouldered their packs, and Nedav helped Achva get the donkeys out of the hold. Nedav waited on the path at the top of the riverbank while his new friend made inquiries as to the availability of a boat bound for the City of Ur.

A frown creased Achva's face as he walked up the steep bank where Nedav sat on the grassy knoll, casually leaning against one of the donkeys.

"Uh-oh, you don't look very happy, friend. Problems?"

Achva nodded. "Evidently boats rarely travel to Ur. There is a large boat that travels the rest of the way down the Euphrates and then turns to travel up the Tigris, but it only makes the trip once a month and the men say that it left two days ago. However there is a smaller -- they say much, much smaller -- boat that goes once a week to carry supplies to Ur and other ports along the way. It will leave about four days from now."

"That's good news for me! Now do come, then, go into Enoch with me. You can help me find a place to stay. It will be good to have more hours together. Come on Uri, it is barely after high noon. Let's see this great City together."

The other man stood hesitating for a few minutes. Things were not going exactly as he had planned, for he had discovered that it would be necessary to ferry the donkeys across the river and travel a day to a day and a half west in order to find stables for his donkeys. He would be able only to take two donkeys with him on the boat to Ur. He explained the situation to Nedav.

"So, let's do it! I'll help you to take your donkeys to shelter and then you'll still have time to visit the City with me."

Making a sudden decision, he nodded his agreement. They arrived at the stables late the next afternoon and Achva was pleased to find that they appeared well run, clean and decent. An old-looking young woman appeared to be in charge and, much to his surprise, she quoted him a fair price for sheltering his beasts. The woman, who gave her name as Rhoda, motioned to a young girl to fetch cool drinks for the men.

Three children returned, each carrying an offering. There was a very, very sweet apple wine taken cold from its container in the swift running stream, several chunks of goat cheese, and crusty brown bread obviously baked that morning.

Both men immediately reached into their money pouches but the woman shook her head. "We are not so poor that we cannot offer hospitality to strangers. Perhaps you would like to bed down in the stables, there is clean straw, and you would be terribly late tonight getting back to the river. Those wharfs are not a safe place to be at any time, and at night only evil goes on there."

The children gathered around her and she whispered that they could get treats for themselves. Laughing gleefully they ran back to the small house. "Don't forget to give some to Zane also." She looked younger as she sipped her own drink and relaxed on a bench that had been made by placing a rough board over two tree stumps. There were several such benches in the little apple grove nearby. Achva wondered to himself if this could be a place of meetings.

Speaking suddenly, as if she thought they might be wondering, Rhoda said, "Zane is a very old man who was left on Oren Rock to die. My children and I found him about a year ago while we were searching for our wandering goats that had gotten loose after we purchased them in the City of Enoch. He was tied to a fir tree. He is blind and his eyes are constantly rummy. When I found him his body was covered with running sores. I think that he probably was a wicked old man who lived a horrible life in Cain's City. The gentle citizens of Enoch frequently carry their old to Oren Rock when they don't want to be bothered with them." She spoke this last with a tinge of irony mixed with sadness.

"Nasty and smelly as he was, much worse than my goats," she laughed gently, "I just couldn't go off and leave him there. We made a litter out of sticks and carried him to the house. The ferryman almost refused to bring us across the river, but money helps I gave him weak wine and treated his sores, and after a few days he was able to begin eating gruel. When I thought he was strong enough, I scrubbed that foul body with my good lye soap and hot water. Oh did he ever yell and curse me! He said that he would rather die alone on the Oren Rock than endure what I was doing to him. Of course, by then he had a full belly.

"I had to be very stern with him at first about his language. I had never heard such talk in all my life. His mouth was more foul than his body. I assured him that I would scrub that foulness out of his mouth with my lye soap, if he didn't speak in a decent manner. Now he is much mellowed, and the children are fond of him."

The men were silent for some time after her story. Achva was certain that he saw Nedav wipe away a tear.

Achva cleared his throat before he spoke. "Where is your husband, Rhoda?"

"He was a rower on one of the large boats back when they traveled the river at night. One night there were bandits. They attacked the boat and killed most of the men; the women and children were carried off. That was three years ago."

She nodded towards a tousle-headed boy who had sneaked back, face smeared with jam, to climb onto his mother's lap. "I was pregnant with him, although I didn't know it until a few weeks later."

"So is it just you, the old man, and the three children?" Nedav inquired gently.

"Five children," she corrected. "The older boy and girl are in the fields, helping our servant to hoe."

Once again her voice assumed that soft storytelling tenor that the men had enjoyed previously. "The servant is really a case somewhat like Zane's. We had traveled to the docks to buy fish and grain. I imagine that you noticed the poor creatures tied to posts outside the City gates. That is called the 'Wall of Punishment'. Well, they were literally dragging this woman to the whipping post. She was pleading her innocence. The authorities said that she had stolen her mistress' jewelry. Her mistress was a very wealthy woman and was not required to prove the crime, merely to state it. I looked into the condemned woman's eyes, for condemned she was; no one survives those beatings! I believed that I could see goodness in those eyes. I asked how much it would cost to redeem her and," again that gentle laugh, "that day we bought Elza instead of fish.

"We tell her that she is a beloved member of our family. I think of her as the mother that I never knew, for mine died when I was five; but she says that she will forever be our slave. Isn't that silly?"

Nedav looked thoughtful. "I have for many years longed to see the great City that is called Enoch. After hearing your tales of how people are treated there, I wonder if I shall like it so very much."

Rhoda shrugged her shoulders. "There are hundreds who would live no where else. As for myself I am grateful that my beloved husband was able to obtain this country place just one year before he was killed. We make a decent living here and I rarely go into Enoch. I no longer take the children with me, and I never venture out after dark. I have relatives who live there and they shelter me when I go."

She paused, hesitated, and then asked the question that obviously had been troubling her. "Are you both seeking a trade in Enoch?"

Nedav nodded, "I do, but Uri is a scholar and travels on to Ur in order to teach them about the stars. I know much about horses and I go to Enoch to seek work."

"Well then, I shall give you a wax token to carry to my uncle so that he will know I sent you. He will have a place for both of you to sleep and I feel certain that he will be glad to have an honest man to take care of his horses. You must leave very early in the morning, before the sun rises, or it will be after sundown when you enter the City. I cannot believe that men such as yourselves would enjoy the pleasures that Enoch has to offer at night."

She awakened them the next morning before first light; slipped cloth bags containing food into their hands and bid them hurry on their way.

They were quiet as they traveled together, both absorbed in their own thoughts.

Nedav suddenly burst out with great emotion, "I must see her again, Uri, for she is a remarkable woman. Do you not also see that she is remarkable?"

"Remarkable," Achva agreed, "and I feel certain that she will be very grateful to have someone bring supplies to her. She seemed none too pleased at the prospect of visiting the City."

Nedav was grinning broadly as the two men and the two donkeys entered the wide gates of the City.

So this was The City. This was reputed to be the very first City, having been founded early in the history of mankind. It was said that the murderer Cain had started it as a small settlement, named it after his first-born son and, in between his wanderings over the earth, proudly watched it become the largest City known to man. Perhaps he was also proud of its reputation for evil.

It was nearly dusk as the two young men walked past the various streets of trade. Both men were surprised that each individual street housed but one type of trade. There was a street with numerous shops of candle makers; one with row after row of knives and weapons for hunting; one that proudly displayed every type of basket imaginable; one that sold cloth, every kind of cloth; cloth so soft that it felt like a baby's skin. The men marveled. Each street was filled with its own wares and it seemed to the men that there was no end of objects to be purchased.

Other streets focused on foodstuffs: chickens plucked and hanging from lines, fish piled high on slab tables; there was a street that had cheeses and milk, puddings and pies, and on and on it went, street after street after street. Then there were other streets, different, set back away from the rest; quiet now in the late afternoon sun.

"What is sold there?" inquired Nedav of a passerby.

A man laughed lewdly. "Flesh is sold there young man. Human flesh. Women of any age. Young boys. Small children. What ever your desire, you will find it on the Streets of Pleasure! Come tonight after dark and bring plenty of money."

"Hurry my friend," urged Achva. "Let us find Rhoda's relatives; surely they are of a more decent sort."

Carefully following the crude map that Rhoda had drawn them, they came to a wide bridge that was built over a small river. They crossed the bridge and found that there were houses situated in large yards. A tall rock fence surrounded each yard. The air was purer here and there was a blessed quiet. Just as the first star appeared they found the gate with the metalwork that Rhoda had described.

"Nedav, this is amazing!" Achva said excitedly. There is a gate in the area where I grew up that is exactly like this. "This has to the work of Tubal-Cain!"

"Well, I don't know who Tubal-Cain is; but that is a magnificent gate, that much I do know." As Nedav spoke, he rang the bell on the post and a servant hurried to see who would be at the gates at the setting of the sun.

The two were welcomed into the house and there was rejoicing to know that Rhoda was well and thriving.

A woman dressed in bright gauzy cloth, wearing the longest earrings that Achva had ever seen, and with her eyelids painted a strange purple hue, shook her head in wonder.

"I just don't understand why she insists on living in that terrible, desolate place when she could live in this wonderful house with our uncle."

The uncle appeared just as the woman finished her statement. He shook hands with each of the young men and greeted them warmly.

"Welcome to the house of Maimon. Thank you for news of our dear Rhoda. We see her seldom, and she never brings the children into the City. We love her very much, but we do find her attitude about the City strange. Oh well, country people have strange ways, I guess. Come join us for the evening meal. We have wonderful cooks."

Achva was stunned to see the flesh of many different animals at the table. The people in Adam's settlement ate only the meat of fish and chicken. All other animals were treated with respect and; although they might be harnessed for heavy work chores, they were never used for food. It was true that hides were taken from dead animals, but they were not killed for such. The only animals that were put to death before their time were the animals used for the sin sacrifice.

Apparently Nedav was not used to these strange meats either, choosing rather to heap his plate with vegetables, grains and fruits. The men exchanged looks. Oh well, City people have strange ways.

The uncle consulted his overseer, who said that he would most certainly welcome a man who knew horses. Nedav was delighted with the offer of a job and a place to live. The overseer found, much to his pleased amusement, that Nedav would neither be visiting the houses of harlots, nor the shrines of the prostitutes, nor, most certainly, (Nedav blanched very pale when this activity was mentioned) not the area where *any animal* could be obtained for 'pleasure'.

The uncle noted that the men drank sparingly and then of the weakest wines. He whispered to the overseer that he believed that they had a rare find.

The overseer nodded and said in an aside, "If only our new young friend doesn't develop a taste for your young niece, who dearly loves the wares of the City, and who certainly has an eye for young Nedav tonight."

The uncle smiled sadly, "Peri is somewhat slow witted and likes her trinkets, but she is not evil. Not yet anyway. Maybe this house has not totally given over to the murderer. We know so little about the God known as Yahweh, but somehow, someday, I believe that this house will know Him."

The overseer looked earnestly into the face of the older man. "How can that be, my master and friend? I cannot find this God anywhere. I have looked in all of the stalls of the City. I have visited the temples and every altar, even down to the ones in the poorest section of town. I can find no God named Yahweh."

The uncle turned his head toward his servant. "Do you think, Zahid, could it possibly be? Could this be a God who has never had his likeness carved?"

Both men looked wistfully into the fire that burned cheerfully in the grate, giving warmth to the coolness of the early summer's eve.

Zahid showed the two guests a clean, snug room built in the rafters over stables. Nedav was delighted.

"You know, Uri, all my life, well anyway all my life since my mother and grandmother were killed by stampeding horses when I was a little boy; all that time I have felt that whatever holy powers there might be had turned their back on me. Since I met you on that boat I seem to have a change for good in my life. Meeting you was good. Meeting Rhoda was good, he blushed as he revealed this, and now I have a good job and a wonderful place to lodge."

"You have one more thing, Nedav, and I hope that you will count it as good."

"What is that Uri? What other thing do I have?" Nedav looked puzzled.

Achva walked over to one of the two donkeys that he had brought with him. "You have a donkey. It is a gift. I want you to have him. Treat him well. His name is Gibar. Now, goodnight. The dawn will be here soon and I must be on that boat by noon."

That night, for the first time in many years, Nedav fell asleep with tears shining on his face.

He arose early and did his chores and then asked permission to escort 'Uri' to the docks. Zadid agreed but insisted that two strong guards from the house go with them. "You are both innocents, Nedav, and I'll not have my new horse man killed so soon. I will trust you not to linger in the City."

The time came much too soon for 'Uri' to start on the rest of his journey. Now, alone on the shore, Nedav waved a last goodbye to

Achva. "I'll come see you in Ur someday, Teacher Uri," he called. "Be safe. Don't get lost in those stars!"

The 'teacher' watched his friend for as long as he could see him. The boat had disembarked what few passengers it had at the port of Enoch. They were mostly a poorer class of people than had traveled on the boat that had brought Achva here. Nevertheless they were excited to see the sights and literally ran toward the shore. Even as the boat traveled far from the dock, Achva could hear the noise, and smell the smells, that came from beyond the marble gates.

He surreptitiously bowed his head and silently prayed for his friend. He asked that Father God place His hand upon the young man, keep him from evil and from harm, and bring him to knowledge of the one true God.

❋ ❋ ❋ ❋ ❋

The first port south of Enoch found the few remaining travelers changing from the small boat into an ancient even smaller one. Achva was convinced that this must be the original craft that first traveled the big river. By the time the lumbering craft finally reached the port of Ur, river travel had lost all exhilaration for him.

Lest someone had followed him from the boat, Achva found lodging for his donkey in the stables outside the City, and went directly to the Tower of Learning. He obtained one of the guest rooms for rent there and determined to begin his search for Enoch on the morrow. He fell gratefully upon his bed and gave a prayer of thanks that the floor was not moving beneath him.

The City was built entirely out of white stone and the rising sun struck the building with such blinding force that Achva on awakening shielded his eyes from the glare. His room had several large windows that were covered with gauzy white cloths. Achva watched the curtains blow languidly in the early morning breeze.

Yawning and stretching he pushed himself up from his comfortable cot and went to the basin to wash his face. After setting his chamber pot outside his door, Achva decided to explore his surroundings. Certainly this was a pleasant room. There were gracious touches of luxury everywhere.

He looked out the easternmost window into the garden below where beauty and serenity bid him come and join. His senses were immediately captured by melodious sounds. Birds were singing, water splashing, and even monkeys added their joyful whistling tunes to the symphony as they played merrily in the trees. With his sforzando call suddenly shattering the peace a large bird who had been admiring his fan of bright blue tail feathers in the mirroring waters of the pool, took his vanity to a safer location in a nearby tree.

Achva laughed softly as he paused in his descent down the stairs from the balcony. He spoke gently to the breeze blowing in the bird's direction.

"No wonder that you are so vain. Your coat reminds me of the story that Father Adam tells us about Lucifer. God made him a beautiful coat even before he was created. Be careful now; don't get so vain that you get cast out of this paradise!"

The garden, complete with blooming shrubs, masses of flowers and a pool with a tinkling waterfall, was centered in the large courtyard. The buildings surrounded the courtyard where Achva had found a room to rent, and a balcony ran completely around the upper rooms. Achva suddenly was assailed by a smell that not only touched his senses but also made his stomach growl hungrily. He smelled breakfast! Remembering that he had not eaten since early afternoon of the previous day, he went in search of this tantalizing aroma.

Underneath an awning in the far southeastern section of the courtyard, Achva found the treasure. Numerous young men, whom Achva assumed to be students, were beginning to gather around large vessels of cooked grain, boiled eggs, flat bread, strong herbal tea, raisin cake, and fruit.

"Good morning," Achva spoke cheerfully to a busy maiden as she scooped hot cereal into a bowl. "May I purchase some of that?"

The girl smiled. "I do not work here. I too am a student, but the bowls and other eating utensils are on that table." She pointed and Achva looked to where they were. Seated nearby were a middle-aged couple handling a moneybox. "Pay them and you can eat your fill."

"Thank you." He grinned at her. "I may be here all morning, I'm starved."

She lifted one eyebrow. "Won't you be late for class?"

"Oh I'm not a student. Not yet anyway. Actually I hope to teach. I know about the stars and moon, and uh ..things."

Her tone became very dry. "I'm sure that you do. Goodbye."

Embarrassed he called after her. "I wasn't trying to be forward. Please don't leave."

She simply tossed her hair over her shoulder and hurried off.

Achva shrugged and found a bench along a path in the garden. He spread out his ample breakfast and gave thought to how he could safely go about locating Enoch.

As the sun rose higher in the sky the courtyard filled with students, both male and female. All wore a type of tunic. Only a difference in the color of sash distinguished the dress. The sashes were yellow, green, red and a few blue. Some older men had sashes of a deep purple. Achva was interested to notice that students with like sashes tended to group together.

Suddenly a hush came over the garden. Even the monkeys were quiet. All eyes turned to a gate leading from the centermost building of the Tower of Learning. A small, serious looking man walked through the gate and towards a secluded, slightly elevated area of flat rocks that held a table and several benches. He nodded briefly to the congregation of purple sashes, but appeared too lost in thought to speak. His white robe touched the ground and his sash was sewn with each color of the other sashes. Around his shoulder hung a cape-like garment of deep purple.

He ascended the few rock steps leading to the platform and raised his arms as if in benediction. His voice was surprisingly deep for such a small man.

"Good morning fellow sojourners on the path of learning. Let us greet the day."

It appeared that everyone responded in unison, with words previously learned: "Good morning, Teacher of Light; and good day to the Sun in the heavens, our symbol of learning."

"I am Ur, and I will speak." Clearly, everyone expected this to follow the greeting. Still hungry, Achva was encouraged to see the teacher's arms remained aloft. Perhaps he would speak briefly.

"Those most experienced along the path of learning," Ur intoned, "are to be the most respected and the most helpful. Those who are new with us are to be encouraged: remember, knowledge and wisdom are the right of all who faithfully travel the path."

Without a signal the vast assemblage responded:

"We will follow faithfully."

The great Ur continued, clearly commanding everyone's rapt attention, "We have yet to think all the thoughts available to man. We will learn and we will teach; we will judge our peers, and we will listen to their judgment; we will uphold and defend our honored teachers; we will encourage and defend our fellow sojourners upon the path of learning. We will always seek the light, follow the light, and share the light. I am Ur, and I have spoken."

His message finished, the man lowered his arms, greeted the purple sashes with a handshake and took his place at the table. Immediately young servers attended his every need.

Conversation began once again throughout the garden as students finished their meal and began leaving, apparently eager to attend their lectures in the various classrooms.

"Excuse me," Achva approached one young man with a yellow sash, "but can you please tell me if the man who just spoke is really Ur?"

The student looked stunned. "But, of course, everyone knows that. He is Ur. The greatest teacher in the world. He founded this marvelous school and this City. He is worthy of all respect and honor."

"Thank you," Achva said meekly as the man walked away with his nose in the air.

Achva hesitated only a moment and then walked over to where Ur was enjoying his morning meal with the purple sashes.

He approached the platform and stood silently, waiting.

Soon a dozen pair of eyes were fastened on him.

Ur spoke. His eyes did not miss the tattered clothes that the young traveler wore. "Have you need of something young man? I will be glad to direct you to the office for needy students. No one is turned away because he is poor."

"I have no need of funds, Father." Ur blanched at this provincial term of respect for an older man. "I do, however, have something that you might find useful. I have a program of study of the heavens. At your leisure I would like to present it to you. I think you will find it worthy of your valuable time."

Ur appeared somewhat dumbfounded that so shabby appearing a fellow could speak so boldly. He regarded the young man for a long moment without speaking.

"You have traveled far. Where is your home country?"

Achva decided to be as candid as possible. "I am called Achva. I live in Mivtzar. I have traveled here to share my knowledge of the stars. Father Adam has heard of your place of learning and desires to know more about it and wishes for us to share the knowledge gleaned by our villagers. I have brought you gifts and greetings."

Ur surreptitiously waved his hand behind his back to shush the snickers of contempt that he heard coming from the purple sashes.

"Come to my office directly after the sun begins its descent from its highest point in the sky. I will have time to hear you then." He turned and motioned toward the gates. "My office is inside those silver gates; you will see it once you enter. You are welcome, Teacher of Mivtzar. If you are able to teach me something, I will be happy to present you with a purple sash."

Achva thanked the great Ur for his time, bade a grinning goodbye to the purple sashes, and whistling a bright tune, walked out the garden gates.

Just as he exited the gates, Achva's attention was caught by a ball of fluff that, for some unfathomable reason, had what appeared to be a tail attached to it. Achva could not be absolutely certain of that because the 'tail' was moving back and forth so madly that it was difficult to tell what it was.

Achva squatted down and clicked his fingers. Immediately the ball of fluff was on top of him: a mass of perpetual wiggles and a very busy wet tongue.

Laughingly Achva picked the puppy up and held it in his arms. "And where did you come from, little one?"

A plump woman selling flowers from a nearby cart called to him. "You are welcome to take that mutt. Some farmer came through here last week and dumped off the entire litter. That one is the last to be claimed. Probably because she was the runt and such a funny looking creature. I suspect that her momma was wed to a bunny rabbit."

"Come home with me sweet one. I shall call you Yafa, and after you are cleaned up you will be worthy to be called 'pretty'."

He quickly retraced his steps, begging scraps from the food vendor in the courtyard, gathering a bowl of water from the pool and finally, securing 'Yafa' on the balcony next to his room. He placed the donkey blanket for the little dog to lie on. The dog sniffed carefully; apparently approved of donkey smell, turned around and around and lay down. She sighed a doggy sigh for she was happy to be the owner of such a nice man and content to be well fed. Satisfied with her change in status, she immediately fell deep into dog slumbers.

Careful to keep to the southern wall of the courtyard so as not to be seen by the men still at their breakfast, Achva once again left the gates and began to explore the City.

The contrast with the City of Enoch was colossal. The streets were quiet and orderly. Signs with symbols on them pointed in different directions. Achva studied the signs and headed in the direction that indicated clothing was for sale.

The City was built on a pattern of squares. In the center of each square was a small park with a pool, a fountain for obtaining a drink of water, and benches for resting. Flowers and shrubs were abundant everywhere. According to the symbol at the gate leading to the square this was the 'Square of the Clothiers'. There were numerous shops of apparel, and it was obvious that the owners' homes were built above them. The buildings were white and spotlessly clean, with boxes built outside every window so that flowers could cascade down the walls.

There was also a place of refreshment. Achva noted that there were numerous old men sitting in the sunshine, drinking cool drinks and visiting with one another. He ordered a fruit drink for himself from the open-air counter and looked back to the square.

"Newcomer aren't you," one man stated matter-of-factly.

Achva agreed and then asked what shop would be selling tunics for young men. "I can pay," he added quickly, noting the man's scrutiny.

Entering the shop he was amazed to discover tunics, robes and shifts of every color imaginable; made of materials that Achva had never seen before. He selected a shift of a soft dove color and a deep blue tunic to cover it. He admired a belt made of silver and adorned with small flecks of gold, but just in time, remembered that Guryon had urged him to do nothing to draw unwonted attention to himself. "Keep a low profile," Guryon had said, "Always keep a low profile."

"I wish to bathe and then dress in these new clothes for a special meeting. Is there somewhere that I can do that?" he asked as he paid the proprietress.

"Where are you lodging?" she inquired.

"I am staying at the Tower of Learning and I have a meeting with Teacher Ur after lunch." He tried, unsuccessfully, to keep the feeling of importance out of his voice.

"Baths are provided as a part of your lodging. They are much nicer than the public ones and you will still be fresh for your meeting. By the way, I saw you looking at the narrow silver belt. It goes very well with the clothes that you bought."

Achva wavered. "I guess that I'll just wear this one." He indicated a well-made leather belt.

"That is a nice belt. Very well made and appropriate…for work clothes. People do not dress lewdly here like in Enoch, but neither do they dress like they just came in off the farm. I will sell the belt cheaply enough. You should have it with your new clothes."

Achva thought seriously for a few minutes. After all, Guryon *had* warned him not to draw attention to himself. Perhaps he should buy the silver belt after all. He nodded suddenly and took the money out of his pouch.

The woman looked him over carefully. "Two squares east of here there is a place where you can have your hair and beard trimmed, and one square beyond there are shops selling sandals. You will want to look your best for such an important visit."

He thanked her, and as he was leaving she called out, "My name is Gana, come later this week and tell me how your visit went."

"I will, I will, and thank you. You have been a wonderful help!"

The baths were every bit as delightful as the shop proprietress had described. There were separate baths for men and women, much to Achva's relief. He knew that this was a City of 'modern thought' but enough was enough!

Ur barely recognized the splendid young man who stood before him as the ragged Achva who had so brashly barged into his conversation this morning. This young man was well-groomed, *splendidly* groomed, with properly oiled hair and beard, trimmed nails and clothes that would cost the average farm worker a week's wages. His curiosity about the man was suddenly greatly charged. "I see that you brought your drawings, Achva. Place them on the table by the window. The light is best there."

Two hours later the Teacher sat down in his favorite chair, a bemused expression his face.

"This is astounding. What a gift you have! Your family must be proud beyond belief."

Achva shook his head ruefully. "No sir, I'm afraid that they only tolerate my scratchings because they love me. I have a wonderful family; but I come from the lineage of Tubal-Cain, and I'm the only male who doesn't know how to make metal into something beautiful! I am clumsy, careless and ruin every piece of metal I touch. My younger sister works metal far better than I do. I tried pottery and with even worse results. I study the heavens because I can do nothing else."

"Achva, my son, I am going to tell you a story that I've never told anyone else. Many, many years ago I lived in the City of Cain. I came from a very wealthy family that pampered me and encouraged my every whim. At the age of fourteen I decided that I wanted to make beautiful gates like the one at the House of Lamech. Tubal-Cain was already a great teacher whose fame had spread far and wide; and, in spite of my mother's tears, I persuaded my father to send me to school there.

"My father paid the fees for my tuition and I'm certain that they had been doubled because Tubal-Cain declared that he had no time for teaching babies, and pampered ones at that. I promised him that I would work as hard as anyone if only he would allow me to learn metalworking.

"I did work hard. I truly did. I simply had no gift for working with my hands. After a few months of disrupting classes, ruining expensive materials and nearly driving my Teacher to madness, I was kicked out of school. I mean literally. Tubal-Cain, in a fit of rage, threw me, my bags and my bedding out into the street. He said that if he ever had to look at my 'lily white girl's hands' again, that he would personally throw me into the hot molten lead! I believed him and ran squalling home in disgrace. I wouldn't leave my bedroom for weeks.

"One day my mother came to my bedroom door and said that my teacher had come to visit me. I couldn't imagine why. Surely he didn't want to heap more abuse on my head. Could he possibly have had a change of heart? Was he willing to give me one more chance? I doubted it. I looked at my hands. No change there. My heart was pounding nearly out of my shift as I went slowly down the stairs to see what he wanted.

"First off he apologized for being so rough to my person. I nodded and said that I understood that I had upset him very much. He agreed that I had, and we both just stood there for a moment. He went on to tell me that while I was his student all he could see were my mistakes. He was constantly offended by the waste caused by my seeming carelessness and my ineptness with materials. I nodded again and, having heard this many times before, I wondered what had possessed this busy man to come all the way to my home in order to berate me again.

"He continued to talk, but suddenly he was listing what he called my 'good characteristics'. He pointed out that I was very clean in my work and my living habits; I always picked up after myself and kept my work area neat. He said that I seemed to have a gift for organization and for motivating others. It was true that even when I had no faith in my ability to carry on, I could somehow inspire others to do well. He stressed that these were rare and unusual gifts for a man to possess, and that I should consider how to use them.

"I will never forget how he looked at me and said, 'Ur, you are a young man who motivates others to follow their dreams. Find a way to sell *that* and you will always make your living.'

"Years later when my father died from a knifing in the streets, I thought of the words of Tubal-Cain. Enoch had become a raucous place to live, and we were a house of gentle people. I sold my father's estates and traveled to this land, bringing all of my people with me. There were no boats traveling in this direction but I hired a private one and came to where the Euphrates empties into the sea.

It was here that I decided to build a City for gentle people. I dreamed of building a City that would reflect the goodness and best of mankind, and I would build a school where men could learn to use their minds. I believe that if men use their minds it will not be necessary for them to use force. So you see, it was your ancestor, Tubal-Cain, that set me on the path that led here."

Achva shook his head in wonder at Ur's story.

"Isn't it amazing how Yahweh works His will in the lives of people!" he said enthusiastically.

Ur was suddenly very still as, with his back turned to Achva, he toyed with objects on a low shelf. Suddenly he turned and looked Achva directly in his eyes.

"You are a God-fearer then. You believe in Yahweh?"

The voice held a tone that Achva could not totally decipher. Was it sadness…not anger…and yet perhaps dismay?

Achva suddenly realized that silence had hung in the air for several minutes.

"Yes I am most certainly a God-fearer. Tubal-Cain moved his family from Enoch to Mivtzar to learn about the one true God. He became a God-fearer and he has taught us carefully down through the generations. I know Yahweh as the One God, the Creator of the Universe. I personally know Adam who is the first man ever created."

"Well, yes, uh.. um, of course. That's all well and good; but now, Achva, we scholars must always keep an open mind about these things, you know. A narrow mind is a dangerous thing."

Both men were once again silent.

Ur abruptly cleared his throat, "I am very impressed with your study of the heavens. I would like for you to accept a purple sash and become a teacher at the Tower of Learning. Would you consider a temporary post, say a six-week course of study, where we can get to know each other? If all works out we could consider a more permanent post at that time."

Achva turned and looked out the window into the courtyard. What a chance this was! To be able to actually teach those things that only he had been captivated by in the past. His trip to Ur had taken much less time than he had originally planned and he had yet to find Enoch. A teaching assignment would give legitimacy to his stay here. He turned back to face Ur.

"Sir, thank you for this wonderful opportunity, and I gladly do accept with pleasure."

"Excellent! You will obtain your purple sash and white tunic from Gana's Clothier Shop. I will see that students are aware of your class and we will plan for your first session to begin two weeks from the first day of the next week."

"Sir, I have another question. It is about the written language. I have seen symbols throughout this City, but I see no evidence of an actual written language. Is that limited only to the scholars, or do you yet possess a written language?"

"I don't believe that I quite understand your question, young man. We have excellent scrolls with our symbols drawn on them. That is how our students study."

Achva made a decision.

"Master Ur, please allow me to show you one more thing. I believe that, when fully developed it will greatly aid the process of education."

Achva began unrolling several scrolls that were in his leather tote bag. He spread them out on the library table; and the Teacher looked on, his curiosity piqued. Whatever could this interesting young man be up to now?

"You see here that I have made twenty symbols. Each symbol represents a sound that we make when we speak. Here is a simple word which I have made by putting two sounds together," he continued as he picked up another sheet of papyrus. "Here is a list of words made by putting two or three sounds together. They are simple words, and when put together they make rather simple sentences; but I believe that it is a start towards a written language whereby we can communicate effectively."

He pronounced the sounds and pointed to the marks as he did so, then he put the sounds together and showed Ur the short words. Ur studied the sheets.

"I see the idea. This is amazing. This too must be taught to our students, Achva. What a fine mind you have. You simply cannot keep your ideas to yourself. You believe that your 'Yahweh' gave you these gifts; that may well be. Wherever they came from, certainly they were meant to be shared.

"Here is a clay tablet with my seal and inscription on it. Take it to Gana. She will know to make your purple sash that only Teachers are allowed to wear. Go now. I have much to think about. How very wrong was my first impression of you. I must never again rush to such fast judgment. You are shaking my perception of many things, young Achva. Leave me to my thoughts, now. Return to me when you possess your tunic and sash. I will convene my staff and we will plan your induction into our society of Teachers. You have, indeed, taught me something."

Chapter Ten

The Search

The sun was low in the west as Achva walked toward his own room. He reminded himself that he must make arrangements with the proprietor of the guest house, for it was evident that he would be here for several weeks. He was whistling as he climbed the steps to his balcony. Yafa was jumping excitedly in her enclosure as he walked over to her.

"Come my new little friend. Come Yafa. We will find some supper and take a nice walk as the stars come out."

Achva was up at the break of dawn, wanting to escape the courtyard before it filled with students. He placed Yafa in a wool carryall.

The carryall had contained his robes that he wore at home in Mivtzar. They were finely made and showed that he had come from a well to do family. He chose a cream colored shift and covered it with a tunic embroidered in dark green. He smiled as he placed the silver belt around his waist.

He headed immediately for the Square where he had gotten his hair cut. He pulled the cord that rang the bell thus causing a chain reaction of shutters flying open and a head sticking out from the window above.

"So alright already! Stop that jangle. So you can't even wait until the sun is up to get your hair cut? Hey! What's the idea---I cut your hair yesterday. So you need a daily haircut now?"

"Please come down into your shop, good sir. I have a job for you."

Achva heard mutterings from above as the man was obviously dressing, answering questions from his wife, and finally, stomping down the inside steps.

The man glared at him as he threw open the door. "So what is this job you have that you can't even let a man rise at a decent hour?"

"First, let me assure you that I will pay you well." As he spoke Achva flashed several small gold pieces. "I want you to trim my dog's fur and bathe her."

The man's bellowing brought his wife running down the stairs with a large knife in her hand, which she was waving threateningly in the air.

"What is it? What is it? Are we being robbed? What is the matter?"

"Silence woman! We are not being robbed. This crazy man wants me to give his ***dog*** a hair cut and a bath!"

By then the woman had seen the gold coins. She hastily put the knife under the counter and smoothed her hair. "Now, now Gev, let's not be too hasty. It seems a gentle little animal. You trim it and I'll bathe it." As she spoke she picked up the coins and put them in the money jar.

Mumbling under his breath something about ruining his reputation, Gev picked up the dog and Achva very carefully held the animal still while the barber wielded his cutters.

In the meantime the woman had warmed water on the cook stove and as she gently bathed the dog she crooned to it like it was a child.

When Yafa was dry and fluffed she was worthy of her name. The three humans praised and petted her as if she were the one who had accomplished the deed. The barber looked quite pleased with himself and was actually smiling as Achva carried the dog out of the shop.

Next, Achva visited the leather shop and purchased several thin strips of leather, and then proceeded to braid them into a harness and leash for Yafa.

When pressure was applied to the leash, Yafa immediately sat down on her haunches and refused to move. Keeping a taunt line on the leash, Achva placed a piece of cake at his feet. Yafa changed her mind and ran over to eat the morsel. Having done so she looked up at Achva expectantly. He showed her another piece of cake and then tugged on the leash. She moved. Soon she was walking proudly at Achva's side as if she had been born wearing a halter and leash.

He then went to the woodcutter's shop and showed him a design that he wanted carved into a flat piece of wood. Giving careful direction as to the finishing of the piece, he left to go to Gana's shop.

He came to an abrupt halt as he entered the shop; instead of seeing Gana, as he had anticipated, he was greatly surprised to see the young woman whom he had offended in the courtyard of the Tower of Learning.

Her brown hair hung to her waist in one long braid. She was assisting a customer in selecting a finely woven tunic.

After completing the sale she looked in Achva's direction, surprise showing on her face.

"You!" she exclaimed.

"I didn't know that you worked here. I am looking for Gana."

"She is my aunt. I live with her and help her with this shop. She has gone to the weavers to purchase material. How may I help you?" She spoke coolly.

He handed her the seal.

"The great Teacher Ur told me to give her this. He said that she would know what to do."

The girl blanched. "You *are* a teacher!"

"Yes, I know about the stars and moon and, uh.. things."

Her face suddenly went from white to very red; she cast her eyes downward.

"Sir, I do apologize for my wrong assumption. You must think me terribly vain. I will give this seal to my aunt. You must be fitted for a white tunic and my aunt does all of that..."

"I do all of what, Zahava?" asked the older woman as she entered the shop by the back door. At her side was an older man whose arms were laden with materials. He hurried on into the back storeroom.

Achva smiled at Gana, and gently took the seal from the girl's hand.

"Hello, Gana. I told you that I would come back to give you a report about my visit with Ur. He sent you this."

She laughed happily.

"Zahava, this young man has just become a teacher at the Tower of Learning! Isn't that wonderful!"

She turned back to Achva. "Tell me your name, young man, and I will be pleased to introduce you to my niece, who is a student at the Tower."

Zahava spoke up. "His name is Achva and we met yesterday in the courtyard. He was pleasant to me and I insulted him."

Gana looked from one to another and laughed again. "Well, Zahava, you do have a way with men."

"It was my own fault, I fear," confessed Achva. "I certainly didn't look the part of a scholar in my dirty traveling clothes. I'm afraid that I was the brash one. I would like to make it up to your niece by taking her to the refreshment booth for a cool drink of fruit wine. With your permission, of course."

"By all means, out of here both of you. When you return, Achva, my man will measure you for your tunic. Congratulations on your appointment. I look forward to learning all about the subject that you teach."

Achva and Zahava looked at each other and broke into laughter. Gana watched them leave the shop with a puzzled expression on her face.

A short time later they were sitting in the shade of a large tree sipping a cool fruit drink.

"How is it that girls attend the Tower of Learning? Where I come from, women teach the girls, and then only the things that they need to know about maintaining a home and taking care of animals or sick people. Of course, there are women who are shopkeepers, but none attend our advanced schools."

"Actually, there are not a great many girls even in the City of Ur that seek higher learning. A few go to listen to the poets and singers. Most are not enrolled technically, although enrollment is open to women. Teacher Ur is very firm about that."

"What are you learning?"

"I am learning to do sums and keep accounts. My aunt needs someone to keep her accounts accurately. She hired a man last year but he was dishonest. I talked her into sending me to the Tower of Learning so that I could be the one to keep her accounts. There is a City tax to be paid, and she has some charitable causes that she likes to donate to. The bookkeeping is getting more involved every year as the shop grows. It appears that I have a good head for figures.

"The Teacher has a new method of teaching us, and he makes it very interesting. See these six stones. Well, now I am going to lay them in a row and put five additional rows of stones next to them. We have always counted all the stones to get the total amount, right?"

Achva nodded.

"Our Teacher has shown us how to get an answer without adding all of these stones together. We take the one row of six and multiply that row times the total number of rows, which is six."

"I don't understand. What is multiply?"

"It is a way of combining numbers without counting them individually. It makes adding sums much quicker. Look at the six stones: if I take them two times we know that the answer is 12; five equals 30 and finally, six times six equals 36. See? Simple."

"I still don't understand. How do you *know* that six times six is 36 without adding them up?"

"Look at my hand: Suppose I want to multiply 8 times 6. I close the fingers of both hands. Now I open 3 fingers on the left hand. The 5 closed on the right hand and the 3 stands for 8. Now I open 1 finger on the right hand. The 5 that were closed and the 1 now open on the right hand stand for 6. Now 3 fingers should be open on the left hand and 1 finger open on the right. This stands for the 10's digit of the answer. The open fingers add up 3 plus 1 equals 4. There are 4 10's in the answer. The closed fingers give the 1's digit. There are 2 fingers closed on the left hand and 4 fingers closed on the right hand. When I multiply these I get the 1's digit. When I do that, I see that 4 taken 2 times equals 8. I add the 10's and the 1's. There are four 10's and eight 1's so I have my answer which is 48."

Achva shook his head as if to clear it. Watching him Yafa stood up and shook her head too.

Zahava laughed at the sight. "It will become more clear as you use it. Perhaps it will even help you count the stars!"

"Tell me about this great Teacher of Sums. Is he from Cain's City also?"

"No, although I was certain at first that he was, because of his name. He is from an area many miles west of here. He grew up by the seashore and then he moved here to build a fleet of ships that will sail on our seas. He is a God-fearer and he..."

Achva abruptly cut her off. "What is his name?" he inquired almost roughly.

The girl looked surprised. "His name is Enoch, like the City, only he isn't anything like the City.

He is kind and good and fun, and even funny. I really enjoy his classes and..."

"Enoch," Achva breathed. He suddenly let out a loud laugh, jumped up from where he was sitting, and did a little dance.

"Enoch, your Teacher. My Enoch, your Teacher! I can't believe it. I have found him. Thank you Yahweh!"

"Achva, if it wouldn't be too, *too* much trouble, would you kindly tell me what on earth you are talking about?"

"I'm sorry, Zahava. I didn't mean to be so rude. It's just that Enoch is a kinsman of mine and I was sent here to find him. I had no idea how to go about finding him, and here you are telling me that he is your Teacher. This is wonderful. Please, do you know where he lives? I must see him as soon as possible."

"Well, I don't know exactly where he lives, but I do know that he had a home on the seashore. He teaches classes on shipbuilding, and I've heard that sometimes he takes his students to the shore where they are building an actual boat."

"But, where is the sea? I have walked all over this City and I have seen no indication of a sea; although I have seen lots of sea birds and sometimes it does seem as if I can smell the sea."

"Have you seen the bridge in the middle of town? Well that river empties into the sea. There are small boats that will take you there; it is about six miles away. Enoch rides his horse to class two days a week. The rest of the week he spends working on his boats. Except for his

Sabbath; and on that day he does no work at all. It seems that Yahweh requires that one day a week be spent in worshiping Him."

❋ ❋ ❋ ❋ ❋

Achva wondered if somewhere, somehow, this sea joined the one where Rina and Abir had settled. The sand was whiter here, he decided, and there was an abundance of seashells. He would take some of the pretty ones back to his mother and sisters. Perhaps he would be so bold as to take one for Adam to give to Eve. He watched the waves lap against the shore; the white foamy tops cascading back into the sea after rising high into the air. The tide was out and Achva could see a line along the sand where the high tide reached.

He laughed at Yafa who had chased a gull out into the water, and had been sprayed by a large wave for her efforts. She shook her fur furiously and barked a threat of revenge, before bounding over to him for comfort and protection.

The house was built well away from the sandy shore but high enough that the view must be awe- inspiring. Achva stood at the water's edge and looked up the slope at the small house. To the west of the house was a large wooden frame that appeared to be holding a partially finished ship; the likes of which Achva had never seen before. It was huge; far too large to sail on the river. The deck was at least 75 feet above the water line. It was astonishing. How in the world did Enoch hope to get it in the sea?

The house was built of a type of brick that looked as if it had been made from the white sand of the beach. It sat up on, well what *did* it set up on? Tree trunks. That was it. It was held off the ground by tree trunks that had been sunk into the ground just above the shoreline. There was a ladder that allowed a person to access a wooden deck in front of the house. The back seemed built into the hillside that formed behind it.

"Well, Yafa, I guess we better do it. I don't know about you but I feel like running all the way back to the Tower of Learning. I mean, will you please explain to me, my furry friend, how I go about convincing this man that he has to return to Mivtzar just because Adam says so? Well, come on, we are in this thing together."

Achva climbed the ladder and observed the deck. There were pottery containers of flowers, a bell with a cord for ringing, a table of sorts made from a large stump, with smooth rocks for seating and a large cage made from bamboo containing a huge bird that had evidently been injured and was recovering. Achva called a brave 'hello' into the cool darkness of the open door.

"Hello, yourself, friend. I saw you walking on the beach and wondered if you were looking for me. Are you a student?"

"My name is Achva. I come from Mivtzar with greetings for you; that is, if you are Enoch of the line of Seth."

With his eyes beginning to adjust from the brilliant glare of the sunshine to the semi-darkness of the room, Achva was able to observe the man standing before him.

He was of medium build, his wind-tossed, sandy colored hair hung in gentle disarray to his shoulders. He had nothing on from the waist up; and on his lower body he wore a type of garment that fishermen often wore and called 'breeches'. His muscular body was tanned a dark brown, but his eyes were as blue as the sea.

He looked deep into Achva's eyes, drew a breath and said, "Welcome to my home, Achva of Mivtzar. I am indeed Enoch of the line of Seth. What manner of greetings do you bring, to have traveled so far to deliver them?"

Suddenly Achva was at a complete loss for words. He reached into the small leather pouch which he always carried attached to a cord hanging around his neck, hidden by his clothes.

"Father Adam sent you this. He wishes you to accompany me back to Mivtzar. He says that we must be there by the Harvest Festival."

Enoch held the soft leather pouch in his hand without opening it. He suddenly shook himself and looked at Achva. "Please forgive my rudeness. Sit down here on this divan. You have traveled far. Where are you staying? Are you hungry, thirsty?" He hurried over to a jug sitting on a small table and poured his guest a drink, slopping it out on the wooden floor as he handed it to him.

Achva smiled at Enoch and suddenly felt at ease, precisely because Enoch was so ill at ease. "I am staying at The Tower where I have been offered a teaching position for six weeks. I will be glad to join you for lunch, as it has been several hours since I took breakfast in the

Courtyard of the Tower. My dog is Yafa and she will be glad to join you too. This is a very good drink, thank you. What is it?"

"It is a wine, fruit juice really, made from pomegranates. I don't care for the heavier drinks. It will spoil if not fermented, but it is a mild drink, and excellent when fresh. There is more if you wish."

Apparently realizing that he was rambling, Enoch suddenly got very quiet, sat down on a bench and observed the leather pouch.

"Whatever is in this pouch must be quite important for you to have come all this way."

"Yes. Father Adam stated that it is very important."

Enoch took a small knife, ripped open the stitching and removed the ring bearing the insignia of the line of Seth. He looked at it for a long time, saying nothing.

Achva sat silently, not moving, scarcely breathing. He had seen a ring just like this on the finger of Adam. His father had once told him that only those men selected by God to represent the holy line of Seth wore the ring. There were six men who wore such a ring and now Enoch would be the seventh. Father Adam had taught that someday, through that line, the Man who is the Shekinah Glory of God would come to crush the head of Satan and be the human lamb of sacrifice for all mankind. The ring had a raised + in the center of it. On one side of the crosspiece was a man and on the other side was a woman; the piece that ran vertically had a tree in the center with a coiled serpent below it and a lamb above it. The + piece was raised in the gold so as to make an imprint if placed in hot wax. Achva had seen Father Adam use his seal to place a wax imprint over papyrus picture letters that he sent to people.

Enoch had tears running down his face. He spoke, but Achva was not at all certain that he was speaking to him.

The voice was barely above a whisper, "Why? Why me? Please not me. I have six older brothers. Surely it must be one of them. Surely not me."

Trying hard not to stare at Enoch, Achva looked everywhere else but at him. The house had one room. It was a large room with many windows, and a ladder that led up to a door in the flat roof. The windows had bamboo shades that could be let up or down and probably, along with the outdoor shutters, were pretty effective at keeping unfavorable weather out. There was the table, a brick oven built into the brick wall, like those at home, several wooden chairs and benches, the divan upon which Achva was sitting, and a large worktable that contained stacks of papyrus sheets with sketches on them.

Enoch suddenly spoke, causing Achva to start. "I must be alone. Where can I find you when I am ready to talk?"

Achva gave him directions and hastily climbed down the ladder. Just as he had started to walk up the path, Enoch called him. "Friend Achva," he called.

Achva walked back to the base of the ladder and looked up. Enoch tossed down a cloth sack that was rather bulky. Inside Achva found a round loaf of bread, several cooked fish, and a large raisin cake. When he looked up to say his thanks, Enoch had disappeared back into the coolness of the house.

The two figures, man and dog, took a long walk along the beach. Achva absentmindedly picked up shells and put them into his pack. Yafa seemed to sense that her master was troubled, and would frequently run up to him as if to make sure that he was all right.

The beach changed from sand to pebbles to boulders, with bluffs overlooking the vast sea. Achva found a large flat rock, spread out the lunch he had been given, gave thanks, and then shared it with his little friend. He sat for a while until the sun was low in the sky, staring out into the blue, blue waves of the ocean.

The following morning, with a resurgence of his normal ebullient spirit, he whistled a joyful tune as he headed for Gana's clothing shop. He had stopped by the woodcarvers and picked up the order he had left there several days before.

The bell jangled merrily as he went into the sweet coolness of the pleasant little shop. "Hello, Teacher Achva!" Gana called from the back of the shop, as she heard him greeting Zahava.

"I hope you don't think that your robes are ready just yet. I've barely had time to get the purple dye for the sash, it is very rare you know." Achva had just begun to explain that he had come for another reason entirely, when Gana entered the room and began excitedly exclaiming about his tunic.

It was of the wild cranberry color that was made from the berries growing in the boggy areas between Mivtzar and the Sea of Amir. A variant shade of this red was used only by the Shalomshamars, but this lighter shade was very popular with the young people where Achva had been reared.

"I have never seen such a lovely red. Do you know what goes into the making of it? Is it rare in your country? How can I obtain it? I *must* have some of that dye!"

The young man laughed. "Slow down, Gana. I can't keep up with your questions. I know very little about dyes, but I do know that the berry is gathered from the shallow pools of water several miles from my home. I know that the women cook it and add some other ingredients to make it this color. It is all pretty secretive, I think; but some recipes are shared. I haven't seen any of the berries around here though, now that I think on it."

While Gana was still fingering his tunic, he told her gently, "I have brought you a gift."

She immediately stepped back and the look in her eyes was like a child. "A gift! You have brought a gift for me. Oh quick, show me. I almost never get gifts."

Achva handed her a parcel wrapped in dried leaves and bound with a thin cord made from hemp. Zahava drew close as Gana excitedly unwrapped the gift.

She held up a sign about two feet by four feet long. It had two holes in the top of it with a leather rope tied from one hole to the other. The sign had three symbols written across the board, they were set in a carved picture of a flower garden.

Gana looked at Achva questioningly. "It is very beautiful, Achva, but what are the marks?"

"These marks are your name in a written language. Gana means 'garden' and that is what your sign says. I have placed your name in the picture of a garden, so that all may know that this is your shop. Someday there will be a written language for everyone to read, but today your shop, here in Ur, is the very first one to have a real word placed outside its door. Your name, Gana, is the first word that the world will get to know by sight."

The older woman's face was beaming with joy. "Thank you, Achva. Please, Zahava, get Iddo; he must hang this for me right now. The world must not be kept waiting another moment."

Zahava reached over and squeezed Achva's hand by way of thanks and hastened to find her aunt's shop man. Half an hour later the sign hung outside the shop and several other shopkeepers had come to admire it. They had many questions about the marks that Achva called 'letters' and all wanted to know what the marks for their names were.

"Another day, another day," laughed Achva and took Zahava's hand to pull her close to him.

"Let's go somewhere for lunch, I want to talk to you alone."

Zahava spoke a few words to her aunt who nodded and flashed Achva a warm smile.

The couple walked as far as the river before finding a refreshment stand to their liking. Truth be told they had been so engrossed in conversation that they passed several stands without even noticing them.

The sun warmed them as they sat on the grassy bank, throwing scraps to Yafa who begged prettily.

"That was a wonderful thing that you did for my aunt."

"Your aunt is a wonderful woman."

"Yes, she is. I have known that all of my life, but I am thrilled when someone else realizes it."

"Do you mind if I ask a personal question?"

"You mean, why am I living with my aunt instead of my parents?"

"Well, yes actually. I have wondered."

Zahava leaned back against a tree and closed her eyes. Her face was unreadable. She began to speak: "I was born in the City of Enoch; the first child born to my parents who were decent, hardworking and poor. They loved me very much. My mother's younger sister lived with us.

"When I was about 12 years old, my father had his storehouse full of the thick carpets which he made for rich homeowners. He had sold the entire lot to a merchant who lived in a place far east of Enoch. The man was to send his servants to pick up the carpets within a month.

"In the meantime my father had purchased a new home for us. We had been living with three other families in one room, and my father had worked for years to provide us with our own place. We were thrilled to have our dream come true. My mother was expecting another child within a few weeks, and everything seemed perfect.

"The warehouse where the carpets were stored burned to the ground one night. A night watchman lived just long enough to tell my father that all the carpets had been removed before the fire was set. The man died of burns. When the servants came there were no carpets and no money. My father had lost everything. He begged the buyer to allow him time to replace the carpets, but the man knew that it would take years for him to do that.

"My father was sent to the authorities and placed in the dungeon. My mother and I were to be given as slaves to the buyer from the East."

She stopped speaking for a few minutes, covered her eyes with her hands. Achva did not move or speak, giving her time to collect her emotions. She finally took a deep breath and began again.

"That night my aunt packed three bags and said that we were leaving Enoch. My mother cried and begged to not leave my father, but my aunt was very stern with her. Aunt Gana told my mother that she must think of her children. I remember her asking my mother. 'Do you want to see your little girl used for sex by all the men of the City?' That was when my mother agreed to escape.

"My aunt took all of her own money, which she had earned by long years working in the shop, and bribed a merchant to smuggle us out of the City. He made a false bottom in his hay cart, put us in it and covered us with hay. He told the gate guards that he had been ill and unable to feed his animals for several days. They allowed him to pass through the gates.

"When he was several miles away from the City he placed us on a fishing boat traveling down the river. He brought us about half way to Ur, and we traveled the rest of the way on foot. My mother went into labor a week after we arrived here, and both she and my baby brother died.

"My aunt had brought all of the sewing supplies that she could carry and had enough money left to buy material and rent a room where we lived and worked. I had learned to make stitches when I was a tiny girl. Both of us worked night and day until we suddenly found that we were successful. If it had not been for my wonderful aunt, I know that I would have suffered horrible things."

By the time Zahava had finished her story, her face was wet with tears; and when she looked at Achva, she was surprised to find that his face too had tear streaks.

The next few weeks were very busy ones for the young, newly vested Teacher at the Tower of Learning. He looked handsome and professional in his white tunic with purple sash, and he couldn't help but feel the importance of the position. After many years of feeling like a misfit in his world, he somehow sensed that he had found a niche that suited him. Teaching came easily to him. He was pleased to discover that the students were grasping the concept of a written language, and his classes on the heavens were the most popular ones in the school.

He saw Zahava as frequently as he could. He enjoyed her quick mind and cheery disposition. She increasingly showed interest in Yahweh, and Achva answered her questions gladly. Starting with the Garden, he told of the wonderful life that Adam and Eve had there and how they lost it, bringing death into the world. He spent many hours giving a thorough account of the history of the world since then. Zahava marveled at his knowledge and his memory. One day he confided to her that he was putting this history into writing, so that all generations would know it. She had many questions, some doubts; but through her friend's answers to her questions, she found a hope that she had never known before.

"You actually know this same Adam and Eve?"

"I do."

"I don't understand. God said that they would die and yet, according to you, they still live."

"Their bodies show the process of death. They look much older than your aunt or much older than anyone you know. Adam says that death will come to them, when Yahweh wills it."

"Is he afraid?"

"No, not at all," Achva's voice showed his own confidence. "He believes that those who trust in Yahweh and serve him will live forever after they experience death here. He believes that there is an eternal Garden called 'Heaven'."

"You give me so much to think about, Achva. I have never really talked to a God-fearer before. Enoch is a God-fearer and he doesn't hesitate to tell of his belief in what he calls 'the one true God'. I know that he has long discussions with students who travel to his house on the beach. As one of the few females in his class, I knew that it would not have been appropriate for me to go to his beach house. Sadly, there was no time for deep religious discussion during class time. I want to believe. I really want to believe."

"You can talk to Yahweh," Achva assured her. "Even though you do not see Him, He sees and hears you. I believe that if you ask Him to do so, He will reveal Himself to you."

"I will try to talk to your Yahweh, Achva. I will tell you if He answers."

The only dark cloud was that he had heard nothing from Enoch, and the six weeks was rapidly drawing to a close.

He knew that Enoch had turned his classes over to a junior teacher and had not been seen in Ur for several weeks. He longed to talk to the older man again but knew that it was up to Enoch to contact him.

Returning to his room one evening in late summer, Achva was surprised to find his balcony door standing open. He entered cautiously, and there sat Enoch studying the maps of the heavens that Achva had left spread out on the table.

Without turning around, Enoch spoke casually. "You have a great gift my friend, and much to offer the Tower of Learning. Will you be staying here permanently?"

Pausing just a moment to swallow his surprise, Achva replied, "No, I must return to Father Adam with the report of this journey. If he gives his blessing, however, I shall return here. I want to continue teaching; and I find that, even with all of its decency and goodness, this City needs to know Yahweh as much as Cain's City does."

"You are discerning as well as gifted. When do we leave on our journey back to Mivtzar?"

Achva glanced at Enoch's hands. There was no ring on the finger. "You will accept the appointment then?"

"I have spent much time in prayer. Actually I have spent much time explaining to God why he has made a mistake in telling Adam to choose me. I only know that I must talk to Father Adam in person.

"I have left my shipbuilding business in capable hands, and my assistants will continue to teach my classes. I hope to return here by next spring."

Achva nodded with understanding. "The summer recess will begin on the day after Sabbath. There is a boat going upriver two days later. Guryon warns that we must travel very inconspicuously. I have a donkey here and I have traveled under the name of Uri. Perhaps you should trade your horse for a donkey and take an assumed name also. There are evil forces that would like to destroy the Godly line of Seth."

Enoch smiled at his younger companion. "Perhaps your special friend, Zahava, would tend my horse for me?"

Blushing, Achva looked somewhat abashed. Did the entire campus know about his feelings for Zahava? Did he dare declare his feelings to her before he left? If he did return, where was a follower of Yahweh in this City to perform the marriage rites?

Realizing that his thoughts had drifted, he suddenly returned to the matter at hand. "We can ask her after I explain that I must go back to Mivtzar. I, uh, I really haven't exactly told her yet that I'm leaving."

Enoch looked around the ample room. "I have already said my goodbyes to my house on the beach. I will remain here with you. You are my guide and I am willing to do as you tell me." He smiled as he added, "Teacher Achva. Or perhaps I should say, Traveler Uri."

Chapter Eleven

Going Home

In spite of the feelings of apprehension that gnawed in the pit of his stomach, the day that he told Zahava that he was leaving was a good one for Achva. He told her of his feelings, and that he would like to make her his wife; but that he would not be able to return to Ur without the blessing of Father Adam.

Zahava smiled sweetly at Achva and assured him that she believed that their marriage would take place. She said, in a quiet and gentle voice, that she would wait for Achva until he returned or sent for her.

She lifted her lovely head, and her shining eyes looked into his. "My heart is forever bound to yours," she said, "and I know that your God, your Yahweh, will make a way for us to be together."

Achva very solemnly placed a silver ring on the finger next to the little finger of her right hand. "I pledge myself to you forever."

They stood for a long moment looking at each other, and then walked back to the shop where the wooden name plaque hung proudly overhead.

"I asked your aunt's permission before I asked you to be my wife. Now we must ask her blessing."

The blessing was joyfully given. "I will work her very hard in the shop, Achva, so that she will not have time to mope while you are gone!" Gana teasingly assured him.

The time came for departure. Enoch and Achva had been invited to a special dinner in their honor, held by Ur. Gana and Zahava were there, but few others because Achva had explained to Ur the need for secrecy.

Achva and Ur sat together in the balcony overlooking the garden.

"Will you return to Ur, Achva?"

"That is my wish and my intention. I will not do so without the blessing and permission of Father Adam. He lives in constant communication with Yahweh, and to disobey him would be to disobey God."

"Will Enoch also believe that he must obey this Adam?"

"Enoch will obey Yahweh. If he truly believes that Adam speaks for Yahweh, he will do as instructed."

"I would like to meet this powerful Adam. I have never known such a man."

Achva smiled. "Adam is the most gentle of men. He knows that his disobedience in the Garden of Eden caused hardships for all mankind. He takes that burden very seriously, and he longs for every person to walk faithfully with Yahweh."

Both men sat silently together for a while. The music drifted pleasantly out of the windows of the house, and soft laughter and shreds of gentle banter could be overheard.

Achva suddenly took a different approach to the conversation.

"I have some fears for the city of Ur, Great Teacher."

"Fears for Ur. How can that be Achva? Ur is a city of gentle and contented people."

The young man nodded. "Yes, that is true, and the people in Ur are industrious and thrifty. Many have accumulated wealth. Everyone here makes a comfortable living. There is no poverty or misery anywhere because the people of Ur are generous as well as kind.

"However, there are gangs of thieves forming in the land between Cain's city and Ur and to the easternmost areas. The gangs are ruthless. Your city has low stone fences, meant only for keeping out wild animals. Your gates are shut at night, but you have only meager patrols. Your police force is basically a group of men and women who offer assistance to strangers and those in need. You have no real protection from attack.

"But that was my plan, Achva. I wanted a city of light; a city to contrast with the darkness of Cain's city. I have that. I have a gentle city. To have armed guards here would change the entire setting."

"Darkness always seeks to overcome light, Great Teacher. Would you have your people slaughtered in their beds by those who walk in darkness?"

Ur sadly shook his head. "I would not have that. What do you suggest?"

"I will be pleased to ask the leader of our troops to send you a legion of Shalomshamars. Guryon is one of Adam's sons and he is wise, gentle, and fierce if necessary. He has trained excellent soldiers. They are disciplined and will bring no disrepute to the City of Ur. However, it is a rule that if we send Shalomshamars to protect a city, we must also send the Proclaimers to teach about Yahweh. Would you allow the Proclaimers to teach at the Tower of Learning?"

Ur's face took on a hard look. "And will the Shalomshamars enforce the acceptance of this teaching with the sword?"

Achva looked shocked at such a suggestion. "Never. Absolutely never would such a thing happen. No man or woman can be forced to accept Yahweh. Only those who choose to know him are welcomed into the family of God. He wants no forced worship. The teaching would be open only to those who chose to attend. The Shalomshamars would be here to protect the people of Ur from those who would destroy the good. The Proclaimers would be here to teach about the one who is Good."

"Forgive me, Teacher Achva, for mistrusting your motive. If your leaders will send such help it will be gladly accepted. In the meantime I will set builders to reinforcing the walls of our city, and I will arm our police force. Please let me express gratitude for your suggestion." Having thus agreed, the men returned to the festivities of the evening.

* * * * *

In those days the coastline of the sea came very close to the outskirts of the city of Ur. Just a few miles above the city the smaller Hiddekel River joined the Euphrates; and after the two merged, they formed a mighty protective wall on the eastern side of the city before rushing into the sea.

A gently flowing river called Gihon branched off from the Euphrates before it joined the Hiddekel, flowed through the city and continued on a meandering course through the lands southwest and beyond.

The two travelers waited with their donkeys and packs for the boat, as it made ready to leave its port above the confluence in its return up the River Euphrates. They each had a donkey which they had ridden and one apiece to carry their packs. They were dressed in coarse garments and could easily have been traveling merchants.

Achva, now that he really was a teacher, no longer chose to present himself as one. He called himself 'Ira'. Enoch became 'Itai'.

The two men kept to themselves, avoiding the rough crowd on the boat and talking as little as possible. Achva didn't like the looks of the shifty eyed youngster assigned to tend the animals, so the men stayed just outside the animal keep where they could maintain watch.

Travel upstream was very slow and the boat master predicted that, including stops at various ports, the trip from Ur to Enoch would take about six weeks.

Achva reminded Enoch that they were expected to be in Mivtzar by the Harvest Festival. "That is about 12 weeks from now. If the boat trip to Cain's city takes five or six weeks, that should be the slowest part of our trip. There are many swift boats traveling from Enoch to Eliakim, and two men can quickly traverse the rest of Going Home by donkey. It will be close but I believe that we can make it."

When they had been two weeks on the boat there was a three-day layover at a port on the western bank. The two men decided to spend the time resting in the hills where both they and their animals could stretch their legs. They made arrangements with the captain, fetched their animals and packs and gladly left the boat. Along the river were huge trees. Most had been growing there since the beginning of time. They grew very densely, and beyond them were lush meadows that led up into gentle rolling hills. It was in these hills that the men made their camp.

It was good to be off the smelly boat, away from the cursing of the rough men, and away from the rocking of the water. The donkeys were delighted to munch on the grass and drink from cool streams. Yafa chased every bird in sight, barking with the sheer pleasure of not being tied up. It was a welcome retreat.

Both men had placed their bedding where they could watch the rising of the full moon. Their talk was somnolent as they watched the arrival of the first star of the night. Rays of pink sun streaks made glorious tracks across the western sky as the sun went down.

"Such an unworthy little boat," Enoch mused.

"So, that is how you would like to spend your life, my friend, making really fine boats to travel on the rivers?"

Enoch sat up abruptly. "Not the rivers, Achva, I mean 'Ira'. I want to build great ships that can float on the open seas. Can you imagine being so far out on the water that you couldn't even spot the shore? It would be glorious to view the sea from that aspect. Travel from one coast to another would be much, much faster than by land. Even that rickety old tug we are on goes faster than a man can walk. At least most of the time."

Achva looked doubtful. "I don't know, er, 'Itai', I think that I prefer having both feet well placed on the solid ground. I went out on fishing boats a few times on the sea of Amir and it was frequently difficult to spy the coastline. I didn't like that feeling much."

Both men laughed at their differences and snuggled down in their bedding to enjoy a night of peaceful rest.

The boat was to continue on its journey upstream at break of dawn the fourth day. The men left their camping spot about noon of the third day. Just as they reached the base of the hills and started across the meadows they spotted smoke rising above the giant trees.

"What is that smoke coming from I wonder?" Enoch thought aloud.

The men tied their donkeys and Yafa to the trees at the western edge of the forest and trod noiselessly to where they could view the dock and the boat tied there.

They saw only charred destruction. The boat was burned. All of the little huts that formed the village along the river had been burned.

The area appeared completely devoid of living activity. The men approached cautiously.

There were numerous dead bodies lying around. Enoch and Achva covered their noses with scarves to avoid the stench. The bodies were not intact. Heads were severed, arms were gone and many bodies were disemboweled. All were burned. The carnage in the burned huts was the same. There were no women or children in sight.

"Did you hear that?" Achva asked quietly.

"I think that I may have heard a groan," Enoch replied. "Let's look under that pier. It doesn't appear to have been totally burned."

The men made their way carefully to the pier and pulled away some burned and fallen timbers. There in a very small boat, mostly submerged in the water, lay a badly wounded man.

While Achva ran to fetch a fairly intact tarp, Enoch began gently talking to the semi-conscious man.

"We are friends and we are going to help you. Don't try to move. We are going to lift you onto this tarp…easy now Acc…'Ira'. Now, together … up you go. … Easy. Easy. He has lost consciousness."

"Is he alive? Is he breathing?"

"I can't tell. Don't stop. Let's get him to the donkeys. There may still be robbers in this area and I have medicine in my saddle bags."

Enoch suddenly caught his breath. "He is alive. He is trying to talk. … Don't move friend. Don't move. We will be as careful as possible. We must find a safe place to shelter you. Just be brave. Hang on. … Oh dearest Yahweh, please help us. Help this poor man to live. Give us strength!"

"Amen and amen," whispered Achva.

"Here 'Ira' let's use this branch to carry him on. Grab that straw from the horse pen over there."

Achva ran to a nearby deserted horse pen and pulled out a bundle of straw. There was a horse blanket lying abandoned in the pen. He grabbed that also. He ran back to where Enoch was attending the man. Together they placed the straw on the branches of the fallen limb, laid the blanket over it and then the man on the tarp on top of that. They worked together to pull the limb to safety.

It seemed to take forever to reach where they had left the donkeys.

"Next time we do this let's leave more clues to help us reach where we left our animals," Enoch breathed heavily after several false turns through the woods.

"Agreed," gasped Achva.

Then suddenly Yafa barked and they headed for the sound.

"Good dog. Good Yafa. Hush now. We're here and we don't want to be found."

The pup immediately hushed and rolled over in submission, tail wagging furiously.

Achva was surprised to find that Enoch had an entire supply of medicinal herbs in his bags.

"Are you also a doctor, 'Itai'?"

"No, but my mother lived much of her childhood in the 'Village of Peace and Hope' which was originally founded by Aluma. All of the girls there were taught the healing herbs and, because I was interested my mother passed the teaching on to me."

Enoch continued, "Bring me water from where it tumbles over the rocks in the spring. It will be the purest there. We must wash his wounds."

Both men carefully tended the injured man. When they turned him over, they found a deep slash in his back, made by something very sharp such as a large knife or sword. Enoch cleaned out the wound. He then poured an ointment in it and with many tiny stitches sewed it closed. Achva watched in amazement.

When they had done all that they could to repair his injuries, they covered him carefully with clean blankets, tied the tarp as a shelter over him, and only then took time to meet their own needs.

As they drank their tea and ate their meager supper, Achva remarked soberly, "We would be dead too had we not left the boat."

"Praise Yahweh for your need for firm ground, my friend. I do believe that our travels on the river are ended for a time. Let us take turns standing watch tonight, and tomorrow we must make an overland map. Study your heavens carefully tonight, for our prospects of getting to Mivtzar depend on your knowledge of direction."

For seven days the men drew maps. Enoch calculated distances from Achva's memory of his trip down the river. At the end of the week they felt that they had a fair knowledge of how to get back to the home of Rhoda where they hoped to find shelter, supplies, and the rest of the donkeys.

On the fourth day the injured man opened his eyes. Each day the two friends had changed his soiled cloths, spooned him broth and water, and treated his wounds.

His voice sounded harsh and strangled from the smoke that he had inhaled. "Are they gone?" he rasped fearfully.

"They are gone. We have been taking care of you and you are safe with us. There is no one left there but you, and I am certain that they had no idea that you were left alive. You may call me 'Itai' and my friend 'Ira'. Those are not our real names, but that is how you will know us for now. We will leave this place in the morning. If you are well enough, you may talk more then. Sleep now. Save your strength. We have a long journey."

During the evening the men constructed a litter from poles, and the following morning they attached it to the back of the donkey. They placed the now fully coherent, but still weak, man on the litter. As they did so he reached out and took their hands.

Tears filled his eyes. "My name is Tam. I praise you for your goodness."

"Praise Yahweh, not us, but we do accept your thanks. We too are grateful to be alive. When going home becomes too rough, call to us and we will stop."

Yafa carefully watched the entire procedure. She then trotted over and licked Tam's face, climbed up on the litter next to him, lay down at his waist, sighed, and looked up at Enoch and Achva as if to say, "Why aren't we moving. We are ready now."

Laughing, the little group started on its way.

For many miles they traveled along the back side of the trees, following the route of the river. Several more times they smelled smoke, but stayed carefully along their chosen route.

Gradually Tam regained his strength and was able to ride on the donkey for short periods of time. The story that he shared was amazing to Enoch and Achva.

He told what he remembered of the attack on the port. Apparently it happened the morning after the two men had left the boat for their trek to the hills. Tam said that ten or twelve heavily armed men came upon the port from across the river. They attacked early in the morning while everyone was still asleep.

As if he knew that his rescuers would find his story difficult to believe, Tam dropped his eyes as he talked. "I have never seen men like these before. They did not look like mortal men. Each man was over eight feet tall. They were huge and their skin was nearly colorless. Their eyes looked a strange reddish color in the morning sun and they had stringy yellow-white hair growing long down their backs. They were brutal beyond belief. They killed and maimed with wild abandon. They tied the women and children together and took them with them.

"I was asleep in my fishing boat when I heard the screams and smelled the smoke. I had planned to fish as soon as the sun came up. I jumped in the water and hid in the reeds. When they spotted me, a man ran out and slashed my back with his sword. I held my breath and went under the water. I stayed there until I could no longer hold my breath. When I came up everyone was gone. I managed to return to what was left of my boat. The next thing I knew, I was being tended by you."

Tam, exhausted from his recalling, slept soundly. As they prepared for the night, Achva turned to face Enoch. "Was it the fever talking? Did the fear and the fever imagine such men? Could it be possible?"

Enoch studied the map that lay folded in his hand.

"Ur once told me a strange tale. It was the final thing that helped him decide to leave Cain's city. There was a large festival honoring all of the 'gods' of the city. There were many people sacrificed, and bonfires lit at all the shrines. It is said that one 'goddess' made a huge shrine and lay upon the ground before it inviting the 'god of her world' to place a child within her womb. The tale is told that she became pregnant and nine months later brought forth a male child that was so large it split her asunder being born. She died, but the child lived and thrived. He grew into a man such as Tam described. He was named 'Nephil'.

"Ur said that he never saw the child, nor the man that he was reputed to have become. He only knew that he had no desire to remain in such a wicked city."

After nearly three more weeks of travel they spotted an encampment of several people. There were tents pitched and some type of covered conveyance behind the larger tent. Two burly looking men stood nearby. Two women were milling about and a very fat man was reclining by a tree outside of the tent.

"Hello there," called Enoch. "May we approach? We come as friends."

The women looked up and turned anxiously to the reclining man. With some effort he stood up. It was obvious that he had been drinking much wine. He motioned for them to draw near.

Greetings were exchanged and the man introduced the older woman, (not much older than the young one, but with a hard face) as 'my woman'.

The younger one was introduced as his daughter. She was barely more than a girl. Enoch thought that she had the saddest eyes that he had ever seen. There was more though, in those dark eyes, was it determination? Not boldness but perhaps a touch of bravery. Aware of his scrutiny, the girl whom the father called Raisa, dropped her eyes. Enoch quickly averted his.

The young women were cooking a mess of vegetables in a large pot over an open fire. There were several rabbits roasting on a spit. Rabbit, although not hares, was one of the few meats, along with chicken and fish that the God-fearers would eat. The three men looked at the fare hopefully.

The host, called Oz, offered to share his meal if the men had money with which to pay, and the three travelers gladly accepted.

"Where are you headed sir?" inquired Achva as the girl served his food.

"To Enoch, that wonderful city of our great Leader, Cain," the man beamed.

Enoch choked slightly on his meat. "Are you moving there?"

"No, not a move, I own a little farm about twelve days journey from here. I am simply taking some merchandise to the city. It belongs there."

Everyone followed the direction of the man's eyes. They noticed that a large cage was tied just behind the tent. The cage, which evidently contained some type of wild animal, for growling noises could be heard coming from within, was covered with thin gauzy covers. Air could enter, but it was not possible to view what was in the cage. The cage was on wheels and obviously had been pulled by the young horses standing nearby.

The man continued, "The boat to Enoch will dock at the river landing tomorrow, where it will leave on the day after. We will continue to Enoch by river travel."

Achva started to speak, but Enoch nudged him. He quickly closed his mouth.

After the meal was over, the girl took a large kettle to the nearby stream to fill with water.

"I must also fetch water for the donkeys. May I go with you?" Enoch asked kindly. "'Ira' will stay with our friend who was hurt in a hunting accident." Enoch looked meaningfully at the two men who each gave a slight nod of his head.

Raisa nodded. "You may join me, sir. The stream flows best in this direction."

After drawing their water the couple sat on the large rocks by the banks of the stream listening to the birds sing their joyful songs.

Enoch spoke in a very quiet voice, "Please do not think me bold or forward. I mean you no harm, but I believe that there is something amiss in your camp. You appear to be carrying a terrible burden upon your heart. My companion and I are God-fearers. We honor and worship the true and only God, Yahweh. Is there a way that we can help you?"

The girl searched his face for a long time. Her eyes filled with tears, which she allowed to fall, unheeded down her pale cheeks.

"I have never had a man to speak with such kindness to me. You are correct in your assessment. There is much evil in our camp. My father --- and he is not really that, but he is the man who married my mother when I was very small and he has raised me. Or at least he has always lived at our house and allowed us to wait on him hand and foot. My mother died, from his many beatings, about two years ago. Then he found this woman in the city of Enoch and brought her home. I do not believe that they were ever married. Such covenants are not required in the city of our noble leader, Cain."

Her last words were spoken with bitterness.

"What is the animal in the cage and why is it being taken to the city?"

"That *animal* is my sister. Nearly two years ago my 'father' sold her to one of the shrines as a prostitute. He received enough money to purchase his little farm. Not that he works it. He has a cruel slave master and several slaves to do that. He sits and drinks his wine, eats his food, takes his 'woman' into his bed and yells at us all. During her time as shrine prostitute, my sister had a child and the infant was sacrificed to the gods of the city. Yakira lost her mind when the baby was killed. She quit eating and began cutting on herself. She ran away and when the guards found her they sent her home to us. A few months ago my father was notified that if he wishes to keep his farm he must send a replacement virgin for shrine prostitute. I am to be that replacement. Yakira is to be placed on Oren Rock to die."

As she spoke the final sentences the tears dried upon Raisa's cheeks. Her voice became flat and emotionless and her eyes lost all luster.

"Raisa, this terrible thing must not be allowed to happen. My companions and I are going to a city far, far away from here. It is called Mivtzar and it is a city where the most high God is honored and men treat men with respect and goodness. The human father of us all, Adam, lives there and directs his people with love and tenderness. Will you travel with us? The trip will be long and arduous, but I know that Yahweh will be with us. You and your sister will find safety and shelter there. No man, or woman, will ever be allowed to harm you in that city."

"How can this thing be?" she responded. "You see his two men servants. They are strong and as cruel as my 'father' and love to do his evil bidding. They will kill us at his slightest word if we try to escape."

"I have a plan. Please trust me. Follow my instructions and move when I tell you to move. Let us return to camp now."

Raisa walked thoughtfully beside Enoch for several yards; suddenly she stopped and looked determinedly into his face.

"I will do whatever you demand of me. I will do anything to escape that place and will cooperate as long as my sister is with me. She is terrified of anyone else. If I tell her not to cry out she will be silent."

As if in afterthought she added, "I take her every night to the creek to bathe."

"Excellent. Tonight when your 'father' and the men are beyond observing you, take her and all of your things to the creek. Wait for us there."

"Are you going to kill them?"

"No. Just make them very, very sick. For a while they will probably wish that they could die, but their death lies in the hands of Yahweh, not mine."

When the pair returned to camp with their heavy loads of water, the man and 'his woman' were in the tent making loud noises. Achva looked up at Enoch and raised his eyebrow. Tam was asleep on a pallet, Yafa snuggled nearby. The two male servants were seated near the cage playing some type of game with dice and pegs.

Keeping his voice very low Enoch said, "Raisa, please go to your tent and pack all of your things without being obvious. 'Ira' and I are going to gather firewood for the camp fire tonight."

'Ira' looked with surprise into the face of his friend and promptly joined 'Itai' in his search for fallen wood.

During their trek in the woods, Enoch shared Raisa's story and told of his plan to aid in their escape. Achva quickly agreed.

"I have a strong potion in my medicinal supplies which will cause even the biggest man to sleep for a least a night and a day. We must get the man and his servants very drunk tonight and at the end of their drinking I will pour my potion into each of their drinks. When they are snoring we will make our escape."

"What about the woman?"

"She is also of an evil disposition. Raisa says that she has attempted to teach her many evil things and believes that it is a great honor to serve in the temple shrine. She served there herself for several years and joyfully cast babies into the fire. We will drug her and leave her with her lover."

By the time the man and woman came out of their tent to eat the small evening meal, Enoch and Achva had a roistering fire going.

The man roared his approval of the immense blaze and thirstily accepted the heavy wine that Enoch offered him. Unknown to Oz the wine that Enoch and Achva were drinking was greatly weakened with water. After Oz was deep into his cups, Achva strolled over to the men guarding Yakira. They hesitated only briefly before accepting Achva's offer of drink.

The plan worked even better than the men had dared hope. Shortly after drinking the drugged wine the men and the woman were snoring loudly.

Enoch and Achva put Tam to work cutting the top off the bamboo cage, creating instead a low wagon with bars that would hold packs and people. They both busied themselves with throwing every thing into the fire that they would not be carrying. When the tents were taken down and carefully folded they placed them, along with all of the food stocks in the wagon. The horses were taken to the meadow and released to freedom. The men were stripped naked and the woman left with only a brief covering. When they woke they would have little to aid them in their travels.

The two pack donkeys were harnessed to the wagon and Enoch fetched Raisa and Yakira. They were placed on pallets at the head of the wagon and the gauzy material was secured to protect them from the elements. Next was placed the foodstuffs and gear, leaving a narrow aisle for passage. At the very end of the wagon was a narrow ledge for Tam to lie on as he continued to convalesce. Yafa looked hopefully into Achva's face to see if she too was allowed to ride. Achva laughed, hugged the little dog close, and placed her on a bed of hay.

The two men rode ahead of the donkeys, each with a lead rope in their hands. The donkeys, which had never pulled in tandem before, were mostly cooperative and eventually caught on to their job.

Leaving their route by the river the men began following the northeasterly direction of their maps, praying to Yahweh that they would find the home of Rhoda.

They had calculated that it would take about two weeks to find where Achva, known at that time as 'Uri', had left the other donkeys in care of Rhoda and her family. They traveled through forests, over hills, across creeks, past meadows thick with grazing deer, and finally into an orchard with trees heavy with fruit. It had been three weeks since their great bonfire.

"Does any of this look familiar?" Enoch asked softly so as to not frighten the others.

"I traveled here by the road from the river, and back the same way. I really saw very little of the surrounding land. According to our calculations the farm should be in this area, but I could have made a mistake. I just don't know. It all seems rather familiar. I remember that there was an apple orchard, but these are pear trees."

"Let's make camp tonight," Enoch suggested, "and look for a dwelling in the morning."

Even before opening his eyes the next morning, Enoch knew that someone was standing over him. Very cautiously, he carefully opened his eyes to reveal a wild looking old man and two ragged children standing over him wielding clubs and a rusty sickle.

"Hello," he said cheerfully. "Good morning. You are up early. It is a beautiful morning. …Achva where in heaven's name are you… Would you folks object to my sitting up a little bit? I just want to be friendly. Here I go now. I'm sitting up. Uh…boy please don't swing that thing. It could hurt someone."

The young boy took a step closer holding the sickle in the air with a menacing attitude.

About that time Achva emerged from a stand of trees where he had evidently been attending to his morning needs. Yafa was with him and began barking furiously. The three strangers turned to look in that direction. Enoch jumped up and grabbed the sickle from the boy's hand and the girl began immediately striking wildly with her club. The old man looked very confused and made no move to do anything, just held his hand to his mouth and made sobbing noises.

Achva began to shout, "Children, children stop this ruckus! It is I, 'Uri', come to fetch my donkeys. Stop now. Behave yourselves. Where is Rhoda?"

Everyone was suddenly silent. Raisa held Yakira close to her at the front of the wagon. Both women looked at the scene with some amazement. Tam had moved in a protective manner towards the women to offer his services if they were needed.

The girl suddenly stepped forward. "Is it really you, 'Uri'? We thought that you were robbers. Marnin, Marnin, it is 'Uri', come to fetch his donkeys."

"I can hear you Bina, and I'm not blind like Zane here. Put down your club, Zane. I knew all along that there was no danger."

Achva turned to Tam and the women. "Here I am known as 'Uri'. Someday I will explain it all. Come now let's go to the house."

"No!" warned the boy. "You must not come to the house. Mean men are watching our house. It is not safe. Bina you stay here and keep Zane here too. I will fetch mother and the children. Don't make a fire and please be very quiet. I will return as soon as I can. The sun is barely beginning to come up. Perhaps the men are still asleep."

Enoch, Achva and Tam carefully hid the women, wagon and animals in the tall, thick brush. Giving Tam a sword and leaving him with the women, the other two went back to the area where they had awakened to find the children.

The sun was well into the sky when the sound of singing voices drew near. Two women and three small children were leading ten donkeys that had large wicker baskets tied on their sides.

The younger woman called out clearly, "Here, Chofit, this is a good place to start picking pears. These look good and ripe. Be careful not to bruise them for they will bring a good price in the market."

Leaving the servant and the children to pick pears, the woman quickly looked all around her and then headed in the direction where the men were hiding.

"Rhoda," whispered Achva, "It is 'Uri', with friends; we are over here."

"Oh 'Uri', how we have been hoping that you would return. There are men from Cain's city at our house. They say that our home belongs to them now. Nedav came here often to visit and he got in some kind of trouble in Enoch. He has been falsely accused of some terrible deed and is in the dungeon there. So are several of the servants of my uncle. Now the cruel men have come here to take away all that I have.

"They are waiting for me to harvest the fruit and then they will take us all to the city. They say that they will allow me to sell the harvest and redeem Nedav, but I know that they are lying. They want us to do the work and when the harvest is complete they will steal it and sell us as slaves. Oh, 'Uri', what are we to do?"

At this point she fell weeping into Achva's arms and he held her awkwardly in an effort to comfort. "How many men are guarding your house, Rhoda?"

She snuffed her tears, "Six. I fixed them an especially nice breakfast hoping that they would not follow us to the orchard. Marnin is hiding in the trees by the path to warn us if they should come."

Achva looked at Enoch. "Well, 'Itai', have you any more strong potion?"

Enoch nodded. "I believe that what I have will make a nice luncheon brew for them. 'Uri', get Tam and the other women. We must all work quickly filling 14 of the baskets with fruit. Leave six of them empty, for they will need to contain something else. It appears that it is time to take our fruit to market. Hurry now. Let's get to work."

A few hours later Enoch shared his plan with Rhoda. She and the servant, Chofit, and the oldest girl, Bina, were to return to the house and prepare lunch for the guards. Enoch had a powder that would be mixed with their food and when they began to show the effects from that, the drugged wine would be given to them. Enoch made Rhoda repeat all that he had told her then assured her that he and the others would be there shortly to tie the men up with ropes.

"Be calm, Rhoda. Tell the others to show no fear. This is your only chance. Be steady as a rock. The men must suspect nothing."

Nodding bravely, the three left for the house in order to feed the men.

Once again the plan was successful and the men were stripped of clothing and weapons, and tied firmly to trees deep in the forest. Another wagon was found and all of the household utensils were loaded into that, covers placed over the load, and hay piled on top of that. Baskets of chickens and ducks hung from each side, and a flock of goats were tied to follow behind.

When Rhoda, her five children, servant woman Chofit and Zane were gathered into the front yard, next to all their worldly goods, Enoch explained what he must do. Rhoda sadly nodded in agreement.

Tam was given careful instructions for taking Rhoda, her household minus Marnin, and Raisa and Yakira to Eliakim. They were to wait there until the full moon of the following month, and if Enoch and Achva were not there by then, Tam was to take his little group on to Mivtzar. Enoch and Achva had given him a message to take to Adam if they were unable to complete Going Home. Indeed, Achva had encouraged Enoch to go with the group. He feared that he was going in direct violation of Guryon's instructions to keep the chosen lineage safe.

Enoch would hear no part of leaving Achva. "If I am indeed the chosen one of Seth's line, then it is up to Yahweh to keep me safe. If I am killed, it must be His will. I am not going to leave you to do this task alone."

Goodbyes were said and Tam took his group into the hills that led to a northern port along the Euphrates River, but a safe distance from the port of Cain's city.

When the group was well out of vision, Enoch, Achva and Marnin set fire to the house, barn and all outbuildings. Enoch had explained that nothing must be left for the use of evil men. The boy had bravely helped light the fires.

All of the baskets were filled. Three with weapons, one with clothing and provisions, one with Achva and one with Marnin. The remaining fourteen were heaped with pears covered by straw. Enoch set off towards Cain's city with his strange procession. They traveled the remainder of the afternoon and night, arriving at the ferry landing well before sunrise.

The ferryman came out to see what the commotion was all about and regarded the fruit with interest. "Quite a harvest you have there. Should bring a good price in the city. Would you be willing to give me a basket in exchange for your fare over the river?"

Enoch agreed, the deal was settled and the donkeys passed over the water in safety, long before the first ferry trip was scheduled to be made. Enoch was grateful for the cover of darkness.

By sunrise Enoch had set up his stand at the outer edge of the sellers market. The booths were very near where the dreaded dungeon sat in all of its ugliness and grime. The dungeon had been placed close to a branch of the river so that refuse and debris could make its way into the fetid water. At the end of the day, sellers would throw their spoiled produce into the water and at night many kinds of creatures came to feast on the mess.

Enoch tied six of the donkeys to logs provided for such and began selling the fruit from the baskets. The fruit sold quickly for it was of fine quality. At noontime Enoch filled a container full of fruit, removed a skin of wine from the pack, and walked over to where the outer guards were standing. He informed them that he had fruit and drink to give to the prisoners being held there from the house of Maimon.

The guards began calling to the others along the guard walk. "Come and see what nice gifts our friend Maimon has sent to his servants!" they jeered. The other guards gathered around grabbing the fruit and making rude jests. "Go away merchant, before we put *you* in the dungeon! This food will be eaten by better men than the servants of Maimon."

Enoch walked off as each of the guards began feasting on the fruit; juice spilling down their faces as they passed the skin of wine back and forth. Shortly thereafter the other merchants let down their awnings and lay on their mats for their afternoon nap. When all was quiet Enoch struck the sides of two of the baskets. Achva and Marnin climbed quickly out. Marnin was still a boy, gangly but strong from years of hard work since the death of his father. Enoch warned him to do exactly as he was told. The boy, frightened but determined, agreed.

The men pulled all of the donkeys close to the gate of the dungeon. They left Marnin in charge of the donkeys and told him to act as if he were unloading foodstuffs for the prisoners. When their friends were found they would be sent to Marnin and he was to quickly hide them in the empty baskets. Enoch and Achva found the guards just as they had hoped: fallen over in a deep stupor. They took the keys, placed the guards in a cell and after stripping them of their clothing, and placing their own merchant garments on them, locked the door. They then dressed in the clothing of the guards, and carried their weapons from cell to cell looking for Nedav. The lower dungeons were at water level and were dank and horribly dark. Huge rats ran across the floor as the men entered.

'Uri' called for his friend, "Nedav, are you in here? Can you hear me? It is 'Uri'."

Carrying lighted torches they continued to look from cell to cell with no success. There were no guards on the lower levels and it was soon easy to understand the lack of need for such. Enoch and Achva were shocked to see that many cells contained dead bodies along with living ones. Those who were alive looked out at them with eyes long dead.

As he was turning to leave the lowest level of the prison, 'Uri' heard someone call his name. He hurried over to the sound. It was the servant, Zahid. "Zahid, I have found you. Where are the others? Where is Nedav?"

"He is in the cell directly above us. There are several others of the household with him. I am here with six more of our servants. We are all to be killed in three days."

"Well, my friend, I guess that we had better hurry then if we are to escape that appointment. Here, this key seems to be working. This is my friend whom, for now we call 'Itai'. Follow 'Itai' to the donkeys and change your clothing there. I will rescue the others."

It took Nedav several precious minutes to realize that the man in guard's clothing was truly his friend, 'Uri'.

"Come, Nedav, hasten, tell the others that I am to be trusted. We have no time to waste. The afternoon nap will soon be over and the merchants will awaken. The guards may start coming around. Come. Please help me help you."

Shaking himself, Nedav quickly embraced his friend and then motioned for the others to follow him. When they reached outside those gone before had changed from their prison clothing and were well hidden in the empty baskets. Nedav and Achva quickly changed clothes and joined them.

"Can we burn this place down too?" pleaded the young Marnin, looking at the horrible prison as he climbed into the last empty basket.

Enoch covered him with blankets and straw. "I wish that we could, son, but I don't think we had better do that. We released all of those poor wretched creatures that we had time for. Come now let us get away from here."

Enoch hurried his team back to the ferry where the ferryman gratefully and with much surprise accepted a generous payment for the trip to the western side.

"Your fruit sold well?"

"Yes, I was able to fill the baskets with much needed supplies for our farm."

"Do you go home to pick more?"

"Apples next time." said Enoch. "Our next trip will be to sell apples. If anyone asks we will be coming through next week with a load of apples."

"Bring me the first picking, will you?"

"Count on it, friend. Good bye."

Enoch led his pack animals the rest of the day and all night before stopping at woods well north of the city. The men climbed stiffly out of their baskets, stretching sore limbs as they did so.

"Wait here in these woods until we return," instructed Achva.

"'Itai', your face was seen by the guards and merchants. It is too dangerous for you to return to the city. Marnin and I must go for the uncle. If they are not being held prisoners in their home, we have a good chance of getting the family out without rousing suspicion."

Enoch settled his group safely in the woods, and then asked Yahweh's protection on 'Uri' and Marnin as they went on their mission.

The evening shadows were rapidly falling as they set out to find Maimon's house. The man and boy found a small craft tied outside a fishing hut. Borrowing it, they made fast time traveling down the stream of the river. Nightfall was once again fast approaching as they neared the city.

'Uri' began explaining his plan to Marnin. "I knew a man in the City of Ur who told me about the canals, which he planned and helped build throughout Cain's city. He told me that the main canal leading from the river into the city has a large gate that allows water to enter a basin. This basin acts as a holding area so that when more water is needed for the city canals, the gate is opened from the basin into the main canal. That way the supply of water does not overwhelm the banks of the canals. He told me that there is a small, mostly deserted, canal further north of the gate that was used for many years before the gates were built. The canal there is shallow and overgrown, so only small craft can enter. That is what we are looking for. Keep a sharp look out. It will be on the eastern side of the river and will be difficult to spot."

They paddled very close to the eastern bank, grateful that there was no other river traffic that night. The entrance to the small canal was all but obscured by vines and leaves, and could have been completely missed by the travelers but for the cooperation of a sleek beaver.

The animal, spying the boat, quickly jumped from the bank where he was working on his own engineering project, into the water and swam toward the east. Achva and Marnin pushed away sticks and mud with their oars, and slowly made their way into a narrow canal, not much more than a ditch, that flowed north and then turned southeast into the city. There was an old, untended sluice gate at the spot where the little ditch turned south to join a larger canal. With only minimal effort they were able to remove this gate in order to enter the larger canal. They carefully replaced the gate after the little craft was through and Achva tied a white cloth to the top of it for easy visualization. The new canal eventually adjoined the large estate belonging to Maimon. There seemed to be no guards around.

The evening shadows finally closed in around them, leaving the new moon to light their way with a tiny sliver of waxing crescent and even that was frequently covered by clouds. With what they hoped was great stealth, they slipped silently up the terraced gardens leading to the main house.

'Uri' could see Maimon seated at his large work desk. His head was down on his arms. His entire body showed complete despair.

"Maimon," called 'Uri' softly. "It is I, 'Uri', friend of Nedav; are you safe?"

Maimon, startled, looked up and hastened over to the shadows of the door where 'Uri' crouched.

"Quickly, come into the upper room." He grabbed 'Uri' by the sleeve of his tunic and pulled him up the stairs. Marnin followed.

Taking the two into an inner room, he locked the door and only then allowed himself to look at them. "I can't believe that you are here. Horrible things have happened to us. Many lies have been told about us. Nedav and my servants, including my dear Zahid, are being held in the dungeon and are to be killed tomorrow morning. I must pay all that I have in gold and make a pledge for yearly taxes or I will lose this house. Poor, stupid Peri is to be given to the Sun god on the Festival of Days. She is terrified. As are we all." He placed his head in his hands and began to weep.

"There is no time for weeping, my friend. All of the prisoners from this house are rescued and in a safe place. You must gather the rest of your household with the least amount of noise. Take only what you truly need. We must travel quickly. Have you boats? I think our chance of escape is best by water."

"There are twenty-two humans and six tame animals in this household. I have six boats that will hold eight people each. They require four rowers each. I have mostly women and very young or old men in the house."

"They will have to manage. Is your house being watched?"

"I think not. I'm sure that the city fathers are convinced that we are too weak to resist."

"Good. Gather your household. Tell them to pack quickly and lightly. Their things will mean nothing to them if they are dead. In two hours we will meet you at your dock. In the meantime Marnin and I have work to do. I need your strongest men to help us load your few livestock onto your barge."

Rejecting the large excursion barge that would not fit between the banks of the narrow escape route, 'Uri' helped the men remove a long narrow door from the barn. They lashed it round about with reeds and leather straps to form a sort of wall around the edges of the narrow barge.

"I wish that I had some of 'Itai's potion for these animals," muttered Achva to himself.

"We will lash them well to the deck, sir," assured the young men who were leading the animals onto the makeshift transportation.

Achva stationed two huge horses on either side of the canal and tied long leads from them to the front of the barge. Behind this he securely lashed the six small boats, one after the other. He placed the small craft that he and Marnin had used at the very back of the six. When the animals were safely loaded on the barge, and the household members in the boats, Achva took the lead walking along the bank. The men guided the horses and by some miracle the whole contraption moved. Everyone had been issued a weapon of some kind. Achva looked at the frail women and men and prayed that they would never have to use those weapons. He was gratified that there had been no whimpering or crying. No one clung to that which could not be brought along. Remembering his fondness for Yafa he let all of the household animals travel with their owners. The people seemed comforted by that.

Marnin, who had previously been given his instructions, was to join them where the canal narrowed, one part turning back into the city and another branching off in a northerly direction. There was a bridge there and they would wait under it until he came. No one asked what the boy's final assignment had been.

About an hour later a huge red glow lit up the night sky, and shortly thereafter Marnin joined the line of boats. Achva praised Marnin for a job well done. "That will keep the city's attention for a while, I hope. Now we must be very quiet when we pass close to the Watergates for there are men housed there who open and close the gates. They may be active tonight if more water is needed for the fire."

Indeed the strange train of watercraft had barely made it through the old sluice gate, and saw it closed behind them, when they heard the cranking of pulleys at the second Watergate.

"Keep the boats moving," whispered Achva. "Hurry now, I can see their torches!"

The men of the Watergates had eyes that night only for the city. It seemed as if the entire eastern edge of Cain's city was burning down.

"The fields must have caught," muttered Maimon.

"So be it. It is the will of Yahweh. Careful now. We draw near the river. We must cross over to the western shore and that will be dangerous."

"Men!" he called. "Swim the horses over to the far side. We will tie them there and come back for the rest of the animals. It will be impossible to hold the raft against the current. Each man or strong boy is to help get the small boats across and then come back to help the other animals swim across."

The job was nearly an impossible one. Two cows were lost and went bawling down the river in the rapid current. Achva was relieved to see one crash against the shore and scramble up the bank apparently unharmed. He could not tell the fate of the second. The goats, sheep, several cows, crates of ducks, geese and other small livestock were landed safely on the western shore.

Achva could not explain even to himself why he struggled so hard to rescue these animals; he only knew that he wanted to leave nothing behind in the evil city.

The barge had been left at the mouth of the ditch where they had found safe passage. "Materials for your dam, Friend Beaver. May Yahweh bless you for your assistance. Farewell." Having blessed the beaver, Achva the last one away from the eastern shore, turned his back to the red sky.

He allowed his group the briefest of rest before heading them on to the road where they had left Enoch.

The current was too swift for the unseasoned group to paddle against, so when they reached the dock where Achva and Marnin had borrowed the little boat they left the others also, tying them all together.

Marnin chuckled to think of the wonderment of the fisherman when he came to fish and found that his one boat had become seven!

There was great rejoicing when Achva and his group were reunited with Enoch and his group. Everyone clapped and cheered when the two old friends, master and servant, Maimon and Zahid joyfully fell into each others arms and gave glory to Yahweh for their safety.

Enoch pulled Achva aside. Grinning he indicated by his eyes a young man about the age of Marnin who was standing quietly aside petting a donkey. "That fellow over there just kind of got picked up along the way."

"What do you mean?"

Enoch's grin spread. "It seems that when he came running out of the prison with others that we had released, Marnin grabbed him, pushed him into a basket and told him to keep quiet. The poor fellow didn't utter a sound until we made camp and discovered that he wasn't part of Maimon's household. He has no family and has asked if he can remain with us. His name is Sagi and he seems an innocent sort. He had been put in prison for stealing a loaf of bread from a delivery wagon. He said that he was hungry and hadn't eaten for days."

"I can believe that; he is skinny enough. *'Enoch':* such a wonderful city that Cain has named for his first-born." Achva placed his hand on Enoch's shoulder and tightened his grip, " I appreciate that you give a totally different meaning to the name of Enoch, my dear friend. Yes, let Sagi travel with us. Guryon will take his measure. Now let us go on to Eliakim and get the rest of our travelers. What's one or two more, anyway!"

❋ ❋ ❋ ❋ ❋

Guryon trudged heavily up the slope where Adam awaited him in the arbor. Had it been four long months since the young Achva had been sent on his journey to find Enoch and bring him home?

Adam sat with his face toward the morning sun, the early shadows playing with the leaves behind his back.

"Good morning, Guryon," Adam spoke without turning.

"And a good morning to you, my Father. I wonder how early I would have to rise in order to be up before you."

"I don't seem to need much sleep these days. I keep wondering where they are. I wonder if I sent Achva to his death, or worse, into that evil city of Cain to forsake the call of Yahweh. Perhaps he has deserted his Faith. Many, many thoughts march through my mind."

"Four days until the Harvest Festival, Father. I firmly believe that Achva is trustworthy. If he does not come, it will be through no fault of his own."

Both men sat silent for a long time.

A sudden shout interrupted their reveries.

A young Shalomshamar came running up the slope from the eastern side yelling breathlessly.

"There is a group coming around the bend of the road outside the city gates. There is a score of soldiers from Eliakim and they are escorting Enoch and Achva and at least fifty other people. They have at least 30 donkeys and cows, chickens and geese and…."

Just then the group came into view and entered the gates through which lay the villages of Mivtzar. There was cheering, singing and much laughter. Women and children were dancing in the road and colored cloths used as banners were flying everywhere. Surely that was no voice but Achva's, young once again and calling, "We're home. Hey everyone! We're home."

Guryon, his face unreadable, turned with his best military manner to report to Adam: "Well, Sir. Achva seems to have returned. I am so very glad that I encouraged him to keep a low profile."

❋ ❋ ❋ ❋ ❋

Enoch sat tensely on the bench outside the meeting room. He could hear the voices of the Proclaimers as they prayed quietly in the next room. He knew that in an anteroom adjoining the flower garden there were also many women praying.

Because of the solemnity of the occasion, the men had come to a special, called prayer meeting; but the women's prayer room was always open to those who wished to spend time alone with the Father.

There was a door that opened into the garden and a gate that allowed passage to and fro without disturbing, or being observed by, the Proclaimers.

The beautifully carved wooden door to the inner room opened, and Jared appeared.

"The Council of the Elect will see you now, my son."

Enoch stepped just inside the room and stood for a moment, allowing his eyes to adjust to the dimness. The room had one high window along the end; it was about six feet long and two feet high and nearly touched the ceiling. No one could possibly observe what took place inside. There were many candles lit throughout the room, and on the wall opposite the window was a large replica of the seal of Adam. Enoch glanced at the drawing of the man, woman, tree, lamb and serpent, and remembered the ring which Adam had sent through Achva.

When he entered the room, Enoch felt the overwhelming force of the presence of God. He suddenly fell to his knees.

"Stand up Enoch, we are but men here," declared Adam.

The young man stood, but tears were running down his face. He looked at the six men in the room: Adam, Seth, Enosh, Cainan, Mahalalel, and Jared, his own father.

Seth spoke: "You are chosen, Enoch. Your seed will continue the godly line. The Shekinah Glory will manifest himself through your generations."

Enoch was offered a chair and, trembling, he sat down. "But why me?" I have six older brothers, and at least two of them are Proclaimers and have sought to follow Yahweh. I am but a shipbuilder with dreams of travel and glory. I am not a holy man."

Mahalalel spoke gently. "You, like each of us, are but a chosen vessel. It remains to be seen how God will mold and shape you for his Glory. But be advised, He will mold and shape you. Sometimes it is a painful process; always it is a process of change."

Enoch took a deep breath and squared his shoulders. He had felt a bit brash when Achva had approached him with the message from Adam. He had told himself that he had but to travel back here and explain to the Council of the Elect that he had other plans for his life. Here in this room all brashness disappeared. He bowed his head for a long moment. When he raised his head, his voice was barely above a whisper, "I submit to the judgment of the Council; and therefore, I pray that I am submitting to the Will of God.

"Kneel before God, my son," directed Adam.

As Enoch knelt, each man, beginning with his own father, Jared, and finally terminating with the Father of All, Adam, came forward with a small vial of oil. Placing a hand on the young man's head, each prayed for Enoch and anointed the bowed head with oil. With tears, oil and prayers Enoch, son of Jared, seventh in the line from Adam, was commissioned into the godly line of Seth.

Chapter Twelve

Raisa

The first rays of sunshine were snuffing out the brightness of the stars as the gibbous moon scurried off to another place in the heavens. The voice of the dove announced that a new day was dawning. Raisa stirred on her mattress of rushes. Stretching her slender limbs, and rubbing her hands over her face, she finally, reluctantly, commanded her eyes to open.

Yakira was sleeping peacefully on the mat next to hers, her breathing still slow and steady. Even after six months, Raisa found their peacefulness difficult to believe. They were safe! She glanced around their tidy home with approval as she smoothed the soft covers neatly over her bed.

The little house was made of wood, bricks and mortar; the floor was made of large smooth bricks. There was a space for sitting, where guests could be welcomed, with a tiny kitchen off the back; and then to the right of that room was the bedroom that she shared with her sister.

Her sister. That was Raisa's biggest joy. Yakira no longer cringed like a frightened animal. She laughed and sang, and sometimes put flowers around her neck and danced. Raisa smiled to herself. Yakira would never again be the person that she had been before her terrible experiences in the City of Enoch; she was now a six-year-old child in a woman's body, but at least she no longer screamed at shadows or howled at the moon.

Reflecting on this, Raisa threw her cloak over her shoulders and stepped out her back door which overlooked the western valley. She could not yet feel the sun's rays on her back, for the sky contained only the promise of the glory to come. She looked up into the heavens where the moon was continuing its descent into the west. She wondered about the bright red 'star' that shone so effulgently to the upper left of the moon. Why was it so bright? Why was its color different from the others? So many mysteries. So much to learn. But for now there was peace. And time.

Here in the vale of safety, which Aluma so many years ago had founded for the wounded, Yakira had found peace and healing. She was always willing to do her little household tasks, and then would go from house to house helping others, who had saved simple chores for her, that she might feel needed.

After dressing, Raisa tended to her needs in the community outbuilding. To the young woman, this was the most surprising part of the little village. The building housed two sections: one side contained a long stone bench; covered with a hard, white material which Raisa believed was called 'marble'. The bench had openings where a person could sit and relieve herself. Each opening was a private closet separated by a curtain. The room was meticulously clean and kept from unpleasant odors by fresh or dried flowers which sat on pretty tables, and bunches of herbs hanging from the wooden beams of the rafters.

The other section of the large room was reached by a set of stairs that accessed a balcony room about six feet higher than the closets. It contained a large sunken bath where the women could cleanse their bodies, swim, or just go to relax at the end of a hard day's work. Raisa knew that the water from the bath was released each night to flush out the large pit below the closets into a tube. This then flowed down the hill into a larger covered pit, where it was treated with lime, and processed back into the earth.

For the cool months, there were four large fire pits built into the stone walls. High windows allowed the sun and air to enter, but afforded privacy.

The water for the bath, and also for the nearby building which contained the men's bath, came from a storage tank on a platform further up the hill. Water from the mountain stream could be channeled into this as needed. The entire process fascinated Raisa.

She tended to her morning needs, and then hurried back to her little house for a simple breakfast.

During the past six months, she had gone daily for training in the tasks of homemaking. Growing up as she had, motherless, unloved by a violent, drunken substitute father, she had been poorly trained in the lessons needed to achieve a properly run home. The Village provided training for such young women, and Raisa worked hard to learn all that she needed to know.

Today would start a new aspect of her training. She was to report to the gardens in the valley below and be taught the skill of raising vegetables. The message had come to her a few days ago that on this day she would meet her teacher at an appointed place.

She was able to leave her sleeping sister with equanimity because she knew that others in the village would watch out for her. When Yakira awakened, she would find her breakfast already prepared.

So it was with a peaceful heart and adventurous spirit that Raisa hurried down the mountain path to the valley below. The air was crisp, even chill; but she knew that the sun would provide warmth to change the early spring day into a gentle one.

Stopping a moment to catch her breath, and to consult the crude papyrus map that had been sent to direct her steps, the girl looked across the fields, seeking the area where she was assigned.

She knew that soon the men with their teams of oxen would be plowing the fields, but right now no one was stirring. The sun had just broken the horizon and was glorious in its arrival.

Then she saw her. A tall woman, her head covered with a blue scarf, her shift revealing the outline of her slender body; she carried a basket strapped to her back. Looking across the field, she spied Raisa and waved a cheerful hello.

Raisa waved back, started in the woman's direction; but then stopped still in her tracks, her mouth hanging open, the call of hello frozen in her thoughts.

Surely it couldn't be. No. No it simply could not be. It just looked like her. It was too silly even to be worthy of a passing thought. But yet. But yet, it looked so much like her. She had resumed walking as the jumbled thoughts tossed in her mind; and when she drew nearer, Raisa realized that indeed her teacher was none other than the Mother of all Living, the Queen of Mivtzar, Eve.

Raisa approached the serene woman and knelt.

"Mother Eve," she breathed.

"My word, child, do stand up!" Eve exhorted.

Trembling, Raisa stood.

"We have much to learn during the next six months, my child. The first thing that I want you to learn is that you never, never bow to me. I will be your teacher. I work, as does every other woman who lives in Mivtzar. I would also like to be your friend."

Numb with wonder that so exalted a person would be teaching her such menial tasks, the girl could only stare at Eve in awe.

She had been introduced to Adam's wife during the Harvest Festival, when the entire group from Achva's journey had been introduced and welcomed into Mivtzar. The Council had explained the rules for living in the area, and each person had promised to live faithfully by all of them. At one point, Eve had graciously walked through the group, taking each person's hand and grasping it in a warm and caring manner. Raisa had thought her the most beautiful woman she had ever seen. Eve's once golden hair was now as silver as the moon on a starlit night; but her face was still smooth and creamy, like the petals of a pale pink rose. Her eyes were a clear, sapphire blue and her body tall and supple. Rhoda had whispered to Raisa that Eve was over 650 years old! Enoch had taught them that Adam and Eve were the very first parents, and had been placed on this earth, fully grown, by God the Creator.

"This is our plot to work," continued Eve, as though oblivious to the girl's shocked expression.

Raisa looked at the area Eve was indicating. The plot, probably a little more than ½ acre in size, had been turned by the men with oxen, but still was full of rocks, sticks and large clumps of soil.

"We must break up all the clumps, get out all the weeds and grass, and remove the rocks and sticks. It will require at least two weeks of hard work before our soil is ready to be planted; but that is just as well because the ground is not yet warm enough to receive our seed.

"We will begin each day's work with prayer, and I am pleased at the early time which you chose to begin today. I would like for you to be here at this time each day. On the fifth day of the week we will meet at the Garden of Prayer, where we will take our turn tending the flowers and plants during the morning hours, have lunch and fellowship with other women, and then share spiritual training and prayer during the afternoon. On the sixth day you will remain at home to tend to the tasks that are required there. On the Sabbath you will rest and worship our God. Does this plan appeal to you?"

"Oh yes, Mother Eve, it sounds just perfect," the girl sputtered enthusiastically.

Eve smiled her beautiful smile and, placing her arms around Raisa, gave her a warm embrace. "Please, just call me Mother," she said tenderly.

Raisa was amazed at the strength of the older woman. It was all that she could do to match the pace that her teacher set. They stopped midmorning for a brief break, drinking water supplied by a cool stream nearby. The work went slowly, oh so slowly, but the conversation was a balm to the girl's young soul.

At midday their lunch was brought to them by giggling young girls from the village. There was bread still warm from the oven, large slabs of cheese, and hard-boiled eggs; grapes, figs and apples dried from last year's harvest; with goat's milk which had been cooled in the stream. No food had ever tasted so wonderful to Raisa, and she devoured every crumb offered her.

"Oh look, we have raisin cakes for our mid-afternoon break," exclaimed Eve with as much enthusiasm as a child. The women giggled, stashed their treat for later, and placed the jug of weak wine in the stream to cool.

The morning of the fifth day dawned cool and wet. Raisa threw a long scarf over herself and started for the path leading down the mountain. When she arrived at the copse of trees where the path began, she was startled to see a man seated on a donkey and holding another by its reins.

"Hello, Raisa," he called. "Come ride this beast, and cover yourself with this dry garment"

"Enoch! How are you? What in the world are you doing here in this weather?" she asked as she accepted the leather hooded cloak and gratefully climbed on the donkey.

"Eve sent me. She said that she knew you would come, regardless of the wet conditions, and she was afraid you would become chilled."

"But, Enoch, why did she send *you*? I mean, I really appreciate your coming, but there are numerous young boys who would have saved you the trouble."

"Well, knowing Eve, I suspect that she had a reason; but most of all I think that I was in the right place at the right time and got snagged. Anyway, I was glad to do it. How have you been? I haven't seen you since the Harvest Festival. How is Yakira? Has she adjusted?"

The two continued their conversation down the mountain path and into the village. Both were amazed, when they arrived at the home of Adam and Eve, that the trip had gone so quickly. Neither had really been aware of the cold wet clouds.

Eve greeted them at the door.

"Come in, come in this house. God bless you both."

She nodded toward the woman who helped with the cooking. "Geela and I have a huge breakfast ready, and I expect both of you to help eat it."

The young people laughingly agreed and were pleasantly surprised to find that Nedav, Achva, and Rhoda with her five children, were also present. Maimon was there as well; and Yafa, much to Raisa's amusement, had her place on a little pillow by the fire. It was a fine reunion with good food and a renewal of acquaintance.

After everyone had eaten until unable to eat another bite, Father Adam raised his hand for attention and the talking ceased immediately.

"I believe that someone in this room has an announcement to make. Nedav is there something that you wish to tell your friends?"

Rhoda blushed a deep pink, and Nedav stood up with a broad grin on his pleasant young face.

"Father Adam has given me permission to ask Rhoda to become my wife, and to ask Bina, Marnin, Aryeh, Avital and Arella to become my children. They have all agreed and we will become a family next month."

Enoch, Achva and the uncle, Maimon, each shook hands with Nedav and then hugged him. Then they shook hands with each other and hugged each other. Raisa hugged Rhoda and Eve and even the flustered Geela. Yafa barked and ran circles around everyone. There was much laughter and many tears.

Adam spoke. "Usually we make marriage commitments at the Harvest Festival, but I see no reason to wait. Our Planting Festival will be a fine time for this special occasion."

Eve nudged Adam. "Don't you also have an announcement, my husband?"

"Well, now that you mention it, I believe that I just might. This time next year, if Yahweh is willing, Eve and I will be making a journey to Ur. It has come to my attention that another member of this party has a desire to take a wife and there seems to be a shortage of priests in that great City of knowledge. I guess I will have to go take care of this matter.

"Enoch has agreed to draw up plans for private boats to transport our party down the Euphrates. We will be taking a legion of Shalomshamars to provide protection for the City, and numerous Proclaimers to provide knowledge of our God. Enoch will be preaching throughout the City, and Achva will be firmly establishing himself as a teacher at the Tower of Learning. We plan to spend one year in the City and return home the following spring. It should be quite an adventure. I certainly look forward to meeting the man ,Ur, about whom I have heard so much."

Raisa spoke up shyly, "I hope that your travels are less eventful than ours were as we came here. I understand that Ur is a beautiful City; but I cannot imagine any place more beautiful or wonderful than Mivtzar. I am grateful to be here, and I am especially grateful to know Yahweh as my God. It is my prayer that I never have to leave this wonderful place, but I am very happy to know that knowledge of Yahweh will at last be taken to Ur."

After the long breakfast, the women left for the Garden of Prayer. Because of the wetness, their work was limited to tending the flowers and shrubs that grew under the sheltered areas; but the weather did not deter numerous women from bringing food and attending the luncheon.

Although she had heard about the weekly lunch at the prayer room, this was the first time that Raisa had attended. She was thrilled with the fellowship. After the luncheon, the women gathered in the Room of Prayer to be taught lessons by Eve. Her voice, though never seeming to rise above a gentle tone, carried to the farthest corner of the large room.

Raisa listened to every word as Eve told stories of life in the Garden, and how she and Adam were able to talk daily with God. She shuddered when Eve described the cunning of the serpent, and wept openly when the first-born lamb of Mother Ewe was sacrificed. Much too soon the day was over.

As she said her goodbyes to the women, Raisa was once again surprised to find Enoch waiting for her.

"You didn't take your donkey," he said, handing her the reins.

"But,... it isn't actually *my* donkey. You just loaned it to me this morning."

"Well. You see, I meant to tell you, Raisa, it actually is your donkey. I bought it from Achva so that you will have transportation to come to the village. It is a long walk and this little donkey badly needs a friend. His name is Koby and he seems to have a sweet disposition. Please accept this gift from me."

Raisa stood for a moment looking into his eyes. For some silly reason her heart was pounding so loudly that she was afraid he might hear. She lowered her eyes and spoke softly, "I do accept this gift, Enoch, and may Yahweh bless you for your generosity. Thank you very much."

That evening she sheltered the little animal in the lean-to that held her few chickens. She stood for a long time stroking his sleek coat. Yakira had been beside herself with excitement when she met Koby. Raisa had sent her with a few coins to purchase hay from the big barn where such things were sold; and for once Yakira had gone straight to her assignment and come straight back, without becoming distracted along the way. Raisa praised her highly, and both girls delighted in feeding the newest member of the family.

❋ ❋ ❋ ❋ ❋

The rocks made a large pile along the edge of the clearing and the women knew that eventually the larger ones would be used in making buildings and the smaller ones crushed to make mortar. The clods were broken and returned to the soil and the weeds pulled, dried and burned.

The ground warmed and the precious seed was planted in long straight rows. Raisa was thrilled when the tiny sprouts began showing their heads through the soil; and she attacked the weeds with fervor, resenting their encroachment on her fledgling plants.

One day, after it seemed that the weeds were winning the war, Raisa plopped down by the brook next to Eve. She scooped up the cool water to wash her face and, removing her sandals, placed her feet in the water. Giving a sigh of relief as she was cooled by the stream, the young woman harshly pronounced her sentiments about weeds, their prolific nature and their worthlessness.

"I don't understand why there have to be weeds!" she exclaimed. "We work and work to get the seedlings to grow; and for each one, six weeds crop up without any effort. You can't eat a weed, they smell bad and they take soil and food away from the things you can eat. It just doesn't make sense. Why would God do that?"

Eve moved to a nearby tree, rested her back against it, and looked at Raisa with sad eyes.

"There were no weeds in the Garden, my dear. The soil was fine and turned easily under our hands, and when we planted seeds they grew strong and true. It was a beautiful sight: all of the different vegetables, berries, herbs and everything good to eat. It was so much fun watching them grow.

"In that Garden we had every seed-bearing plant that God had placed on the whole earth, and every tree that yielded fruit with its seed in it. We had no concept of how wealthy we were.

"But, when we sinned…you remember how I have told the groups of women about that…when we sinned, and had to leave the Garden, it seemed as if the entire world was suddenly weeds. Beyond the gates of the Garden was nothing but wilderness. There was great beauty but everything was untamed.

"God had told us to gather our stores of seeds, which we would have planted the next season in the Garden, and take them with us. After we had traveled for several days in the direction that the angel had indicated, we found a place to settle for a bit. There was a little cave which sheltered us and a brook near-by. This was east of the Euphrates and the river was too deep for us to cross.

"Adam said that we must get busy and plant our seed so that we would have food. We had taken a few chickens with us for eggs and a couple of goats for milk and cheese. We had caught them but they were strangers to us.

"None of the animals could talk to us any more, we didn't recognize the ones we caught; only Horse. He stayed with us for some reason, even though his mate and children ran away. He never left us and helped us for a long, long time before he died. It was as if he tried to talk to us with his eyes. He never balked, or complained; he simply faithfully served our needs as best he could. He helped till the fields, carry our loads, give us rides. He was a wonderful friend. I don't know why he continued to trust us, when we had failed him so miserably and provided him with such a difficult life. He was certainly a faithful creature.

"Well, anyway, we began to work the land, just as you and I have had to do. We planted our seed, often having to carry water from the river to keep it watered. We worked very hard and for the most part we were able to accept our new life. At least I tried to because Adam was so very brave, and I didn't want to fail him again.

"The seed broke through the ground and we rejoiced. We danced around our little plot like we had danced in the Garden. We sang and laughed and thanked God. And then the weeds came. Every morning there was a new crop. We had little time for anything else but to fight weeds. It was as if the wilderness, the desolation, had declared war on us. At night, sometimes, I imagined that I could again hear the derisive laugh of the Dark One.

"We worked and worked; and one morning I decided that I simply could not, would not, do it any more. I stayed in my bed in the little cave with my face to the wall. I wouldn't speak to Adam. I kept my eyes closed and wouldn't move.

"I stayed there for days, only moving to relieve myself; and that soon became a rare necessity because I had quit eating. I didn't comb my hair, or wash my face, or speak to my husband."

A sob from Raisa broke the moment of ensuing silence as Eve remembered those long ago days.

"Oh, those horrible, horrible weeds!" the girl cried. "They are so destructive."

Eve took her hand, looked into her eyes, and said gently, "It wasn't the weeds in the field that were destructive, my dear, it was the weeds in my heart. The horrible weeds are those that are allowed to grow in the human heart. They take up space where the good seed could be growing, but provide no nourishment for the body or soul; allowed to grow they become the domicile for the Destroyer. A tiny sprout began to grow in my heart as I listened to the voice of the Destroyer, and continued to grow and grow and grow as long as I nurtured it. At any point in time I could have, through God's grace, ripped that ugly old weed right out of there, but I kept watering it with my sorrow and grief.

"When Adam tried to talk to me; to tell me how much he needed me, my reply was that God had told us that if we ate of the fruit of the forbidden tree that we would die. I had eaten and I wanted to die. I said that life was too difficult and that I wasn't going to live any longer. So I lay there, oblivious to my husband's need, and let the weeds grow in my soul."

"But…there are no weeds in your soul now, Mother. How did you survive that awful time?" the young girl spoke in pleading tones, longing to be given hope.

Eve's eyes regained the far-away look. "It was while I was lying with my face to the cave wall that I began to feel movement within my womb. I realized that there was a child growing within me. It was then that I knew it was not yet my time to die; that God wanted me to live, to survive until He would say that my life was finished.

"I remembered all the baby animals that had been born in the Garden, and I thought about how each one looked like a replica of its parent. I wondered what my child would look like, and if it would be a replica of myself or of Adam. Suddenly I wanted life to go on. I wanted to meet the little person who was growing inside of me.

"As you know, that little one was Cain. He was our first-born and oh how we loved him. We worked very, very hard to provide him with a home. Before many years had gone by we had another son, Abel. Our little cave home was full to the point of being crowded.

"Adam loved to look off to the west and see the mountain range. He often expressed a desire to see those mountains, but the river was too deep for us to cross. One autumn morning when we awakened, the strangest thing had happened; the river was only waist deep. Several fallen trees had jammed a bend in the river, and there was only a trickle of water getting through.

"We gathered up the animals and placed our packs on them, put the boys on Horse, and waded the river. We felt absolutely triumphant to be on the other side. It took us two more years of traveling to find the cave that is part of Aluma's Village. Adam knew then that he had found the place where he wanted to made a home, and we have lived in this area since that time.

"There has been much joy, but oh Raisa, there has also been deep, lacerating pain. Cain chose to allow the weeds of bitterness to grow in his soul. By becoming angry with God, he chose the most poisonous weeds of all; and he allowed them to destroy his soul. There was nothing that his father or I could say or do to direct him to God. He rejected everything that we believed in. When Abel chose God, Cain, in his jealousy, chose to kill his own brother. Then he chose to kill his children by introducing them to the way of death.

"When God does call me to depart this life, I will die knowing that death came because I sinned. God has forgiven my sin. He has accepted my tears and my repentance, but nothing that I can do can undo that selfish decision I made in the Garden. Let me assure you, dear little daughter, that no matter how enticing the path to sin may look at the time, it brings nothing but grief and death in the end. God's way and God's time is always the better way."

Both women sat quietly together for a long time. Suddenly Eve started. "My goodness, Raisa, look at the sun! If we don't hurry home you will be riding Koby home in the dark and my husband will be sending out a search party for me. Go home, my dear child, go home. We have talked the evening away.

"Tomorrow I want you to stay at home. We will take a longer rest time this week, for I am weary. Take Yakira on a picnic; go see the wild flowers blooming in the fields. Have a fun day. Forget weeds for a few days. I love you my dear; you have greatly blessed my life."

Eve gave Raisa a strong hug and a kiss on the cheek; then she was off, fast-paced, for her home.

Raisa stood for a moment blinking back tears. How could *she* possibly have been a blessing to the Mother of all mankind? What a privilege it was to know Eve at such an intimate level. She never ceased to marvel that this wonderful woman had chosen to take her, Raisa, under her wing. Once when she questioned Eve about it, the First Woman smiled a secretive smile and said simply that Adam believed God had a special task for Raisa in life.

With the fading sun still warm on her back, Raisa turned Koby toward the path that led home. She thought about what Eve had said. She wanted to find God's will for her life more than anything. She halted Koby beside a huge tree. She touched the tree and wondered if it had been standing since God first called the earth into being. The tree felt warm and alive under her touch. Raisa knelt beside the tree and looked up into the sky. One lone star had appeared.

"Father God. Yahweh. Thank You for sending the men to rescue my sister and me from Oz. Thank You for not allowing me to be sent to the City of Enoch to be used as a vessel of sin. I want to serve You. You have been so very good to me, and I worship and praise You. Show me Your will, dear God. Give me a heart that is tender and willing to serve wherever You would have me serve. Please don't let weeds grow in my soul. I want always to be Your child, dear God, Amen."

Raisa knelt by the tree for a long time. She felt a warmth on her head but was unable to know that a golden light, the Shekinah Glory of God, was hovering just over her.

Chapter Thirteen

Ur

Adam and his sons declared, at the top of their voices so as to be sure and be heard, that there must be a whole nest of bees in the wagon behind them, because they heard a constant buzz coming from that direction. The ladies just laughed and waved at them.

Eve felt a sense of excitement and anticipation that was rare for her serene spirit. She was going to ride a boat down the Euphrates River all the way to Ur! Best of all she was going to share the adventure with her seven daughters. The First Couple had issued invitations for all of their children to join them in their trip to the majestic City of Ur, and each one had been able to accept. What a family reunion it was!

Rina was serving cakes to each of her sisters from the ample supply of food that she had brought from her home on the Great Sea. Eve smiled with pleasure. How good it was to see her seven 'girls' together again. Her mother's heart paid no mind to the fact that each of her daughters was several hundred years old. They were all here and they were beautiful. Rina, Simcha, Tori, Nehama, Leeba, Chaya and Bracha were as excited as their mother to be on this journey.

Suddenly, as they rounded a curve in the road and began the descent toward the river, silence fell on all the wagons. There in the harbor sat the splendid fleet of boats, which had been the final outcome of Enoch's hard labor. Never before had there been such a glorious sight on the Euphrates. Rina's husband, Abir, had been appointed as River Captain in charge of the Fleet. He had, after all, many decades of experience with fishing boats on the sea that bore his name.

Eve's voice held awe as she told her daughters, "I find it difficult to believe that this busy river is the same one that your father and I waded across so many years ago. Look at the size of it!"

Rina reflected on the numerous groups going with them to Ur. There were 500 Shalomshamars; Enoch, Achva and one hundred Proclaimers; Adam, Eve, the seven daughters, seven sons and all the spouses and at least 200 people who had volunteered to come along as servants.

There were also wagons full of gifts, and animals: scores of animals that would be presented to the City Fathers of Ur.

Besides all of this there were the rowers; four sets of rowers for each boat. Each set of four would row for a six-hour period, followed by twelve hours off. The boats were to go non-stop to the City of Ur.

Rina shook her head in mock dismay. "Poor Ur," she remarked, "when he sees this multitudinous group he'll probably decide that *we* are the invaders."

Eve nodded. "Fortunately, your father sent messengers ahead several months ago to give warning that we would be spending a year in the City of Ur. Ur himself sent back a message of invitation. He said that facilities would be provided for all who came."

"It must be quite a City!" offered Chaya. "I can hardly wait to see it."

"*I* can hardly wait to be safely past Cain's City," declared Bracha, and everyone agreed.

Leeba, who had watched her mother's face change at the mention of Cain, reached over and took her hand and squeezed it.

No one spoke again until the boats had been boarded. The great general, Guryon, had carefully seen to the billeting of his troops before returning to his father's boat. There were troopships of Shalomshamar before, after, and to each side, of the passenger boats.

"Quite a show we must be making," mused Adam.

"That is exactly what I want, Father," replied Guryon. "I want those who would do us harm to think it over very carefully before they decide to commit suicide."

"But, Brother," questioned Doran, "if we leave all these troops to guard the City of Ur, how can we guarantee our safety when we return home?"

"I have a plan. We will not discuss it at this time, however. There is safety in secrecy."

The brothers all nodded in agreement.

Unlike other boats on the river, Abir's fleet did not put in at Cain's City, the Port of Enoch. Hundreds of people were gathered along the boardwalk as the fleet passed. Many waved and called friendly greetings; but some had angry expressions on their faces, and some shook their fists at the boats.

The City smells and sounds permeated the clean air about the boats as they passed by. Abir urged the rowers to increase their speed for the stench was nearly overpowering.

"What is that?" asked the beautiful Nehama. Her look indicated a large boulder at the outskirts of the City: on it men, women and children, even infants, were tied flat on their backs to stakes.

"That must be Oren Rock that Rhoda told us about," Eve sadly responded. "That is where the undesirable people of the City are placed to die."

"Aluma wouldn't have liked that very much, would she mother?" Tori added.

"I rather suspect that the reason she worked so hard to rescue every creature possible, whether man or beast, was due to the evil that she saw in that wicked place, my daughters. She was a kind and loving person, and the wickedness of that City finally destroyed her life."

As the boats traveled on the way, by day and night, Guryon's sharp eyes spotted many dangerous looking men skulking along the river banks.

"Father, I am very glad that we do not have to stop along this river, for I perceive that there are many evil and menacing men who would love to do us harm," the general reported.

"My heart and eyes tell me that you are right, my son. We *must* proclaim the message of God. We must pray that hearts will be made tender and lives will be changed by our message."

Eventually the eyes from the forest became fewer and fewer, and the towns became smaller and smaller. It seemed that most people preferred living close to the 'exciting' City of Enoch. It was rumored that *Ur's* City was dull and stuffy. This reputation suited the travelers just fine.

The Port of Ur was well north of the great City itself, due to the fact that when the Euphrates was joined by the Tigris, the waters became rapid and unsafe for boats to traverse. A branch from this extensive river continued to flow through the City, but the larger body of water chose a southwesterly route to the sea.

After docking at the Port of Ur, the travelers spent the night aboard ship; arising while it was still dark in order to arrive at Ur for breakfast. This was all according to Adam's instructions; and if it seemed a bit peculiar to his children, no one ventured to say so.

When the many boats off-loaded, just before the confluence of waters, there were numerous horse drawn vehicles from Ur assembled to transport the group.

Eve had greatly surprised her daughters when, after they had carefully bathed and then dressed their hair, she brought out a new gown for each of them. Never, in all of their long lives, had they worn, or even seen, gowns of such opulence. Although made to cover the body with the utmost modesty, the gowns were of vibrant colors and a lightly delicate material unknown to Mivtzar. The material had been shipped, many months before, to Eve, from Gana. Eve had urged the village seamstresses to secrecy; and when the work was completed, she had carefully packed the stunning gowns away for this occasion.

Guryon sent 200 Shalomshamars ahead of the group to announce the impending arrival of the main party, and to set up tents for encampment of the soldiers outside the gates of the City.

The founder of the City that bore his name had just finished an early breakfast, and was seated on the balcony that overlooked the large courtyard of the Tower of Learning. He was enjoying the last of his hot mulled wine and recalling a conversation between himself and his closest advisors the evening before.

Ur's sister Renana, the hostess for his frequent formal dinners, had prepared a lovely dinner for the six men who formed the inner circle around him. As the man responsible for the great civilization called "The City of Ur," he had met to discuss, at great length, the completion of the arrangements needed for all the guests that were soon to descend upon the great City.

Kaniel, the second most powerful man in the City, shook his head ruefully; "I still find it difficult to believe that you have invited all those country bumpkins to spend a year in this City. They are certain to be an embarrassment to themselves and to the elite families of our fine City. You amaze me, Ur; whatever were you thinking?"

Barth, the youngest and newest member of the group, spoke up somewhat timidly: "But Kaniel, remember how we were blessed by the presence of Enoch, and while I do admit that he never dressed with much care, he certainly was a man of great intelligence and much talent."

"That is true," agreed Gidel, a rather pompous little man who had a habit of raising his voice more loudly than was actually necessary, as if by so doing he could compensate for his small stature. "However, he did live like a recluse out by the seashore with his boats and dreams. He seemed a rather odd fellow to me."

Kyle, Achva's closest friend in the group, walked to his friend's side as if in defense. "When Achva was scrubbed and dressed appropriately, with much thanks, I might add, to Ur's friend, Gana, he became one of our most popular teachers and made an enormous contribution to our great place of learning. I am fascinated with his writing of the language and his study of the heavens. He may be a 'country bumpkin', Kaniel, but he certainly is a brilliant one."

"Is it true that their leader, a man called Adam, actually claims to be the first man placed on earth?" asked Efrem incredulously.

"It is true!" Zer interrupted as Ur had begun to explain, "I heard Enoch say this very thing. They are all God-fearers you know, and I'm sure that they plan to try and force their superstitious beliefs on all of us. Aren't they planning to bring a thousand or more of their preachers?"

"Now, now, Zer," entreated Ur, "let us not give place to exaggeration. You know as well as I do that Adam asked permission to bring 100 of their 'Proclaimers', as they call their religious teachers. They will simply tell their stories and explain their beliefs. Certainly no one will ever be forced to accept their religion. After all, we at the Tower of Learning do pride ourselves on our open minds."

"The best and truest religion is no religion at all," grumbled Efrem. "Man is his own god and creates his own destiny. *That* is the teaching of the Tower of Learning. We reject anything that causes man to live in bondage and fear. That is why we chose to leave the evil teachings of Cain's City. Now we have openly invited a man here who is clearly a megalomaniac, and not only have we invited him and 100 of his minions, but we are allowing 500 of his soldiers bearing arms to enter our City."

"Just a moment, men!" Ur's voice was unusually stern. "Which is it? Are the people who are coming to visit us from a far away place, country bumpkins who will show their ignorance of anything erudite and embarrass us all; or are they leaders of such knowledge and skill that they will overthrow our City? Please listen to yourselves, because you are all talking like a bunch of nervous old women. If this is the wisdom of my closest group of advisors, may Adam's God show me mercy."

Without giving the men an opportunity to reply, Ur continued, "The soldiers, or Shalomshamars as they are called, will not come into the City, except when they are granted leave, a few at a time. They will be making encampments on each side of the City and will be training any of our young men who volunteer, how to defend themselves and others. Each of you knows full well that our environs are in constant danger from raids. There are numerous groups of cutthroats and bands of thieves roaming the lands outside our gates. We have recently had women carried off and men slaughtered as they have tended their fields. It is only a matter of time until the groups band together and attack our City in force. Are you so foolish as to think that our great learning will keep evil outside our gates!"

None of the men spoke for several minutes and when they did the subject had been totally changed. After about 30 minutes of desultory conversation, the men paid their compliments to the hostess and their goodnights to Ur.

As they were starting out the door, Ur spoke once again: "There will be an early dinner and reception in their honor on the day in which they arrive. It could be any day now. Can I count on each of you being there and making them welcome?"

Zer stepped back into the room and placed his arm across his friend's shoulder. Looking squarely at the rest of the men, he stated in a firm voice, "We would each one still be in the bondage of Cain's evil City if it were not for your vision of this wonderful place. We trust you completely, and you may count on our total loyalty. Now and always."

The men walked back into the room and placing a hand in turn on the shoulder of their leader, each vowed his allegiance.

Ur, smilingly reflecting on the memory of the evening, was suddenly jarred back to the reality of the moment. Someone was pounding loudly on his door.

"Just a moment!" he called as he drew his dressing gown over his nightclothes. "Don't pound the door down. I am coming."

The youngster at the door was nearly breathless from running. "Sir. I have been sent to tell you that there are hundreds of armed men outside our gates. They say that they come in peace and that a man, whom they call 'Adam', and his family, will be here for breakfast. They have spears sir, and other weapons; the sentry at the gate says that they are called swords. I don't know what they are called but I wager that they could cut a man's head off with one swipe. They say they come in peace sir, but I surely don't know. They are all lined up in rows outside the gate and their leader says that many more are coming, and could they put their tents up in the fields. Sir they have weapons and everything, and sir I just don't know...."

Ur himself looked a bit stunned at the news he had just received. How did they get all the way to the gates without him realizing it? For breakfast, the boy said. Hundreds of people for breakfast! He hadn't really expected them until next week, or even the week after that. How in heaven's name had they traveled the Great River that quickly? What must be done now? He must think. That was it. He must think and he must act. He was Ur. He was the leader of this great City of learning. He could certainly handle having a few unexpected guests for breakfast!

"Be still boy! Stop your yammering and run tell the cooks that the students will be given only bread and cheese for breakfast this morning. They must prepare a feast for our guests.

Tell them to set up tables for at least 300 people and to do it quickly. Now stop shaking and do as I say. We have company coming. Don't stand there like a … like a country bumpkin!"

The boy fled and Ur stood dumbfounded for only a moment more.

He then ran to his private chamber to complete his morning toilet, yelling for servants as he did so. He sent messages to each of his advisors and ordered them to instruct those officials under them. There would be a formal breakfast in the Courtyard, and anyone not participating wholeheartedly would be sent…would be sent…back to the City of Cain; that's where they would be sent!

He turned to a young female servant who stood trembling as she awaited orders from this great man who seemingly had suddenly gone raving mad. "Don't just stand there. Go fetch Gana! She will know what to do. And get my sister. Tell her to come right now. Hurry, be quick about it, or I'll take one of the soldiers' swords to you myself!"

Miraculously the food was prepared and the tables set; fresh flowers adorned the courtyard, which had been swept clean and the flat stone walks sprinkled with flower petals. Ur surveyed the group standing in readiness before him. His shoulders began to relax. How nice they all looked. He knew that everyone, including himself, had been forced to dress quickly and preparations had been improvised in haste. There was a sharpness in the air as if it had been charged by some outside force, but everything and everyone was in order.

Suddenly a ram's horn sounded and the gates were thrown open wide. Ur and his dignitaries hastened to the receiving stand just as the parade of visitors came formally into the City. Leading the procession were six young boys blowing horns with ribbons streaming from them. They were followed by several columns of Shalomshamars in full military dress. The gold on their belts, and the jewels in their swords, gave evidence of the wealth of their homeland. Next came Enoch and Achva and several teachers from the School of the Proclaimers. They were standing in a small vehicle pulled by two white donkeys. Directly behind them were the 100 Proclaimers, who walked with quiet dignity and bestowed warm smiles on the crowds of people who had gathered along the road. Behind them, riding in a wagon pulled by a team of six gray donkeys, were the sons and daughters of Adam and Eve. They waved happily to the cheering crowd. Gana, standing on the receiving stand with the City officials felt a warm rush of approval as she caught sight of the beautiful gowns that the girls were wearing.

Suddenly the crowd was silent. Six more boys with horns broke forth with a resounding strain. They were followed by six young girls who were scattering rose petals in front of the next vehicle. A man and woman stood together in a small rolling vehicle that had been plated with gold, and was being pulled by two magnificent white horses. The woman had on a gown that appeared to have been spun with gold threads; her long silver hair was worn in plaits that were wrapped around her head. Nestled in the top of the plaits was a thin gold crown set with precious jewels.

The man stood straight and tall. His cloak was fastened around his shoulders by a silver clasp that had a strange engraving on it. In the center of the clasp there was a raised +. On one side of the crosspiece was a man and on the other side was a woman; the piece that ran vertically had a tree in the center with a coiled serpent below it and a lamb above it. The + piece was raised from the silver background and plated with gold.

The man's hair, silver with streaks of a remembrance of a darker hue, hung long down his back and was secured with a leather thong. His beard was neatly trimmed close to his face. Resting on his head was a crown, wider than his wife's and profusely set with precious stones.

Ur, standing at attention on the reception stand, turned ever so slightly to his council of advisors who stood by his side.

In a muffled tone he said, "As soon as they get near enough I will introduce you to these country bumpkins."

❋ ❋ ❋ ❋ ❋

Three days later a tall young man stood silently across the tree-lined boulevard from the shop with the wooden sign over the door. The little dog sat at his feet, stealing impatient glances at her master's face. She seemed to be asking, "Why this wait? You know she's in there. Let's go find her!"

Achva would have been hard pressed to explain why he was hesitant to walk across the street and embrace his beloved. His mind was churning in many different directions: it had been well over a year since he had placed the ring on her finger and they had pledged their love to one another; her feelings might have changed for him; perhaps another had taken his place; he had looked in vain for her during the reception speeches, but not once had she appeared. Why? Furthermore, he had found no chance to talk alone with Gana; indeed, was it his imagination, or had the aunt avoided him?

Finally, as if in exasperation, Yafa barked.

Achva reached down to pet the dog, just as she bounded out of his reach. He looked up in time to see Zahava standing in the shop doorway and Yafa leaping into her open arms.

"I just hope that I get as warm a welcome," he muttered under his breath. He straightened his shoulders and walked across the street.

Zahava gave him a somewhat tentative smile and then bit her lip as if uncertain how to act. Their eyes met and suddenly both were shy.

"I looked for you at..."

"The shop needed my..."

Both had begun to talk at the same time.

Achva suddenly reached out and grabbed Zahava's hand and pulled her through the door. "I'm taking her for a while; we'll return in a bit," he called to Gana, who had a broad smile on her face.

They didn't speak at all until they had reached a secluded spot by the river. They found a bench and sat down. Yafa, panting heavily from the swift walk, looked into both their faces with a silly doggy grin and then lay down, contented, at their feet.

He had held her left hand tightly all the way as they walked; and now he reached for her right hand and looked, just to make sure. The ring that he had placed on her finger was still there. He let his breath escape in a sigh of relief.

"I've never taken it off," she whispered.

"Then why didn't you come to the reception and the parties afterward? I looked and looked for you. There was no way for me to leave before today; it would have been a slight to our hosts."

"I did come. At least I came to the crowd at the gates when you entered. There was such splendor, such wealth; I had no idea that you were rich, and it frightened me. I thought that I knew you. I assumed that you came from a small village and had to work as I do."

Achva began to laugh.

He drew the young woman into his arms and tenderly kissed the top of her head. "Zahava, I am not a rich man. Well, at least I am not any more rich than every other man in our village. Actually though, Mivtzar is not just one village but a series of villages, and I suppose that if you put them together they would justify their name that means 'fortress' and they *would* make a rather great City. It just *feels* like a village. Every person in Mivtzar has to work. Why even Eve, the mother of all living, goes out into the fields to plant and to harvest. Small children work. We all work. We all play. We all worship. We are a family. No one is allowed to be idle, but no one is forced to work beyond his endurance either.

"But, Achva, the jewels, the gold, the dresses!"

"Yes, well…let me assure you that we do not dress like that at home. I had heard that we had stores of gold and jewels, but this is the first time in my life that I have ever seen them. I don't really know why, but I do believe that Father Adam was making a point. I rather suspect that he wanted the City fathers to sit up and take notice."

He grinned at her. "Which, I think you will have to admit, they certainly did."

She looked deep into his eyes. "It was the most splendid procession that I have ever seen. Even with all of the wealth and glitter, everyone looked, well, pure. I felt unworthy."

His face became very still. Very serious. "My beloved Zahava, none of us are measured by what we wear, or what we own. Our measure is taken by Yahweh according to what we are, inside. Wealth cannot make a pure person soiled; nor can it make a soiled person pure. Purity begins in the heart, continues in the soul, and finally lives forever in the spirit. Only a person who seeks to know the heart of God can be truly pure.

"I desire to make you my wife. Father Adam wishes to meet you before I will be allowed to do this. He will ask you questions about your relationship with Yahweh. If he feels that you are ready, you will be turned over to the Godly women, those led by Eve, for instruction in what we know as Truth. When the time is right, we can be married by Adam, here in this City. Are you willing to be subject to the laws of Mivtzar, even here in Ur?"

Her eyes glittered as she spoke, " I am willing, my own love, I am willing. It is my desire to serve Yahweh, and to become your wife."

❋ ❋ ❋ ❋ ❋

In the weeks that followed, the visitors from Mivtzar settled into their own routine in the City. The Proclaimers were divided into several groups, each containing ten men, and were given buildings that had been set aside especially for their use throughout the City. There they taught about Yahweh, as they knew Him and His story. Evening classes were also taught, and at the beginning of the dusk that heralded the Sabbath, all who wished to met to worship. No work was done on the Sabbath day by any of the God-fearers. Ten of the Proclaimers were selected to teach classes at the Tower of Learning. Any who wished to attend were invited and all difficult questions were welcomed.

The Shalomshamars had fortresses around the City. Each fortress housed 100 men. There were 100 of the men who served as teachers of new recruits. This unit of raw recruits was kept separate from the City, and was housed in an area that had been made as private as possible. It was hoped that the training of soldiers for the City of Ur would be kept secret from the evil men who were forming gangs.

Hundreds of young men volunteered to receive one year of training such as Guryon had instituted many years before in Mivtzar. Ur and his advisors had requested that, after graduation, the new Ur soldiers would be called, not 'Shalomshamars' but 'The Magen', a name indicating that they were protectors. Their uniforms would be made of a pattern similar to the Shalomshamars but of gold and black, with a headpiece of beaten metal. Upon graduation each would take an oath of loyalty to defend Ur and its environs, and would be presented with a shining new sword.

The women who had come from Mivtzar met with the women of the City and did what women have continued to do throughout the ages: they shared ideas on childcare, cooking, gardening, homemaking and beauty.

They also were given a building in which to meet, and there in the large courtyard they planted a flower garden. Although some species of flowers were different, it felt much like the Garden of Prayer at home. It was there that Eve taught the women about the very first Garden and about Yahweh who had placed man in it.

At Adam's encouragement the City walls were extended to include a large field where vegetables could be planted. Each family was to send a representative to plow the fields, plant the seed, keep it weeded and cultivated, and finally to harvest the crops.

Guryon, who had sent some of his Shalomshamars to oversee the project, explained that, for a City to be safe from those who would take it over by force, it must be self-reliant. There must be an unmolested supply of food, a constant and safe source of water, and trained soldiers.

The City of Ur, which had heretofore been a collection of independent families cooperating with one another, was rapidly becoming a community unit that depended on each other. It was, Barth said in wonder to the mighty Kaniel one day, like it was becoming a family.

Zahava, having been questioned carefully by Adam, was sent to receive instruction from the women at the new Garden of Prayer. She still helped her aunt with the shop, but managed to find time each day to attend the sessions held on various aspects of married life, as taught by the women of Mivtzar.

She saw rather little of Achva, as he was one of the busiest teachers in the Tower of Learning. He and Enoch taught a joint class on the heavens, which included mapmaking and mathematical facts. He also taught classes on writing, and a direct result of this was that almost every shop in Ur displayed a sign that announced its type of business.

They did spend each Sabbath afternoon together, and it was on one such afternoon that Achva laid out his plans to her. It had been agreed by the City Advisors and Adam that the God-fearers, those from Mivtzar and those new converts from Ur, would be allowed to observe their various festivals in the field just outside the main City gate.

Each spring there was a Festival of Planting when the people gathered to thank God for bringing them safely through the winter months and for providing them with seed for the new plantings. Children born during the past year were presented in dedication to God. His blessing was sought for the coming year, and hearts were rededicated to Him.

For many years the marriage ceremonies had taken place only during the Harvest Festival, but the population had grown so large in recent times that this was no longer practical. So, for the last several decades, the Spring Festival had also witnessed the pledging of the wedding vows. Furthermore it was a time when couples were allowed to announce their commitment to one another and to begin plans for a wedding at the Harvest Festival.

Achva and his fellow travelers had arrived in Ur during the month of Adar; the Spring Festival would take place at the beginning of the month of Ziv. On the last night of the Festival Adam would announce to the group gathered there that Achva, son of Jared, and Zahava adopted daughter of Gana, would join their lives together before God during the Harvest Festival that year. From that point on, it would be permissible for friends and family to give them gifts for their household, and for Zahava to begin stitching her wedding gown. They would be treated like a married couple in every way except that of the wedding bed. The silver ring, which Achva had placed on Zahava's right hand, would be moved to her left hand, indicating that she was a wife by promise. When the wedding vows were made, a small gold ring would be added to the silver one.

❋ ❋ ❋ ❋ ❋

Enoch smiled as he heard the stamping of feet on the front porch of his beach house. Adam, Ur and Ur's Advisors had arrived for their day of rest and meeting.

"Welcome!" he called. "Come on in and help yourselves to refreshments."

Ur stood for a moment on the porch looking out at the cerulean sea. "What a wonderful view you have, Enoch. I can't imagine why I don't build myself a house overlooking the sea. It is very serene here. I could certainly use a little serenity. I used to believe that a life lived in temperance and kindness would bring contentment, but lately I seem to stay in turmoil. I simply don't understand why."

He continued to stare wistfully out at the vast blueness, as the others went inside and helped themselves to generous portions of the sumptuous breakfast that Enoch had prepared for them. Sighing, Ur finally joined the men inside, casting an unfathomable look at Adam.

When appetites were satisfied, the men looked to Ur to begin their discussion.

The summer was well past and soon the Harvest Festival would take place. Many of the citizens of Ur had professed belief in Adam's God and were going to make sacrifice at the coming festival. The Advisors had talked to many of the converts regarding their newfound belief and had been surprised to discover how deeply the roots of faith had already grown. Search as they would they were unable to detect any evidence of coercion by Adam's people.

Ur turned his gaze to Adam. "Your people have done wonderful things for the City of Ur. The wall has been enlarged and completed. Our young men are rapidly becoming capable of defending us, and we have never before had such an abundant harvest. The new wells bring more than ample supplies of fresh water throughout the City. If need be, we could be completely self sufficient for several months. We have much to be grateful for. Your coming here has been a good thing for us."

"It is also obvious that you have brought a new found faith to hundreds of our citizens," Kyle added quietly. "Places of worship are springing up throughout the City, and the large number of God-fearers have presented our council with a request that the Sabbath day be declared a day of rest for the entire City."

"That is preposterous!" exclaimed Gidel angrily. "We cannot have any *one* religion dictating rules for this City. Just because a group of fanatics follow this man who claims to have once talked to some god; a god who made the world for the express purpose of placing him on it, doesn't mean that we are going to adopt their ways."

The men suddenly became very quiet and all except Adam and Gidel sat with downcast eyes. Gidel glared at Adam, and Adam calmly and serenely looked into Gidel's eyes. Was Gidel mistaken or did Adam have amusement in his eyes. Gidel shifted his own eyes away.

Ur looked up and spoke. "We have all heard your story, Adam, and I have no question about your sincerity. I am certain that you *believe* that you once lived in a beautiful Garden where animals talked and God came to visit you each evening. I know that you believe that you and Eve were the first people to inhabit this earth and…"

Adam interrupted "Excuse me Ur. I must correct one fine point there. I was placed in the Garden and I spent some time naming all of the animals as God had instructed. When I was finished I realized that everyone there had a mate except myself. When God realized that I was sad, He asked me what the problem was, and I explained to Him that I could not find my own mate.

"God told me to lie down on the bed where I had been created and I did so. He touched me with his hand and I must have gone immediately into a deep sleep. Father Sheep later told me all that had happened while I was asleep."

Some one snickered but Adam ignored him and continued his story.

"While I was sleeping God removed a bone from my side and from that bone He made me a mate. He woke me up and presented me with my beautiful wife. I called her 'Eve'; she was to become the mother of all mankind."

"But later God made you leave that Garden?" questioned Barth, his young face incredulous.

Adam nodded sadly. "Yes, we disobeyed. We brought sin to the Garden. We brought death to the Garden. We could no longer live in that holy place."

Zer spoke quietly, looking deep into Adam's eyes. "Wasn't that a terribly harsh action for this Heavenly Father; this God of Love that you would have us believe in?"

"No, Zer, it was a righteous act of a righteous God. He is a righteous and Holy God and cannot dwell where there is sin. He does provide a way for us to be righteous, but it is through blood sacrifice. God has promised that someday He will send a perfect sacrifice: a Redeemer for our sins.

"The most difficult part of our leaving the Garden has not been the hard work or the weeds or even losing our relationship with the animals that we loved so. The horrible burden that Eve and I must bear for all of our days, is watching some of our children choose evil over good. It breaks our hearts to realize that we have borne children who will be eternally separated from God. The City of Cain is a wicked, sinful place, but those people who dwell there are no more separated from Holy God than the good people of this City of Ur who do not serve Him."

"Wait just a minute!" bellowed Gidel. "Are you telling us that God rejects good people just like He does evil people? Surely you don't equate that bunch of animals in Enoch with the fine people of Ur!"

Ur grabbed his arm. "Sit down, Gidel, and calm yourself. Let Adam explain this thing to us."

Adam waited a moment before speaking. "Gidel I do not mean to insult you or any of the citizens of Ur. It is just that none of us is really good; not when we compare ourselves with God anyway. When we reject God in our hearts we cause a wall of separation to come between Him and ourselves. He won't tear that wall down because He respects our right to choose. We are the only ones who can tear down that wall. Unless we do, we are forever separated from Him."

"We have all known people who have died, Adam. Do you believe that there is a life beyond this one?" asked Kyle.

"Yes, Kyle, I do. I believe that those of us who serve God will live forever with Him. I believe that we will once again live in a perfect Garden, but this time no one will sin. Not ever."

"But Adam, perhaps having come from that Garden originally, *you* will never die. If you have already lived over 600 years like you would have us believe, perhaps you won't really die." Efrem looked a bit smug when he challenged Adam with this thought.

"Well, Efrem, you are not the first to make this suggestion. The tempter in the Garden made this same false observation many years ago. I can assure you that I have watched my body 'die' every year of my life. I don't know when my body will be placed in the soil. That is in God's hands. I do know that when my body dies my spirit will live forever in His presence. I know that He is a worthy and true God. I have failed Him many times but He has never once failed me."

No one spoke for several minutes. Enoch, and the young men who worked with him, had finished their tasks in the kitchen and had slipped softly out the back door and down the beach to make some preparations for their guests.

Barth suddenly turned to Adam, his young eyes full of earnest questioning. "Why did you name your Enoch after Cain's son, Enoch. Doesn't that name represent all that is evil to you, and don't you consider this Enoch to be part of a holy line?"

"You have asked well, Barth. Please allow me to answer the last part of that question first. "After Cain killed Abel, their mother and I were left with several daughters but no sons. One night in a dream the angel of the Lord came to me and promised that there would be another son born to us, and that through his line would come the One who would defeat the sin-bringer. Eventually Seth was born and from his seed God indicated that Enosh was to continue the holy line, and then was chosen Cainan, Mahalalel, Jared and now Enoch. Enoch is the seventh son of his father and seventh in line from the beginning of time.

"At first it was difficult for Enoch to accept that he is the chosen one to continue the holy line; but friends, it is not up to us to question God. He had a plan in place and it doesn't depend on our worthiness; only upon His Sovereignty.

"As each of you knows we choose names for our children because of the meaning given to the word we use. The meaning for the word 'Enoch' comes from the word which we use for narrow, and we sometimes use this word to mean initiated or even, trained or disciplined. Cain's son Enoch was initiated into what Cain believed to be the 'freedom' of sin.

"God's meaning of Enoch, that narrow way, is the way that He chooses for us to travel. It is a godly way: a way of obedience and discipline. This is the meaning of the name that Jared chose for his son."

Adam took a coin out of the pouch hanging from his belt. "Each side of this coin could have an Enoch inscribed on it. We could observe one side of the coin and decide to spend it on that which corrupts, or, we could turn it over and choose to buy that which edifies."

Each man appeared to be seriously considering these words and once again silence descended on the group.

Adam walked to the window and looked toward the beach. "Come look, my friends. The young men have prepared a bathing area for our pleasure. I have been blessed to enjoy your bathing facilities made from stone. Now let us all enjoy this beautiful facility which God has made."

The men joined him at the window. The young men had constructed an awning along the beach and from the awning were attached long drapes of a gauze-like material; dozens of different colors flapping in the breeze. Here the bathers could rest from swimming and have protection from the sun and insects. The men nodded in approval and voices were raised in delightful anticipation.

Gentle waves, topped with foamy white splashed in quick abundance along the sandy shore. The blue water was absolutely clear revealing numerous little fish and water plants. It did not drop to a depth of more than six feet for several hundred yards away from the shore. It was a perfect place and a perfect day for swimming.

There was a second tent and inside were tables filled with cool drinks, dishes of fruits and piles of sweet cakes; fine fare for refreshing a man after he had his fill of swimming. Both tents contained colorful couches surrounded by potted palms and vases of ferns and flowers. Musicians were seated on benches and, at a slight raise of the hand by Adam, began to play invigorating songs.

Ur turned to look at the elder man, "Well, Adam, I do believe that you have attempted to provide us with a glimpse into your memories of your beautiful Garden. What a lovely picture you have provided for us, and I, for one, am ready for a cool swim!"

The Advisors agreed with one voice and Adam led the way to the first tent where robes and shifts were removed leaving each man, except for Adam, clad only in a brief loin cloth.

Adam slowly removed his robe and stood at the center of the men still wearing a thin shift. He smilingly pointed to Barth's naval. "Isn't it fascinating to realize that you were once attached to your mother by a cord, and when that cord was severed it left that cavity. I remember how amazed I was when Eve gave birth to Cain, our firstborn, and I had to tie and cut the cord. Not having been born that way, and of course, not having such a cavity, nor did Eve, I was very interested in how birthed babies looked."

As if what he had just said was of no consequence, Adam began to hum as he pulled his shift over his head. He kept his back toward the men and made as if to walk to the water's edge.

Gidel spoke in a demanding voice. "What do you mean that you have no such cavity? Turn around here and let us observe!"

Still smiling, Adam turned.

The men looked.

Adam's skin was smooth.

Gidel reached over and impudently pulled the cloth down until it barely covered Adam's private parts.

"Gidel have a care!" warned Ur.

Gidel stood back, obviously shaken.

Kaniel spoke in a hushed voice. "You say that Eve is just the same?"

"She is indeed. However, on that point, you must accept my word, for I assure you that I will not place my wife on display. Those of you who are married may ask your wives about Eve, for they too will be bathing this week."

Zer bowed at Adam's feet. "I believe you Adam. Adam…my father. I know that you are indeed the Father of all mankind. I acknowledge Yahweh as my God. As the only true and living God."

One by one each man kneeled before Adam and confessed their belief in the one true God. Only Gidel remained standing.

Slowly, with ashen face, he too knelt.

Adam spoke.

"Let it be known, my sons, that you do not kneel to me. I am but a man. A man created in the image of the perfect God, but a man stained by sin. You kneel now in the presence of God and it is to Him that you make your confession."

After some time Ur stood. He looked at Adam. "I feel as if I want to be washed. As if I need to rinse off this old sinful nature."

Adam stepped into the water, moving several feet out into a deeper area. He held his hand out to Ur who moved to his side.

Lifting a hand up to heaven Adam asked God to receive Ur and to cleanse him from sin. He then asked Ur if he was willing to be submerged in the water. With tears running down his face Ur agreed.

Each man came forward for baptism. When the ceremony was finished Adam looked up to see one more man at his side. It was Enoch.

"Me also, Father Adam, please submerge me."

Adam took Enoch into his arms and held him in a warm embrace for several minutes. He then prayed over the young man and baptized him in the name of the Creator, Yahweh.

❋ ❋ ❋ ❋ ❋

The voice of the turtledove sounded across the land. Winter was over. Adam walked through the courtyard, speaking to the various students as they were busily planting flowers in the freshly dug beds. He paused for a moment to survey the area where the students and faculty gathered for many meals and special olfaction. Feeling a bit of nostalgia already, Adam looked for long moments at each building, statue, and water pond; he hoped to impress the images so fully unto his memory that he could recall them long after his departure.

It was early morning of the day before Sabbath. Adam was meeting Ur, Guryon, Enoch, the inner circle of the Advisors, and Adam's six other sons, and seven sons-in-law. Today Guryon would reveal the secret route that the group would be using to return to Mivtzar.

Adam was slightly surprised to discover that his feelings were mixed about returning home. He missed the sweet hills and gentle slopes of Mivtzar. It had been home for so long that Adam felt an aching in his chest to return there.

However…however, the trip to Ur had been wonderfully successful. God had blessed their every endeavor. They had watched hundreds of persons pledge their lives to Yahweh. Each one of them had expressed a desire to be washed in the waters of baptism, and Adam felt assured that Yahweh gave His approval to this new outward manifestation of 'having sins washed away'. The City that had once been only a place of great learning was now a City of devotion to Almighty God, and to all things godly.

It seemed that the attacks by the bandits had escalated in direct proportion to the spiritual growth of the City, but the attacks had been faithfully withstood by the newly trained young soldiers. Little by little, the Shalomshamars had turned the defense of the City over to the brave and well prepared Magen.

A voice called from the balcony above. Adam looked up. Barth, cheerful Barth, God-fearing Barth called out: "Father Adam, come up and break bread with us. Renana has prepared a feast!"

Laughing, Adam felt a surge of youthful agility and took the steps two at a time.

The large room was filled to overflowing and all eyes turned to the inaugural man as he walked into their presence. All stood to greet him.

"We have waited, Father, for you to bless our food," said Gidel, no longer pompous but with a quiet, gentle spirit.

Adam, lifting his hands and face toward heaven, pronounced blessing on the meal, gave thanks for the year that he had spent in Ur, and asked that Yahweh give both the group returning to Mivtzar and the group remaining behind special protection and continued growth in their spirits.

❋ ❋ ❋ ❋ ❋

Adam and his fellow travelers stood on the banks of the narrow and shallow body of water that branched off from the larger more tumultuous river leading away from Ur.

Yesterday's Sabbath had been a blessed day of prayer, rejoicing, and rededication of lives. In the early dawn, the City streets had been lined with hundreds of well-wishers waving good-bye; young children had rushed into the crowd thrusting bouquets of flowers into the hands of their departing friends.

For the general knowledge of the people, it had been rumored that the travelers would be returning home by the same route that they had used to come to Ur. Unknown to the City, hundreds of the soldiers slipped into tents outside the City and changed into common clothes, their weapons underneath their robes. The smaller soldiers dressed as women, their heads and faces completely covered as if to be protected from the weather. Among much pomp, with wagons laden with gifts from the people of the City, this group boarded the ships at the dock of Ur.

The group that broke off and headed for the southwest were unnoticed by the cheering crowds. They too were dressed in traveling clothes but carried only the necessary provisions for their trip home.

Achva and Zahava had stood hand in hand as they waved goodbye to the departing family. Zahava's hand rested protectively on her belly that was beginning to swell with the child growing within.

Enoch and Achva had both shed tears as they had embraced goodbye. Achva had decided to make his home in Ur where he would continue his teaching in the Tower of Learning. Grieving as he said goodbye to his friends, Enoch explained that he felt Yahweh's calling was for him to return to Mivtzar.

"I know now that God has called me to continue the chosen line that leads to the Redeemer, but I must pray and seek His will in my life. I am not certain what Yahweh wants me to do. I must know in my heart and spirit what He wants. I must obey Him at any cost."

Achva looked into his friend's eyes. "We shall meet again my dear friend. I will bring Zahava to visit Mivtzar after our child is born. We shall break bread together once again."

Now Enoch stood with others by Adam's side and looked with interest at the shallow river. There were large bodies of reeds growing on either side of the water; and just beyond those were small trees whose long willowy branches hung down and touched the tops of the reeds.

Adam looked at Captain Abir; his face reflected the question in his mind. "But where are the boats, my son? Are we to wade all the way to Mivtzar?"

Abir smiled at his father-in-law, and then looked at General Guryon, who nodded. Abir clapped his hands with one authoritative sound and suddenly dozens of small, flat boats began to emerge from the reeds.

They were unlike any boats that Adam had ever seen. Each boat was built to hold six passengers; three per bench facing each other in the middle of the boat. At both ends of the boats were Shalomshamars who stood as they propelled the craft with long poles. In unison each man would place his pole into the shallow bottom of the river, give a great shove, and allow the boat to glide for several yards before repeating the movement.

An awning was rigged over the boats to protect the travelers from the elements of weather. The benches allowed room for the travelers to stretch out for sleeping, and other boats carried relief troops for the pilots.

General Guryon directed his words to Adam and those at his side. "For the past year I have sent troops down this river to clear debris and, at some points, to reroute the course of the water. There were no bands of evil men spotted, and, as a matter of fact, the land along this river is almost totally unsettled. We will have a slow, not terribly comfortable, but God willing, safe, trip home. We will arrive less than 100 miles away from home."

Adam placed his hands upon the General's shoulders, "We thank you, General Guryon for your careful planning. We have no complaint to make about any of these small discomforts that we may be asked to endure. It will be a good day when we arrive safely home, and it is due to the diligent work of your troops that we may anticipate this. May Yahweh bless you, my general, my son."

❋ ❋ ❋ ❋ ❋

Chapter Fourteen

Enoch

Enoch smiled as he looked down at his three sleeping girls. His beautiful young wife, Raisa, looked almost childlike in her repose. How different from the haunted young woman he had chanced upon years ago, and helped to escape from the evil Oz.

Now she was able to run with happy abandon, playing games with their two little daughters, or sing blithesome songs as she worked at household tasks. She gave of herself wholly and joyfully in every way. He blushed slightly in the moonlight as he carried this thought to include their lovemaking.

"Yes. . .well, enough of those thoughts, Enoch my man!" he whispered to himself.

Indeed, not only the two sleeping little ones, but also Raisa's slightly bulging body, gave evidence of the freedom they felt in their love.

"Thank you, Yahweh, for You have given me so very much. Help me to serve you in every way. May my every breath be drawn to praise you," this too whispered. Whispered as if to the stars, but in reality to a dimension far beyond the trillions of the starry hosts.

Dawn would soon come, and with it perhaps the arrival of his dearest friend, the man closer to him than any of his brothers. His companion, his confidant, his fellow adventurer: Achva, was going to be his near neighbor!

Achva was bringing Zahava and their four sons to live in Mivtzar. Traveling with them were twenty scholars and their families from the Tower of Learning at Ur. Achva had asked, and had had been granted, permission to establish a learning center in one of the villages of Mivtzar.

Enoch was thrilled. How good it would be to walk and talk, to discuss and pray; to once again share thoughts with his dearest friend.

For safety reasons, the little group had traveled the same shallow river route that Adam and Enoch had taken from Ur.

During the past years a small port had grown up at the terminus of the river. The port was at the point where the river emptied into a large lake and from the lake a larger river went straightway to the Great Sea.

Enoch had been so excited at the prospect of seeing his friends again, after these many years, that Raisa had suggested they make the journey to the port and welcome the family there. She had heard so much about Zahava that she felt as if she were already a dear friend.

It had been a glorious trip for his young family. The girls had loved traveling on the little donkey; and their eyes, dark like their mother's, had sparkled each morning on awakening with anticipation of the forthcoming day.

Raisa had not left the villages of Mivtzar since her arrival several years before. She had amazed even herself when she suggested that they travel the nearly one hundred miles to meet the boats.

For years she had not felt safe at the idea of being anywhere but in Mivtzar; but since her marriage to Enoch, five years before, she had begun to rely less on Mivtzar and more on Yahweh. She knew that whatever happened to her, she would be eternally in God's care.

Yakira had looked frightened when her sister had explained to her that it would be a few weeks before she would see her again. She soon relaxed though, for the women of Aluma's Village, where she now lived in her own little house, assured her that all would be well.

Joy had radiated Raisa's face as she left her sister. How amazing it was that Yakira had learned to trust. What a wonderful gift that was.

Streaks of pink were beginning to lighten the sky in the east. Enoch stirred the embers of their campfire in sudden anticipation of breakfast.

Yawning and stretching her lithe arms, Raisa opened her eyes and watched her husband as he began preparation for the meal. The air was slightly chill and a little damp from the night air. She pulled a cloak around her shoulders. The child, also awakened, moved inside her. She smiled and gently patted her belly.

"How beautiful my husband is," she mused silently. "He is a young man, only 65 years old, but mature enough to be wise." She studied his build: he was not as tall as some men, more of a medium build, muscled and strong; and his sandy colored hair hung unusually long down his back. His blue eyes were kind and loving, always tender when they looked at her. How well she remembered the day that Eve had found her busily working in her flower garden, and announced that she and Adam felt it was God's will for Raisa to become the wife of Enoch. Raisa had been speechless. She well knew that Enoch was of the chosen line, and she felt nearly overwhelmed with the idea that she would be God's instrument whereby this line was continued.

She had stood somewhat in awe of Enoch, but now knew that even those of God's special line, those who had a special calling, were still human beings just trying to find their way. Her husband was not perfect, but he was kind, loving, faithful and godly. When he became impatient or thoughtless, he was quick to ask for forgiveness.

Slipping quietly out of bed she stole stealthily up behind him and threw her arms around him. "You are my captive sir; I have just taken you prisoner."

Laughingly Enoch turned and gently wrestled his wife to the ground. "Now who is the prisoner? You must be very certain, fair warrior, that you can overpower your enemy before you attack him!"

In mock dismay she protested, "But sir, please have mercy on me. I cannot be taken prisoner for I have children to feed and a demanding husband to please. If I do not have his breakfast ready on time he will surely beat me!"

Enoch stood, pulling Raisa to her feet. "Show me this monster who would dare to mistreat such a beautiful young woman. I will do him great harm. He should be grateful to have such a devoted wife. I, on the other hand, have a wife who lies abed until the sun is high in the sky. Indeed I have to prepare breakfast myself!"

Both were laughing as they embraced. What a wonderful day this was going to be.

Later, as Raisa made certain that the girls were clean and groomed, she wondered aloud if the boat would be here early this morning, or perhaps this afternoon. It had been expected yesterday, but Enoch said that it was entirely possible that they were a day late getting started, or perhaps delayed by weather along the way.

He whistled as he broke camp and loaded their equipment on the donkeys. Excitedly the family started down the narrow trail that led to the shallow river.

They had been waiting on the pier that was adjacent to the port for about thirty minutes when they saw a man, obviously injured, using a donkey to pull a raft up the river. There was something on the raft covered by blankets. The man was weeping and calling for help. The guards from the port began running toward him. Enoch's voice became stern. "Take the girls and go inside the port."

"...but Enoch..."

"Do it now! Do as I tell you. Here. Guard," he called one of the younger Shalomshamars, "take my family inside and protect them."

Several hours passed before Enoch came back into the port building. His face was ashen. His eyes were cold and hard.

"The man was able to tell us what happened before he died. The group was attacked by the sons of the Nephilim. All are dead."

Raisa gasped. "No, Enoch, NO! Not Achva, not his family. Please, no."

Enoch stood woodenly, unable to help her with her grief.

"Achva is dead, Zahava is dead. Even brave little Yafa is dead. All of the scholars are dead. The children were carried off as slaves. Only Yahweh knows what will become of them. The man said that the Nephilim bragged about how strong they are. He said that they tied up their captives and tortured them before they killed them. They chanted and danced and dared the Shalomshamar to come into their mountains east of the Tigris-Euphrates valley. They challenged them to a 'great battle'." Enoch turned to the soldiers who were standing behind him.

"Bury the bodies up there on that bluff for they will not withstand the 100 mile trip to Mivtzar."

He then turned to another soldier. "Take my wife and daughters home to Mivtzar. I charge you to see that no harm comes to them. Give an account to Adam and to Guryon."

He turned to Raisa who was sobbing soundlessly. He gently placed his hands on her shoulders and looked into her eyes. "I must be alone. I must try and come to terms with this horrible thing.

When my soul is calmer, I will return."

He did not look back as he walked towards the hill country that lay in the distance.

❋ ❋ ❋ ❋ ❋

Raisa had just finished mucking out the little stable adjacent to the house when Adam appeared in the yard. Hastily she smoothed her hair out of her eyes and attempted to wipe the dirt off her shift.

She approached Adam hopefully. Perhaps there was word of Enoch. Five full moons had come and gone since that appalling day on the riverbank. Nearly half a year.

"I came to make sure that you are well, my child. There has been no word of your husband."

Raisa swallowed the lump in her throat and nodded. Lifting her sad eyes to the face of the Patriarch she spoke softly, "I have cool apple juice in a jug in the spring. Would you enjoy some?"

Adam made an attempt at heartiness, "That sounds wonderful, my child, I can think of nothing that I would like better. I'll sit my weary bones down on this bench while you fetch it."

They drank the cider and munched raisin cakes. Talk seemed dear.

"The child will come soon, I believe," Adam commented, noting the size of the young woman's belly.

"Indeed, soon. I should give birth before the next full moon."

Adam stood and placed his hand on her head. "God give you strength my child. Have faith in Yahweh and in your husband. They are together right now, talking things over. Yahweh will send him home when it is time. Be patient. Be patient."

Adam looked like an old man as he walked away. Raisa stood and went into her cottage to prepare the evening meal. She would set a place for Enoch, as always. Perhaps tonight he would share the meal with his family.

❋ ❋ ❋ ❋ ❋

The man sat by the mountain stream, his head in his hands. He was naked for he had washed his few rags in the stream and laid them on the rocks to dry in the sunshine. He was thin beyond words and his once golden hair was drab and matted.

A stranger seeing him would have thought him one of the mad ones, for his face had a drawn and angry look. Even now, after all these months, the tears ran down his face; and the grief and rage boiled up inside.

He heard the Voice.

"Enoch"

Turning, he fell to his knees and threw his arms over his eyes to protect them from the blinding light.

"Why do you grieve so for your friends, my son? Do you not know that they live in peace and safety in my house? They do not need your tears. Rather, give your tears for the ones who did this deed, for they live without hope and without peace."

Enoch jerked himself up from the ground, and just as quickly fell back to his knees, once again shielding his eyes.

"Tears for those murderers!" He exclaimed in anger at the Creator of the Universe. "Why? Tell me why; explain to me *WHY,* would I cry for those monsters? They are not even human! They are evil beyond imagining. Who would shed tears for them?"

Suddenly the form of a Man stepped out of the Light. "I weep for them," He said softly. "I long for their return. They were formed in the image of God and now the Evil one is remaking them in his image. Listen to me, Enoch, for I have work for you."

The Man showed him scenes from great cities of the earth. In these cities there was only violence and sin. Babies were thrown into fires during frenzied worship of false gods. Human flesh was bought and sold, and nowhere was there love or kindness.

Then Enoch saw a boat being built. It was unlike any boat that he had ever seen.

"Am I to help build this boat, Sir? I am a good boat builder you know."

The Man smiled. "No, my son. Another will build this boat in the appointed time. Watch now and see how the boat is filled."

Enoch was amazed to see animals enter the boat, and then the man went in with his family. When they were in, God shut the door.

A hard rain began falling on the earth. Once again Enoch was amazed for he had never seen water fall from the sky like that. Thousands upon thousands of people were drowned in the water but the boat did not open its doors.

Enoch turned to the Man. "Sir, what does this mean?"

"These people must have every opportunity to hear about Yahweh. You must go into every town and every City to tell them that God the Creator loves them and longs for them to turn from their sin. Even when you are weary, and when no man wants to hear, you must continue to tell them. God has chosen you for this task. You must be faithful."

"Sir, I cannot do this of myself; for I hate them. There is no love in me for these people. However, if You will love them through me, if You will give me a portion of Your love, then I will go. I will be faithful."

"There will be springs of love flowing from you, my son. I will give you but a small portion of my love and it will over flood your heart. Rest now, for you must have strength to return home. Your son will be born on the day of your return. You will call him Methuselah, for when his days are ended the judgment will come."

Enoch suddenly could not keep his eyes open and fell asleep where he lay.

❋ ❋ ❋ ❋ ❋

Raisa took a step backward, straightened her shift, smoothed her hair and regarded the work of her hands. She had risen before dawn that morning with an overwhelming surge of energy. She had fed and watered the animals, gathered eggs, weeded the garden, picked fresh vegetables; she had awakened the girls, fed and dressed them, and pushed them out the door to play. Then she turned her energy toward her already clean house; curtains were washed, pillows were aired, cupboards were cleaned, floors swept and scrubbed, and fresh flowers placed in a large jug on the table.

She called the girls in from their play, cleaned their hands and faces, fed them their lunch of bread, cheese and fruit, and put them down for naps.

Finding the house cleaned to her satisfaction, Raisa placed her freshly risen bread in the stone oven to bake, put vegetables in the pot and placed it over the coals to simmer. She added a handful of barley to give more substance to the meal and looked pleased with her efforts.

"Now," she reflected, "I had better do a little clean up of myself, for this may be the day that my husband returns home."

Giving the sleeping girls a last quick glance, she picked up a clean shift, along with some soft towels, and headed for the bathhouse.

Feeling refreshed, and now somewhat tired, Raisa sat in the courtyard of her house enjoying the warm rays of the sun as it continued its descent toward the horizon, its work nearly done. She ran her fingers through her hair to comb out the last droplets of water. "Lucky sun," she smiled, "your brother, Moon, will be showing himself tonight, and my work still won't be done!"

As if to prove her point to the sun, she stood and stretched; then hearing two little girls awake and softly calling for 'mommy', she went back to her duties.

Having set the table carefully for the evening meal, Raisa turned to call the girls in from their last play of the day.

She stopped to listen for a moment. What in the world were they squealing about? Their dog, who was the most obedient of animals, was barking loudly.

What were they yelling? Could it be...Yes, yes it was! Abba, that's what the girls were screaming. Abba, Abba: their father was home!

Raisa dropped the pottery on the table, totally unmindful that it had broken to bits.

She ran into the yard just as Enoch, carrying two little girls in his arms, was coming up the stone walk.

Tears were running down both their faces as they regarded each other. Gently he lowered the girls to the ground and gently he took his swooning wife into his arms. As he carried her into the house he noticed that the back of her shift was very wet.

She labored for six hours; and in the end a big, squalling baby boy was ushered into the world. His face was red and his eyes tightly clenched as he screamed his protest at being thrust so abruptly into this strange environment.

He had a mass of red hair; and he deigned to open his bright blue eyes as his mother tenderly offered him her milk-filled breast. His countenance cleared; and as he greedily sucked, he seemed to appraise the situation with a new acceptance. Maybe this wasn't going to be so bad after all!

His father held the tiny hand in his own large one. "Hello, Methuselah, welcome to our house. You are much beloved and wanted. Together we have a world to tell about our Lord; so eat your fill, for we must soon be about our Father's business."

❋ ❋ ❋ ❋ ❋

As had been told them in the Garden of Eden, Eve and then Adam died. Eve lived 900 years, and a very lonely Adam lived for another 30 years.

His generations of grandchildren visited him often during those last 30 years, and he was especially cheered by the loving Methuselah; but his wife, bone of his bones, flesh of his flesh, was no longer there, and the light had gone out of his eyes.

All but three of his sons and daughters gathered to place their father's body deep into the interior of the cave that had been his first home in Mivtzar. During the next few years their own sons and daughters were called upon to do the same for them, and the original persons of the earth passed away.

Enoch preached throughout the earth. He had other sons and daughters; but Methuselah, his flaming hair blowing in the wind, was the one to follow him in his travels.

It was Methuselah, at the age of 300, who returned to the family one day with a shining countenance. He found it difficult to find the words to convey his experience to his mother. He explained that his father had been deep in conversation with the Lord when suddenly the Shekinah Glory of God came down and enveloped Enoch. Methuselah watched in awe as the two dear friends simply walked off together. He had waited, but they did not return.

Her eyes filling with tears, his mother embraced her eldest son and simply nodded. Looking at him for a long moment she touched his face in a gesture of love, and went back into the house to knead the bread dough.

The End

Printed in the United States
97547LV00006B/24/A

9 781425 982775